APOCALYPSE MACHINE

Also by Jeremy Robinson

Standalone Novels
The Didymus Contingency
Raising The Past
Beneath
Antarktos Rising
Kronos
Xom-B
Flood Rising
MirrorWorld

Nemesis Saga Novels
Island 731
Project Nemesis
Project Maigo
Project 731
Project Hyperion
Project Legion (2016)

The Antarktos Saga
The Last Hunter – Descent
The Last Hunter – Pursuit
The Last Hunter – Ascent
The Last Hunter – Lament
The Last Hunter – Onslaught
The Last Hunter – Collected Edition

The Jack Sigler/Chess Team Thrillers
Prime
Pulse
Instinct
Threshold
Ragnarok
Omega
Savage
Cannibal
Empire (2016)

Cerberus Group Novels
Herculean

Jack Sigler Continuum Novels
Guardian
Patriot

Chesspocalypse Novellas
Callsign: King
Callsign: Queen
Callsign: Rook
Callsign: King 2 – Underworld
Callsign: Bishop
Callsign: Knight
Callsign: Deep Blue
Callsign: King 3 – Blackout

Chesspocalypse Novella Collections
Callsign: King – The Brainstorm Trilogy
Callsign – Tripleshot
Callsign – Doubleshot

SecondWorld Novels
SecondWorld
Nazi Hunter: Atlantis

Horror Novels (written as Jeremy Bishop)
Torment
The Sentinel
The Raven
Refuge

Post-Apocalyptic Sci-Fi Novels (written as Jeremiah Knight)
Hunger
Feast (2016)
Viking Tomorrow (2016)

APOCALYPSE MACHINE

JEREMY ROBINSON

For Matt Frank.
Together we will usher in a kaiju renaissance.

1

ABRAHAM

T.S. Elliot got it wrong. The end of the world doesn't begin with a bang, or a whimper. It begins with a toe prick.

"God damn, son of bitch!" Kiljan Árnason falls to his side, the blow cushioned by layers of clothing and a thick down jacket. He clutches his boot, hisses through his teeth and swears again, "Mother fuck! What was that?"

The four people with him—three scientists and myself—have a good laugh at his expense, not because we're sadistic and enjoy seeing people in pain, but because our long-bearded Icelandic guide has done us the courtesy of cursing in English. His thick accent somehow transforms his broad, 6'4" tall, hair-covered frame into something adorable, rather than fearsome. His Viking ancestors might have split us in half with an ax for laughing at him, but as he rolls on his back, still clutching the boot, Kiljan chuckles along with us.

When the surprise wears off, and he tears away his gloves and unties the laces of his right boot, the laughter fades. He's genuinely injured. Not mortally, but when you're hiking across a glacier that rests atop the caldera of a subglacial stratovolcano more than fifty years past due for an eruption, a guide that can walk is preferable.

The glacier, Vatnajökull, is the largest in all of Europe, covering eight percent of Iceland's landmass. Its average depth is 1300 feet, but over volcanic calderas such as the one under our toes, it reaches down 3000 feet. The volcano beneath us, Bárðarbunga—Bardarbunga to non-locals—is one of the largest in Iceland, and like the other thirty volcanoes in the region, it still roils with activity. In 2015, an offshoot of the volcano burped lava and toxic steam over a swath of land the size of Manhattan. But that six month eruption was little more than a pressure release. A true eruption, the kind that transforms landscapes and alters weather around the world, could still be building. That's why our little band of volcanologists and geologists is hiking across an ice cap in search of the perfect location to set up camp and start running tests like ice core samples, as well as air quality and seismographic readings.

A lot of what we're doing out here is theater, designed to garner public attention to a potentially serious threat. As a journalist for *Modern Scientist*, I'm here to chronicle the expedition and ruminate on any discoveries made. If the study's findings are mundane, I'll write a character piece, focused on the lives of scientists in extreme environments. I'll pepper it with facts about what an eruption would look like. And I'll remind people about the chaos caused across Europe in 2010 when Eyjafjallajökull, Bardarbunga's sister volcano, blew her top, closing airspace over twenty countries and keeping ten million travelers on the ground.

But if the study finds evidence of the opposite, that Bardarbunga is building toward an eruption, the story will take on a tone of Biblical end-times prophecy. I'm hoping for something in the middle, portending doom, but for some future generation—preferably after my sons have lived long lives. If Bardarbunga erupts in a significant way, all of Europe will feel the effects. Between earthquakes, tsunamis, poison gas clouds, hot ash and glacial flooding, several hundred thousand, perhaps even millions of lives will be threatened.

"What happened?" Holly Interlandi, one of our two volcanologists, asks, crouching beside the fallen giant. Dressed in snow pants and a parka, she has trouble bending down. She nearly gets us laughing again, but we're sobered by the pained look on Kiljan's face.

"Felt like a bee sting," the big man says. "On my toe."

"You do realize that there are no bees to—" Phillip Kim clamps his mouth shut when Kiljan pauses unlacing his boot—long enough to give the man a look that suggests some of his Norse instincts remain intact. Phillip is a know-it-all kind of guy, and he takes it upon himself to educate the expedition, at all times, and on all subjects. To make things worse, his proper British accent makes him sound hoity-toity, even when he's being down to earth.

"I do not need a volcanologist to teach me about my own country's wildlife," Kiljan says. His boot comes away with a sucking sound, unleashing a cloud of steam from the sweat-dampened, wool sock.

Phil opens his mouth to speak again, no doubt to recommend moisture wicking socks or to warn of frostbite, but he's silenced once more, this time by the sight of blood.

"Dios mío," Diego Rodriguez says, crouching down next to Holly. The man is a geologist, but he's also the closest thing we have to a medic, with basic first aid and CPR training. He removes his sunglasses, takes a close look at the blood stained toe and then slides out of his backpack. "I'll disinfect and bandage the wound, but we need to get your foot in a sock—a fresh one preferably—and back in your boot before..."

"It is not as bad as it looks," Kiljan assures him. He pulls his foot up close to his hairy face and spits on his injured toe. While Diego gasps and the rest of us wince, the Nordic man wipes his toe clean with the end of his black scarf.

For a moment, I can see the small puncture wound, already surrounded by a ring of purple, but then a bead of blood emerges and trickles away.

Diego removes a small first aid kit from his pack, opens it and removes a package of sterile gauze. He tears it open and offers it to Kiljan. "Hold it on. Tight."

The big man presses the gauze to his toe, wincing in pain.

"Turn it over," Diego says, waggling his hand at the injured foot. "Show me the other side."

Kiljan twists his foot around, and the scientists all gasp again. I do, too. I might not be an official scientist with a PhD in one 'ology' or another, but I've got the mind and constitution of one. I just couldn't decide on a single field on which to focus, so I write about them all. My stomach twists as purple spreads beneath the thick toenail.

Diego clears his throat, more to control his gag reflex than to get anyone's attention. He points to a small rise at the center of the nail. "It went nearly all the way through." He clears his throat again, this time covering his mouth with his hand, trying not to be obvious about it. If he looked up, he'd see the rest of us doing the same thing.

Kiljan lifts his foot toward Diego. "Bandage it, and let us be on our way."

Diego, leaning away from the foot, shakes his head. "A simple bandage isn't enough. Not for long. It seems likely the bone is split. If it gets infected..."

My mind's eye paints the picture for me; Kiljan's phalange cleaved like a log, fractured bits of bone shifting around in his flesh. I turn and step away, nausea sweeping through me. Several deep breaths later, convinced the expedition is over before it truly began, I ponder the new story angle: *Scientists Rescue Icelandic Guide from Glacial Demise— Oh yeah, and Volcano Doom.*

But should I take part, or simply observe? I'm supposed to write the story, not be part of it. But this...

If Kiljan can't walk, we'll all have to pitch in to get him back to the superjeep—a rugged, oversized jeep with massive tires, used to traverse the lunar landscape surrounding the glacier. The airspace in this region is closed, but maybe they'll make an exception for an injured local? Kiljan has the sat phone, so it's his call, literally.

"Right," Phillip says. "That's about all I can take of that. You lot are on your own." He steps up next to me, arms crossed, lips pursed, eyes aimed at the horizon, where the most brilliant, sunlit white glacier meets the deepest blue sky.

Guilt creeps up on me. I wasn't abandoning Kiljan the way Phillip did, I was simply trying to not vomit on him. Shame tugs my eyes to the ice. *Go back and help,* I tell myself, but then I quickly argue. *It's a wounded toe. What can I do?*

Salvation comes in the form of a toothpick sized spire of deep black, streaked with dark red, protruding from the ice in front of me. Another step and it might have punched a hole in my foot, as well. I crouch down, raising my sunglasses to look at the slender spear, now hidden in the shade of my bulky, arctic-garbed torso. "I found it. What he stepped on. I think."

Phillip stands beside me, but doesn't bother crouching. "You can't be sure of that."

It's a statement. Not a question. And it crawls under my skin. I motion to the vast white glacier surrounding us. "Do you see any other spikes sticking out of the ice?"

His silence says he doesn't.

"Let me see." Holly crouches down beside me. The discovery either trumped the maternal nature that led her to Kiljan's aid, or like us, she's seen more blood than she's accustomed to. Rocks don't bleed. Though it could be argued that volcanoes spew the Earth's blood.

After a quick glance back to confirm that Diego hasn't also abandoned his patient, I shuffle to the side and take my shadow along with me. Bright sunlight gleams off the revealed ice, forcing my eyes shut. I pull my sunglasses down and blink until the green afterimage fades. When I can see clearly again, Holly is leaning down close to the ice, looking at the spike.

"I don't think the red is blood," she says, sliding a gloved finger over the barb. She holds the finger up, first to Phillip and then to me. The digit is clean. "It's just red coloration."

"Closer to a maroon, don't you think?" Phillip says.

Holly smiles at me without looking back at him, and I try not to laugh. But fail.

Phillip's eyebrows billow like mushroom clouds, rising steadily higher onto his forehead. "What about this amuses you, Mr. Wright?"

"Abraham or Abe, please," I say. "People might get the wrong idea if you keep calling me Mr. Right."

It's an old family joke started by my father, but I haven't used it in a while. At least not with this group. My full name is Abraham Lincoln Wright. I had patriotic parents with high hopes for their son. They both died when I was nineteen. Car accident. I miss them terribly, but part of me is glad they were spared the disappointment of having a son with such a promising name become a science writer for a magazine/soon-to-be webzine.

Phillip scoffs and rolls his eyes.

"Abe," Holly says, probing the prong with her gloved fingertip. "Focus."

She's the only one of our crew that I'd met before, and she has seen my sarcastic side. She also knows—we both do—that Phillip doesn't understand sarcasm. Or humor in general.

I lay down on the ice and look at the small spike from the side. The new angle provides no new insights. It's slender and sharp, broadening slightly where it emerges from the ice.

Holly pushes on the barb again. "Is it bending or moving? At all?"

"Not even a little. It's wedged in there tight."

"Right, then," Phillip says. "Let's dig it out, so the next unsuspecting sod that comes along doesn't step on it."

I lock eyes with Holly. Both of us want to point out that the odds of someone walking along this very same path, ever, is highly unlikely. I can see it in her eyes, the jab on the tip of her tongue. But she has more self-control than me.

"It's hardly scientific," she says, changing the subject with a tone that also scolds me for even thinking about mocking Phillip again.

"An archeologist might study it in situ for a time," I say, having spent enough time on dig sites to know the protocols. "But, we're not archeologists. We're not here to study spikes rising from the ice, and he *does* make a good point." I glance up at Phillip. "Bravo, good sir."

Holly takes my chin in her gloved hand and pulls my face away from Phillip's glower. "Unless this is a rock. Something welling up from below. Then it *is* what we're here to study."

"This ice cap is stationary," Phillip says. "Not to mention nearly a thousand meters deep. For objects from the bottom to find their way to the surface—"

"Lava tubes," I offer. "Rising up through the ice. Upside down geological roots."

"We know what they are." Phillip shakes his head. "There would have been thermal venting. Someone would have noticed."

"Vatnajökull is thousands of years old," Holly argues. "For most of that time, it hasn't changed, but 168 square miles of ice have deglaciated since

1958. The ice is melting. The human race has seen to that. New layers are uncovered every year. This might be the first time this...whatever it is, has been exposed since the beginning of the iron age."

"Humph," Phillip says.

"I'm *agreeing* with you, Phillip," Holly says, reaching up and flexing her fingers, open and closed. "Give me your ice ax."

"You are?" Phillip sounds both genuinely surprised and delighted. He pulls his ice ax from the side of his pack and hands it to her.

While Holly goes to work on the ice, digging and scraping, I stand and check on the others. The big man's toe has doubled in size, thanks to the copious amount of gauze and tape wrapped around it. Despite all the extra padding, Kiljan winces as Diego slides a sock over the injured foot. It's going to be hell getting his boot on again. Diego is right. Kiljan can't continue, which means we all need to head back. Three scientists and a writer alone on the barren ice pack might make for a good story, but I doubt it would have a happy ending. The story would probably have someone else's byline, since I'd be frozen solid along with the rest of them.

It also means that the mysterious spike jutting out of the ice is the closest thing to a scientific discovery we're going to make. "How long until we can move?"

"Ten minutes," Diego says, though he sounds unsure.

"We will go nowhere," Kiljan says through grinding teeth. His toe hurts more than he wants to admit.

"Are you *trying* to be ominous?" I ask.

He grins through the pain. "We cannot walk through the night. We will camp here. Leave in the morning."

Diego nods and looks pleased by the decision. None of us are athletes. The trek has already taken a toll.

"Abe," Holly calls. "Come see this."

As I stand, Diego looks back at Holly with eager eyes. He has yet to see the object of our fascination.

Kiljan shoos Diego away with one hand and picks up his boot with the other. "I do not need a wet nurse. I can put on my own shoe." He sounds gruff, but it's an act of kindness. Scientists with new discoveries are like children on Christmas morning. Anything short of opening the box and making a mess right then and there is a disappointment.

Holly moves to the side at our arrival. She's dug out a foot deep crater around the object, which looks like a black, ten inch tall, upside down carrot with a severe case of freezer burn, not to mention weird red veins running through it.

"What is it?" Diego asks.

Holly scrapes away ice crystals until there's just a sheen of frozen water remaining. Breathing heavily, she leans back, places the ice ax down and shrugs.

I lay down on the ice, viewing the strange spire from the side again, seeing subtle streaks of pink, like veins, crisscrossing the surface. *Or is it just distortions from the ice?* As though drawn to the thing, I remove my glove, reach out and wrap my hand around the inch-thick stem. Numbing cold burns through my hand.

Water drips between my fingers, melted by my body heat. I close my eyes, resisting the urge to pull my hand away.

"What are you doing?" Holly asks.

Melting the ice, I think, but don't answer.

I *can't* answer.

The scent and taste of salt tickles my nose and mouth.

Ocean waves crash against a rocky shore, the sound like thunder in my ears.

Tall grass tickles my outstretched hands, blown by a warm breeze.

"Abe."

The voice is faint. And not Holly's.

"Abraham."

I open my eyes.

Iceland is gone.

2

A gull squawks, hovering like a kite in an ocean breeze. The way it hangs there feels unnatural, like a moment frozen in time. But it's still calling out, its orange tipped, yellow beak opening and closing, its unblinking eyes focused downward. I follow its gaze, past the endless ocean, blue splashed with whitecaps tossed by the same wind that holds the bird aloft. Then past the rocks, craggy and blemished by patches of white barnacles. And then to the beach. Sand stretches down to the water, where a layer of smooth, round stones mark the high tide line.

I slip out of the tall grass surrounding me. The thick blades slide through my hands, sharp enough to cut. The sting of a bloodless wound draws my eyes to my hand, and then lower. I'm naked, my far from toned 'dad bod' revealed for all to see, but I feel no shame at it. When I look up again, I'm standing on the rocks, overlooking the beach. The grass is behind me now, bending in the breeze atop a short, sand-covered hill that divides the beach from the rest of the world.

How is this possible? I think, boggled by the moment's surreal vibe. *How did I get here?* Memories slide back into place as my mind comes

to grip with the new surroundings. I was in Iceland. Kiljan was hurt.
We found something in the ice.

I touched it.

And then...I woke up here.

I didn't *wake up*. I was never asleep. I was laying down when
I closed my eyes, dressed in winter gear, and when I opened them
again, I was here, standing and nude.

Fear nudges its way into my chest, wrapping its hand around my
heart and squeezing.

"Don't be afraid."

I flinch away from the voice, wondering how someone was able to
get so close to me. After stumbling over the jagged rock and nearly
slipping in a patch of seaweed, I steady myself and turn toward my
company, staggered by who I find.

"Ike?"

He lifts his hands away from his hips and grins, saying 'Here I am,'
without saying a word.

Except it isn't Ike. Not really. The face is the same—close enough to
recognize—but Ike, my son, is still eight years old. The person standing
before me is a man. And there's a long scar on his cheek that isn't there
now. My mind spins with possible explanations, dipping into science, both
real and fringe, from stories I've written over the years. Teleportation. Time
travel. Out of body experiences. Lucid dreaming.

I lock on that last possibility. *I'm unconscious,* I decide. *Dreaming.*

I wrote about lucid dreaming three years ago, about how dreams
can be controlled. The trick is that when most people realize they're in
a dream, they get excited and wake up. But there are ways to stay in the
dream, like jumping up and down, or waving your arms in circles. Then,
you can fashion the dreamscape into your very own fantasy world. But
it takes practice. And a lot of it. I performed the techniques for three
months, keeping a dream journal and failing every night, until I found
myself standing at the edge of a lake, beneath the most magnificent
nighttime sky, and thought, 'This is a dream.' When a duck swam at me,
I willed it to become a dog, and it did. Then I turned the dog into my
wife. And then, with a thought, my wife stood before me, naked, at which

point I woke up, disappointed and alone in a motel room. I left that last part out of the article. The point is, I recognize this place. It's a dream, and now that I've acknowledged it, I can take control.

"Wake up," I tell myself. When nothing happens, I close my eyes and shout, "Wake up!"

The dream remains. While I've never *had* to wake up from a lucid dream before, I was told that this was a simple and surefire way to do so. "Wake. Up!"

"You are awake," my aged son says.

"This is a dream," I tell him.

He shrugs. "Yet, you are awake." He clasps his hands behind his back and turns to look out over the beach, smiling like some kind of Buddhist monk, content with the world. "A vision, perhaps?"

"Great," I say, dragging my fingertips over my cheeks. "Now even my dreams are sarcastic."

"They're like grains of sand, don't you think?"

Dream Ike has definitely been smoking a little too much of something. What part of my subconscious could he possibly represent? "It's a beach," I say, turning toward the sand. "Of course it's..."

The sand looks strange. It's moving. The separate granules shift into strings that merge and bend in varying colors and forms, becoming individual shapes. The beach stretches to the horizon, filled with lumps of...of hair. Faces turn up, looking at me with something close to reverence. Some are white. Some are black. Most are something in-between. But in all of them, I see familiar features. Sometimes in the nose. The cheek bones. The chin. The hair. The further back I look, the more muted it becomes, but there's no denying that I am a part of all these people.

"Who are they?" I ask.

"Your children," a new voice says.

My second son, Ishah, stands to my left, as aged as his half-brother. The pair were born from two different mothers, two months apart, and they look nothing alike. While Ike is a blend of his second-generation Korean American mother and me—a black man of South African descent—Ishah's mother is as pale as I am dark, leaving him a shade of brown that makes his blue eyes pop. I look from one boy...man...to the other. They don't look much like their child selves, but I see them beneath the stubble and age lines, and I see myself in them the same way I do all those faces in the beach.

"This isn't possible," I tell them.

"All things are possible," Ike says.

Ishah takes my hand. "Out of the ashes, a nation will be born."

"What ashes?"

"The world will burn," Ike says.

"It has been evaluated," Ishah adds.

Ike takes my other hand. "And has been found wanting."

"Evaluated by who?"

A new voice rises up behind me, carrying the thunder of crashing waves with its every syllable. "The machine."

Ike's grip tightens. "The Ancient."

"Death." Ishah holds me back, as I try to turn around and see who's there. "And rebirth."

The ocean recedes as though it was a tablecloth yanked away by a magician. Millions more bodies are revealed, all looking toward me. The water rises up at the horizon and rushes back in. The earth quakes. Fissures open up. Beyond the beach, lava bursts into the sky, smoke billowing black as the world shakes around us.

I look out at all those faces, water and lava closing in from both sides, and I see devotion. "No," I say. "Stop!"

I close my eyes. "Wake up!"

When I open them again, the ocean is calm. The lava is gone. The beach is sand. And my sons are missing. Overcome with emotion, I fall to my knees and feel a stab of pain, as the jagged rocks dig into my flesh.

"Abraham," the roaring voice behind me says.

I turn around slowly, and I see a writhing black shape. It rises up above me, reaching out two flowing black arms, holding a blazing hot staff between them. I cower beneath the figure, which is as impossible to ignore as it is to look at directly.

"What do you want!" I scream, raising a hand in fear.

The form rushes down at me, thrusting the rod into my open hand. The air fills with the hiss of burning flesh, and I scream. Steam sprays out from between my fingers. My flesh boils and pops. I scream again, but am quickly silenced by the emergence of a face, concealed by roiling smoke, but filling me with a sense of relief.

"Abraham," the voice says again, a waterfall of sound cascading around me. "I am with you."

The pain returns with a sharp vengeance. I scream again, snap my hand away and leap back, staring into the surprised eyes of Holly, Phillip, Diego and Kiljan. I'm in Iceland again, though I'm pretty sure I never really left.

Holly reaches out for me. "Abe..." Her eyes travel down to my hands, one clutching the other. "Let me see your hand."

Suddenly aware that the pain has not yet faded, I look down at my right palm and find a band of burned, blackened skin stretched across the middle of my hand.

"Where I held the staff," I say.

"I would hardly call it a staff," Phillip says. I look from him to the spike jutting out of the ground. Memories collide with the dream. I reached out and took hold of it. I wasn't burned by heat, I was burned by extreme cold. A dream after all. "How long was I out?"

"Out?" Diego asks.

"Unconscious."

Holly lifts my hand, inspecting the wound. "Abe, you grabbed it, held on for a few seconds, said something and then screamed. You never lost consciousness."

I stagger back and plop down onto my butt, sitting on the ice. "What did I say?"

"Veneno mundi," Kiljan says, his baritone voice reminding me of the dark force's watery growl.

"What the hell does that mean?" I ask.

"Poisoned world," Phillip says. His translation is followed by a wet gurgle. All eyes turn to the sound's origin at Phillip's feet. The small hole that Holly dug is now partly filled with water. Phillip leaps back. "What the bloody hell?"

We stare in silence, waiting for it to happen again. And then, just as I notice that the water is steaming, a thin stream of bubbles roils to the surface.

Diego kneels down beside the slowly growing puddle. He holds his hand over the water as more bubbles churn the surface. "These bubbles aren't gas," he says. "The water is boiling."

3

There isn't a single member of our expedition who needs to be told what boiling water atop Vatnajökull means, especially when it's originating from what I'm now positive is an ancient lava tube. Bardarbunga is going to erupt, probably before I have time to upload the story to my editor. The region is geothermally active. There are vents and hot springs dotting the landscape surrounding the glacier, reminiscent of those in Yellowstone Park, but not on top of three thousand feet of ice. The heat and pressure required to push boiling water to the surface means we're standing on a powder keg. It also means that a good portion of what we thought was ice beneath our feet is actually boiling water. And the longer we stand here, the weaker the ice will get.

Kiljan rams his foot into his boot, shouting in pain. He ties the laces fast and pushes his bulk onto his feet. "Leave your packs."

"But it will be night before—" Phillip stops when the puddle gurgles again. "Yes, of course. We don't have that long. But we mustn't leave empty-handed."

We shed our packs and pocket whatever basic survival gear we might need for the return hike—water, rope, energy bars, first aid. Phillip assaults the spike, now rising from a foot deep puddle, with his ice ax. His first strike glances off the top and strikes water. Ice hisses where the water lands, kicking up steam.

"Phillip," Holly scolds. "Not now!"

"This will be our only chance to collect a sample," Phillip argues. "You were right about the formation's significance."

Kiljan limps around us. "If you wish to leave this place with your lives, follow me now. I will not wait."

Diego pockets one last water bottle and starts after Kiljan. He claps his hands at the rest of us. "Let's go! Vámonos!"

Phillip cocks his hand back and takes another whack. The ice ax connects with the spike, just above the waterline, where the spire is only a quarter inch thick. From the resounding clang and jarring impact, you'd think the stone jutting from the ice was actually rebar. Phillip hisses through his teeth and pulls back from the puddle. He drops the ice ax and holds his arm. "It's like hitting a brick wall with an aluminum bat."

Holly takes her fellow volcanologist by the coat and drags him away. "Now! Move!"

Defeated by the ancient stone spike, Phillip relents.

I recover the ax and step after them, stopping for a moment to look back at the black-red spire.

"Abe!" Holly shouts at me. They're twenty feet away and speeding up to catch Kiljan, who has broken into a limping jog.

I kneel beside the gurgling puddle holding up the ice ax. "What are you?" I say to the small spike, watching the puddle around it inch its way closer to my knees. My memories of the dream world are as fresh and clear as every real experience during the last fifteen minutes. Wanting to know what caused it, and suspecting the old stone, or perhaps something in it—microbes, an electrical current, something new—was the cause, I haul the ice ax back and strike.

The hard metal blade connects with the very tip of the spike, the serrated edge bumping over the thin formation and then connecting solidly. The millimeters thin rock—if that's what it really is—has taken my hardest hit and remained whole.

Or has it?

I lean in close, steam collecting on my face. There's a thin scratch on the surface. Determination takes root, and I raise the ax again, eyes on the spike, aiming for the same spot. But I don't swing.

The scratch is gone.

Healed.

"What the..."

"Abe!" Holly shouts. *Not shouting,* I think, *screaming.*

I don't turn toward her to see what she's warning me about. I don't need to. I'm already looking at it. Straight down. Between my knees. The glacier beneath me has turned translucent, like ice on a lake. And through its clear, wet surface, I see bubbles.

I nearly stand to run, but decide that would be a mistake. I don't know how thin the ice is. Could be a foot. Could be inches. Either way, it's getting thinner by the second. Putting all my weight in a small area could send me shooting through the ice. So I crawl, still clutching the ice ax. I move slowly at first, trying to disperse my two hundred pounds over three contact points at all times. When a geyser of steam spews into the air behind me, I shout and crawl-sprint, watching bubbles roil beneath me. I can actually see the ice thinning now, absorbing cracks and imperfections as the water rises, threatening to cook me alive like a lobster. I haven't eaten a lobster since I heard one scream, as it was placed in boiling water. I wonder, for a moment, if my scream will be as high-pitched.

When the ice beneath me spider-webs, I shout out and nearly start sobbing. Sudden heat scalds my left knee, and I hear the scream, not as high-pitched as the lobster's, but far more anguished. Lobsters are primitive creatures. They eat, poop and procreate, driven by instinct more than any kind of mind. But me...I have two sons and their mothers, Mina, my wife, and Sabella, who I call Bell. She's my...it's complicated. But I love them all, and that deep sense of loss, for my boiled self and for my family, who I know loves me, bubbles out as a pitiful wail.

And then I'm lifted. Propelled really. The ice below me gives way to boiling, steamy water, but I'm no longer there. I see glacial ice beneath me again, and then I slam down onto its blessedly hard surface. Before I fully understand what has happened, I'm lifted once more and placed back on my feet. "Move," says the mountain of a man who saved my life. Kiljan shoves me so hard that I nearly fall back down. Instead, I turn the tumble into a run, and obey.

When Kiljan sidles up next to me, grunting and wincing with each step, I slip the ice ax into my belt and look up at the big man. "You came back for me."

"I have not lost anyone before," he says. "I did not want you to be my first."

"Uh-huh." I smile at him. "And if it had been Phillip?"

He chuckles and winces, but doesn't reply.

"Admit it," I say. "You like me."

The glacier answers for him with a loud *pffft*. We're a hundred yards from the small spike, and the puddle now looks like a pond. A jet of steam erupts from the center of it, rising high into the air, before freezing into snow and being carried off by the wind.

"Faster," Kiljan says, lumbering ahead.

I'm not entirely sure running is going to help us much. Near as I can tell, we're at ground zero for an impending eruption. But I'm desperate to see my family again, to hold them in my arms and tell them all how much I love them. So I run faster, despite the burn already settling into my chest. I'm no athlete. None of us are. And the air consumed by our desperate lungs is frigid, fighting with each breath to lower our body temperatures and slow our retreat.

When Kiljan and I catch up to the others, just a quarter mile from the steam vent, they pause for a breather, hands on knees, lungs wheezing.

"Can't...breathe," Phillip says, gulping air like he's just surfaced from the ocean after nearly drowning. I know how he feels. My heart is pounding. I feel lightheaded, and I'm seeing spots dance on the fringes of my vision.

"You can breathe when we are off the glacier," Kiljan says, slowing to a walk, but not stopping.

It takes us four hours to trek five miles, slowed by frequent stops and scientific arguments. Someone in good shape, and who's accustomed to the cold, might be able to cover the remaining distance in an hour. We'll be lucky to cover it in two, which is around the same time the sun will set. If that happens before we reach the superjeep, we're going to be in trouble. Of course, there's also the chance that molten lava could consume us all at any second.

When Holly and I pass Diego, he forces himself to follow.

"Move it, you old codger," I say to Phillip, but he just waves me off. "Need another—"

The ice beneath us quakes. Some unseen and distant part of the glacier cracks open, the sound like a gunshot, rolling over the icy plane.

Phillip groans and brings up the rear.

We move like this for more than an hour, stopping just twice to drink, breathe and stretch. Both times, we're propelled back into action by the rumbling volcano. It's no longer beneath us, but it's still capable of killing us instantaneously, with poison gas, glacial flooding or good old fashioned pyroclastic flow—a mix of 1000-degree gas and powdered stone that rushes away from a volcano at 450 mph, enveloping everything in its path. It's a horrible, yet very fast way to die, as the residents of Pompeii discovered when Vesuvius erupted in 79 AD.

The sun is low in the sky ahead, forcing our eyes to the ground as we trudge along, our energy nearly sapped. My legs ache, but not nearly as badly as my lungs, which feel blistered and torn. With every step, I feel lower to the ground. I fight off thoughts of stopping and laying down to sleep by picturing Ike, Ishah, Mira and Bell. They become my world. My goal.

Stay alive.

Get home.

"Stop," Phillip says. "I can't go on."

I turn my eyes forward without lifting my head. Phillip stands a few feet away, his legs teetering like pine trees in a storm. He's pitched forward, hands on knees, head dipped toward the earth, which I notice is dark gray now, not glacial white.

Where are we? I think, and I look beyond Phillip. I see Holly ten feet ahead, smiling back at us, and Diego further on, leaning against something solid, black and cast in silhouette, thanks to the setting sun. Diego tilts his head back, draining a water bottle.

"Phil," Holly says. "We're here."

"Here, where?" Phillip says, standing and staggering until I reach up and catch him. We stumble a bit before balancing and lifting our hands to block the sun. With the sun blocked, the superjeep is easy to see. Its bulky frame fills me with relief.

"Thank God." Phillip staggers past Holly and collides with the vehicle's side, arms outstretched to embrace the vehicle. He flinches back when the engine roars to life. Kiljan is already behind the wheel, waving us on. Despite the long, exhausting trek, the man hasn't lost his sense of urgency. And with good cause.

It feels like we're half a world away from the melting ice and churning subglacial caldera, but in geological terms, we're still at ground zero. Pompeii was a little more than six miles from Vesuvius, and it would have taken the pyroclastic cloud just forty-eight seconds to envelope the city. At five miles from the caldera, we'd have even less time, assuming the eruption jettisons material in our direction. Most models predict Bardarbunga's ash and gasses will travel east to west, descending on the UK and Europe. But that doesn't mean we're safe. Not remotely. Even if six miles is considered the standard 'safe zone for habitation.' Tell that to the residents of Pompeii, and the more than 25,000 people killed by volcanoes since 1980.

Kiljan juices the gas, prodding me along with the engine's roar. I hobble to the tall jeep and open the back door, where Phillip and Diego are already waiting, looking half asleep. Holly has a hard time climbing in, so I shove her from behind and close the door behind her. I have my own struggle climbing in to the tall, front passenger's seat, but Kiljan reaches across, grabs my arm and hauls me inside.

Blessed heat rolls over my exposed skin. I lean forward, melting the frozen moisture from my face.

"Buckle," Kiljan says.

"I will, I will." The vehicle's heat, despite just starting to warm up, feels like a hot flame against my skin. But I can't pull myself away.

"Buckle, now!" Kiljan shoves the transmission into *Drive* and hits the gas. I'm flung back into my seat, lost in the chaos of the moment. And then I see it, out the windshield and then the side window, as the superjeep peels around in a circle; a cloud of ash and smoke launches skyward on the horizon.

Bardarbunga has erupted.

And we all know what's coming next.

Ignoring the pain wracking my whole body, I yank my seatbelt down, and after three frantic tries, I clip it into place. As the superjeep peels back onto the path that brought us to the glacier's edge, I look back again. I see a wave of distortion—kicked up snow and stony grit—rolling toward us. Gripping the armrest to my left and the 'oh shit' handle above me on the right, I shout, "Hold—" but my voice is cut short by the shockwave's impact and a cacophonous *boom*.

4

I'm looking down at the gritty, rock strewn ground through the superjeep's windshield. The back end has lifted up, propelled by the shockwave. Holly tumbles from the back seat, falling between Kiljan and me. My left hand snaps up from the armrest and catches the thankfully lithe woman's shoulder, keeping her face from crashing into the dash, but stretching my muscles to the limit, and then beyond. I shout in pain as sinews snap, but no one notices because all of us were already screaming.

Just when it seems the superjeep will hit a 90 degree angle and topple onto its roof—a death sentence for all of us even if we survive the crash—Kiljan slams his foot on the gas. The big front tires of the four-wheel drive vehicle are still in contact with the ground, and when they churn against the rough surface, we're launched forward. The forward motion pushes the back end down, and keeps us from flipping, but we remain upright for several horror-filled seconds, until the rush of air dies down and the back of the superjeep slams back to the earth.

The vehicle's oversized tires and forgiving shocks absorb much of the impact, but Kiljan quickly pushes the superjeep to its limits. He's plowing over rocks and crevices large enough to stop most trucks in their tracks.

I watch the speedometer needle move steadily clockwise. I attempt to convert kph to mph, but give up when the needle nears the numbers in red. Our trajectory takes us downhill, and will continue to, until we leave the mountainous region. On one hand, that's a good thing. Our retreat will be a speedy one. On the other hand...

I squish my face against the passenger seat's burning cold window and look back, up the steady grade. Gray stone catapults into a clear blue sky. My sigh of relief catches in my throat when the gray horizon rises up higher. What I thought was more barren stone is actually a pyroclastic cloud.

"Kiljan..." I say.

He glances in the rearview. "I see it."

The cloud is churning up into the air, but also rolling down the incline. It's still miles behind us, but it's massive and shoved steadily outward by the world's most powerful combustion engine.

Pebbles flung by the initial explosion rattle off the roof and the hood of the vehicle, falling like hail. It's loud enough to keep anyone from talking. We clear the falling debris quickly, putting more miles between us and the volcano, but not the expanding cloud.

As Kiljan maneuvers around a boulder that even the superjeep can't tackle, we drive perpendicular to Bardarbunga once more, and I get a clear view of the eruption. Gray smoke, soot and earth rises several miles into the air, spreading out wide in a mushroom cloud that dwarfs any created by man. Orange streaks of lightning crisscross the sky as dust and debris generate enough static electricity to power a city.

"This has to be the largest eruption in recorded history," Holly says, hands pressed against the window, eyes wide with a mix of fear and admiration. Every volcanologist dreams of being this close to an eruption. The downside of that dream is that most volcanologists close enough to witness an eruption like this, don't survive to tell the tale.

I place my hands against the glass, sharing Holly's awe. As soon as my right hand touches the glass, I yank it back, hissing through my teeth. I look at the glove, wondering what the burn across my palm looks like now. A slave to curiosity, I pull the glove from my hand and look at the wound, now bright red. It had been black, and I had mistaken it for frostbite at first. But the spike had been hot, not cold.

No, I think, *that's not right either.* It had been cold to the touch when I first reached out for it. It was even covered with a thin film of ice that my body heat had melted. But when I snapped out of that vision, or whatever it was, the spike had become scorching hot. *A coincidence,* I tell myself, but it's hard to believe. The alternative is that physical contact with the spire triggered the reaction, and as a result, the subsequent eruption. But that makes no sense either, because Kiljan had the thing jammed in his toe and nothing happened. That pretty much leaves me with some kind of supernatural explanation, which is to say, no explanation at all.

Beeping pulls my attention away from the view and my thoughts. Kiljan has the satellite phone in his right hand, dialing with his thumb, while he steers with the left.

"Two hands on the wheel," Phillip insists from the back seat. "Ten and two, for God's sake!"

Kiljan puts the phone to his ear, glancing at me for a moment while he waits for whoever is on the other end to pick up. The look in his eyes, determined but full of doubt, chills me. We're roaring away from the volcano now, easily twelve miles out, but the big man still isn't convinced we're in the clear. I twist around and look out the rear window. The massive pyroclastic flow, lit in hues of orange by the setting sun ahead of us, rolls steadily downhill behind us. It's not moving at 450 mph, but even at a fraction of that speed, it will eventually overtake us. Perhaps within minutes.

Kiljan's conversation is loud, fast-paced and completely unintelligible, as he's speaking in his native Icelandic. When he hangs up, he looks simultaneously defeated and more determined.

"Who was that?" Phillip asks. "Who were you speaking to?"

"Airfield," Kiljan says, and I find myself nodding. The small airfield is the fastest way out of the region. If we could get airborne, it would be our best chance of survival. Perhaps our only chance. "There is one plane remaining." He glances at each of us. "But no pilot."

Phillip looks frozen in horror.

Diego sags forward a little bit. "Mierda."

"But..." Holly starts, and then just shakes her head and looks out the window.

"I can fly."

The words escape my mouth before I've really considered them. I have a pilot's license. I got it three years ago, when writing a piece about how easy it is to do so. Took all the classes. Passed the tests. And flew a plane for the required number of hours, while a *Modern Scientist* photographer snapped photos of me. It was a popular piece, and part of why I get to go on expeditions like this one, but I haven't flown a plane since. Nor have I had any real desire to. I put on a good smile for the camera, but I hated every second of it, knowing that one wrong move could send us plummeting to our doom.

Phillip scoffs. *"You?"*

"Unless you have wings or a teleporter," I say. Part of me screams at myself to shut-up, to withdraw my claim and tell Kiljan to keep driving. But I know where that path ends. We all do. Even Phillip, who crosses his arms, but swallows his complaints.

Kiljan tosses the phone into my lap and puts both hands on the wheel. My head slams into the headrest, when he shoves his injured foot down on the gas pedal. The superjeep roars even faster, fueled by hope. Possibly false hope.

I turn my eyes down, zoning out as I imagine a thousand different scenarios involving the plane and our deaths. A jarring bump rattles my thoughts, and I suddenly see the Sat phone resting on my lap. I lift it up and turn to Kiljan, "Do you mind?"

He looks at me like I just passed gas with a volume and stench only attainable by a hippopotamus on a fiber-rich diet. I take that as a 'yes,' and dial home. There are several clicks as the signal shoots into space, bounces across a network of satellites and then zips down into the landlines leading to New York. Five shrill rings are followed by the sweet, still high-pitched voice of an eight year old boy. "Hello?"

"Ike, buddy, is that you?"

"Dad?"

"It's me."

There are too many things I want to say to him. About his birth. His life. My failings as a father. About his mother. And about the future. But there isn't time for all that, so I just say, "I love you, Ike."

The boy laughs. I can picture him rolling his eyes. In public, he's not affectionate. At home he's all hugs. But even then, getting him to say those words every parent wants to hear, it's like the rarest gift. So when he says them now, "Love you, Dad," I start to cry.

Working my damnedest to not become a blubbering fool, I say, "Can I talk to mom?"

I hear a muffled, "Mommy!" on the other end, followed by, "Dad is on the phone!" Then his voice is clear and loud again. "She's coming."

There's a ruffle of movement and Mina's voice threatens to make me weep again. She's normally reserved and quiet, but not now. "Where are you? Tell me you're not there."

The eruption must have made news already. Most of the world might not know about it yet, but Mina keeps track of where I am and what's going on around me when I'm away.

"We're about to get on a plane," I say, feeling guilty for glossing over the truth. I look in the side view mirror. The wall of smoke rolling closer calls me a liar. I keep my eyes on the view as I talk, watching the billowing formations, laced with lightning and lit by the sun. Seen through a television, it would be beautiful. "I was just calling to..." *Shit. To what? Say goodbye? Just in case? There goes my 'getting on a plane' story.* "...to tell you both that I love you."

"There is no plane, is there?"

"There is," I say. "I promise there is."

"But you're not there yet."

"We're on our way." An aberration at the bottom of the churning cloud catches my attention. A line of undulating white separating the gray earth from the gray smoke streaks toward us, outpacing the cloud.

"Can you give me to Sabella?" I ask.

When she pauses, I add, "Hurry."

"Love you, too," she says, and I hear knocking. The house is a duplex. On one side is my wife of twelve years. On the other is my, for lack of a better word, *mistress* of eight years. It's a long, complicated story around two impossible pregnancies and what has become a polyamorous relationship. We're not polygamists, or part of a religious cult. Far from it. But when a series of unintended circumstances resulted in both women carrying my children at the same time, I couldn't abandon one of them, and neither of them wanted me to. While they don't love each other in a romantic sense, we are all one family now, and Ike and Ishah are the closest brothers—or half-brothers—I've ever seen.

During the transition, I tap Kiljan's shoulder and hitch my thumb backwards a few times. While he looks in the rearview, the three scientists in the back seat crane around to see what I'm motioning toward.

On the phone, I hear a door open. "Hey Min—" Bell's voice cuts short. "What's wrong?" That Bell can see that normally hard-to-ruffle Mina is upset means she *really* looks upset.

Mina starts to talk, "Abraham is—"

Then Bell's voice is loud in my ear. "Baby, what's happening?"

I smile at the obvious differences between the women. They even speak at different volumes. "Volcano. No biggie."

"Don't play," she says. "Mina looks worried. Like, really worried. You always said you'd give it to me straight if you were ever in trouble."

She's right. I did. But I never thought I'd be in trouble when I said that. Still, total honesty is how a relationship with two different women works. "I'd put my odds of getting out of this at sixty percent."

"Dear Lord Almighty," she says. Bell, unlike Mina and me, is a church goer. A true believer. Despite our strange familial lifestyle that she freely admits is 'living in sin.' And while I don't share her beliefs, her earnest love of God, the Bible and all the things that go along with that, have helped me realize that Christians aren't nearly as bad as the politicians who have hijacked the religion.

"Bollocks!" Phillip shouts. "It's glacial flooding!"

"It's gaining on us!" Diego adds.

"Who was that?" Bell asks. "Who did I just hear?"

"Colleagues," I say.

"Why are they shouting?"

"Because our odds just reversed."

"Oh, Lord Jesus."

"Listen, baby. I love you."

"Love you, Abe."

"Give the phone to Ishah."

"Ishah!" Bell shouts, and I can hear the warble in her voice. "Daddy's on the phone!"

I hear his small voice asking questions as he approaches, but it's lost in a burst of static. "Daddy...you...where..."

"Ishah?" I say, and then I shout into the phone. "Ishah!"

"—addy?"

The signal cuts out. "God damnit!" I start to dial the number again, but Kiljan stops me with a tap on the shoulder. He points ahead where a small hanger and landing strip emerge at the center of a valley. I recalculate our odds to fifty-fifty, and then look in the side view mirror again. I realize they're not remotely that good. A churning wall of water, just a mile back, cascades down the hill behind us. I clutch the phone in my hand, heartbroken over not being able to speak to Ishah, who is perhaps the most sensitive and intuitive person I know.

Goodbye, Ishah, I think, hoping that if Bell's God is real, he'll convey the message for me. *Love you, son.*

5

"You have got to be joking," Phillip complains, and this time I whole-heartedly agree with him. The superjeep kicks up a trail of dust as it roars down the side of the runway—a stretch of compressed, unpaved earth—headed for a small hanger at the far end. It's not the runway's condition or the hanger that's disconcerting, it's their positioning. To take off, we're going to have to fly *toward* the flood water and cloud of ash rolling at us.

"Could be worse." Diego grips both front seats, holding himself upright as Kiljan hits the brakes. "There could be no airplane."

There still could be, I think, but I keep the dire prediction to myself. It's bad enough that Diego is jinxing us with his positivity. Before the jeep comes to a complete stop, I shove open my door and slide down to the ground. In my mind's eye, I charge to the hangar door, kick it in if I have to, and save the day. Reality is a bitch. When my feet hit the hard ground, my legs wobble and give out. I catch myself on the door, holding myself up. After running for hours across a solid glacier, and then sitting without any kind of stretching, my legs feel like two planks joined by loose chains.

I nearly fall a second time when I grip the side of the door with my burned hand. Steadying myself, I turn my gaze back to the eruption. A mile-high wall of darkness moves steadily toward us, no longer a true pyroclastic flow, but suffocating and blinding and impossible to fly through. It would choke the plane's engine and its passengers. A column of twisting volcanic ash rises up into the upper layers of the atmosphere, moving out in all directions, including directly above us. It's creating a luminous, and ominous, sunset. Furious lightning cuts the sky like multi-headed Hydras lashing out at unseen foes. The lava spewing from the Earth's depths isn't visible from here, but I know it's there, heating up and rapidly melting the glacier. I know, because the result of that rapid melting still rushes toward us, outpacing the cloud. Water turned to mud after sliding over miles of terrain, flowing downhill with enough force to carry bus-sized boulders.

"Can you make it?" Holly asks, squeezing my arm with one hand while holding onto her door with the other. She looks as unsteady as me.

"I have to," I say, and I take a shaky step.

Kiljan, displaying his Nordic strength, limps to the hangar, outpacing the rest of us despite his injured toe. When he reaches the hangar door, he doesn't even try the knob, he just puts his shoulder into it and barrels through. A moment later, the large garage door at the front of the hangar rolls up, revealing the plane: a white and red Cessna. It's a single-prop airplane, not too dissimilar from the one I trained on. But it's not going to work.

There's only room for four people.

Kiljan emerges from the hangar, airplane keys in hand.

"This won't work." I point at the plane with a shaking finger, my feet growing steadier with each step forward. "There's only four seats, and even that will be cramped.

He hurries up to me, places the keys in my hand, and says, "Good luck to you."

"Wait. What?"

"I was never coming with you," he says. "My home. My family." He looks to the east and doesn't need to say anything else. If he didn't abandon us on the glacier, he's not going to leave his family, who are apparently located downhill—soon to be downstream.

"Thank you," I say, and we part ways, him rushing back into the superjeep, me hobbling to the hanger.

Reaching the airplane is hard enough, but climbing inside nearly undoes our beaten group. It takes a team effort to get all of us inside the cramped cabin, Holly and I in the front, Diego and Phillip in the back. The well maintained plane smells like cigar smoke, but the engine turns over on the first try. I start going through the pre-flight checklist that was drilled into me. "Flight controls, free and correct. Altimeter, set. Directional gyro, set. Fuel gauges—"

"There's no time for all that!" Phillip shouts, thrusting his hand at the view through the front windshield like he's trying to fling off a glob of peanut butter. The flood of viscous mud rolls over the valley wall straight ahead, oozing out in all directions, rolling boulders, and heading steadily toward the airstrip. When it envelopes the chain link fence fifty feet from the runway, I push the throttle forward, and the RPM gauge snaps to life.

I don't bother looking for a headset to drown out the buzzing propeller. There's no time for that. Maybe not enough time to take off. We roll clear of the hangar doors, and I shove the throttle forward. The engine coughs once, making my heart skip, but then it roars to life. The airfield on both sides becomes a blur, but I can clearly see the superjeep keeping pace beside us until it reaches the gate, makes a hard right turn and speeds away in the opposite direction.

"Pull up!" Phillip shouts from the back, his voice nearly drowned by the propeller. I can't see him, but it sounds like he's crying. Not that I blame him. We're now rushing straight toward a wall of darkness that, though lifeless, appears like a hungry beast, ready to devour us.

But I don't pull up. Not yet. We're not moving fast enough.

"Abe!" Holly is gripping her seat, still not strapped in. She looks as mortified as Phillip sounds.

"Buckle up!" I shout at her. The plane shakes around us, the din garbling my voice, but she gets the message. She flinches and looks down, and then fumbles with her belt for a moment before clipping it in place.

I pull back on the control stick gently, lifting the plane's nose off the ground. The wings and tail follow, lifted up while g-forces pull my stomach down, twisting my gut and reminding me why I stopped flying in planes this small. The shaking stops, granting a momentary peace, until I see the wall of mud rushing toward us.

We're not high enough yet.

Grinding my teeth, I yank the control stick back, putting us into a steep climb. The engine whines, but doesn't stop. A giant boulder rolls toward and then beneath us, bringing back memories of Han Solo in the asteroid field. Then we're above the flood and rising, approaching the mile-high ash cloud.

Part of my brain registers voices in the cockpit, but the words are filtered out by my intense focus. We're rising at a seventy-degree angle, still headed directly toward the ash, but gaining altitude. I'm sure someone is telling me to turn, but I'm no stunt pilot. To turn around without crashing, I'm going to have to level out first, and that means getting above the plume.

With one hand still gripping the control stick, I reach down and push the throttle. It only moves a little, but the slight jolt of speed pushes me back into my seat.

People are still shouting, and it still just sounds like noise, but now it's irritating me. "Just hold on and shut up!" I shout, leaning forward and gazing straight up. We're headed toward a precipice of gray, above which is a broad open swath of sky with a ceiling of dark volcanic smoke high above.

"We're not going to make it," I say, as the clouds close in.

Diego starts whispering in Spanish, perhaps cussing me out, perhaps saying a prayer. There're no atheists in foxholes, they say. Maybe the same thing is true for scientists in airplanes about to fly into a volcanic dust cloud? I consider this for a moment and quickly dismiss it. The only person, living, dead or deity who can help me right now, is me.

"What!" Phillip pulls on my chair, as he leans forward to shout at me. The seat tilts back from the added weight, pulling me and the control stick with it. Phillip falls back when the plane tilts up at a sharper angle. My equilibrium struggles to make sense of the tilted world, and I have the strangest sense that I'm about to fall backward.

Darkness envelopes us. Tiny particles hiss against the metal body. I imagine the engine's air intake, sucking the stuff down, and right on time, it coughs.

And then, like the baptized rising from the water, we spring free of the cloud and rise into the orange light of the setting sun once more. I feel reborn. Elated. Light. As I level out the Cessna, cheers surround me. The doubtful Phillip pats my shoulder. "Good show. Good show."

"Gracias, Abe," Diego says. "Muchas gracias."

Holly gives me a grin and shakes her head. The look in her eyes says that a hero's reward awaits me when we land, but my life is complicated enough already. Holly is smart, pretty and fun to be with, but I'm a two-woman man.

Exuberance turns to stunned silence. The view through the windshield is apocalyptic. Hell on Earth. The land, for as far as I can see, is covered by the thick ash cloud, which has raced away from the volcano in every direction, chasing a flood of water scouring the terrain clean. Far ahead is a line of luminous orange. Lava. It stretches across the landscape.

"It wasn't just Bardarbunga," I say.

"It looks like the entire volcanic chain erupted." Holly meets my eyes. "That's *thirty* volcanoes."

"That makes no sense," Phillip says. "The release of magma from one volcano should have reduced the pressure on the rest of the system. This kind of eruption is theoretically impossible."

"Reality often turns theory on its head," Diego says, sounding more like the calm, thoughtful man I'd met yesterday. "Makes the impossible, possible. Sometimes even scientific laws are proven incorrect. That's why wholeheartedly embracing a theory—believing that the world's mysteries have been solved—can be not only inaccurate, but dangerous."

"Says the man who works with inanimate rocks," Phillip says.

Far in the distance, a fresh volcanic eruption tears out of the smoke field and billows into the sky.

"Holy shit," Holly says. "Holy shit! It's rising miles into the air, in seconds. That kind of force isn't—"

"Hold on!" I shout, banking hard to the right.

As the plane swings around, I glance out the cockpit window to my left.

And freeze.

My mind struggles to comprehend what I'm seeing. Amidst the rising and falling ash, above and below the burbling lava and the streaks of lightning, there is *something* else. It rises up within the smoke column, dripping lava as it extends miles into the sky. I follow it upward and see the edge of a jagged shape within the smoke, turning. Atop the still rising form, there's a black sphere, and I get the sense that this thing is looking at me. The clouds part for just a moment, and I see a splash of red, made radiant by the setting sun.

"Holly," I say, trying to sound calm. I lean back and point out the side window. She looks past me, but her expression doesn't change. She's seen nothing.

I look out the window again and see the chaotic eruption still unfolding, but nothing else. No shapes, or giant limbs, or eyes.

Another vision?

A shockwave slams into the plane, pitching it to the side. I fight the controls, trying to keep us right-side up. When it passes and we find ourselves still airborne and sky-worthy, I accelerate to full speed and race away from what will become known as Event Alpha, the first day of the world's end.

6

KATI

Kati Takacs breathed deeply, in through the nose, out through the mouth. Each breath was timed with every fourth footfall, her running limbs and her lungs in perfect sync. She glanced at the heart monitor on her wrist, the digital display showing a perfect 85%, which was her target rate for the half marathon she planned to run in a month. She had honed her body into an efficient machine, and took great pride in her physical achievements. The same could be said for her business acumen. In a world still run by men—anyone who said otherwise *was* a man—she built her law firm case-by-case, earning a reputation for no nonsense, and at times, aggressive legal representation. She ran the firm with the same rigid protocols that kept her exercise routine well oiled. Everything in its place.

Every document. Every employee. Every sinew and bone in her body.

All of it was perfect.

A flawless sculpture.

So why am I so unhappy? she wondered, and she watched the heart rate leap forward, scrolling its way toward 90%.

Through sheer force of will, she purged her mind of doubts. *I'm on the right path. I'm successful, wealthy...*

...and alone.

The realization tripped her up, and she staggered to a stop in the center of the single lane road—the only one—stretching from one end of SEAcroft to the other. The small village was the most northwest town in all of the UK, located on the isle of Lewis, in the Uig parish—which was to say, in the middle of nowhere. Kati had summered in the quaint locale as a child, staying in a rented cottage. While her parents had read books on the beach, she had grumbled about being bored. When she decided to take a holiday—the first of her career—at the insistence of her psychiatrist, she returned to SEAcroft, hoping to find her now deceased parents wiser than she remembered. She discovered that little had changed since childhood, about the tiny village, or about her desire for more. For better. She'd spent just one night in the one-and-only local inn, and was already feeling restless.

So she ran.

And now, stopped between an adorable gray stone home and a rolling green field where some sheep had paused munching grass to look at her, she wasn't sure if she was running toward her life, or away from it.

"You all right, luv?" a woman said, her sea-weathered face peeking out from an open window. Her round cheeks were framed by two lace curtains. "Can I get you a drink? Some tea maybe?"

Kati smiled as a long forgotten memory returned. She closed her eyes and saw the woman, twenty years younger and just as many pounds lighter. Kati had been walking this same barren stretch of road leading to the Atlantic Ocean, kicking stones. The woman, this same woman in this same house, had offered her a soft drink. "Fizzy drink, luv?" she'd asked.

Kati's mouth watered at the memory of the grape soda, and the cherry licorice that had followed it. For an hour on a single, boring day on holiday with her parents, this woman had been her friend. While the woman had apparently not changed much since then, Kati had.

"No thanks," Kati said, moving forward.

"I have licorice, too, if that suits your fancy."

Kati paused and looked back. *Does she remember me, too?* she wondered, but she just shook her head and returned to her confident stride.

Leave the past behind.

Focus on the future.

On growth. On strength.

These are the things that create greatness.

"And anxiety disorders," she heard her psychiatrist say. "Go on holiday. Someplace quiet. Reflect on your life. On what really matters. Then reevaluate."

Reevaluating sucks, she decided, and she poured on the steam. She pushed her heart rate to 95%, perfect both for a 10k race and for ignoring tough choices. She passed small homes to her left and more sheep to the right, the treeless landscape otherwise barren. Cresting a hill, she saw the ocean ahead. Its vastness filled her with hope, and she ran for it, pushing forward as the road became something closer to a trail. As a child, she had never explored past this point. Believed it was private land. It very well might have been, but she knew the law. Without a posted sign claiming it as private property, or a fence to keep her out, she could go where she pleased until told otherwise.

Her heart monitor showed 98%. A 5k pace. Something about the ocean drew her in. The way it smelled. The rising crescendo of the crashing waves. The call of seabirds. Maybe *this* was why her parents had come here?

The path led out onto a peninsula, turning right toward what looked like a small compound. A business, or just more solitary residents. She didn't care which, and continued running straight, off the path and toward the sea.

Approaching a cliff that dropped down into the ocean, Kati slowed to a jog and then stopped. Hands on knees, she caught her breath. Then she lifted her head and took it all in. The morning sun warmed her back. A strong breeze rolled in from the ocean, cooling her sweat-dampened cheeks before pushing waves into the rocks below. The scene enveloped and calmed her, blocking out the hubbub of life she left behind on the mainland.

A deep breath brought tears to her eyes.

I shouldn't be here alone, she thought. *Why am I?*

She thought back to lovers come and gone, none of them serious, all of them short-lived trysts. She didn't have poor taste in men, but they clearly had poor taste in women. Each of them. She'd made her body available on occasion, when she'd fancied, but the rest of her had hidden—and still hid—behind steel emotional walls. Walls that could apparently be rusted and cracked by a dramatic ocean view.

As tears rolled down her cheeks, she looked for a place to sit, but paused when the air grew hot around her. The sun hadn't suddenly moved higher in the sky, so the heat had come from the ocean, which was frigid, even in the summer. Her eyes turned back to the water, looking out to the horizon, where a dark cloud marred the view. But the distant storm, blotting out the sky, looked cold, not hot.

And yet, the temperature pushed by the ocean breeze continued to grow warmer. Her nose scrunched at a recognizable, but totally out-of-place smell. She turned around, searching the distant compound for any sign of a pool. She saw nothing, but even if there was a pool, why was she smelling chlorine—from the ocean?

She turned back to the storm, squinting and wondering. The word *ominous* came to mind, but brought a smile to her face. She had completely forgotten about the world and its troubles, but not its technologies. She dug into her pocket, plucked out her smartphone and opened her weather app. She was pleased to see that she had cell coverage, even out here, and she waited for the app to find her current location and update.

A flashing red warning caught her attention.

Disaster Alert — Volcanic Eruption.

Her thumb moved to tap on the message, but she stopped when the scent of chlorine became unbearable. Her nostrils burned. Her eyes watered.

"Oh," she complained, rubbing her eyes and turning away from the ocean. "Oh!"

A shrieking of birds turned her watering eyes to the sky above the ocean. A swirling flock of agitated gulls swarmed skyward, as though frightened. Half of the group headed toward open ocean. The rest toward the coast.

Toward Kati.

She gasped, the sudden deep breath scorching her lungs, as the gulls flying out to sea contorted, spasmed and fell, lifeless into the waves. Backing away from the ocean, Kati watched the inbound birds fall from the sky, one by one, starting with the furthest and moving forward as though something invisible were reaching out and crushing them.

There is *something invisible,* she thought, looking at the distant black cloud, which she now realized wasn't a storm at all, but a volcanic eruption originating in Iceland. But she'd only stopped reading the news for the past day, which meant the eruption had taken place in the past twenty-four hours. For the plume of smoke and ash to already be visible from SEAcroft, the eruption's force must have been catastrophic. Her hand rose to her lips, as she remembered the loud boom that had interrupted her meal the previous evening. She'd assumed it was an errant thunderclap. But now she knew what it was, and understood what was happening to the birds.

It was gas.

Chlorine for sure, probably CO2, and God knew what else was being shoved ahead of the ash, propelled by the distant explosion.

And if there was enough of it to choke the birds in mid-air, there's more than enough to do me in.

Kati wheeled around, facing the village, and sprinted.

Focusing on the path ahead, her legs became a blur. While she normally concentrated on endurance running, because it most resembled the slow, steady climb of the business world, she occasionally sprinted, reflecting times when legal battles were closer to wars. She was a fighter, not prone to giving up. Yet with every breath, the sting of chlorine seeped deeper into her lungs, where it was absorbed and sent coursing through her body.

Routine drew her eyes to her heart monitor. It was pegged at 100%, a fact she already knew because of the pounding in her chest, the ache of a strained heart as unfamiliar to her as breathing chlorine.

She covered the distance between the ocean and the single lane street in under two minutes, but her legs began to shake. She slowed as she approached the line of homes, now on her right. Her chest heaved with coughs, and then for air. *Not air,* she thought, *oxygen.*

Her eyes widened as the sheep on the left side of the road let out a pain-filled bleat. It kicked and thrashed against some unseen attacker, desperate and afraid. Its front legs folded beneath its body, and it ran like that, pushed along by its hind legs for a few more steps before collapsing. It then let out a long sigh and fell still.

The door to the house on her right opened and the familiar face of her old friend greeted her once more, this time with a look of abject horror. The woman tried to speak, but couldn't past her swollen tongue. She fell to her knees, clutching her throat, and then laid as still as the sheep.

No, Kati thought. Move!

Her legs beat against the pavement, but became useless after just a few steps, her body and mind deprived of oxygen.

She stumbled off the road, reaching out for balance and grasping hold of the thin metal wire surrounding the wide-open sheep field. The pain in her mouth, throat and lungs was momentarily dwarfed by a jolt of electricity, coursing from the fence, up through her arms.

Her shout of pain lodged inside her swollen throat. If the air around her was still breathable, it would have done her no good.

She rolled onto her back, gulping.

Dying.

Regretting.

As her vision blurred, she let go of the world she had built. The business. The million pound flat. The expensive dinners. None of it mattered in the end. Her head lolled to the side, and for a moment, she saw the beach where her parents used to sit and read. *I'm sorry,* she thought, as she saw only darkness. *I should have enjoyed it all more.*

And then, Kati Takacs laid still, for the first time in her life, at peace.

The invisible cloud of chlorine and CO_2, ignorant to her passing, continued on its journey inland, propelled by the staggering eruption's influence on the region's weather patterns. High winds swept the gases southeast over Lewis and Harris, the largest of the Western Isles, killing all 18,500 residents and 875 visitors, before descending on northern Scotland, where it thinned and eventually settled in the Highlands, but not before claiming another 235,000 lives.

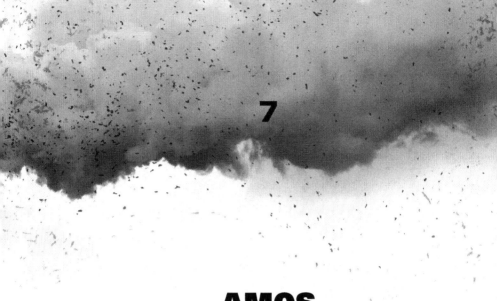

7

AMOS

"Tighter," Amos Johansen told his son, his voice rumbling in his chest. The resonant volume of his words made him sound larger than life, but he knew the baritone had more to do with his smoking than his manly stature. As Nordic men went, he was small. He stood no taller than his wife, an average Nordic woman, and only a few inches taller than Ralf, his thirteen year old son. He hadn't weighed himself in years, but he suspected both wife and son outweighed him.

Ralf rolled his eyes and undid the pile hitch knot, tying the small fishing vessel off once more. "I know how to do this. Better than you."

When Ralf turned thirteen, seven months previously, he suddenly knew everything about everything, including fishing, knot-tying and cooking—tasks Amos had been working on all his life, under the tutelage of his own father, Hagnar. The family had owned and operated the Fjord Sjømat Restaurant for more than fifty years, and Ralf believed himself ready to take on the mantle of owner, operator and head chef all at once.

Amos didn't judge the boy too harshly, though. He still remembered saying similar things to *his* father, though he wasn't allowed to get away with it. Hagnar Johansen was a hard man, who had wielded a switch the way gladiators did swords, brought in record hauls of fish and fried most dishes. Fish were more scarce these days, so Amos cooked with finesse, using locally sourced organic foods that brought in wealthier patrons from the mainland. Beneath the Fjord's sign, in smaller text, were the words, 'Finest Tappas on Frøya,' which locals got a chuckle from, because there were only two restaurants on the island of Frøya—both located in the small town of Kalvåg, and the other still fried everything.

"I'm sure you do," Amos said, sarcasm bubbling to the surface.

If there was anything Ralf loathed more than being told what to do, it was not being taken seriously. The boy stood from his knot-tying duty and thrust an index finger at Amos. "First you make me stay out all night fishing, and for what?" He motioned to the cooler resting on the dock between them. "Five cod. Then you ride me about the knot. And now you mock me? You never take me seriously. You never listen. You don't understand."

If Amos had ever spoken to his father in this manner, he didn't remember it. The memory would have been knocked out of him. And that part of him that was his father's son wanted to find a length of wood and teach the boy a lesson. But it was far too late for such things. The confrontation would be less of a discipline between father and son and more of a fair fight. The part of him that loathed his father, revolted at the idea.

He decided to wield the only real power he held. "You will do as I say, when I say it, or you will spend your summer on Frøya, cleaning dishes."

The boy's mouth snapped closed, but his eyes filled with fire. Ralf's girlfriend lived on the mainland, a traverse over several islands connected by a series of bridges, and then a long drive to Haugeelva.

"Your ancestors would have traveled much further on foot to find a good woman," Amos joked, feeling pleased.

"Maybe I will," Ralf said.

"If you get started now, you might be there in time for dinner."

"It won't take that long." The boy crossed his arms.

Amos smiled at the boy's growing absurdity. "You've walked the distance before?" He patted his own slender belly and looked at Ralf's chubbier girth. "I think not." It was a low blow. Ralf had grown up in a restaurant, eating rich foods at every meal. While Amos's rapid metabolism had kept him slender with little effort, the plump boy had more of his mother's genes.

The defiance melted from the boy's face, replaced by a sudden wash of self-degradation. Tears filled his eyes.

I've gone too far, Amos realized. *Again.*

While Hagnar had been a violent father, Amos made his son cry nearly as often, stinging the boy with his words rather than with his hands.

Venting a sigh, Amos walked to his son, brushed away the boy's protesting hands and wrapped him in a hug. Ralf resisted, but the effort was half-hearted. He was as affectionate as he was overweight.

"I'm sorry," Amos said, scolding himself, in part for speaking cruelly, but more so for losing this battle of wits with his son. Making the boy cry shifted the outcome of this argument in Ralf's favor. Despite the boy's rude and defiant behavior, Amos was the one apologizing. In fact, the sudden reversal got Amos thinking. With widening eyes, he leaned his face around, looking at the side of his son's face, where phony tears framed a more honest grin.

He's manipulating me!

Amos reconsidered the switch for a moment, but movement caught his attention. The pile hitch, tied too loose again, was coming undone.

Ralf stumbled away as Amos pushed him. "The knot, you deceptive buffoon!"

The boy looked ready to launch right back into a second round of verbal sparring, when he glanced back and saw the rope snaking free of the piling. "Shit!" He took hold of the rope, which was about to fall into the water and struggled to pull the small boat back to the pier. "Father, help!"

Amos crossed his arms. The advantage had shifted again. "You can do it without me, can't you?"

"Help me, you asshole!"

Heat and pressure built inside Amos. He strode to his son, fully intending to shove the boy into the frigid Norwegian Sea. To teach him a lesson he wouldn't forget. But when he saw the boy struggling to hold the boat, which was surging away as though under power, worry gripped him.

"Let go!" he shouted, rushing forward and wrapping his arms around the boy's waist before he was pulled in the water. But it was a temporary measure. The taut rope would pull them both in. "Let go!"

"But the boat!" Ralf shouted.

"Let. It. Go."

"It was grandfather's."

"He was an asshole, too," Amos said. "It is not worth our lives!"

Ralf released the rope and both Johansen men spilled back onto the dock. Amos crashed into the cooler, knocking it off the far side of the dock. After colliding with the wood floor, he heard it land, but not with a splash. Instead, he heard a wet thud.

Confused by the sound, Amos rolled over and looked down. Where there had been water just moments ago, there was now only muddy, pungent-smelling seafloor. Exposed crabs scurried over the mud, looking for hiding places.

"Father," Ralf said, sounding astonished. "Look."

Amos pushed himself up and turned around, already expecting to see something strange, but nothing remotely close to what he found. The Frøysjøen strait, which was sixteen miles long and two and a half miles from Kalvåg to the far side, had come to life with a sudden, raging ferocity. The flow of water, which rose and fell with the tides, surged out to sea, fast enough to cover the small, unpopulated islands dotting the straight.

Their small fishing boat was pulled away by the retreating waters, joining a fleet of other boats, some empty, some holding crews of fishermen and lobstermen, shouting for help.

"What is this?" Amos said. His family had lived on the island for generations upon generations. He knew Frøya's stories—the true and tragic along with the fictional and mythical. But not one of them told of waters rushing out of the strait with enough force to pull boats from piers and men out to sea.

Ralf had his own answer. "Tsunami."

"A giant wave?" Amos asked. "That does not happen here."

The boy dug into his pants pocket and pulled out a smartphone.

"I know the definition of a tsunami," Amos complained, sure the boy was trying to educate him again.

Ralf held up the phone so Amos could see the screen, which was displaying a BBC news app. The first story listed under Top Stories had the headline: Iceland's Bardarbunga Volcano Erupts. "Says it's the largest eruption in modern history. That travel is going to be restricted across Europe for weeks. Maybe months."

Amos held up his hands. He knew what Bardarbunga was and understood the ramifications. He'd vacationed on Iceland several times, and he remembered the fallout from Eyjafjallajökull in 2010. "Why didn't you tell me?"

"Like you would have listened."

Anger squeezed Amos's heart, but he held it at bay. "Bardarbunga isn't on the coast. Why would it cause a wave?"

"It released a gas cloud, too," Ralf said. "Killed people in Scotland."

Fear quickly overpowered Amos's anger. "How *many* people?"

Ralf shrugs. "No one has been able to check. But a lot, I guess."

Amos snatched the phone from his son's hand and quickly read the article, which was scant on details and heavy on speculation. But the reality of the situation was impossible to ignore. While Bardarbunga was the first volcano to erupt, more than thirty had since the previous night. *That boom,* Amos thought, remembering the throaty reverberation that had rolled over the open ocean like a passing jet. *We* heard *it.* Prevailing winds and the eruption's force had pushed volcanic ash and gas southeast toward the UK. He looked at a projection of how far the ash would travel. The trail skirted the southern regions of Norway and Sweden before heading into Europe, but a shift in the wind could bring it farther north.

Amos scrambled to his feet and dragged Ralf with him.

The boy pulled free of his father's grasp. "Hey!" But Amos took hold of him again and shoved him toward the red building at the end of the pier. The first floor of the large seaside building was the Fjord restaurant. The second floor was home to Amos and his family.

"Get your mother!" Amos shouted, reaching into his pockets for the car keys.

"What? Why?" Ralf pointed to the tall hills rising up beyond the line of homes and businesses lining the road that wrapped around the island. "The open ocean is on the far side of the island. The wave won't hit us here."

Amos thrust his hand at the now empty strait. "Where the water flees, it will also return. You put too much faith in our seawall." He moved his hand to the now revealed stone wall, covered in seaweed and barnacles. More than a few of the stones had slipped into the mud below. "And we're not fleeing the water. We're fleeing the ash. I do not wish to choke to death, do you?"

Ralf sobered, heading for the back door, while Amos unlocked the car. "Where will we go?"

"North."

"Can we pick up Gayle on the—"

"Get your mother!" Amos shouted. "Your girlfriend has parents of her own. Go! Now!"

While Ralf disappeared into the house, Amos started the car and mentally mapped out their route, heading north to Heggelia, where his brother lived. *But what if that is not far enough?* Amos worried. He remembered an airport near his brother's. Perhaps they could fly out if the skies were still clear?

Both passenger side doors opened. Ralf and his mother, Bitta, climbed into the car, tilting the small vehicle to the right. "What is all this about?" Bitta asked. Her hair was tied in a bun, but somehow still disheveled. She wore a flour-dusted apron and smelled of warm bread. "The loaves will be useless if the stove stays off."

"Close the door," Amos said and stepped on the gas.

Bitta yelped as the door closed on its own and the tires screeched over the pavement. As they tore down route 616, which took them along the coast of Frøya and across several bridges to the mainland, they saw long-time friends and neighbors cramming into their own cars, as well.

"Slow down!" Bitta shouted.

Amos glanced at the speedometer. He was going twice the speed limit. There was no one in front of him. He was leading the pack. Hoping those behind him would follow suit, Amos pushed the gas pedal harder.

The ground shook beneath them. Amos let up on the gas while he fought the wheel for control. Bitta screamed.

"Is the water returning?" Amos asked, eyeing the first bridge ahead of them.

"I cannot see it," Ralf said from the back, looking out the passenger's side window to an empty fjord.

Slowing to turn onto the bridge, Amos glanced left. Homes and farmland stretched out and ended at the base of a rocky hill ascending more than two hundred feet at the island's core. But where there should have been blue sky at the crest, there was, instead, a wave.

The ocean rose up, swallowing the island whole.

As warm piss coated the seat beneath him, Amos pushed the gas pedal to the floor and raced across the bridge.

"Oh, god," Ralf said. "Oh, god!"

To their right, the ocean returned to the strait, hundreds of feet deeper, surging toward them and consuming everything in its path. Amos willed the car to move faster, but the vehicle's 100 mph top speed was 400mph too slow to outrun the rushing waters. One instant the water was rising up behind them and beside them, and the next, it erased them.

The Johansens died instantly, their vehicle and bodies torn into unrecognizable bits strewn over Norway, 100 miles inland. The 500-foot-tall wall of water struck Norway moving at 600 mph. Minutes later, it struck Scotland, scouring hundreds of thousands of poisoned bodies from the landscape and increasing the death toll. Ireland followed with similar results. The island nations stole much of the wave's energy, but a swath of Europe, from Norway to Spain was struck by the wave. Half a day later, the west coast of Africa was hit. And a full day later, South America was slapped, from Venezuela to the most eastern edge of Brazil. With some warning, South American nations were able to partly evacuate affected areas, but across the world, millions of lives were lost.

8

ABRAHAM

Upon stepping into JFK International Airport, I'm greeted by a loud, "Daddy." Then I'm tackled by two small bodies, squeezed and loved by sons who both somehow resemble me without looking at all alike. Mina and Bell follow, hugging more gently, shedding tears of relief that our strange family is whole once more. No one stares. No one judges. The world just lets us be.

That's my fantasy.

And the first part that's wrong is that I'm not stepping anywhere. Not yet. I'm confined to a wheelchair, because my legs are fairly useless. It's been less than a day since fleeing Bardarbunga's eruption, first on foot, then in the superjeep and finally in the Cessna, which carried us to Keflavík International Airport. Thanks to its location on the far west coast of Iceland and the ash cloud's eastern trajectory, the airport remained open, and still does. While floods have consumed much of the island nation's east, the west has suffered only minor damage from a series of earthquakes that rumbled through the land, the previous night. They resulted in a tsunami that killed untold millions throughout Europe.

I close my eyes, confused by a strange cauldron of emotions. I was at ground zero for the world's worst volcanic eruption in modern history and survived. But all those people in Europe, choked by gas and water... It doesn't seem fair that they should perish, while I live.

I'm not ungrateful. My sons still have a father. My wife a husband. And my mistress her love. But I feel guilty for surviving while so many others died. Normal survivor's guilt is triggered when something like a car crash claims some lives while sparing others. The odds of survival are equal and left to chance, or to fate, or Bell would say, to God. But that's not what happened to me. I stood at the point of impact, between metaphorical crashing cars, all odds against survival. And not only did I survive, but the crash extended to the far side of the road, resulting in a pile up claiming the lives of everyone for miles.

I should have died. That I didn't, feels like the very laws of nature have been broken on my behalf. Surviving while so many others perished is an unexpected burden, shouting at me, 'What will you do with your life now?'

My heart replies, 'Go home. Love my family. Live a quiet life.'

But my mind finds this offensive. How can I live such a small, simple life, when it feels like I was spared for a reason, for a purpose beyond my understanding?

As I'm wheeled down the 747's aisle, I decide not to mention these thoughts to Sabella. Mina's logical mind will break it down for me. Help me make sense of these emotions. Bell, for all her abounding love, will add the weight of eternity to my already heavy load.

The eyes of my fellow passengers—Americans escaping Iceland—follow my progress through the plane, as I'm wheeled by a flight attendant. They all heard the story of our escape from the frozen caldera, a yarn spun by Phillip upon our arrival at Keflavík, where I landed—nearly crashed—the Cessna, without permission. We were arrested, but freed upon Phillip's dramatic retelling, in which he was elevated to heroic status, and upon our very dire predictions for the volcanic fallout. We were, after all, the only experts in the area to witness and survive the eruption. And they had much bigger problems on their hands—the kind that determine the very lives and deaths of nations, never mind individuals.

I get a few nods from men I don't know. Smiles from the women. Wide eyes from the kids.

"Are you a hero?" a little boy asks me.

"Surviving doesn't make you a hero," I tell him as I pass.

Then I hear Holly, who's being wheeled out behind me, tell him, "He saved us all."

"Really?" the kid asks, as if by 'all' she meant the human race.

"Really," Holly says, and I suppose she's right. Deigo, Phillip and Holly are alive because of me. Kiljan, who knows, but I wish him well.

The journey through the jet bridge is silent. The flight attendants just smile and push Holly and me, side-by-side. Holly smiles at me, takes my hand in hers, and squeezes. As we approach the doorway ahead, I hear a sound like angry bees coming from the far side.

Holly squeezes again. "For real. Thank you."

I squeeze back and offer a smile.

It's the most she's going to get, though I can see she'd appreciate more. "Maybe we'll work together again."

"Count on it," she says, and frees my hand from her tightening grasp.

The doors open.

Light explodes in our faces.

Voices assault us from every direction, the cacophony sounding like an alien language, roaring. A waterfall, resounding. I flinch at the memory of the black figure, placing its staff into my hand. Its voice. Then my hands are raised, blocking the light strobe.

"Look," someone says. "He *is* hurt."

Lights flash faster. Photographers are taking pictures of my gauze-wrapped hand like it's Taylor Swift's panties. The waterfall takes on a new tone. Questioning me. About Iceland. Bardarbunga. Europe. Holly. *What?* I managed to leave a frozen-turned-fiery hell behind, only to enter a new kind of modern hell, where the people I love are held at bay by a throng of hungry reporters. They're jostling over sound bites like hyenas over a kill, yapping and pushing, ready to pounce at the first sign of life.

I'm thankful when a man in a black suit steps between me and the reporters. "Back. Give them space. Everyone back."

But then a particularly resilient reporter breaks the line, thrusts a microphone in my face and asks, "Mr. Wright, how do you think you survived, while so many others in the region—"

The man in the black suit descends on the reporter, yanking him back by his shirt collar and shoving him back in line. Then he lifts a badge and says, "Secret Service. The next of you to interfere will—"

"Freedom of the Press!" the reporter shouts, stepping up to the tall, black secret service man, but not making physical contact. "What gives you the right to..."

I miss the rest when a second suited man, who looks like a Tom Cruise clone, wrests control of my wheelchair and whisks me away.

"What's going on?" I stretch my neck up, looking through a glass wall for Mina or Bell. They were supposed to be here. "Where's my family?"

"They'll join you later," the man says.

"Join me? Where?" I twist back and forth, searching. The reporters, still held at bay by the large secret service agent, have quieted down. Holly is being wheeled behind me by a third agent. A woman.

Then I see them, waving and frantic, on the far side of the glass partition. My family. Ike leaps onto a bench, looking worried, while Ishah clings to Bell's neck, supported by her hip. He looks like he's been crying. I reach a hand out to them, but it's slapped down.

"Watch it," the agent says. I'm about to complain when we pass through a doorway and I lose sight of my family.

"Where the hell are we going?" I ask, gripping the wheels with both hands, but forced to let go when the friction burns one hand and the gauze covered hand just slips. Then I see where we're going—not the ultimate destination, but a mode of transportation. We're on a jet bridge, approaching the open door of a plane. The two men waiting for me are dressed in U.S. Air Force uniforms. Their steady gazes and shaved heads intimidate me, but I'm still too angry to care. I find the wheelchair's brake and push it hard against the wheel. Forward momentum tips the chair forward. As I lean toward the floor, I plant my feet, push hard and rise—a few inches.

I stumble to the side and crash into the jet bridge wall. Thick hands catch me, while rough hands grab me from behind.

"I've got him," says a new voice. One of the Air Force men. He's older than most active duty military men, his salt and pepper hair hidden by the short haircut, but visible in his mustache.

"Your problem now," the short secret service agent says, before doing an about-face and motioning to the woman pushing an equally stunned, but less indignant Holly. "We're done here."

Without a word, Holly is abandoned and has to slow the wheelchair on her own.

"Sorry about them, Mr. Wright," the Air Force man says, then he nods to Holly. "Ms. Interlandi. I am Major David Gibbs." He looks me in the eyes. "You're not a light man, Mr. Wright, mind if I sit you back down?"

Working together, we get me back into the chair. I'm able to walk some, but not without help. Another day and I should be fully mobile again, though it's going to hurt, maybe even worse than today, but I plan on being medicated by then. I lean back in the wheelchair seat with a groan. "Where are you taking us?"

"I'm going to tell you everything I know," Gibbs says. "Everything. With the hopes that we can avoid further incident."

I can't promise I'll play nice without hearing what he has to say, so I just wait in silence for him to speak.

"Deal," Holly says for me.

"Our destination is Washington, D.C. My mission is to fly you both there, where a second Secret Service team will pick you up."

When he falls silent, I ask, "That's it?"

"That's it. That's all I know, but given your recent experiences in Iceland, and the Secret Service treatment, my guess is that you're both headed for the White House. The world is in a tizzy, and you both were firsthand witnesses."

While it makes some kind of sense, I don't appreciate the surprise, or being torn away from my family. "My kids are out there. My family. They took me away before I could even speak to them."

Gibbs steps behind my chair and starts pushing, while the second, silent U.S. Airman pushes Holly. "Understand your frustration, sir. And I will look into it for you. But the situation is fluid. The death toll is climbing. And while the fallout is primarily affecting Europe, the whole world is going to feel it. I've been in the military for a long time, sir. Where you and I might see tragedy, others will see opportunity. If there was anything I could do to help avert further loss of life, I would do it." He pauses to look down at me, his mustached grin upside down. "Wouldn't you?"

"They told me my family would join me later," I say.

"Like I said, I'll look into it." He wheels me into the plane, and we turn through a door just wide enough for the wheelchair. Two U.S. Marines salute the Major as we enter and step aside to reveal what looks like a plush corporate jet outfitted for Marines on the go. While the seats at the front of the plane are intact, the rear has been converted into a mobile weapons locker. A special forces unit could probably climb aboard and be ready for just about any mission upon landing.

Then I realize where we are. A friend of mine wrote a piece about it years ago. But it had just been speculation based on rumor and legend. The story told of how the U.S. Marines adopted the luxurious Gulfstream IV, after it was damaged by a tornado. During its repair, some of the accoutrements were kept, but much of it was gutted and converted to a mission-ready plane that moved Marines, weapons and cargo during 476 sorties, without being identified as a military asset. Legend no more. This is the real thing. "The Gray Ghost."

"You know your planes," Gibbs says, impressed.

"I know a little about a lot," I say.

Holly stands from her wheelchair, takes a shaky step and slides into the nearest seat. "He knows *a lot* about a lot."

"I have a feeling that quality is going to be in high demand," Gibbs says. "Now find a seat. We're going to be in the air and back on the ground inside an hour."

"That fast?" I ask.

"Let's hope it's fast enough," Gibbs says with a deep frown, and I realize I've been lied to. He knows more than he's said, and whatever it is he's not telling me, it's not good.

9

Despite the growing list of unanswered questions and unvented anger, I fall asleep only five minutes after liftoff. Rest had been impossible on the flight from Iceland. Frenetic energy buzzed through the passengers like an agitated specter, keeping eyes wide and mouths speculating. So when I leaned back in the plush executive chair, a remnant of this vehicle's former corporate life, blanketed by the white noise of the engines, I closed my eyes. For the first time since wrapping my hand around that black and red spike, I rested.

Briefly.

I jolt awake as the wheels touch down, frantically clawing at the armrests as inertia pulls me forward. I'm held in place by a seatbelt I don't remember buckling. Before we've come to a complete stop, the two Marines seated in front of me unbuckle, stand and turn around, with the single-minded efficiency of synchronized swimmers. Then they separate, one headed for me, the other for Holly, who just woke up.

"Come with me, Mr. Wright," the nearest of the two big men says. His tone suggests I better find my legs, and fast, or he's going to man-handle me. But is he an ass, or just in a rush? Either way, I don't want to know what his meaty hands feel like, so I push myself up with a groan. My knees wobble for a moment, but I remain upright, clinging to a seatback.

"Move it, Mr. Wright," Holly says in a deep voice, hobbling past me with a grin. The Marine following her doesn't seemed pleased by the impression, but it lightens my spirits and ignites my competitive spirit. If Holly can walk on her own, so can I.

Limping on both legs looks funny, like a tall, Indian Runner duck, wings folded down, body wobbling from side to side. It hurts, but the image keeps my spirits lifted. Slightly. I still don't know what's happening, or where my family is.

We're whisked into a black SUV with tinted windows. I half expect to be greeted by some shady Smoking Man, but the back seat is empty. Blue and red lights strobe from the windshield, pushing traffic out of the way, and we're treated to a very fast, psychedelic, tour of Washington, D.C. And then we're underground. It happens so fast, I miss the transition, and I flinch back as we race down the well-lit concrete tunnel.

Tires screech. Doors open from the outside. Men in suits, wearing coiled white comms in one ear, motion for us to exit.

"This way," one of them says, leading us to an elevator, its doors already open and waiting.

"If you all went into fast food, you'd make the—"

A glare silences me.

Inside the elevator, I take a moment to stretch my legs, pulling my feet up behind my butt. Before I'm done with the second, the doors open and the agent steps out, motioning for us to follow. Holly gives me a nervous glance, but then follows the man.

On slowly limbering legs, I follow. The journey is a short one, ending at a door guarded by two more Secret Service agents. One of the two agents twists the knob slowly and pulls the door open without making a sound. Commingling voices slide out of the room beyond. *It sounds like a party*, I think, and then I step over the threshold and realize there is nothing festive about this room, or the people in it.

The long, rectangular room is occupied by a large wooden table, currently covered in open documents and laptops. Flat-screen monitors are mounted around the room, taking up wall space like a grandmother's family photos. White light from the ceiling makes most of the room's occupants—generals, advisors, elected officials, some of whom I recognize

—look pale, even those who aren't already white. When I see what's on the monitors, I realize it might not be the light making them look pale.

Scenes of death and destruction surround the room, displayed on the monitors. Some are newsfeeds from around the world. Some are satellite images, though many of those are blotted out by clouds of ash. I saw the eruption first hand, and understand its destructive force, but this is the first time I've actually seen the fallout.

"Oh, god," Holly whispers next to me.

I keep my mouth shut, but share the sentiment.

This is unreal.

Our escort motions to a line of chairs against the wall. All but two, at the far end, are occupied. Traversing the maze of limbs and moving bodies would be a challenge if I felt fresh. I get more than a few annoyed looks as I bumble my way to the far end of the room.

My legs quiver as I lower myself into the seat. Then everyone stands up. Before I comprehend why, Gerrald McKnight, the President of the United States, walks in and stops by his chair, which is directly across from me. He pauses long enough to give me a sidelong glance, no doubt wondering why I'm the only person who didn't stand upon his entrance, and then he takes his seat. Relief settles over me when the room sits with him.

The President looks tired, but nothing close to how I feel. Sure, he's pushing seventy-five and has a roller coaster of wrinkles and honest-to-god jowls, but his sharp blue eyes say he's also hopped up on coffee. Probably the best coffee money can buy.

"What's the latest?" McKnight asks, his voice deep and rough.

"Sir," says a man seated beside the President. His face looks familiar, but nothing else about him stands out. His light blue shirt, loosened tie and gray hair match more than half the men in the room. He clears his throat. "Casualties are estimated at upwards of ten million."

The President wilts, sickened by the number. "Anything they need. Offer it. I don't care how much it costs and whether or not they're an ally. In a situation like this, I don't care about borders."

Two men in military dress, the only two still wearing their jackets, sit up a little straighter, but keep their mouths shut. Open borders flow in both directions, and there are bound to be refugees.

"Uh, sir..." The man speaking is Harry...Something, the Homeland Security Advisor. "We don't know how this is going to play out yet. Russia could—"

"Harry," McKnight says.

"Sir. If the winds change direc—"

"Harry." The President leans forward on his elbows. "While I recognize your concerns, I really do, we cannot turn our backs on a crisis this vast. Wind shift or not, we are in a position to provide aid and save lives. How many nations have agreed to take part in the aid coalition?"

"Twenty-two," says the President's Chief of Staff, Sonja Clark, who looks fresh and poised. "China is still on the fence."

"I want aid on the ground in the hardest hit regions by nightfall. If you have to fly in from the Mediterranean and drive the rest of the way, so be it. Everywhere else by morning. Ted, John, make it happen. Now."

The two military men stand and offer a synchronized "Yes, sir," before heading into an adjacent room.

"Now then, let's get back to the matter of what the hell happened." McKnight motions to the man I recognize most in the room, Robert Scarlato. He's the Assistant to the President for Science and Technology, Director of the White House Office of Science and Technology Policy and Co-Chair of the President's Council of Advisors on Science and Technology. Basically, he is the guiding force behind the United States' scientific programs, and I've had the pleasure of interviewing him three times. He's progressive, kind and brilliant, but like most scientists, he's a specialist—plasma physics and astronautics—which has resulted in a budget increase for NASA.

Scarlato scratches his gray beard with both hands, adjusts his glasses and takes a deep breath. "I'm afraid we don't know much more than we did an hour ago. A massive Icelandic eruption involving a chain of volcanoes has sent a plume of ash over most of Europe, grounding flights. It also unleashed an invisible cloud of chlorine and CO_2, which made landfall in the UK shortly before Iceland experienced a series of earthquakes, resulting in a tsunami."

"We've heard all this," McKnight says, sounding weary. "Is there anything new? Anything at all? Is this done? Are we out of the woods?"

"When Eyjafjallajökull erupted in 2010 it lasted four months." All eyes in the room, including mine, turn to Holly. She purses her lips for a moment, caught off guard by the shifting attention, or perhaps her own blurted words. She straightens herself, and continues. "That was a relatively small eruption from a single volcano. What we have here is a major eruption from more than thirty volcanoes, all buried beneath a massive glacier. There's no way to know how long the eruption will persist, but even if it stopped now—and it's not about to—the effects will be felt around the world."

"And you are?" McKnight asks.

"Uh," Scarlato says. "This is Dr. Holly Interlandi, a volcanologist, and Mr. Abraham Wright."

I lift a few fingers in greeting. "I know a lot, about a lot, I'm told."

Scarlato's smile makes him look like he just crapped his pants. "They were studying Bardarbunga when the eruption began."

"The survivors I've heard about," McKnight says.

Scarlato nods. "I asked for them to join us. I thought they might have insight about—"

"Understood," McKnight says, and then he motions to Holly. "How did we not see this coming?"

"There were no warning tremors. Bardarbunga was quiet."

"Isn't that unusual?" McKnight asks.

"Unheard of," Holly says, "but no longer important. The poison gas cloud and tsunami, not to mention the glacial flooding scouring Iceland clean, are tragic. The loss of life is astronomical. But I'm afraid it's just the beginning. The ash cloud covering Northern Europe is going to spread. When Eyjafjallajökull erupted, the ash cloud reached Siberia, rising 30,000 feet and blocking the sun for a week. Twenty countries closed their airspace. Eyjafjallajökull ejected 9.5 billion cubic feet of ash. Yesterday's eruption has likely already eclipsed that number, and over the coming months we're likely to see upwards of eight hundred billion cubic feet of ash, reaching far higher into the atmosphere. It will cover the *entire* northern hemisphere, including Canada and the United States. It'll take years to settle."

"What exactly are you saying?" McKnight asks.

Holly squirms in her seat. She doesn't want to say. Who would? So I decide to bail her out. I raise my hand, "An ice age, sir."

"You're shitting me." McKnight turns to Scarlato, but the science advisor looks like a wide-eyed ghost. The physicist hadn't figured this out yet.

"Without sunlight," I continue, "temperatures will drop. Fast. Crops are going to fail. This year. Famine will follow, affecting the entire northern hemisphere. This coming winter will be the worst in recorded history, and probably won't end. Not until the ash settles and temperatures rise. Glaciers will return. Landscapes will be remade. Some of the southern states might be sustainable, but the North is going to ice up. Anyone who doesn't migrate south risks starvation and freezing. If I were you, Mr. President, I would hold off on sending aid to other nations. There's a good chance you'll need it here in the next few months, if not sooner. And you can bet that once the Aid Coalition members south of the equator realize they're about to receive billions of refugees, they'll be putting their time and money into sealing up borders."

That's dire enough, I decide, and I leave out what will likely follow all of this. When the planet's most powerful nation, with a military capable of taking on the world, no longer has a place to call home, you better believe we'll take a new one. Central and South America won't stand a chance. Europe will colonize Africa once more. Russia will invade Asia. While half the world freezes, the other half will be consumed by the fires of self-destruction.

"Does anyone disagree with this?" McKnight asks, searching the faces around the table. Some shake their heads. Some stare down at the table, no doubt thinking about what my news means for them and their loved ones. "Robert?"

"Sorry, sir," Scarlato says. "I should have—"

"Save your apology," McKnight says. "Is he wrong?"

"No," Scarlato says. "I don't think so."

"Let's meet again in an hour. I want ideas. Contingency plans. Get me more people like them." He points at Holly and me. "We need to get ahead of this. Today. You're dismissed."

People burst into action, filing out of the room, talking on phones or to each other. McKnight turns to Sonja Clark. "I'm going to talk with

Ted and John." The generals. The military. I hate to think that what I've just said will hurt people in Europe, but there's little chance that aid would do any good. And my family's here. It's selfish, but I'd do just about anything to keep them safe. "Take them to my office."

I nearly fall out of my chair when I see McKnight looking at me. Then his now cold eyes are blocked by Clark's power suit. She's tall, a little plump and staring down at me through thick rimmed glasses. "You made an impression."

"I just told it like it is," I say.

"My advice..." She motions for us to follow her. "...keep doing that. Because if you're right, about even a fraction of what you said, what you say next could alter the human race's future."

10

The maze of elevators and hallways combined with a flurry of activity has me confused. Other than the occasional flash of recognition—a bust of a long dead president; a painting seen in a photo, printed in a magazine—I couldn't tell you if this was the White House or some other gaudy government building. But then we're whisked through an open door, into a room that is easily recognizable because of its oval shape and layout. While the Oval Office's decor might change from president to president, the Resolute desk has been in place since Jackie Kennedy had it put here for JFK, in 1961. The two couches facing each other at the center of the room, resting atop a navy blue rug bearing the presidential seal, also seem to be a mainstay. Though I'm sure they're replaced every few years. They sure as hell look comfortable.

Clark leads us into the room, strutting her stuff like a supermodel, despite her size—good for her—and despite the fact that the world is falling apart, which isn't such a great reflection on her character.

Having little pride and less energy, I take a seat on one of the couches before being offered, and I find myself tilting to the side. A Secret Service agent closes the door behind us, silencing the voices and the footsteps from the hallway and rooms outside. My head hits the cushion just as the world goes quiet. I exhale slowly. My body relaxes.

"I am with you," a booming voice says.

I flinch up in my seat, blinking my eyes. McKnight has just entered the room, allowing a momentary burst of voices back in. Then the door is shut and the aged president walks around the room, heading for his desk.

Holly is seated across from me, looking a little overwhelmed. She leans over the coffee table between us. "I think you fell asleep."

"I just closed my eyes."

"Five minutes ago."

While McKnight riffles through some pages on his desktop, I motion to Clark with my hand. "Any chance we could get some coffee?"

Holly opens her mouth to speak, but is interrupted by the side door opening. A woman in a pantsuit rolls in a tray with a coffee pot and an assortment of china cups. I apparently slept through Clark requesting the brew's delivery. The woman picks up a china cup and turns to me, but is cut short by Clark. "You can go."

Without a word, the woman exits the way she came, and without waiting to be offered, I stand and help myself. The first cup is medicinal. I pour the coffee close to the top, take a sip to test the temperature and then chug it down black. By the time I'm done refilling the cup, I can already feel the caffeine hitting my system. Two sugars later, the President clears his throat and steps in front of the Resolute desk.

I hand the next prepared coffee to Holly, and then I go to work on another for me, four sugars and cream. My small spoon clinks out a musical ditty as I swirl it round.

The music ends when McKnight says, "What you're about to see is classified. Only a handful of people have seen it: the satellite analyst who found it, his supervisor and the general he forwarded it to, Ms. Clark and myself. Everyone in that chain has been previously vetted and approved to view and protect the contents of top secret materials. You two have not. So I'm going to ask you a question, and please understand that our conversation is being recorded and any agreement you offer will be considered legal and binding."

My coffee cup hovers halfway to my lips. *What the hell?*

"You will not, under any circumstances, reveal the subject matter or content of what you see, hear and discuss here today to anyone outside of this room. Doing so will be considered an act of treason, and you will be prosecuted to the fullest extent of the law. If you agree, stay where you are. If you don't, you may leave now."

Holly and I make eye contact. She looks unsure, but remains seated. The stakes are high, but with a setup like that, who wouldn't stay? I turn back to McKnight and shrug. "We're good."

The President stands and heads to the couch opposite me. He sits at the center of the couch, beside Holly, and then pats the empty seat to his left. When I join him on the couch, sipping my coffee, savoring the flavor and sugar-zing, a flat screen TV mounted where I'm pretty sure a bookcase used to be, turns on.

Clark steps up next to the couch, pointing a remote at the TV. "These satellite images were taken during the initial eruption. Each image is a second apart. The aberration appears in the fifteenth second."

Aberration? A rapid-fire slide show plays on the screen, two grayscale images per second. It looks like a high res animated gif of a volcano, as seen from space. The rising smoke of several volcanoes billows high into the sky, moving west to east, filling the right half of the screen.

"That's Bardarbunga," Holly says, pointing to the center of the screen, where a white glacier, not yet melted, meets gray earth.

We're down there, I think. Somewhere in that image, there are five tiny people speeding away in a superjeep.

Then the monotonous rise of smoke and ash shifts, spinning to the side, as though something has moved through it.

If I were standing, I would sit. The best I can do is to shrink back into my seat.

"What the hell was that?" Holly asks.

"We were hoping you might be able to tell us," McKnight says. "You were there."

"Well, I certainly didn't see anything like this." Holly sounds indignant, like a joke is being played on us.

I for one, am not laughing.

"Can we zoom in?" Holly asks.

"That's coming," Clark says, and the stitched together video goes black. It's then replaced by a zoomed-in version that slowly replays what they've dubbed, 'the aberration' frame-by-frame, for five frames, revealing five seconds of my life that I thought were delusions. Another vision. An illusion created by shifting clouds, static lightning and fear-fueled adrenaline. None of which, by the way, can be captured on video, by a satellite.

The images scroll by, two frames a second. The object slips in and out of sight pretty quickly.

The video replays, this time one frame per second.

Then again at one frame per ten seconds.

And then once more, one frame per ten seconds, but each frame has been sharpened. A curved shape, clearly not a cloud, emerges from the smoke, but still partly concealed by it. The next frame shows it breaking through, into the open air. The edge looks serrated, like a curved Ginsu knife slicing through the ash plume. The next image makes Holly gasp, and shrinks me back into the couch. The shape struck by the setting sun, now has depth and a stone-like texture, like a shell of some kind. If I didn't know this was a satellite image of something huge, I would have guessed that it was some kind of ancient sea creature, like a horseshoe crab, crawling through a geothermal vent on the sea floor. The next frame shows a lightning strike, sparking against the surface, confirming that it is a physical object within the smoke column.

"What the hell?" Holly says. "Seriously, what the hell?"

The final image shows the shape concealed by smoke again.

"What are the dimensions of this thing?" Holly asks.

Clark moves back two frames, freezing it on the clearest shot. "There's no way to confirm the overall size, though we're pretty sure what we saw was just a small part of the whole. But the portion that emerged from the smoke..." Clark's calm and professional demeanor falters for a moment, but she sucks it up, raises her chin in defiance to some unseen force, and says, "A mile, from one side to the other, give or take five hundred feet. We're still trying to figure out how high off the ground it was."

"Well, I..." Holly takes a deep breath and lets it out. "I definitely did *not* see that."

"You may not have," McKnight says. "But I think one of you did."

I shrink back a little bit more. I don't want to be here. I don't want this to be real. I just want my family back.

McKnight turns to me.

Holly leans forward, peering around the President at me.

"Miles," I say, leaning forward to place the now shaking china cup in my hand upon the coffee table. "It was miles high. Two. Maybe three. But I didn't have time to really calculate it. I barely had time to register what I was seeing."

"*What?*" Holly says. "Why didn't you say something?"

"I had already had one...delusion," I say. "I thought I was seeing things."

"What kind of a delusion?" Clark looks down at me, suspicious.

"It was more like a vision," I say. "When I touched a...holy shit." I motion to the TV. "Are there any color images of this?"

McKnight shakes his head. "Just black and white."

I stand and walk closer to the screen, eyeing the strange shape cutting through the smoke. "It was black, but streaked with luminous red. Deep red. Almost like blood..." I turn to Holly. "...and exactly like what we found in the glacier."

"You think that small spike was a part of *this*?" Holly asks.

"Hold on," McKnight says. "What spike?"

Holly quickly breaks down our find, how Kiljan discovered it, and my contact with it. "I thought it was stone," she says. "The end of a lava tube."

"But it wasn't," I say, making my own conclusion. "And the eruption...it didn't start until *after* I touched it."

"You *touched* that thing?" McKnight asks.

I hold up my bandaged hand. "When I snapped out of my vision, or whatever, my hand was burned and the water beneath us was boiling. Holly...I think...what if we triggered it?"

"Triggered it?" She sounds doubtful.

"Woke it up. I don't know."

"You think that thing is...alive? Is it a creature?"

I shake my head. "I don't know. When I saw it, it was rising into the sky above us. Its body, or part of it, was tilted toward us. There was a black circle, like an eye." My voice fades to a whisper. "I thought it was an eye."

Silence as three sets of eyes stare at me, weighing my sanity. They flinch when I blurt out. "Do you have the seismographic data?"

Clark heads for a laptop sitting atop the Resolute desk. "The magnitude of the eruption was—"

"Not for the eruption," I say. "For the earthquakes that preceded the tsunami."

After a few clicks of the laptop's track pad, she picks up the thin laptop and brings it to me. I slump back down on the couch beside McKnight, my legs feeling numb. Laptop delivered, I scroll through the time stamped seismograph data, stopping when I reach the first earthquake represented by a series of tall, jagged lines. The quake registered a 6.2 on the Richter scale. Powerful, but not uncommon. I scroll some more and find the second quake. A 6.1. Then the third quake. A 6.3.

Not aftershocks. Each quake was an individual event taking place at slightly different locations. Knowing the first quake happened at the eruption's epicenter, I use the coordinates on the readout to plot a path. Each quake, separated by a mile or two, moved from Bardarbunga to the coast. I zoom out, looking at the series of quakes in sequence, and at the timestamp. "Holy shit."

"What is it?" McKnight asks, though I can tell he's not really sure he wants to know.

"These aren't earthquakes," I say, looking from one person to the next, seeing my fear reflected in their eyes. "They're footsteps."

11

MARGRET

Margret Dieter couldn't sleep. She was lying in bed, staring at the ceiling, numb. She thought about the millions of people who had died, some not far from her home in Büchen, Germany, located twenty-four miles southwest of Hamburg, which had been flooded by the tsunami as it surged down the Elbe river. The small town of just over 5000 people sat at the fringe of the giant wave's reach. Water had roared down the river, eight miles south of the town, scouring less fortunate towns from the map. But Büchen had survived unscathed. From the water, at least. Shifting winds had brought the ash cloud south from Iceland, flowing down through Europe and swooping around toward Russia like a great, murky sickle.

Earlier in the day, when she had set out to survey the damage along with her two dogs—Bruno, a black Labrador and Ottis, a yellow Labrador—the air had felt rich and saturated with moisture. Refreshing. But then she had reached Basedow, another small town like Büchen, but no longer standing. Homes and businesses had been crushed or swept away to be bundled at the base of various hills.

And the bodies... Some could be seen amidst the debris, torn apart, hanging limp, baking in the sun. Others had been strewn across the landscape, their clothes torn away by the raging waters, their bodies gleaming in the morning sun.

That had made it real.

That had broken a part of her mind.

While others in town had rushed into neighboring communities, looking for survivors, Margret, Bruno and Ottis had walked home. The early morning light that had warmed her face felt like a gift.

But it didn't last long.

A mile-high wall of darkness slid through the atmosphere, following the tsunami's path. It crossed over the town and spread in every direction until the sun, and any trace of blue sky, had been replaced. Flecks of gray ash fell from the sky like hell-scented snowflakes. With every passing hour, the land grew darker, descending into a kind of blood red twilight.

Margret turned her head, looking at the clock. It was 4:00 pm, but it felt more like 9:00 pm. Through the bedroom window, the thick soupy sky swirled, endless and featureless. When a hiss scratched against her window, she realized that the ash and smoke weren't just filling the sky above her, but stretching all the way to the ground.

Her bed groaned as she slid to the edge. Both dogs stood, tails wagging, waiting to see if they were going to be petted, fed, walked or played with. Without looking, Margret reached down for both dogs' heads and rubbed her hands over them, scratching behind their ears, eliciting delighted grunts.

The dogs started licking her fingers when she stopped. But Margret didn't respond. She didn't coo to them, call their names or crouch down to kiss their noses. She stood still at the window, unable to see much beyond her own yard. She could make out silhouettes of buildings, including the town's center, just a mile away, but the view she was used to, being on the second floor of a home built atop a hundred foot hill, was gone. It was replaced by a sea of dark red haze.

She didn't turn away from the monotone view until the dogs stopped licking her fingers. Bruno and Ottis were notorious lickers. Some people enjoyed it. Some people detested it. Margret was simply accustomed to it in the same way she didn't notice her home's dog scent. But its absence was noticeable. She looked down at the dogs. Both were craning their heads from side to side, ears perked up, eyebrows twitching. In dog body language, it was the equivalent of pondering a mystery.

But what mystery? Certainly not the volcanic smog. *It's the smell,* she thought, noting the scent of rotten eggs for the first time.

Ottis tilted his head in the opposite direction and whined. Bruno joined in.

"What is it?" she said, reaching for the dogs.

Both dogs snapped back to normal, tails wagging, tongues flapping. She crouched down, and the dogs assumed their positions on either side, her arms wrapped around their necks, scratching their backs.

"What's with you two?" she asked, and the dogs responded by licking both sides of her neck. The pair was back to normal, but a little too excited. *Like they're relieved,* she thought.

Both dogs went still. Tongues withdrawn, ears lifted, eyes shifting back and forth.

"Seriously, Ottis..." No response. "Bruno..."

Her hands stopped scratching their backs. Trusting their heightened senses, she closed her eyes and listened.

A thunderous boom drew a high-pitched shout from her and sent both dogs cowering to the floor.

The din's source was revealed a moment later, when a streak of orange lightning cut through the red haze, letting her see the distant town a bit better. Shapes moved on the roofs of some of the flat-topped buildings.

People, she realized. *Why are they outside in this mess? What are they looking at?*

Thunder followed the lightning, and the dogs took up defensive positions under the bed. Margret would never tell anyone, but she hated thunderstorms and she sometimes hid under the bed with the dogs. But this wasn't a typical storm. There was no rain to begin with, and there was something else...a kind of energy.

Is that what the dogs were feeling?

A subtle vibration moved through her feet. She'd heard that people about to be struck by lightning sometimes felt a tingling sensation before it happened, so she leapt onto the bed with a yelp, and both dogs started barking. But the lightning didn't come. Instead, a distant peal of thunder, long and rolling.

"We need to get out of here," she told the dogs, their snouts peeking out from under the bed, sniffing wildly. She had planned to head south in the morning, but if the ash grew thicker, she wouldn't be able to drive. Maybe not even breathe. A mental checklist began to form in her mind: clothes, toiletries, food, water, dog food, leashes.

The dogs started whining again, despite the lack of thunder and lightning. Margret got on her hands and knees, looking both cowering dogs in the eyes. "What? What is it?"

A vibration moved through the floor, stronger than the last and coupled with a vibration moving through her hands and knees.

"It's thunder," she said, looking out the window, waiting for more flashes of lightning. There was a flash and a boom, and that was it. The home didn't shake. Her eyes remained locked on the window, watching for flashes, distant or close.

The dogs whined.

The floor shook.

"It's *not* the thunder," she said to the dogs. "Is it?"

She walked to the window again, craning her head in both directions, seeing nothing but endless dark red haze. Her fingers tapped a beat against the glass, while her forehead created a smudge.

There's nothing out there. Nothing I can see.

Her bare feet slapped against the bedroom's hard wood floor. Back and forth. What to do? Where to go? *I should have left earlier. I can't leave. I have to.* Fear and anxiety bubbled past her shaking lips as a barked sob that drew both dogs from beneath the bed.

Margret sat on the mattress as both dogs flanked her, tongues back in action, comforting their master, like they did when her son Carl had passed, and a year later when Louis had left her. "You two will never leave me, will you?"

The house around her seemed to leap in the air. The cushion pressed against her, lifted her up and then dropped away beneath her. She landed on her back, staring at the ceiling once more, each breath a shallow, panicked gulp.

What was that?

All around the house, precariously balanced items cascaded to the floor. Pans fell in the kitchen. Dishes followed. Something tumbled in the closet. One of the dogs peed.

Go outside and look!

I can't see anything! What good would it do?

Drive away! Now!

But I can't see.

The house shook again, groaning as a wave of energy rolled beneath it. More dishes broke. A window shattered. Car alarms filled the air. Neighbors shouted.

"It's an earthquake," she told the dogs, wiping away tears and remembering hearing that it was an earthquake that had kicked off the tsunami. She tried the television, but its screen remained black. The power had kicked off six hours ago. *What the hell is happening?*

Panic rose, a demon from hades, sinking its talons into her chest, dragging her down. Confused and broken, she tried to think about what to do, how to save her boys. Where was the safest place during an earthquake? *Nowhere near it*, she thought, and then she considered the closet again. *A doorway? The tub? Under a table?* It was one of those. Maybe all of them.

She decided on the dining room table. It was hardwood, had survived English bombs in World War II and was large enough to accommodate herself and the dogs. As the shaking reduced, she took one last look out the window and stood still.

A new kind of darkness slid into view. It looked like a tree trunk, but with joints. For a moment, she thought it was close by and moving slowly. Then she realized that she was seeing something far away, moving very fast. Night fell so suddenly and completely that she wondered if she was losing consciousness. Hands on the cool glass for balance, she watched the unfolding scene, unable to turn away.

Darkness surrounded her home, for as far as she could see, except for dead ahead, where a blood red horizon showed the moving limb.

Limb...

The word resonated.

It's like an elephant's leg, she thought, *but covered in plates. And big.* Far too big to be believed.

I'm hallucinating, she decided. She was being poisoned by the sulfuric stench now wafting into the house through the broken window. *Just like those people in Scotland.*

Lightning crackled, lighting up the town and the massive shape descending toward it. Thick flesh crushed buildings underfoot, enveloping half the town beneath its girth. The ground shook when it made contact, but the massive pad spread out, dispersing weight across the land. And then, all at once, something within the massive shape settled. The ash cloud swirled up into the air and outward, disappearing for a moment, and then it was lit up by a fresh streak of lightning. The billowing shockwave leveled the parts of town not yet crushed, and then moved further, racing toward Margret's house.

She didn't have time to even think about what to do. The shockwave slapped the side of her house with a thunderclap that she heard for the briefest moment before both of her eardrums burst. Glass shattered, stabbing her arms, chest and face. The floor beneath her slid away, knocking her to the floor, where both dogs lay. She could see them, howling and terrified, but she couldn't hear their high-pitched yelps.

The house shifted around her, the walls canted at an angle.

Get out, she told herself. *You have to get out, now!*

She sprinted to the door and down the stairs. The dogs, injured but loyal, charged down with her. At the bottom of the stairs, she was knocked back when the slower moving shockwave coursing through the earth rolled beneath her home, cracking the foundation to dust and yanking joints apart. Margret pulled the front door open just before the house tilted back and collapsed behind her. She and the two dogs remained standing in the doorway, the open door framing them.

We made it, she thought, looking for her car.

The small vehicle, just large enough for the boys and her, looked undamaged, but the roads...

She looked down the street, which was crumbling and crisscrossed with fallen street lamps. And her dogs. Both of them. Sprinting away like they were on a track.

She called for them. "Ottis! Bruno!" But she couldn't even hear the words, and given the dogs' lack of reaction, neither could they.

Just as a new kind of despair settled over her, she felt a wind pressing down on her. Pressure squeezed her. Air rushed past and away. The darkness above and around her became absolute.

Solid.

Heavy.

Crushing.

Her last thought was of Bruno and Ottis. *Run, boys. Run!*

The weight pressing her into the ground was so intense that blood, bone and sinews were compressed to liquid and then separated at the microscopic level. Margret Dieter existed one moment, and then, in the next, was obliterated.

12

ABRAHAM

The White House feels like a beehive. People crawl over and past each other, buzzing information, shaking limbs as they talk, gesticulate, tap, swipe and shuffle. My sudden advancement from science writer to Assistant Science Advisor to the President of the United States came with an ID badge, Top Secret security clearance and a seat at the table for as long as the current crisis persists. I don't think everyone here understands this yet, but that's going to be a long time.

My stomach clenches.

A *very* long time. Ice ages don't come and go like nations. They last hundreds of millions of years with intermittent periods of glaciation. Most people don't know that we're still in the midst of an ice age that began 2.6 million years ago. It's end has been kick started by humanity, but nature is already reversing the damage done. By this time next year, an endless winter will start rebuilding the glaciers that retreated from North America 22,000 years ago.

But who knows if any of us will be around to see it.

I have no concrete reason to think this way, but the appearance of something unimaginably colossal, moving about beneath the ash cloud, has laced this catastrophic natural disaster with a sense of otherworldly apocalyptic doom. I really want to wave my hand and declare my footstep theory as hogwash, but I was there. I saw it. And the satellite images confirm it. Bardarbunga wasn't just a volcano. It was a resting place.

For something that defies logic.

I try to find comfort in the books surrounding me. The smell of old paper is familiar and soothing, the writer's essential oil. The uneven shapes dull the sound of nervous chattering filling and echoing around the building's solid walls, floors and ceilings. The old book spines lining the shelves have titles like *Lincoln*, *Ulysses S. Grant*, *Truman* and *Nixon*. Actually, there are three books sporting Nixon's name. Not a single Michael Crichton novel in the mix. I'm surrounded by historical texts covering the formation of the United States to the more recent past.

Will any of this matter? I wonder. *Will any of it be here in ten years?*

So much for comfort.

I look into the eyes of four American Indian chiefs, their paintings hung on either side of the men's room. The men look regal, decked out in traditional garb—feathers, horns and beads. Three of the four look like good natured guys, the kind that wouldn't make you feel uncomfortable if you bumped into them outside a bathroom. The fourth, Patalesharro—Generous Chief—looks like he knew what was coming, that the age of American Indian freedom was coming to an end.

"Pawnee," I say, reading his tribe's name. One of the few American Indian tribes deemed 'friendly' by the U.S. government. Hence the painting in the White House...beside the men's room. I stand face-to-face with Patalesharro, feeling like I'm looking in a mirror, not because we look alike, but because the sadness and anger in his eyes is a reflection of my own.

Or maybe he just had gas.

"Mr. Wright," a deep voice says, turning me around. It's a Secret Service agent I don't recognize. His bulk is blocking the door, but I can see familiar faces peeking around him. "Your family is here, sir."

"Daddy!" both boys shout, shoving their way past the surprised agent, who's looking at my sons like they're a terror cell loose in the White House.

I let out an "oof!" when Ike and Ishah reach me, wrapping arms around my waist and pummeling my gut with their heads. I rub their backs, missing when they were small enough to pick up. Granted, I could lift one of them, but at times like this, I like to give them equal attention. It doesn't matter that they have different mothers. They're both my sons, and I love them equally. I rub their heads, and look down into their faces, seeing very different reflections of myself. Ishah, like me, has curly hair, but the brown color matches his mother's. Unlike my tight cut, his is grown out into a loose afro that looks almost bohemian. But his brilliant blue eyes look like mine. Ike's sharper features are topped by smooth black hair and brown eyes, also like his mother, but the shape of his face reminds me of my father. For a moment, I see them grown up again, tall, stubbled and strong, and I wonder about the vision's accuracy. Could my mind conjure up my future sons and picture them accurately? If science writing still exists in the future, that might make an interesting story.

I kiss the boys' foreheads and turn to greet their mothers. Bell is first. Arms reaching, smile broad, she seems to bounce across the room. Her hands clasp my cheeks, and she plants a kiss on my lips. "We've been scared."

"You don't need to be," I lie. "Everything is good."

She sees through it and gives me 'the squint,' but she must realize my falsehood was more for the boys' benefit than for hers. "We'll talk later," she says, stepping to the side.

Mina glides across the room, her lithe body hardly moving vertically with each step. Her arms slide around my waist, and her head leans against my chest. From an outside perspective, the hug might look robotic and lacking the obvious affection of Bell, but I feel Mina's body relax in my arms. She's been carrying a lot of tension, and while she and Bell are great supports for each other, I still have a major role to play in both their lives—as strange as that might be. Mina tilts her head up, meeting my eyes. She looks near tears, but puckers her lips and invites me to kiss her, which I do.

When I raise my head, the Secret Service agent's air of unflappable authority has been replaced by a flabbergasted expression. I've seen it before. We all have.

"It's complicated," Bell tells the man. "You'll live."

When the man's expression deepens, I sense the boys becoming uncomfortable, and that is something Mina, Bell and I do not want to happen. I step closer to the man, and say, "There are stranger things going on tonight, don't you think?"

His eyes flick to mine. "Uh, yeah. Yes, sir."

"You can go," I tell him.

"I, I can't, sir. I've been assigned to your, uh, family."

Great. "Then can you wait outside, Agent..."

"Huber," he says.

"Agent Huber, can you give me a minute to catch up with my family? In private?"

He looks around the room, at the books, at the paintings and at the sabers mounted on the wall.

"They won't touch anything," I tell him, my second lie in the last few minutes. He gives a reluctant nod and exits, closing the door behind him. I turn to my family. "Everyone okay?"

"We flew in a helicopter," Ike says.

"And a limo with bulletproof glass," Ishah adds.

"Wow," I say. When I all but demanded McKnight bring my family to me, I didn't think they would get the red carpet treatment. Most of the people here, aside from the President himself, don't have family in the White House. But they weren't yanked away from their lives, either. As far as I know, I'm still not getting a paycheck for being here. Not that it matters. Banks might not be able to hold much more than snow in the near future. "Hey," I say, looking around the room. "I've heard that some of these books have dollar bills hidden in the pages. Why don't you two see if you can find them."

The boy's eyes widen, and they hustle to the shelves filled with old books.

"Just be gentle," I whisper, eying the door where Agent Huber exited. "The other rule is if you ruin the book, you have to buy it with any money you find."

While the boys flip through the pages gently, as requested, I head for the far side of the room and sit on a couch that looks antique, but also brand new. Bell sits beside me and Mina pulls and turns one of the chairs around in front of the couch, so it faces me. At home, we'd call this kind of meeting a 'pow wow.' Seated across from the Native American chiefs, that feels inappropriate.

"You're afraid," Bell says, glancing at the boys. They show no reaction, replacing books carefully and inspecting the next.

I give a subtle nod.

"Is it this volcano business?" she asks. "It's bad, isn't it?"

Another nod. "As bad as volcanoes get. World changing."

"Are we going to be all right?"

"For now," I say. "But I'm not sure what the future holds. For us, or anyone else. The good news is that we're pretty much in the best place we could be to stay ahead of it."

"What else?" Mina asks, her laser-focus eyes burning through my layers of defense. "You are...shaken."

"Did I tell you that I have top-secret security clearance now?" I ask. They stare at me.

"That means there are things I can't tell you." We're alone, and the door is shut, but only a fool would believe that any conversation inside the White House is truly private. "As much as I might like to."

They get it. I can see it in their eyes.

"But what I said before still applies. This is the best place for our family to be right now. And I intend to keep us here, but to do that, I need to stay useful."

"You do what you need to do," Bell says. "We'll be here, and I'll be praying for you."

Mina takes my hand. "You won't leave us."

"Not a chance."

She looks at the boys, who are looking discouraged and have started stacking the books they've already checked. "They need you as much as we do."

"I am with you, and..." My words trigger a flashback. The figure standing over me. The rod in my hand. Was he a father figure?

A knock at the door startles me. I flinch back to the here and now, seeing concern on both women's faces, and then the door opening

behind them. Agent Huber enters first. He quickly spots the boys'
activity, points his finger and growls, "Hey—"

A wrinkled hand adorned in expensive rings reaches up and
pushes Huber's accusatory finger down. "Calm yourself, Bruce." Susan
McKnight, the First Lady, enters the room, smiling at the boys. She's
the grandmother everyone wishes they had, pruned, casual, friendly
and all about the kids. "Are you boys interested in history or has
someone set you on a wild goose chase?"

"Both," Ike says, and glowers at me. "I think."

The First Lady chuckles, and turns to Bell and Mina. "Ladies. I've
had a room prepared for you all. If you'd like to come with me, I think
your...husband's attention is required elsewhere at the moment."

Bell would normally correct people when they call her my wife.
She's sensitive to the fact that the title belongs to Mina, but she keeps
her mouth closed, probably because she doesn't want to offend the
First Lady in her own home.

When Sonja Clark steps into the room, behind the First Lady, and
simply motions with her head for me to follow her, I stand. "Duty calls."
I kiss both Bell and Mina on their foreheads, telling them both I love
them, and then doing the same to the boys. "I'll see you all later."

I smile at the First Lady as I pass, and she squeezes my arm. "You
have a lovely family."

"Thank you, Mrs.—"

"Call me Susan."

I smile. "Thank you, Susan."

I re-enter the beehive hallway, mixing in with the scurrying aids,
politicians and agents. Clark is waiting for me, holding a tablet. She
holds it up as she leads me toward the West Wing, where the Oval
Office and Situation Room are both located. She holds up the screen
for me to see. It's a satellite view of Europe, the ash-free countries of
the Mediterranean still recognizable. But it's cast in hues of blue and
green, with several splotches of yellow, orange and red.

"What is this?" I ask.

"Thermal imaging of Europe." She points to several hot spots on the
coast of the Mediterranean. "These are cities." Her finger travels north,

into the ash cloud obscuring the nations located there. "These are not. Most of Northern Europe is without power. Communications are down. Governments have gone silent, and our own overseas assets are either clueless, dead, unable to make contact or in the dark. Literally. So what we need to know is, what are these hotspots?"

I take the tablet and stop in the middle of the hallway, oblivious to the people moving and talking around me. *Please God, let me be wrong.* Finding recognizable bits of coast here and there, I fill in the map's black spaces, mentally tracing out the UK, Spain, France and Germany. "Shit."

"What?" Clark asks. "Abraham, what?"

Her use of my first name pulls my eyes away from the screen. "Nuclear power plants. Most are built on the coast. They would have been flooded by the tsunami. The flood waters might have helped keep things cool for a while, but as the ocean recedes, the remaining water is going to boil off quickly. If they haven't melted down already, they're about to. And when that happens, the winter we're facing is going to be nuclear."

13

I'm a bit relieved, upon re-entering the Situation Room, to find that the U.S. Military has figured out what the hotspots are across the northern European coastlines, without my help. I'm less relieved by the fact that they have no idea what to do about it. Mostly because I don't either, and by the way they're looking at me as I take a seat against the wall, I can tell they're hoping I'll give them a place to start.

"Mr. Wright," a general whose name escapes me says, but he's old and gray, and serious in the way you'd expect generals sitting around this table to be. "You're aware of the situation?"

I nod.

"Can you—"

"A problem like this isn't solved in a room like this," I tell them. "It's solved in laboratories. You don't need a scientist, you need *all* of them. When Chernobyl melted down in 1986, radioactive contaminates spread northwest to Sweden and Finland, and west, into Europe. Radiation increased to one hundred times the normal background as fallout fell to the ground, the water supplies and the crops. While much of it dissipated within a week, there were serious health effects for people living within eighteen miles of the meltdown, and for those tasked with cleaning it up.

Mutations. Cancer. Cataracts. Mental illness. The list of effects is long, and the number of affected in the hundreds of thousands. That was from a single meltdown in a less populated area.

I motion to the large wall-mounted display showing the hotspots hidden beneath a shroud of volcanic ash. "What we have here is, what..." I quickly count the hotspots. "...seventeen nuclear power plants on the verge of melting down, if they haven't already, with no one left alive to stop it. When Chernobyl melted down, they lost reactor number four. That is to say, *one* of four reactors. That disaster could have been four times worse. And while seventeen power plants is bad enough, there are far more reactors—"

"Thirty-two," Robert Scarlato says, looking up from his laptop. He looks happy to have contributed to the conversation, but then sheepish when that number is all he has to offer.

"The northern coast of Europe will be uninhabitable for thousands of years, and the North and Baltic Seas will be contaminated for who knows how long."

"What about the UK?" someone asks, as the room continues to fill.

"Between the poison gas, the tsunami, quakes, the ash cloud and seven nuclear power plants melting down? With the exception of Ireland, which is currently protected from the radiation by wind and ocean currents, the UK is probably a total loss. Even if there are survivors inland, the ash prevents air travel, and you'd have to get past the radioactive coast to reach them. If evacuation is on the table, focus on Ireland."

McKnight shakes his head. "We're going to conserve our resources. I've never liked the every man for himself mentality, but our commitment is to the American people first. If this comes our way, we need to be ready."

"Will it?" Sonja Clark asks. "Come our way?"

"The ash," I say. "Yes. And if the radioactive isotopes bind with the ash in the atmosphere, it's possible we'll have radioactive fallout. In Alaska. Maybe on the West Coast. But there's a good chance it will encounter weather systems and dissipate by then. But given the current trajectory of the ash cloud, it seems likely that Northern Europe and a portion of Russia will be significantly contaminated. Those closest to the meltdowns will die quickly, and painfully. Those further away will fall ill in the next few years, but will probably die from the endless winter they're about to face. Ocean currents will keep contaminated water from reaching the East Coast, but fishing in the North Atlantic and Arctic Oceans probably won't be a good idea for a long time. But like I said, it will take teams of scientists *years* to truly understand the ramifications of this many nuclear meltdowns.

"The one course of action I can recommend without further delay is the shutting down of all active nuclear reactors worldwide."

A man I don't know, wearing a suit and tie, objects. "Twenty percent of our energy comes from nuclear power. Millions of people would be in the dark. Other countries depend on nuclear power for a vast amount of their energy consumption. They'll never agree to it."

"Better to be in the dark, than melted," Clark says.

"Robert," McKnight says to the senior science advisor. "Look into that. I want to know how fast it can be done, how many people would be affected, and projections on how we would be affected by a similar disaster along either or both of our coastlines."

When Scarlato scribbles a note and says, "Yes, sir," McKnight sighs and with a deep, growly voice, says, "Now."

"Y-yes, sir." Scarlato fumbles with his belongings, gathers them up and heads for the door.

McKnight leans back in his chair, rubbing his face. When he removes the wrinkled digits, he looks even more tired. "General Alonso..."

"Sir," the gray haired general says.

"Any update from our forces in Europe?"

"Those in the clear are as in the dark as we are. Borders are closing. Countries are preparing for the worst. We've called back everyone we could, but we suspect our people in Northern Europe and the UK are facing the same odds of survival as the locals."

"God damnit," McKnight whispers. He looks ready to beat his fist against something. Those seated near him lean away. He might be old, but he still looks strong enough to pack a punch. He closes his eyes and takes a deep breath. When he opens them again, his focus looks deadly. He looks at those seated around him, meeting their eyes, daring them to not speak. "How do we get ahead of this thing?"

The answers come in a torrent, ample in numbers, but none well thought out.

"We need evacuation plans for all major cities."

"Refugee camps in the south."

"Radiation units in Alaska and the West Coast."

Radiation units? These people are just spinning on my words from predictions to actions.

"Close the Mexican border," someone says, and I laugh.

The room falls silent, like I've just used the 'N-Word' at a Black Panthers meeting. All eyes turn toward my rapidly wilting smile.

The President raises his eyebrows at me, silently demanding I speak.

"First of all," I say, "you want to keep the Mexican border open. Wide open. If possible, start tearing down walls and fences. If a significant portion of the U.S. population needs to head south, a few border crossings aren't going to get the job done, and there is a very real chance Mexico, and the rest of Central America, isn't going to be happy about a massive population increase. In fact, they'll probably treat it the way we would."

"An invasion," General Alonso says.

"You'll probably want to start moving ground forces south to the border, if you can do it without being seen." I feel uncomfortable giving advice that includes military action, but if Mexico doesn't play ball, hundreds of millions could die. If the U.S. has to put the smack down on the Mexican military, the end justifies the means. Maybe. Either way, people are going to die. Millions of them already have, or are in the process of dying. At this point, war is inevitable. "Second, all of the other suggestions are Band-Aids."

"I don't follow," McKnight says.

"They're treating the symptoms," I say. "Not the cause."

"We can't fight a volcano," Alonso says. "Or radioactive fallout."

"Again, those are symptoms. They're not the cause."

"You're talking about the aberration," McKnight says.

I wonder how much everyone in this room knows about the aberration, and decide to guard my answer. "I am."

The confused looks on most of the faces in the room confirm that this subject is still a closely guarded secret. Only Alonso and Clark seem unconfused by the subject matter. And I understand why. Natural and manmade disasters are horrifying in scope and because of their potential to kill people by the millions, but they still make sense. They're part of reality. A giant...something...miles tall, wide and long, strolling across the Earth's crust, setting off volcanoes, tsunamis, earthquakes and nuclear meltdowns... That's supernatural, and it very well could kick off a panic inside the White House—and outside as the news leaks, first to family, then to friends and finally to the networks.

"Give us the room," McKnight says, and bodies shuffle from the room in silence. They're not talking now, but I have no doubt these people will be asking each other about the 'aberration' as soon as the doors shut behind them. When the doors close, I'm left with McKnight, Alonso, Clark and a few more people I vaguely recognize, but haven't spoken to directly. But it's clear that they're in the know. One of the remaining men, dressed in a military uniform, looks like he was chiseled from stone. A real, old-school, shoot-'em-up, get-the-job-done type.

McKnight turns to me. "What are you suggesting?"

"That a concerted effort be put into studying and understanding the...aberration. How it works. Where it came from. Where it's going. What it wants. We need to answer all the same questions we might when studying a disease, or cancer, with the end goal being a cure."

"A nuclear warhead might be all that's required," Alonso offers.

I shake my head. "This...thing...has been living under tremendous pressure for who knows how long. At least since the glaciers formed on Iceland, but probably a lot longer. It survived inside a volcano. And with all the nuclear material currently being pumped into the atmosphere, I'm not sure launching nuclear missiles is a good idea. Also, it doesn't seem concerned about nuclear fallout, does it?"

"You say that like you think it's intelligent," Clark notes.

"It's following a path directly below the ash cloud," I say. "It's imposs-ible to see from above, but in that eternal darkness, it would also be hard to see coming, despite its size. Every action it's taken so far suggests some kind of intelligence. At the very least, strategic instincts. But whether it's intelligent or not doesn't really matter. It still wants, or needs, something. It exists for a purpose. We need to figure out what that is and then use that knowledge to stop it. It may very well be a nuclear missile, but I wouldn't recommend using one—or five—until we know it will work. At the very least, we'll avoid making it angry."

That seems to resonate. Right now, the aberration seems to be out for a very destructive stroll. I hate to think what would happen if it went on a rampage.

"General Stone," McKnight says, and the rugged-looking military man straightens up.

"Sir."

"Assemble a team. The best you have. I want eyes on the aberration by this time tomorrow. As Mr. Wright says, we need to know what we're dealing with."

"Yes, sir."

"And he's going with."

Stone looks momentarily unhappy, but the emotion is squelched by the hard man's years of training and unflappable discipline.

I, on the other hand, nearly pass out when I realize the 'he,' in question, who will be joining this military expedition to locate, identify and study a creature responsible for the deaths of millions, and likely millions more to come, is me.

14

Turns out that while I have no trouble writing convincing words, and can recite facts on a myriad of subjects, I'm horrible at verbalizing why I am the wrong man to send into an apocalyptic hot zone. After all, I had spent my time at the White House showing the President that I was, in fact, the right man to send. And since this is really an exploratory mission, my job being to assess the situation and recommend which fields of science should be directly involved, I'm more qualified than any actual scientist. In the President's words, I am 'quick thinking, knowledgeable, and experienced.'

Escaping the initial eruption and saving the team has somehow convinced the Commander in Chief that I am not only a science-minded fellow, but a man of action as well. I disagreed, vehemently, but soon found myself speaking to an empty chair and General Stone, a man whose course in life seems defined by his last name. He was hard and unmoving, both physically and emotionally, plotting out the mission that would lead me away from my family once more and toward the embrace of doom.

Dramatic, I know, but not an exaggeration.

When I realized the argument was unwinnable, and that in three hours, I would be heading back across the Atlantic, I made a request.

Perhaps my final request. And that has led me to where I am now, standing outside a White House bedroom door with Sonja Clark.

"They're inside," she says.

"How long do I have?" I ask.

She looks at her watch. "Forty-five minutes."

God...

"How are your legs?" she asks. The last day has been a whirlwind. I all but missed the sun's passage through the sky. My body, still acclimated to Iceland time, is telling me it's time to get up, but here, it's the middle of the night. The boys will be fast asleep. Their mothers...who knows? Bell sleeps more soundly than Mina, but given everything that's going on, I suspect both women will have trouble sleeping. Even more when I tell them I'm leaving.

I shift my weight back and forth, stretching both limbs. "A little stiff, but mostly better. If I don't have to outrun a volcano, I should be fine."

Her forced smile looks more like a frown. She and I both know there is a good chance I'll be running for my life again. Hell, I might not even get the chance to run.

"I'll knock when it's time." She twists the door knob and pulls the door open.

Feeling equally desperate to see my family, and terrified to reveal my fate, I step inside the dark room. Clark closes the door behind me, and I stand still for a moment, willing my heart to slow down and waiting for my eyes to adjust.

The White House grounds are well-lit and artificial light seeps through the spaces around the drawn shades, making my transition from light to dark a little easier. There are three cots, all made up like they're fancy beds, no doubt intended to be used by the boys and either Bell or Mina. All three are empty.

On the far side of the elegantly furnished room is a king size bed with a hardwood-framed high canopy. The crystal chandelier overhead, old paintings in golden frames and display cases full of china make the space feel like a museum, like I snuck past a velvet rope to get in here. But none of this strangeness holds my attention long. Ike and Ishah are fast asleep on the bed, framed by their mothers, who are both laying on their sides. There's a gap in the middle, which I have no doubt was left for me.

We don't sleep together as a single unit often. Once, when the boys were younger and frightened during a power outage, and once when we all went camping in a single tent, but it never feels strange. To the rest of the world, we're a circus act, and I understand why, but to us, it's just the way our family is. And to the boys, it's the way we've always been. Bell, Mina and I have always been up front about our situation. None of us intended this to happen. All of us made mistakes. Had Mina and I had a little more faith in her ability to bear a child, that rift would have never formed, and I would have never found myself sleeping on the couch of our surrogate mother. But at the same time, now that we're years beyond the pain of that tumultuous time, none of us regrets what happened. Instead of one son, we had two. Our family became complex, but full of love.

I crawl into the bed, happy to find the mattress firm and unbending to my weight. The boys don't stir when I lie between them. Surrounded by my loved ones, a weight lifts from my body, and I nearly fall asleep. But in that twilight space between consciousness and sleep, my mind's eye replays those brief moments where I saw it—the aberration—slipping in and out of the ash cloud. So big. And alive.

My stomach twists.

My eyes open wide, staring at the ceiling.

You're not here to sleep, I tell myself, and I turn my nose against Ishah's head, breathing deeply. I kiss his forehead, my nose tickled by his coiling hair, and then I repeat the process with Ike. Nine years ago, before the boys were conceived, I believed I would never be a father. It seemed impossible. But then, two of them. Sons.

I glance at each of them, tears welling in my eyes. The emotions swirling through me are complex. Fear, regret, longing, pride. But there is something larger, something blanketing every torrid emotion this horrid situation has conjured. I look at Mina, her soft eyes closed, peaceful in sleep.

I am blessed, I think.

And this thought causes me nearly as much consternation as facing down a colossal monster risen from the Earth's depths. Because to be blessed, to be bestowed with something good, requires a second party. I believe in the power of the mystical universe even less than I do an omniscient God. Reality itself, as defined by science, is incapable of blessing. It provides, or it doesn't. Blessing requires intention.

And if I don't believe in a higher power, how can I feel blessed by something larger than myself?

I turn toward Bell. Her big brown eyes are staring back at me. Her thick lips are curved up in a smile. "You have the look of a man contemplating big things."

Our hands meet over Ishah's back, fingers interlocking.

"You don't have to believe in Him, to be heard by Him," she says, getting a smile out of me.

"There're no atheists in foxholes," I say, recalling my thoughts on Diego's prayer.

Her smile fades. "What's that mean?"

She knows what it means. Understands the saying. What she doesn't know is that I'm about to head toward a battlefront where foxholes are useless.

"It means..." Mina's slender hand wraps around my shoulder and pulls me back, flat onto my back. "...he's leaving us."

I say nothing.

What *can* I say?

I have trouble looking Mina in the eyes, but there's no hiding from her. "You said you wouldn't leave."

"They didn't give me a choice." It's a pitiful excuse, but the best and only one I have.

"When?" Mina asks.

"Soon."

Her fingers find my free hand. I pull both women's hands to my chest, squeeze and then kiss them. I feel ready to break. Vulnerable. General Stone would probably roll his eyes and call me a Nancy, or worse. But this is who I am. I'm an emotional guy. In the early days of our strange relationship, I was plagued by doubts. Would Mina and Bell accept each other? Could we really function as a family? Could I really love two women, and two sons from different women, with the same level of affection and devotion? While Mina and Bell found their natural rhythm, balancing their relationship, and finding joy in the closeness of their sons, who seemed more like fraternal twins than half brothers, I felt lost. 'You have enough love for us all,' Bell had told me, and Mina had agreed. 'None of us doubts that.'

While Mina had felt betrayed at first, and Bell was guilt-stricken because of her conservative beliefs, something drew them together. And they were better for it. Once I saw that, I was too. We had sons—plural—when it seemed none would be possible.

Mina called it fate.

Bell said it was a miracle.

I chalked it up to luck, though I didn't believe in that, either. But it sounds better than being driven by a biological imperative to reproduce. Science, for all its unflappable truth, is cold. Not only does it remove a creator from the universe—Bell argues it doesn't—but it reduces love to a series of chemical reactions. And that's where science and I part ways. Love is the chink in science's armor.

And as I lay in that bed, surrounded by an Old World, gaudy, White House bedroom, I feel more loved than I think any man should. In my heart, I know there is more going on than a simple rush of dopamine, adrenaline and serotonin. In my brain, I have no idea what that might be, and what it might mean.

"Why?" Mina asks.

It's a simple question, but I hear far more. *Why you? Why now? Why are we here? Why did you lie about staying? Why not someone else?*

I turn toward my wife and see an uncharacteristic amount of emotion in her deep brown eyes. They glisten with tears, like she already knows my fate. She and Bell usually balance each other. Logic and emotion. Realism and dreams. Pragmatism and hope. But now, we're all on the same page, feeling...what?

Loss.

I haven't told them what I'm doing, or where I'm going, but they can sense the finality of this visit oozing off of me.

Her question lingers in my mind, and I decide to break my promise to guard our nation's secrets. I tell them. Everything. Words of unnatural death and destruction whisper into the darkness. Their fingers grip mine tighter, as I detail what I saw in Iceland, how it moved across the island nation, plunged into the sea and ended millions of lives. And now, taking the advice I gave him, the President of the United States is sending me to the far side of the planet to figure out what is happening and why it's happening, and hopefully to devise a way to stop it.

I try to reassure them by making a promise I'm pretty sure is a lie. "We'll keep a safe distance."

"How do you keep a safe distance from something that big?" Mina asks.

"We're not exactly sure how big—"

"Miles," Bell says. "You said 'miles.'"

"We'll stay out of its way."

"The radiation," Bell says.

"It could change direction," Mina adds.

They're thinking up all the horrible possibilities that I've already considered.

"You can't go," Bell says. "The boys..."

She stops when a tear rolls down my cheek. Leaving Mina and Bell is hard enough, but leaving the boys again... I know they struggle when I'm gone. Despite the traveling I have to do for my job, we're a close family. And I've been away a lot lately. Too much. After the trip to Iceland I was going to focus on more local stories, maybe even take a lower paying job at a local paper. Or try blogging.

"Sometimes the best thing you can do with your life, is risk it for others." My words sound hollow, like some action hero's last words. I can't help but feel that I have finally and completely failed them all. *At least they have each other,* I think, and then I turn to Bell. "Maybe you could pray."

She slaps my chest, looking angry. "This is *not* the time for sarcasm." It's true. I have teased her about her beliefs before, especially in the wake of one religious scandal or another. Mostly about TV news anchors and politicians, who she says (and I agree) have hijacked the religion for their own gain.

But this is not one of those times.

"I'm not joking."

I'm as surprised as she is. But she nearly falls out of bed when Mina props herself up on one elbow, looks over me and says, "Go ahead."

It would appear that there are no atheists in foxholes, nor in the homes of those who have loved ones in foxholes.

"Jesus," Bell says, closing her eyes. She has a very simple way of praying, like God is right here with us and has been all this time. "Please protect Abraham. Bring him home to his family. But also guide him. Make his mission a success. Reveal this...creature for what it is. Reveal its purpose. And give Abe the wisdom and discernment to understand your purpose in this mess. We give our fears to you. Our anxiety, too. Your will be done."

There's a gentle knock on the door.

"Amen," Bell finishes.

When I open my eyes, I see tears in hers.

"I have to go," I say.

She and I lean over Ishah to kiss.

When I roll the other way to kiss Mina, I'm once again taken aback by her emotion. Like Bell, she's crying, but she's really struggling to control herself. An invisible force clutches my throat, angrily choking me for leaving.

I kiss my wife, then the boys.

A second knock draws me from the bed.

Half way to the door, I stop and turn around. Both mothers are sitting up.

"Love you," I say.

"Daddy?" Ike rises, rubbing his eyes. "You leaving?"

I head back to the bed, greeting him as he slips onto his bare feet. "For a little while, bud, yeah."

He hugs me tight, and then Ishah is there, arms around us both.

Then Mina.

Then Bell.

When the door opens, filling the room with ambient light, we're enfolded in a group hug that puts the corniest Hallmark card to shame. I turn toward the door and see Clark, who looks ashamed for having looked in. I say one more quick round of goodbyes, and then meet her in the hall, wiping away tears.

I close the door behind me, knowing that if I stop again, they'll have to send Secret Service agents to drag me away.

"Sorry," she says. "That was...touching."

"Are they all set?" I ask.

She looks at the door and nods. "Where we go, they go. There were a few complaints, but Mrs. McKnight silenced them. They'll be safe. You don't need to worry about them."

I turn and start walking down the hall, trying my best to feel confident and brave.

Clark clears her throat, turning me around. She points in other direction and offers a smile. "This way."

I'm so screwed.

15

EMIL

The house was quiet.

Emil Chovanec was accustomed to having the kitchen to himself at four in the morning. His wife, Hana, and their three children were sound sleepers. But their absence had left the house feeling empty. *Soulless,* Emil thought, *if such a thing is possible.* As a security specialist for the Dukovany Nuclear Power Station, Emil's job was to secure and protect the four reactors and eight cooling towers—visible through his kitchen window—from all manner of threats. Terrorists and natural disasters were part of the job, but the most dangerous peril faced by the plant was human error.

He liked to say that Dukovany had the highest safety record of all nuclear power stations in the Czech Republic, which was true, but the country had only two such facilities. His other job, the one he took even more seriously, was to protect his family. So when it became clear that the ash cloud from Iceland would blanket the Czech Republic in a chilling, lung-choking darkness, he sent his family south, to Italy. Hana's sister lived in Manfria, on the southern coast of Sicily, which was about as far south as you could travel in Europe without jumping the Mediterranean into Tunisia.

The crunch of his knife scraping honey across the slice of toasted rye made him flinch. Then he remembered that they were gone. There was no one to wake up. *Relax*, he told himself, conjuring a burp and letting it out. *It's like a vacation.*

But it wasn't. He was here, instead of with his family, because it was his job to make sure the four nuclear reactors, still running despite his warnings, stayed functional. Information from neighboring countries to the north and west was scarce. Power was out. Communication came from those with radios, but most people transmitting were asking for information, not providing it. Germany had gone dark, first from the ash cloud that now covered most of Europe, and then from a lack of power. There had been news of a tsunami, caused by the eruption in Iceland, but then nothing else.

When Emil had gone to bed, just six hours ago, Prague had gone dark. Power was failing across Europe, and he couldn't understand why. No one could. But it was their job to make sure that the millions of people depending on Dukovany for electricity wouldn't go without. That was what he was told when he proposed they shut down the facility until they knew what was happening.

Sucking honey and rye crumbs from the knife, he checked his phone. No updates from the power plant, which was good. It meant that everything was operating normally, and maybe he was wrong to worry. He checked his texts. The newest was from Hana, and he'd read it before falling asleep. She and the kids had made it to Italy, and they had learned that the border was being closed. Even if he wanted to join them, he couldn't. But they were safe.

And not asleep upstairs.

He leaned back in his chair and pitched the knife into the metal sink, creating an explosion of noise so loud it seemed to rumble through him. *Early morning jitters,* he thought, and he looked down at his breakfast. Coffee, honeyed rye, slices of cheese and salami and two eggs, hard boiled the day before. As an early riser and late lunch eater, Emil always had large breakfasts.

He bit into the thick toast, the crunch vibrating through his body in a way that felt unnatural. He chewed once and paused, his senses telling him something was wrong. But what? *Is the bread spoiled?* He flipped the toast over, looking for mold. When he found none, he chewed again and felt nothing strange. The honey's sweetness hit his tongue and relaxed him.

Drawn by the bitter smell of his black coffee, Emil picked up the mug, lifted it to his nose and breathed deeply. The scent alone was enough to lift away the lingering weight of sleep. He moved the mug to his mouth, the hot liquid stinging his lips, as he sipped. Then he froze. The liquid jittered, as though blown on. A vibration moved through his body, starting from his feet and butt. Then it faded.

He remained motionless, trying to decide if it was the world around him shaking, or his body. *Did I just have a seizure?* he wondered. When the coffee burned his lips, he pulled the mug away. Placed it on the table. Watched it.

Fingers gripped the table sides, squeezing, waiting.

A rattling buzz filled the silent house. Emil reeled back from the table, nearly falling over. But it wasn't the house shaking, or a seizure, it was his cell phone on the tabletop. Emil smiled at his paranoia, and leaned forward, expecting to see an update from Hana. But the message displayed on the screen wasn't the white text on a green background he associated with a text message. It was black text on a white background.

Work.

The power plant.

He leaned forward, reading the brief message from his counterpart, Bohumil, whose shift ended in an hour, when Emil's would begin.

1.2, 1.9, 2.5 richters. Escalating tremor sequence. Shutdown in progress. They should have listened to you.

Emil stood from the table and moved to the kitchen window. He could see the eight cooling towers, lit from below, and ringed with blinking red lights to keep wayward planes from crashing into them. Steam still billowed from the towers, but no klaxons had sounded. Tremors weren't a problem.

Thumbs moving quickly, Emil tapped out a reply.

Need me there now?

He waited, watching the plant.
The phone buzzed.

Stay on schedule. Will be here for duration.

The plant's on-duty security chief was required to stay on until a crisis was contained, even if his replacement reported for duty. It ensured that nothing was missed, that no detail was lost in the shuffle.

Will do, Emil replied, and he put the phone on the counter. Leaning on the kitchen sink, he watched the plant.

Too little, too late, he thought. It took days for reactors to fully shut down and cool off. They were not like light bulbs. You couldn't just switch them off. The control rods might be able to absorb neutrons and stop the fission process, but the highly radioactive atoms already produced would still be present. Protons, electrons, neutrons, positrons, gamma rays, helium nuclei, burning with energy, would turn the water into a radioactive swill that would take years to break down. A nuclear power plant doesn't need to fully melt down to be dangerous, and a serious earthquake could introduce radioactive liquid into the water table.

The coffee cup rattled and bumped across the counter as another quake struck. The mug slid off the counter and shattered on the floor, splashing Emil's bare feet with steaming liquid.

He barely noticed.

He clutched the sink, keeping himself upright while dishes and pans clattered and fell around him. The shaking pulse of energy rose and fell, rolling beneath the house and dissipating in seconds. Fast, but powerful.

Phone in hand again, he accessed the plant's emergency system, which monitored geological events throughout the region.

4.4 magnitude.

Nearly twice as strong as the last. The sequence was still escalating.

If it continues...

Emil closed the app and opened the text program. He tapped out a message to his wife.

Don't come home. If I don't make it to you, don't look for me. Too dangerous. Love all of you.

His thumb hovered over the send button.

He waited.

Breathing.

Like a sprinter on the starting line, he focused, seeing the race before him, seeing each step, craving the finish line.

But he didn't want to run this race.

Mostly because the gun firing at the race's start was loaded with a radioactive cloud.

The phone buzzed.

It was Bohumil.

Trouble. Hurry.

Emil flicked the message away. His course had been reset. The car. The road. The highway. Austria. Italy. In the perpetual darkness provided by the ash cloud, he felt sure he could find a way through, a way south to his family, who was his primary concern. His job at the plant was serious. Crucial even. But there was nothing he could do against an earthquake, and if another came, stronger than the last, even running might not be enough.

I should go now, he thought. *But if nothing happens, I'll be fired. I'll be jailed.*

Wait, he told himself.

His stomach seized as something moved in the sky. It was like the night itself had come to life, shifting darkness within darkness, hovering like a massive specter over the power plant.

What is that?

He leaned forward, trying to see through the black.

A klaxon sounded. He'd never heard it before, but he knew what it meant. The race had begun.

But he didn't move.

He stood transfixed, as the sky itself seemed to descend on the plant.

Cooling towers crumbled, crushed from above.

The lights at the tower bases illuminated a rough textured, dark gray surface, like the moon itself had fallen from the sky. Then, all at once, they winked out. The entire facility was there once more, and then it was crushed beneath something massive.

Emil's eyes widened.

He tapped the send button on his phone, then dove to the floor.

Scrambled under the kitchen table.

A pressure wave slammed into the side of the house, shattering the windows, blasting glass into the kitchen from where he stood just a moment ago. The kitchen cabinets disgorged their contents, shattering ceramic, glass and china on the floor, and on the tabletop protecting Emil. An earthquake far stronger than the last rolled beneath the house. Emil heard the foundation snap and crack. The house canted to the side.

"Do prdele!" Emil yelled, using language he'd removed from his vocabulary after having kids. He fought against the shaking and shifting floor, pulling himself out from under the table. Glass cut into his feet as he sprinted across the kitchen. Some pulled free when he reached the living room rug. The rest was pushed in deeper.

Running through the pain, he paused at the front door to snatch the car keys out of a bowl. Outside, the weather was warm and breezy, but there was a stench in the air, unlike anything he'd smelled before. Wincing as the firm paved driveway pushed the glass deeper into his feet, he hobbled toward the car. Yellow lights blinked as he unlocked the doors. But he didn't climb inside. The view from the power plant, from where the power plant used to be, pulled his attention again.

The massive object lifted up and away, lit from below by orange light that plumed brighter as the flat, craggy surface rose. A series of dull *whumps* sounded from the flattened plant, and they were quickly followed by the sharp report of multiple explosions. Fire and smoke billowed from the power plant's remains, like four volcanoes.

Or four melting down reactors.

Screaming in horror, Emil leapt into the car and fumbled with the keys, desperate to start the car.

The engine hummed to life and then screeched as he held the turned key too long. He slammed the car into gear and screamed again as he crushed his glass-pierced foot against the pedal. Tires screeched, replacing the foul stench in the air with burning rubber. Then he was on the road and moving, racing an unseen enemy.

When he reached the middle of the now powerless town, his headlights revealed bleary-eyed residents, many of whom worked for the plant. They gathered on the sidewalks, no doubt trying to understand the strange sequence of events that had roused them from bed. He honked his horn and screamed at them to flee, but he didn't look back to see if they listened. Tires shrieked as he wove through the town's center, heading east, charting a mental course to where he could turn south.

The wheel became slick in his hands.

He was sweating.

Drops rolled down his forehead, stinging his eyes.

No, he thought. *God, no!*

His body quivered.

It's anxiety, he told himself.

But he didn't believe it.

And a moment later, his body confirmed it. His head swirled. The road ahead blurred. Vomit burst from his mouth, coating the front window and the steering wheel. The severity and rapid onset of ARS—Acute Radiation Syndrome—symptoms told him that he had already been exposed to a lethal dose. Even if he cleared the area and reached a hospital, there was nothing anyone could do for him. He pulled to the side of the road as the skin on his forearms turned bright red, blistered and popped, covering his skin in hot liquid.

He felt his pants pocket for his phone, hoping to send one last message to his family, but it was missing.

But a moment later, it didn't matter. His vision went black.

He vomited again.

He didn't notice that the car was still moving, speeding up as it rolled down a slight incline. He didn't feel his bowels vacate. He felt burning. Confusion. And then he understood nothing. Forgot who he was.

Suffering from the final stages of rapid onset ARS, the mega dose of radiation affected his neurology, erasing the mind so he was incapable of sensing or processing his own death.

The radioactive cloud climbed into the atmosphere, mixing with volcanic ash and adding its unleashed energy to the dozens of other reactors melting down across the continent, flowing steadily east in the wake of something monstrous.

16

ABRAHAM

"Check your line!" the soldier at the back of the plane shouts. I'm not sure about his name or rank, but he's dressed for war, even though he's not one of the men about to jump. He's not wearing the air filtration mask, goggles or radiation detectors, but the black BDUs, body armor, helmet and sunglasses make him look just as deadly.

"Line secure!" The men around me shout. Each and every one of them is part of the 75th Army Ranger Regiment. Not only are they the best of the best, but they're the most rapidly deployable unit in the Army. When the United States declares war, the Rangers aren't just the first soldiers on the ground, they're already there. They're a no-brainer for a last minute mission on the far side of the world.

I, on the other hand, am not a no-brainer choice. I'm a science writer. Sure, I *do* know a lot about a lot. I've been on rigorous expeditions before, saved the team in Iceland and proved myself to the President, but I am in way over my head. I'm like a Chihuahua running with a pack of wolves.

The man behind me, Master Sergeant David Graham, tugs on the line dangling above my head. The carabiner connecting me to a metal cord running down the length of the ceiling jangles and remains secure. "Science Guy, secure!"

The Rangers gave me the callsign: Science Guy, after Bill Nye, who represents the highest level of science education these guys received. Graham is called Supernatural, on account of his skill level. I think five syllables is a bit of a mouthful, but these things have meaning to the Rangers, and I'm not about to point out nickname flaws to the men assigned to keep me alive.

"Check your equipment!" the soldier at the back shouts, motioning to his chest with the flats of his hands. The men around me check straps, gear and weapons with well-rehearsed efficiency. One by one they sound off, shouting, "Good to go."

Graham takes me by the shoulders and spins me around. He shakes my helmet and goggles. Both are tight. He looks over the facemask covering my nose and mouth. It will filter the air I'm breathing, so I won't have to worry about ash. And if things get bad, I have an hour's worth of air in a small bottle strapped to my hip. He checks the zippers, buttons and clips of my clothing and body armor, which is lined with a thin weave of lead. It adds a lot of weight to the uniform, but it's better than having your insides melted. It's not perfect protection, but it can reduce the effect of what would normally be a mortal dose of radiation and give the wearer—me— more time to get to a safe distance.

If there is such a thing, I think.

The 'aberration' seems determined to melt down every reactor between Hamburg and Russia. Following the seismic trail, it seems to be headed toward Rivne, Ukraine, where the Rivne Nuclear Power Plant's four reactors pump out 2800 megawatts of energy. And we're on course to intercept it, sometime before it reaches the plant during the late morning hours. We have no specific times or locations to go by, because the seismic data is vague—and moving. The GPS trackers we have will let us track it precisely, but until then, it's whereabouts are all guesstimation.

And since we're getting ready to hurl ourselves out of the back of a C-130 Hercules cargo plane, someone is guesstimating that we're closing in on our very large target. I've leaped out of planes before, for work and for fun—before I was married—but I've never done a Low Altitude Low Opening (LALO) jump. While being closer to the ground sounds like a good thing, LALO jumps are often more dangerous. By the time you figure out that something has gone wrong, you're already a pancake.

Graham taps my radiation detector with a single knuckle, like he's a shy, door-to-door, insurance salesman. The green power light remains lit and steady. I'm not sure what that was supposed to check—loose battery maybe—but he seems satisfied. If we come across radiation, which seems likely, the devices will sound alarms via the earbuds we're all wearing. They'll then identify the radioisotope, its source and level. And if that weren't enough, if the level requires action, the devices will identify local shelters using GPS and will supply us Google maps-style directions on the go. Sounds like super science fiction, but I already use the same technology to arrive at every meeting on time.

I'm spun back around toward the rear of the plane and given two firm pats on the shoulder. I would never admit it in current company, but the pats hurt. A lot.

"Science guy is good to go!" Graham shouts.

And I'm not sure why they're all shouting. The comm system we're all wearing lets us hear each other clearly over the C-130's buzzing engines and the rush of wind through the plane's open rear hatch.

When nothing happens, I look back at Graham and start to speak, but I manage only a single syllable before he thrusts two fingers at the open hatch. "Eyes forward, Science Guy!"

I turn forward again and say, "Graham, how—"

"Callsigns," Graham says. "We're crashing the party."

I glance at the soldier standing in the back of the plane. Not only is he concealed in armor, but there is no sign of a name, rank or even country on his uniform. *We don't exist,* I think. *That's why they had me turn in my IDs.*

"Supernatural," I say. "How do we know when to jump?"

"When the light turns green," he says. "And when I shove your ass out the door."

I hear light chuckles from the men around us. So far, they've all been professional and polite, but that doesn't mean they aren't getting a kick out of me.

"Question for you," Graham says. "What's it like?"

"What's what like?"

"You know..."

I *do* know, but if he's going to make me talk about this over an open comm with the nine members of the Reapers, made up of Graham, the squad leader, and two four-man fire teams, not to mention whoever is listening in from the situation room, I'm going to make him say the words.

"Having two wives."

I've never backed down from the conversation, and if I'm honest, I'd rather focus on my family than jumping out of this plane, so I answer honestly. "I'm only married to one of them."

"So the other one is what, like a concubine?"

"That's awesome," I hear one of the other men say.

"No way, man," someone else says. "One woman telling me what to do is enough."

Chuckles fill the comms. And it's a good point. My strange relationship is only possible because we're oddly compatible.

"It's complicated," I say.

"I bet. You—" Graham pauses as a loud *shhh* fills the cabin. Through the open rear hatch, I see a cloud of ash fill the sky around us, blotting out the Ukrainian landscape below. When nothing horrible happens and the plane remains on course, he continues. "You ever get tired of the questions? I imagine you all get strange looks when you're out and about."

It's a fairly sensitive question for a soldier, but then, maybe I'm judging these guys as quickly as people judge my family.

"Only when people bring the kids into it, and really, they're what we're all about. I didn't intend to have two kids at the same time by two different women, but I wasn't about to choose one over the other. It was an easy call for me. Harder for my wife, for obvious reasons, and for my partner, for religious reasons, but it was still the right call."

"Hardcore dedication, man," someone says. "Right on."

I smile and am about to offer my thanks, when someone manages to verbally sucker punch me. "If it's so great, how come you're out here with us?"

"Uh. I was ordered to—"

"You're a civvy," the unseen soldier says. "You could have said 'no.' You could have stayed home with your family. Your two women. But instead you're flying half way around the world into a war zone. Now, the rest of us, we're single and have no children. This is what we do. You? You're a writer. I read your file. And from what I can see, you travel the world far more than you're at home."

"You have a point, Wheeler?" Graham asks.

"I'm just saying, he might be overestimating how much he enjoys having a weird family. Seems like he spends most of his time running from them."

The men fall silent, perhaps waiting for me to reply, or knowing that Wheeler has shifted the conversation from friendly ribbing to uncomfortable truth. And I kind of hate him for it. Not for being rude or an asshole, but because he might be right. And I don't think I would have come to the realization on my own. When I'm away from home, I tell myself there is no place I'd rather be than with my family, and there is some truth to that. I do love them. More than anything else. But I'm also uncomfortable. And afraid. So I keep on taking assignments that require travel, and a lot of it.

Wheeler isn't the asshole. I am.

"Listen," Graham says, his tone sympathetic to my plight. "Let's focus on—"

The plane angles upward so sharply that I'm pushed to the floor. I'm caught under one arm and hauled to the side of the plane, where I grasp hold of a metal handhold.

Engines scream.

The angle increases. I reach for the soldier at the back of the plane—the one not jumping. He leans forward, taking one step at a time, fingers stretching for mine. He's wearing a parachute, and is clipped into a nylon strap attached to the floor, but falling would still hurt. Or worse. The strap is attached at his waist, designed to keep from stumbling out of the plane, but I don't think the designers planned for a near vertical plummet.

Somewhere in the back of my mind, over the roar and chaos, I hear someone, probably one of the pilots, shouting, "Pull up! Pull up!"

The plane's nose tilts up at a ridiculous angle, the engines straining against the vehicle's incredible weight. The soldier's hand, just inches from mine, falls back with the rest of him as gravity tugs him down. He's in a free fall. I don't see any way out of a broken back for the soldier. He'll either be dead or paralyzed the moment that line snaps taut. Concealed in armor and sunglasses, he looks fearless as he falls. Maybe he is. Men like these, who face life and death situations for a job, must make peace with their possible demise, early on.

When a blade flashes, and the nylon cord is severed, I know he's come to the same conclusion as me. Better to fall out and parachute down. But that's not what happens. He flips, head over heels, falling back. Before tumbling from the plane, his head strikes the hard metal ceiling. The blow saps the life from him. The blade falls from his hand. He spirals from the back of the plane, body lax like he's sinking in a pool of water. If he's not dead already, he will be when he hits the ground.

I scream, first for the man falling out of the plane. And then for myself. My feet leave the floor, and I nearly lose my grip, as my wrist twists around. I reach up and grasp the handhold with all ten fingers. Looking up, I see the other nine members of our squad doing the same.

Some of the men are screaming like me, which is good for my ego, but not very reassuring. Others are shouting commands and questions. There's too much at once to make any sense of it.

The plane shakes violently in time with an explosion.

We start spinning.

A long, massive spear of darkness sweeps past the open hatch.

My hanging body turns sideways as the plane continues to twist, the centrifugal force overpowering gravity.

"Reapers!" Graham shouts over the noise. "We are hit! Deploy in three..."

The plane shudders. I feel a sudden drop in speed. *We've lost an engine,* I think. That's why we're spinning. That's why we're slowing down. In seconds, we're going to fall back down, and then exiting this plane through the open hatch might be impossible.

"One!" I shout over Graham's 'two' and relinquish my grip. I fall from the open hatch, twisting as the line attached to me snaps taut, deploying my parachute. I fall into the ash-laden daytime twilight and see the plane above me. It's missing a wing, still spinning, but its climb has stopped.

Graham and three other Rangers drop from the back, but then the 69,300-pound C-130—129,300 pounds fully fueled—with the rest of Reaper squad and two pilots, careens over and falls behind them, plummeting toward the ground.

Toward me.

17

I lose sight of the falling cargo plane and four Rangers when my chute snaps open. My body is flung around so all I can see is what's ahead of and below me, which right now, looks like endless sunlit gray snow. Then I see the ground, rushing up at me, and I don't mean that in the cliché sense of the term that actually means *I'm* rushing toward the ground. I mean, the surface of the Earth actually appears to be rising up below me, swelling and ready to burst, like a frog's vocal sac. As much as the parachute has slowed my descent, the rising ground will still greet my body with enough force to crush my bones.

And then, just as I'm sure I will never see my family again, a wave of pressure, thrust up by the massive shape, shoves against my parachute, lifting me higher, until I match the flat surface's momentum. Boot tips reaching, I try to touch down, but the ground below me falls away.

I look up, expecting to see the plane falling, ready to swat me from the air, but all I can see is my parachute, billowing out hard as the pressure wave becomes a vortex, sucking me down.

I flinch as feet swing into view just over the top of my parachute. Graham swings around ahead of me, controlling his descent.

"Next time you get close, detach the chute," he says.

He sounds calm. How can he sound calm?

The other two Rangers drop down into view. One of them is ahead of us by a hundred feet. The other is to our right.

A line of black, rising up from below and stretching in the sky high above, slides out of the gray mist, swinging toward us. It's massive. Comparable in scale to the Eiffel Tower, but taller, its height indeterminable. "Look out!" I shout, like there is something any of us can do to avoid it.

The black tower—for lack of a better word—cuts through the sky. When I see its trajectory, I scream. Not for myself, but for the man ahead of us.

The streak of black, emitting a red-orange glow through criss-crossing seams, passes just fifty feet in front of me. It collides with the Ranger, sweeping him out of existence. Before I can feel revolt or sadness, or even shock, the wind generated by the massive tower pulls me and the remaining two Rangers hard to the right. Feeling like a kid on a carnival swing-carousel, I'm pulled sideways and given my first glimpse of the sky since leaping from the plane.

I scream again.

The plane is there.

Right there.

Nose down.

Falling toward us.

I see the pilots in the cockpit, fighting for control, despite missing a wing. The plane pinwheels downward as I'm pulled to the side, just out of range of its rotating wing and still buzzing propellers. The C-130 plummets past.

"Give the devil his due, boys," Graham says a moment before the plane reaches the shifting ground below and erupts into a ball of fire.

The heat from the explosion hits me at the same time as the concussive force, which slaps into my parachute and shoves it up, slamming me back into an upright position.

"This is it," Graham shouts. "Get ready to detach!"

The ground rises up once more, the pressure wave leading it pushing the chute higher and keeping me from slamming against it. When the rough, ruddy surface slows to a stop three feet beneath me,

I yank the 'three-ring release' dangling from my right shoulder strap, cutting away the parachute and letting the breeze snatch it away.

I hit the ground hard, bending at the knees like I was landing with a parachute attached. The surface beneath me is unforgiving and jagged, like I've just landed on a large chunk of beachside granite. I roll once and come to a stop on my back, coughing and groaning. An "oof" turns my attention to the side, and I see Graham rolling beside me, much more gracefully. He gets back to his feet in one quick movement. The Ranger off to the right is nearly close enough to drop, but the ground starts moving away from him. A twisting sensation fills my gut, like I'm in a fast moving elevator, dropping down.

The Ranger detaches.

The ground falls away, and we fall with it.

For a moment, it appears the soldier is flying, his downward momentum matching that of the descending surface. But he's not flying. He's falling. And when the ground begins rising again, if it does, he's going to impact at terminal velocity.

"Pull your reserve!" Graham shouts.

The Ranger grips the small handle hanging over his chest and pulls hard. The pilot chute pops out, catches the wind and snaps upward, pulling the reserve parachute.

Fabric expands, billowing out with hope.

And then the ground slows to a stop, reverses direction and erases all hope. The partially deployed parachute does little to slow his descent. I close my eyes when the Ranger collides with the ground head first, but I can still hear the crack of his armor and his bones slamming into the solid ground.

Silence follows.

I catch my breath, clinging to the moving ground, trying not to throw up as the constantly shifting world twists my gut with nausea.

"This is Supernatural. Anyone copy?"

"I copy," I say, and then I realize he already knew I was fine.

I'm the only one who replies.

"Beehive, this is Supernatural. Do you copy?" he says, using the current codename for the command structure above us, monitoring the mission. He takes a moment to crouch by the fallen Ranger, but doesn't bother checking for a pulse. I can see from here that the twisted heap of a man is dead.

The Beehive stays silent.

"Comms are local," he says, looking at me now. "Take a moment. Get your bearings. But then I want your assessment as to what the hell just happened, what killed my men, and where the hell we are." Before I can reply, he starts walking away, struggling to stay upright as the world shifts directions again, tilting to the side. I'm about to ask where he's going, terrified that I'm being abandoned, when I see he's heading for the only real landmark in sight: the flaming wreckage of the C-130 a quarter mile away.

Kneeling on the rough surface, I'm thankful for the body armor protecting my knees and the gloves over my hands. Without them, I'm sure my injuries would be far more substantial and bloody. The ground beneath me is covered in a thin layer of volcanic ash that falls from the sky. But it doesn't stick like snow. The light flakes shift with the breeze and lift away as the ground drops down once more. I brush a section of the ash clean, revealing an obsidian surface, marbled with streaks of bioluminescent red light, giving the impression that the surface is also somehow transparent.

I'm struck by a sudden lightheadedness, and it has nothing to do with the movement. I recognize the texture and color. The spike jutting from the Icelandic glacier. We haven't landed on some kind of quaking landscape. We've landed on the aberration's colossal back.

I look left and right, seeing no end to the barren living world we've dropped onto. If visibility wasn't reduced by the endless ash floating about, maybe I'd see some end to the creature's back, but right now, my whole world is gray sky, this black-and-maroon streaked shell and the orange fireball now silhouetting Graham. His figure warbles from the heat, and for a moment it seems to disappear, like he's been teleported onto the starship Enterprise.

"Graham," I say, blurting out the name, and then correct myself too late. "Supernatural."

"No one can hear us," he says, sounding grim. "Don't worry about it."

"I know where we are."

His silhouette shifts as he turns back to me and starts walking. "Spit it out."

"We're on top of it."

"On top of *what?*"

"The aberration."

Graham stands motionless, his head scanning the terrain around us. He sways as the landscape shifts again.

"It's walking," I say. "We're feeling its footsteps."

"This is its...back?"

"That's my guess."

"But..." He twists around, scanning the area. "I can't see the end of it."

"I know."

I see the faint shadow of a looming tower rising up to our right. It stretches up into the sky, fading away long before reaching any kind of terminus. It's what struck the Ranger out of the sky. Maybe even what hit the C-130. But it's not a tower at all. It's a spine, rising up at an angle from what looks like a hill, but what I suspect is something closer to a massive pore. I point to it. "Look."

"This is FUBAR, Science Guy."

"Very."

"Can we do anything here?"

I take a small kit out of my hip pack. Inside are several sample bags along with a sampling of collection tools, including a battery powered core drill and an old school hammer and chisel. "Maybe." I start with the drill, attaching the diamond tipped core blade and placing it against the hard surface. The drill bit can chew through most any hard stones, steel reinforced concrete and cemented gravels. Aside from the strongest metals, there isn't much it can't chew through. I pull the trigger. The blade spins and slips to the side so fast that I nearly fall over. There's not even a scratch on the surface. "Okay..."

With the drill clutched in both hands, I position the blade on a rough patch. No chance of it slipping here, and once it digs into the rough surface it will keep on going. I pull the trigger again. Sudden sharp pain tears through my fingers, wrists and arms. The diamond tips caught the rough surface, but instead of chewing through, the drill spun free of my hands, nearly breaking my wrists.

Guess I'll try the old fashioned tools.

I discard the drill, place the chisel on the hard surface and give it a solid whack with the hammer. My hand holding the hammer stings from the blow, but once again, I don't even blemish the surface. I place the chisel against a small imperfection, aiming to chip it away. I slam the hammer down with all the strength I have left. The impact sends a jolt of pain from my already aching wrist to my shoulder. The small lump remains intact. I lift the chisel and look at the blade. It's as clean as it was the moment I lifted it from its carrying case.

My mind flashes back to a similar moment in time, two days ago, when I held an ice ax rather than a chisel. The ice ax failed to break a piece away, but it wasn't clean. It was covered in a thin layer of black. I doubt the ice ax was any sharper or more powerful than the chisel and hammer, but maybe, after sitting in the ice for so long, the shell was softer? Or perhaps it was because it struck the very tip of such a thin spike.

My eyes turn back to the distant tower, and I see it in my mind's eye, rising high into the sky, a mile or more, tapering down into a spike thin enough to prick a toe. Is *this* what Kiljan stepped on? What I grasped in my hand?

"I already have a sample," I say to myself.

"What?" Graham asks.

When I look up, he's standing above me. I flinch back, falling onto my ass with a shout of surprise. "A sample. I think I have one."

"You chipped this with a hammer?" He taps his foot on the solid floor and sounds dubious.

"An ice ax. In Iceland. Before all this started."

"Where is it?" he asks.

"If the Secret Service is true to their word, delivered to my front porch. In New York."

"*New York?* If you tell me this whole mission was a waste of time..." The threat lingers, but is never finished.

"We need to look around," I tell him. "There could be more to learn."

"Including a way off of this thing."

"That...would be good." I tug at my glove, removing it from my right hand. It's a tight fit because of the bandage covering my scorched skin, and it hurts as I remove it, but I manage to free my hand a moment later. My fingers tingle as blood rushes back into the digits. I hadn't realized how tight the gloves were.

"What are you doing?" he asks.

"I want to know if it feels similar to what I touched in Iceland." My bare hand stretches out for the rough, black and red surface. "Things like texture and temperature might not seem important now, but—"

My skin makes contact.

"But what?" I hear Graham ask, but his voice sounds funny.

Distant.

Spoken through a wall or a tin can.

I blink, and in the micro-moment of time, the hard black shell sprouts a layer of lush green grass.

My hand snaps up, the tickle of the thin blades still on my skin.

What the...

I look up.

The aberration is gone, and Graham with it, replaced by a sweeping mountainous landscape worthy of Yellowstone Park, but totally unrecognizable.

It's happening again, I think. *Another vision.*

And then I feel it. A presence, rumbling through the very air itself, filling the valley below with the sound of a waterfall. There is either a flood behind me, or the figure in black. I remain locked in place, quivering, not wanting to confront either possibility, despite the fact that I know this isn't reality.

Then something grips my shoulder, and the rushing water voice says, "Let it burn."

18

"I don't *want* it to burn." This shred of defiance feels like the opening salvo of a battle. But nothing happens, to me, or to the forest spread out before me. The pressure on my shoulder is gone. The weighty presence is gone.

I spin around, confirming that I'm alone, standing atop a gray stone cliff, framed by trees all around, the scent of pine and earth tickling my nose. Despite the physical relief I feel at the smoky figure's absence, I'm struck by a strange sense of profound loss.

What's the point of it all? I think.

Pebbles beat out a rhythm as they bounce down the cliff, knocked free by my feet, shuffling closer to the edge.

I *want* to jump.

I'm an emptied vessel.

Without purpose.

"This isn't real," I tell myself, forcing thoughts of Mina, Bell and the boys into my head. They're real. My family is real.

But you left them, my inner monologue says, mirroring the sentiment of the now-deceased Army Ranger who questioned me on the C-130. And like that man, who I did not know, my inner monologue's painful accuracy cuts deep.

As hope leaves my heart, the world around me changes. Pine needles brown at the fringes of several trees, spreading steadily upward. Dead limbs crack and fall away. The brown spreads through the forest like a disease, consuming life, both plant and animal, rotting the ground and then the very air itself, once fragrant, but now death-scented.

The world is dying.

I'm letting it die.

I'm *killing* it.

Burn it, I think. *Let it burn.*

A sudden heat blossoms in my right hand, burning my flesh.

The glowing orange rod is there once more.

"Remove your disgrace from the Earth." The rumbling voice shakes my insides with its sudden and insistent return. But it also fills me again, returning purpose and focus. "Make things anew."

"How?" I ask without turning around, still afraid to experience the presence directly.

The voice is silent. I already know the answer.

"Let it burn," I say, hefting the rod up like a javelin. "Burn it to the ground. Burn it all."

Two quick steps take me to the cliff's edge. I lean my body forward, thrusting my arm out and loose the spear with all my strength and best intentions. The orange rod reminds me of the glowing-hot tracer rounds used to track the trajectory of fired bullets. Following its course through the air is easy. Despite the distance, it soars out over the valley, descending toward the dried out, rotted land below.

The rod pierces the earth, stabbing into the dead land. The brown debris surrounding it smolders and then bursts into flames. The blaze spreads quickly, sliding out in all directions, leaving a ring of charred black in its wake.

The fire spreads faster than the rot, catching, devouring and digesting it, until all that remains is ash.

When the fire continues, consuming the living world beyond the spreading death, I start to doubt what I've done. Animals scurry from the forest. I hadn't seen them there! The flames catch them, igniting them one by one, with the sudden deadly efficiency of moths striking a bug zapper. They shriek, leap and ignite. By the time they hit the ground again, they're nothing more than charred remains, reduced to their most basic chemical elements.

"No," I say, tears in my eyes.

A rabbit springs into the air, trying to vault the flames. Its outstretched body clears the flickering orange, but the heat alone set the soft fur alight. The shriek of its passing lasts just a moment, but it's enough to fully break my resolve. "No!"

The fire spreads toward the horizon, filling the air with smoke and cries of anguish. Heat surrounds me as flames lick up the cliff side and then lunge into the forest behind me.

My legs give way.

Hard rock digs into my bare knees, and for the first time since this vision began, I realize that I am once again naked and shameless. Blood flows from my scraped flesh, oozing out into the rocky crags. I feel no pain. Only sorrow at the world's passing.

"Do not despair," the voice says. "Rebirth requires sacrifice."

"Requires death, you mean." The words are an accusation. "Murder. Genocide."

I think my words, burning with anger and accuracy will put the presence on the defensive. That it will learn the error of its ways and recant. I have come to believe, after all, that I am communicating with the aberration. Why it's bothering to show me these visions, I don't know, but some small part of me hopes it can be reasoned with.

But then it adds to my list of accusations, revealing it fully understands the scope of what it's doing. "Extinction."

I turn to face the figure, thrusting my index finger toward its smoke covered face. "You don't have to do this! We don't deserve this! What gives you the right!"

Unaffected by my tirade, the figure, which is now really just a spectral, undefined head and a limbless body, tilts its head. "The machine is fueled by destruction."

The machine.

The smoky figure spoke of it in the first vision, too. Ike called it 'the ancient.' But am I speaking to the machine? Is that what's walking across

Europe? Maybe the machine is what woke the massive creature? Or Kiljan's blood. Or the ice ax assault? Did that small scale attack trigger a war?

None of this makes sense.

But I know it's wrong.

"Destroying a species isn't—"

"It is the world that burns," the figure says. "Not a single species."

I'm speaking with a sociopath intent on scouring all life from the planet. The depth of its hatred and loathing unhinge me, and words I haven't used since becoming involved with Bell rise from the depths and hiss through my lips. "Jesus fucking Chri—"

The figure billows out like a predatory bird, unfurling its wings, flaring with primal rage. "Fool!" For a flickering moment, I see past its smoky veil, seeing luminous eyes that tear through me—body and soul. Then it descends, lifting me off the cliff and propelling me over the side. Gravity takes hold with sickening quickness, pulling me toward the scorched earth below.

I look back at the figure standing above me on the cliff, its ominous shape taking on the figure of a man once more. It seems satisfied with my fate, watching me plummet to my death.

But will I die?

This is a vision, I think.

I'm still riding on the machine's back. Still with Graham. Perhaps unconscious, but in no immediate danger, if you ignore the potential for radioactive fallout. But last time this happened, I was only unconscious for a few seconds, and speaking out loud.

"Veneno mundi," I whisper, the words yanked away by the wind whipping past me.

Poisoned world.

The machine is fueled by destruction.

I feel the realization tickling my mind a moment before I strike the ground.

Bones break. Everywhere.

My insides liquefy and ooze from pores and burst skin.

And yet, I live. I can hear. And see. And think, despite the fact that I can feel my brain slipping out of my opened skull.

The taste of ash is dry on my tongue. The land around me is charred and dead.

But no longer poisoned, I think, my impending epiphany returning.

The ash twitches.

A coil of green pushes up through it, into the sun.

Leaves sprout.

The plant grows.

Life from death. Rebirth. Poison defeated.

Bare feet step beside the plant, flexing, digging in the ash the way a child does sand at the beach.

I turn my eyes—the only part of me that can still move—up. Two slender legs give way to a naked body that I recognize before my gaze reaches the face. But when I see Mina's kind eyes looking down at me, they're framed by wrinkles. Like with the vision of Ike and Ishah, she has aged.

"Do you understand now?"

"Why are you here?" I ask, and then I address the presence, who I can no longer feel, but who I suspect can still hear me just fine. "Why show me her?"

Mina crouches down beside my dying body. She caresses my cheek with the back of her hand.

The vision fractures, and I see other realities.

An endless green, living ocean. I can feel the toxicity emanating from it.

I know what this is. The Great Oxygenation Event. The very first mass extinction on Earth. Massive amounts of photosynthetic organisms bloomed in the oceans, covering the planet, releasing vast amounts of free oxygen, which was toxic to the anaerobic organisms that populated the Earth 2.3 billion years ago. Nearly all life on Earth was killed, until suddenly, something shifted. The photosynthetic organisms' numbers were greatly reduced, and life was allowed to flourish and evolve once more.

A green wave, hundreds of feet tall, surges through the ocean, heading directly for me. My eyes follow the cresting form toward the top, where the sun glows brightly, blotting out the shape of something massive, moving through the water, shedding waves of material from its back with every step.

The vision within a vision ends when Mina pulls her hand away from my skin. Her fingers come away bloody. "Quid futurum sit. Erit."

She stands, looking like she wants to say something else, but then her face twists up in fear and anger, and she screams at me.

"Science guy! Get the *fuck* up!"

19

Despite the crash of the C-130, the deaths of all those Rangers and my own close call with the brink, the moment I entered the vision-state, the environment surrounding us was calm. I had time to think and observe, to wipe away ash and test a theory—that physical contact allows human beings to somehow communicate with the aberration...the *Machine*. While the theory appears to be validated, Kiljan had his toe impaled by the creature's spine and experienced nothing more than pain. All of this comes and goes through my thoughts with the brevity of a top quark's lifespan, measured in yoctoseconds, and is replaced by a louder, more desperate set of thoughts that coalesces into a simple, three-word expletive.

"What the shit?"

I'm on my back, looking up at an ash-filled sky. But I'm not lying still, I'm sliding backward, bouncing over the shell's rough surface. Graham is dragging me with one hand, yanking my body over jagged imperfections while firing his tan SOPMOD M4 assault rifle in regular three-round bursts.

What is he shooting at? I wonder, as the vision-fog lifts. Our situation doesn't seem to have changed much. We're still on the Machine's back, and I seriously doubt bullets will do the megalithic creature any harm.

"Science Guy!" Graham tugs harder, shaking me, driving his fist into the back of my skull.

"Oww!" I shout, and I'm dropped.

"Get up!" Graham says. "Tangos at your six."

I've never been in the military, nor have I ever really played military video games, so I'm not very familiar with military terms, unless they involve some kind of tech or advanced science. But I've seen enough movies to know that 'tangos' means 'bad guys'—though I'm not really a fan of dehumanizing enemies with terms like Charlie, Gook and Haji. And I know 'my six' is behind me, which is also Graham's twelve.

Did another military force land on the Machine's back? If so, why would Graham be firing at them? His is the only weapon I hear, so if there are people here with us, he's either pinning them down or slaughtering them.

I roll to my stomach, push myself up and get a good look at what's coming our way.

They don't have guns, but they're not human either.

The best way I can describe them is giant, eight-legged mites, or hairy crabs. Their shells match the Machine's back in color and texture, and if they weren't moving toward us, I doubt I'd ever notice them. I don't see any pincers, but their mandibles look prehistorically powerful. In fact, everything about them feels ancient.

Every time one of Graham's bullets strikes a creature, it hunkers down, looking more like a stone than a living thing. But there are no bullet holes. The rounds are being deflected, not even leaving scratches. And once the barrage ends, the struck creatures get back to their sharp-tipped feet and continue toward us. Individually, I would find them no more threatening than a large crab, but these...Crawlers...have a malevolent look in their six, small, black eyes.

And they outnumber us a hundred to one.

Graham swaps out his spent magazine for a new one, his movement fluid and practiced. He aims at the encroaching horde, but holds his fire. "Ideas?"

He's asking me?

But then I realize he's already exhausted his options. Brute force isn't going to help.

"Where did they come from?" I ask.

He motions with the rifle's barrel, at the rear of the advancing wave of Crawlers. Small pore-like holes pock the vast exoskeletal shell. The smaller creatures must have been huddled inside the divots. "They came out just after you went down and started mumbling."

"What did I say?"

"How should I know?" he says. "Sounded like Latin. That's hardly pressing, though, don't you think?"

I focus on the creatures, hoping to glean some kind of clue about their purpose here. I find it in their appearance. Like mites. "They're symbiotic organisms," I declare. "Living off the Machine, scavenging material that collects on its surface, the way pilot fish swim around sharks, picking off parasites. Or the way actual eyelash mites do, eating old skin cells and oil."

Graham takes a step back, standing next to me as the Crawlers close in. I can't see his facial expression behind his goggles, facemask and helmet, but his body language exudes tension. He's doing a good job not losing his mind, though. I feel close to becoming unhinged, but finding a way to classify these things helps.

"So what are *we*, in this scenario of yours?" he asks.

Wishing I had a weapon of my own, even though I know it wouldn't do any good, I say, "We're a food source. Given the size differential between us and the Machine, a better comparison might be bacteria, in which case the bacteria that's already made its home here—" I motion to the Crawlers, now just twenty feet away, "—sees the new bacterial strain—*us*—as invaders. These things might be part of the Machine's physiology."

"You keep calling it 'the Machine.'" He turns his head toward me, and though I can't see his eyes behind his goggles, I feel his gaze like a weight. "You know something I don't?"

"Just something I heard."

"At the White House?"

"In a..." I nearly say vision. "In a dream."

"Well, that's incredibly *not* helpful."

I see a blur of motion reflecting in his goggles.

"Look out!" Before I understand what I'm doing, I shove Graham out of the way, putting myself in the projectile's path. I have just enough time to turn my head and see that the thing flying toward my face is a Crawler. The creature sprang into the air with the energy of an enlarged flea. Its underside flexes wider, and its eight limbs spread open to envelop my face. Of all the ways I imagined myself dying on this mission, being killed by something so much smaller than me wasn't on the list.

Just before the creature strikes my mask, a three-round burst drowns out the sound of my scream and punches into the Crawler's underside. Limbs explode outward, trailing tendrils of white and luminous red gore, which slaps against my facemask. The consistency of toilet paper dunked in milk, the goopy guts stick, until I brush them away. Through the smeared visor, I see the shell spinning by my feet.

There's a pause, as the small creatures seem to watch their fallen comrade's corpse spin around, flinging a pattern of white and glowing red slime that reminds me of the spin-art toy Mina bought the boys a few years ago.

Then, all at once, they start tapping their little legs with frantic urgency. Their undersides flicker red and then glow, like miniature undercar lights.

Graham backs away. "That can't be good."

"I think we should run," I say.

"That's your scientific opinion?" he asks, and I hear the sarcasm.

"Common sense," I say, and then I make a break for it. It's probably not nice of me to run without a consensus, but my odds of survival are much lower than Graham's. Most of my photographers over the years have joked that the best way to survive a dangerous encounter is to be faster than the writer you're working with. It was funny the first time, as the photographer and I stared down a grizzly bear, and the second time, when Bell said it while we squared off against mice in the attic, but it hasn't been funny since. And now, as I stumble-run over a rising, falling and tilting landscape, I suspect that there is a nugget of wisdom buried in the cliché.

When Graham easily overtakes me, I'm sure of it.

"Where are we going?" I shout.

"Hell if I know. You're the one who picked the direction."

"Straight line," I say. "We'll reach the edge sooner or later." I take a quick look back. The Crawlers aren't crawling any more. They're scurrying. Leaping. Building speed as we put a little distance between us. But I don't think they've reached full speed yet, and there's no way to know how far they can run without getting tired.

At my best, I know that I can run miles when certain death is chasing me. I learned that on the glacier. But that was just a few days ago, and I'm already starting to feel the ache return to my muscles. I'm not ready for a long distance slog.

Graham on the other hand, looks like he could run around the globe, his posture and pacing perfect, like he was engineered in Germany.

I shouldn't be here.

I should have said 'no.' Stayed with my family.

Why didn't I?

A shrill beeping fills my ears.

"Is someone trying to contact us?" Despite being thirty feet ahead of me, Graham has no trouble hearing me over the comms, which is where the beeping is coming from. He slows to a stop, staggering a little, as the ground beneath our feet slows to a stop and starts rising again. He bends his knees, absorbing the shift in direction, as he looks down at his chest.

What is he looking at? I think, and then I look at my own chest, where I see the radiation detector. A small red light is blinking in time with the beeping.

Shit.

I look back at the Crawlers, now surging straight for us.

Shit, shit, shit.

An almost sexy, robotic voice fills my ears. "Radioactive isotopes detected. Cesium-134 and Cesium-137 have both been detected in unhealthy levels. At current levels, prolonged exposure could result in fever, muscle weakness, vomiting and other flu-like symptoms. Recommend immediate evacuation in a southeasterly direction."

I look to the sky, trying to find the sun, but it's nowhere in sight. I am lost, in every sense of the word. But Graham is still in control. Consulting a compass on his forearm, he turns around and points. "Southeast."

"Rock and a hard place," I say.

"Killer rocks and a radioactive cloud. But it's a simple choice. I can't shoot radiation."

And with that, he charges directly at the incoming Crawlers.

20

Graham moves with the swiftness and agility of a running back despite the armor and gear he's wearing. I can't pull off that level of physicality, even without gear and armor, but I do my best to follow him. Any other path might lead directly to my demise.

Two groups of Crawlers are tick-tacking their way across the shell-back, scrabbling over the imperfections stumbling me up, with ease. Their broad, flat-bellied bodies and eight legs are tailor made for this environment. The hordes are closing in on us from both sides and zipping together behind us and pursuing.

We can't stop.

Can't change direction.

We're either running toward freedom or directly into a trap.

I flinch when Graham opens fire, squeezing off one round at a time. The bullets ping off the shells of the nearest Crawlers, doing no real damage, but triggering their crouching instinct, allowing us to pass by without being leapt upon.

We run like this for several minutes, with me breathing heavily, Graham shooting any Crawlers that make it past the mental line he's drawn and the Crawlers inexorably closing in behind us. We're a little bit faster than they are, but with the zipper still closing behind us, the horde is just ten feet back, nearly close enough to leap on me. And that's what keeps me moving, despite the ache in my side, the burn in my lungs and invisible knives stabbing into my thighs.

"Science Guy." Graham sounds a bit winded himself. Or afraid. Neither possibility comforts me. He slows a little, letting me catch up. He shoots a Crawler making a mad dash toward him, forcing it to the ground, squelching the red light from its underside. Then he points straight ahead.

A dull line of pink light stretches across our path.

"Is that more of them?"

"I don't think so. It's not moving." He takes another shot, and then swaps out his magazine for a fresh one. "Looks more like a wall."

"How many more of those do you have?" I motion to the magazine he's just loaded.

"After this, just one more. Do you think that's a problem?"

At first, I think he's talking about the limited amount of ammunition he has, and I'm about to declare that yes, clearly, that could be a problem. But then I realize he's talking about the line of glowing pink ahead of us. "Only one way to find out," I say, and I'm proud of how nonchalantly brave it comes out sounding.

"Copy that," he says, and keeps on running.

It's hard to focus on what's ahead when the Crawlers are closing in, too many for Graham to shoot. He picks up the pace, and I'm forced to follow. I don't think I can keep it up for long, but we'll reach the line of pink, which looks like a deeper rose color, now that we're closer and seeing it through less ash. The ground beneath us drops down, making me feel lighter, but when it slows to a stop and rises back up, my weight feels doubled. My knees quiver for two steps and then give out.

I hit the ground hard, but haven't even stopped moving when Graham opens fire. The rapid fire staccato tells me he's switched to full auto, and he's unloading on the horde like Rambo. When I get back to my feet, the nearest Crawlers are crouched down, while the rest attempt to scrabble past.

Graham swaps out his last magazine and says, "Try not to do that again." Then he heads for the glowing wall.

If I could see myself from the outside, I'm pretty sure I'd look like Igor, hobbling after his master, desperate and pitiful. But it's the best my breaking body can manage, and we're nearly at the wall of now red light. The color matches the Crawlers' undersides, which is disconcerting, but I don't see any immediate threats...not including the sea of giant mites still pursuing, and maybe gaining on us.

On the plus side, the radiation detector alarm hasn't declared us dead or poisoned yet. The red blinking light means we're still in the danger zone, but if our armor does its job, we should have time to get away. That is, if we can get back to solid, unmoving land and commandeer a vehicle. Getting to the actual ground might be enough, though. If we're miles high, it's possible the radiation in the atmosphere hasn't filtered down into the Ukrainian landscape. Then again, last I knew, the Machine was closing in on Rivne Nuclear Power Plant. When it gets there, we need to be long gone.

Graham arrives at the luminous wall first, takes a moment to look it over and then turns toward me, raising the rifle. I flinch when he fires, hearing the buzz of a bullet cutting through the air beside my head.

A Crawler snaps back, spinning end over end, spraying its brethren with its slick interior. The slime-covered creatures stop and begin wiping themselves clean. The rest stay on task, closing the distance.

Graham takes a few more shots, slowing the front runners. "Ten seconds. That's all I'm going to give you."

I'm confused for a moment, but then see the 'wall' and understand. We've reached a kind of fault line, where one massive plate overlaps the next. The massively thick, top plate tapers down to what looks like a razor's edge, but it's the stuff between the plates that is really interesting. It reminds me of a glowing pink version of the lumpy green Jell-O salad my mother used to make for Easter. Chunky white cottage cheese-like fluid oozes from the wall, slowly spreading. It's followed by gelatinous red, the biolumin-escence's source. And then there are countless clear spheres with what look like...

I gasp.

"Holy shit."

"Hurry it up!" Graham says, squeezing the trigger a little faster now.

With shaking hands, I free my sample bag and tools, scraping some of the white and red goo into a small vial and following it up with a single—for lack of a better word—egg. This mash of glowing goop most closely resembles a wad of frog eggs.

There's a hiss from the goop, then a loud crack that shakes the shell beneath our feet. The top plate rises an inch, and more of the eggs fill the gap. It's expanding. And then I realize there is a better analogy for the eggs: Fiddler crabs, who carry their gelatinous mash of eggs between layers of shell before flapping them out into the water.

I've just finished twisting the cap back onto the vial when Graham takes me by my belt, giving me a wedgie and hoists me three feet up, onto the upper plate. He climbs up behind me, and he's nearly back on his feet when a Crawler springs up onto his calf. Its sharp limbs clamp down, eliciting a shout of pain from him.

On my feet, I wind up and kick the Crawler's side. If not for the military boots I'm wearing, I think the impact would have broken my toes, but instead, the force knocks the creature free and launches it, tumbling back over the side. I help Graham back to his feet as more Crawlers jump from one plate to the next, continuing their relentless pursuit.

Graham takes two limping steps and says, "That's it. Screw this shit." He removes a grenade from his vest while limp-walking backward. He pulls the pin and says, "Fire in the hole." Then he rolls the thing over the edge and takes a few more steps back, pushing me with him.

The grenade explodes with impressive force, launching Crawlers into the air and hopefully buying us some time.

Without another word, we both turn and hobble away, our pace nearly perfectly matched now. Ten minutes into our flight, I glance back. There are a few Crawlers still in pursuit, visible through the ash only because of their glowing underbellies, but the horde has either been dissuaded entirely, or delayed enough that we can no longer see them.

The radiation detector chimes and declares, "Radiation levels within safe limits," which means we're not going to melt, for the moment.

It's a full half hour later that the plate beneath us shifts in a downward direction, hinting that we're nearing the thing's edge. And it's another full hour before we find it.

The rise and fall of the behemoth upon which we stand is dizzying, now that we're standing near a precipice. It's like the world is flat and has come to an end. The Vikings were right all along. As the Machine rises hundreds of feet, I find myself clinging to Graham's arm.

He looks at my hand, and then my facemask. "You know we have to jump, right?"

"I'd rather jump than fall," I say.

He shrugs. "Fair enough."

We inch toward the edge, shuffling forward slowly. When we reach it, both of us deflate.

"Damnit," Graham says, looking down. The plate we're standing on doesn't just drop away, it angles downward, disappearing into the ashen gloom. If we jump over the edge, we won't fall, we'll slide, hitting who knows what on the way down.

"What now?" I ask, and I'm surprised when Graham launches over the edge. I'm about to curse him out for being impulsive, but then I notice the Crawler clinging to his facemask.

He didn't jump.

He was *tackled*.

I look back.

Flickering red lights switch on in rapid succession, revealing the Crawler horde's arrival. They've been following us this whole time with the bioluminescent giveaway shut off.

Smart little bastards.

One of the nearest creatures launches at my chest. I lean sideways, evading the strike, and the Crawler sails out over the drop off. With one last look back at the encroaching swarm, I follow it off the edge and begin sliding down the rough, black surface of a giant, descending toward who knows what kind of hell, and pursued by a wave of Crawlers that flows over the edge after me like a living waterfall.

21

I was obsessed with sledding when I was a kid. Sliding down a hillside with nothing but a millimeter thick sheet of plastic between me and the slope was my idea of not just a good time, but the best time. Even when the snow began to melt, giving way to frozen dirt and rocks, I would launch myself downward with enough momentum to carry me over the rough obstacles. The sled did little to protect my backside, and I'd go home with bruises and swollen lumps, but they were the price of admission for my favorite kind of fun.

As an adult, sliding down a steep grade, jostled and poked by the rough surface beneath me, and moving at a pace that would make my younger self wide-eyed with envy, I fail to see what I ever enjoyed about sledding. Of course, back then I was sledding down a hillside, followed by friends. Now I'm cruising down the side of a nation destroying monster, pursued by a horde of giant, glowing mites. I don't think my younger self would enjoy this either.

Most of the massive plate's imperfections are angled downward, allowing me to slide over them without being snagged, or impaled. That's a good thing. But it also means gravity is having her way with me, yanking me faster over the giant shell.

A quick glance up reveals the horde, still in hot pursuit. Some of the Crawlers are sliding, belly down, legs splayed wide to stay upright. Most are tumbling like an avalanche of grapefruit-sized stones, bouncing out of control.

I shout in surprise as the surface beneath me falls away. I drop a few feet, impact a new plate and continue downward on a steeper slope. Above me is a fault line, where two plates come together, the uppermost one lifted up by glowing red, Jell-O egg goop.

"Science Guy," Graham says, drawing my attention back to what lies ahead, and downward. I can see him through a thin curtain of ash, which seems to be thinning as we descend. He's twenty feet below, sliding on his back, feet first, head raised, arms outstretched to either side. He's doing a better job of controlling his descent, but he's still bouncing around, being pummeled by the rough surface. The Crawler that tackled him tumbles at his side, spraying white and glowing red goo from its sliced-open gut. He must have stabbed it shortly after going off the edge.

Thank God for the armor we're wearing, I think, and then I say, "Right behind you."

"What's your sitrep?" he asks.

Sitrep? And then I remember Janet Deakins, an expedition leader who'd spent time in the Army before leading Grand Canyon tours, who took a team of biologists and geologists and me down the Colorado. She'd been out of the military for ten years, but still used the lingo. 'Sitrep' stands for 'situation report', which is military for, 'how's it going?'

"I'm alive," I say. "And twenty feet above you. But we're not alone. We've got Crawlers...on my six."

"How many?"

I glance back up. I can't see the end of them in the ashen gloom above. I'm launched by a bump and the number coughs out of me. "Hundreds."

"Can you steer?" he asks.

My child self rears up from the past. Can I steer? "Lead the way."

Graham lifts his left hand from the plate and pushes down hard with the other. The sudden brake swings his body to the right, and he slides away at an angle. I perform the same maneuver, and follow his path. The tiniest hint of a smile forms on my face. Part of me is ashamed by it. Millions of people are dead. Thousands more are probably being killed a few miles below us, victims of the Machine's destructive power. Graham's squad—his friends—lay dead on the plates now high above us. And there is a very good chance Graham and I will be next. But as we shift directions and the Crawler horde plummets straight down, a pin prick of hope draws my smile a little wider.

And then the floor falls away again.

It takes a few seconds to strike the next plate, but the impact is slight, as though I'm hovering a few microns above the shell.

"This is it," Graham says. "Angle your body away from the Machine."

I'm a little surprised he's adopted the name from my vision, but it's as good a name as any.

"We need to put some distance between us and it, before touching down."

Touching down?

It's then that I figure out that we're not really sliding down the side of the plate, we're (mostly) falling beside it.

As are the Crawlers. I see them tumbling out into open space, raining down to the ground far below.

"Are you with me?" Graham shouts.

I turn my focus back to Graham. I can see him beneath me, between my feet. "With you."

"We need to push away," he says. "At the same time, so we don't collide."

Push away? At this speed?

He's nuts. But he's also right. If we fall straight down to the ground, there's a very good chance we'll be stepped on, killed in an earthquake or irradiated by the fallout trailing above and behind the behemoth, not to mention the four nuclear reactors it's closing in on. Once we hit the ground, if we're still alive, we'll need to make a hasty retreat or risk being caught in the plant's impending meltdown.

I lean forward slightly, angling my feet toward the vertical plate. My body lifts fully away from it, and the rough descent becomes a smooth freefall.

"Ready," I shout.

And before I really feel ready, he barks, "Now! Now! Now!"

I shove backwards with my feet, registering the impact with the shell, and then nothing. Or everything. The world becomes a gray-blue blur. I lose all sense of up and down. My gut twists and my mind goes numb. What is happening to me?

Through the onrush of overwhelming sensations, Graham's voice pumps loud and clear into my ears. "You're tumbling!"

No kidding.

"Control your descent!"

I know how, but can't think of it.

"Open your arms and legs, God damnit!"

His precise instructions register, and I realize I've curled up into a tight ball. I open my arms and legs. Wind tears at them, straining my ligaments and muscles. My tumble stops, and for a moment, I find myself falling backward.

That's when I see it.

The Machine.

Through the gray haze, a creature the size of Manhattan, maybe larger than Manhattan, lumbers through the ash. I still can't see all of it. It's obscured by ash, and I'd probably need to be miles away to see the whole thing at once. But it's the most I've seen. Its massive plates are black, but also translucent, revealing shimmering light from within. The plates that cover the outside of its body are split by glowing fault lines, all filled with that thick, luminous, red material.

Eggs, I think, remembering the viscous mass.

Massive coils of glowing red-orange tubes hang down from the Machine's underside, some of them twisting back up in great loops, others hanging loose and open, drizzling vivid pink fluid on the unseen landscape far below. While much of this thing seems very machine-like, it's also very much alive, radiating prehistoric biology and displaying biological adaptations still present in modern day organisms—horseshoe crabs and frogs, as well as ancient creatures, like trilobites.

The Machine's eight massive legs, segmented with large armor-like plates, grow wider at the base, where massive mounds of softer looking flesh spread out, dispersing its incredible weight. It's an extreme example of how an elephant's foot evolved over millions of years; the perfect adaptation for something so heavy, keeping its girth from punching through the Earth's crust with each step. But how did something like this evolve at all? To evolve requires an entire species population and countless generations. Are there more of these things hiding beneath the volcanoes? Are they like cicadas, emerging from their subterranean hiding places every couple of million years? The legs move with graceful efficiency, their stride covering miles with each step. In the seconds I observe it, the thing has nearly passed me completely. While it appears to be moving at a slow, lumbering pace, taking scale into account, I guess it's moving at an easy two hundred miles per hour. And I think it's taking its time. My thoughts drift for a moment, wondering why the wind didn't scour Graham and me from its back.

It's not aerodynamic, I realize. *The air doesn't flow over its shell smoothly. The Machine is punching through the atmosphere, disrupting the flow of air, creating pockets of stability.*

"Science Guy!" Graham shouts, snapping me from my thoughts and back to my current plight.

I twist around, so my stomach is facing the ground, still hidden by ash. Arms open wide, I angle myself away from the Machine and turn my downward fall into an angled glide. Graham is above me now, and further away. I can barely see him through the ash.

"Radiation ahead," Graham says, sounding calm despite the grim notification.

My radiation detector chimes, and the feminine voice repeats her previous warning. "Radioactive isotopes detected. Cesium-134 and Cesium-137 have both been detected in unhealthy levels. At current levels, prolonged exposure could result in fever, muscle weakness, vomiting and other flu-like symptoms. Recommended action... Unknown."

The GPS unit is likely trying to make sense of our rapidly changing position and altitude.

"Maintain present course," the device finally says.

Like we have a choice.

"Secondary recommendation," the voice says. "Repair radiation shield damage immediately."

It's then that I feel the breeze cooling my exposed backside. My pants and the lead mesh within them, protecting me from radiation, must have been torn during our rough slide. When I sense a wet warmth along with the breeze, I realize it's not just my pants that were torn up. Pain follows the realization, burning the back of my legs and butt. My body tenses. Running away from the Machine, and the nuclear power plant it's closing in on, is going to be difficult if my muscles are torn and I'm gushing blood.

Focus, I tell myself. *One problem at a time.*

The ground slides into view, emerging through the dry, gray fog. The land below is both comforting and disconcerting. Comforting because it's solid ground, rather than the back of a lumbering, ancient, megalithic monster. Disconcerting because it's wide-open, green field. We won't have to worry about colliding with houses or vehicles, but it's going to be a slog before we find transportation.

I look left and see the distant silhouette of eight cooling towers rising above the city of Rivne, dwarfed by the Machine closing in, its massive limbs covering miles with each step.

"Pull your chute," Graham shouts, and I don't hesitate.

There's a hiss of wind yanking the small, reserve pilot chute from my back. The wind drags it up, taking the canopy up into the air behind me, where it snaps open and slows my descent.

The green grass beneath me comes into focus for just a moment, as I slip through the ash. Then it's pummeling me as I touch down. Knowing I'm not up to sticking the landing, I go limp and flop to the ground. I'm dragged for a moment, and then the parachute, no longer tugged down by my weight, falls to the grass ahead of me.

Alive, but battered, I roll over in time to see Graham perform a perfect landing, running to a stop. He's a hundred yards away, in the right direction. While I get back to my feet, he frees himself from his parachute rig, discards it in the grass and then waves to me.

"Get a move on, Science Guy. We've got just minutes before that thing reaches the power plant."

I hobble toward him, legs aching and stinging with equal urgency. I shed my parachute gear, and feel a bit lighter, but it's the radiation detector that speeds me up. "Radioactive isotopes detected. Cesium-134 and Cesium-137 have both been detected in dangerous levels. At current levels, exposure for—fifteen minutes—could result in fever, muscle weakness, vomiting and other flu-like symptoms. Recommended action, evacuate immediately in a southwesterly direction."

My hobble turns into a jog, and then a run. "Did you hear that?"

"Thirty minutes is plenty of time," Graham says, walking backwards ahead of me.

"I've only got fifteen minutes," I say, my legs already growing numb from the run. "My suit's torn."

"Copy that." Graham turns away from me and breaks into a sprint. *Is he leaving me?* I nearly shout to him, but he quickly dispels my fears. "I'll see what I can do about transportation. Try not to slow down."

As I look at the open green field ahead, factoring in distance, my current speed and how fast I'll probably be running in a few minutes, I calculate that I've got just under fifteen minutes to live. Or, at least, fifteen minutes until I've been sufficiently irradiated to suffer a slow, agonizing death.

22

Running through the endless field, I glance back at the Machine as it wades through the gray ash cloud, the front of its body now a silhouette, the red-orange glow of its underside diffused to a dull pink. A massive segmented tail trails the ancient creature, covered in spikes. It sweeps back and forth through the sky, stabilizing the Machine's enormous body and leaving cyclones of ash in its wake, the way a whale's movements through the ocean create flat 'footprints.' *That's how we can track it,* I think, and then I realize that both Graham and I forgot that part of our mission was planting a GPS tracker on the monster's back.

Tears form in the corner of my eyes, and I tell myself it's from the wind or the stinging dust and grit in the air, but I know that's not true. It's not even the physical pain wracking my body, as I once again run for my life. It's because I left them. Again. And I wonder if they know why. The idea that I might die out here, away from my family, with them believing that I am ashamed of our situation, of them, breaks my heart.

I need to get back home.

I need to be with them, and never run away again.

I'll do anything, I think, unsure of who I'm mentally conversing with. *Anything.*

Aching pain from my thighs clears my thoughts.

I'm not going to make it.

I try to wipe the blurring tears out of my eyes, but my bare hand slaps against the facemask I forgot I was wearing. I nearly take it off, but resist the temptation. The gear weighing me down is also postponing my death from radiation poisoning.

I focus on my legs. *Faster*, I will them. *Faster!*

Instead of obeying my will, my knees buckle, and I fall to the ground.

Shit.

I crawl, and I find even that difficult.

Shit!

A roar lifts my head. Two glowing, angry eyes bear down on me. Has the Machine spawned smaller versions of itself to scour the countryside? The eyes are bright enough to make me squint. I sit on my knees, hands raised to block the light, and wait for death.

There's a grinding of earth mixed with a deep growl. I don't even flinch as I wait for the end. I'm too tired.

"Get in!" It's Graham.

I lower my hands to find a red Mazda CX-5 skidded to a stop in front of me, the passenger side door open. Graham is behind the wheel, waving at me to get in. I can't see his face behind his mask, but his body language conveys all the urgency that's needed. And I feel it, too. The trouble is, my body is no longer playing along.

I'm about to explain this when Graham is suddenly at my side, hands under my armpits, hoisting me up. *Did I black out?* I'm shoved into the SUV, sitting sideways. The door bangs hard against my butt, as Graham slams it shut. Then he's beside me again, and we're moving. I'm tossed back and forth. Unbuckled and lacking the strength to hold on, I'm at the mercy of Graham's driving, which at the moment has everything to do with speed and nothing with comfort.

A crunching crash and a jarring impact sends a surge of adrenaline through my body and spins me around, so I'm facing forward. There's a ruined, short, stone wall outside the window, and then we're beyond it. Tires shriek over pavement and we're off, racing through the ash-congested Ukrainian countryside.

I glance in the side view mirror, looking back. The giant silhouette is still there, its underside luminous, but as it moves northwest, and we race southwest to escape the radiation, it slowly—very slowly—shrinks in size, fading over the horizon. Normally, at ground level, the average human being can see three miles to the horizon. That distance increases significantly with height, like from the top of a mountain. Miles tall, a walking Mount Everest, the Machine would be able to see a good two hundred miles to the horizon, which also means we will be able to see it rising above the horizon from nearly the same distance. On a clear day. Sans Icelandic ash.

I don't know if I passed out, or if we're simply driving near light speed, but the radiation detector chimes happily and declares, "Radiation levels within safe limits." We've moved beyond the invisible killer cloud following the Machine. At least for now.

Graham reaches up and pulls his goggles and helmet away from his head, letting them fall to the floor in the back seat. He then unclips his mask, which falls to the side, but remains attached to his armor. His tan skin glistens with sweat and hints of a Central American lineage— probably on his mother's side with a surname like Graham. He looks over at me, eyes appropriately wide. "You okay?"

I follow his lead, removing my gear and freeing myself from the mask. "I'm alive." I glance in the side view mirror again. The Machine is still there, and will be until we're hundreds of miles away, or it's fully swallowed by the ash, which is less dense on the ground.

Graham adjusts his side mirror, looking back. "We got lucky."

His compatriots are still up there, dead and burned on the back of an impossible monster, never to be buried, and possibly being consumed by giant mites.

"Sorry about your friends."

Graham drives in silence for a minute, absorbing my apology. Then he turns to me and says, "You did good. Just...tell me they didn't die for nothing."

"We learned a lot," I say. "And we have this." I remove the gelatinous sample from my pocket, holding it up. "It could tell us a lot about what the Machine is."

"And how to kill it?"

"Let's hope."

Tires screech, and I'm pressed against the door. When we come to a stop, I'm surprised to find the rear end of an abandoned car just inches below my window. Ahead of us is a line of vehicles filling both sides of the road, their doors opened, their drivers gone.

Why did all these people give up their vehicles to move on foot?

Graham pulls the SUV onto the shoulder of the road and turns into a driveway. It's a small house with a well-manicured yard—trimmed bushes, potted flowers and bark mulch—giving off a strong retiree vibe and looking surprisingly American.

"Why are we stopping?" I ask.

"Landline," he says. "I'd rather call for an evac than try to drive to the nearest U.S. Military base, which is in Bulgaria, a good six hundred miles south of our current position. It would require crossing two, or three, currently closed borders. And that's assuming your Machine doesn't turn south. There'd be no outrunning it."

"*My* Machine?"

"You named it."

"It was in a—" I shake my head and sigh. I don't feel like arguing semantics. "It's not even a good name."

"We're all machines," he says. "Aren't we? Organic machines."

I shrug. I've met more than a few people that I would describe as robotic, and the Machine certainly carries out its...what? Duty? Function? Purpose? With the same emotionless efficiency of an actual machine. It's as good a name as any, but I decide to add a little flourish. "Apocalypse Machine."

"Fuckin' A." Graham opens his door and steps out. He looks over the roof of the car, toward the distant hulking silhouette. Now that we're stopped, I can feel its footsteps vibrating through the ground, each one an earthquake, tripping seismographic sensors around the world. "If your Apocalypse Machine starts getting bigger, honk the horn."

I still don't like that he's identifying the Machine as being mine, but I don't bother arguing. Instead, I offer a warning. "Try to be quick. When the power station suffers a meltdown—"

"We need to be gone."

"I was going to say that the landlines might not work either, but yeah, I think I've been exposed to enough radiation." As I say the words, the back of my leg starts to sting, like I've been sunburned. I may have been exposed to too much radiation already.

With that, Graham heads to the front door. He tries the knob, finds it locked and with a sudden, fast motion, kicks it in. Then he's inside and out of view, leaving me alone to ponder whether or not I've already been exposed to too much radiation and am already dead—a bona-fide zombie at the actual apocalypse.

23

I sit in the SUV, which has a new car smell mixed with ash and something metallic. *Is that blood?* I check myself over. My legs and ass *are* bleeding, but the wounds are shallow, and the scent in the car smells...rancid, like spoiled beef. The driver's seat is clean. I swivel around. The backseat is coated in a crusty brown layer of coagulated blood. Someone was killed in this vehicle, but not recently. Probably during whatever chaos led to the traffic jam. I wonder if Graham got rid of the body, or if—

"Hey!"

My head snaps to the house. Graham is standing in the shattered doorframe, waving me in. Before I can complain, he slides back inside the home.

Knowing our lives hang in the balance, I open the door and slide down onto my feet. My calves cramp up and I nearly go down, but I manage to take a step and then another, pausing at the SUV's hood for a moment. I perform a few quick stretches, which hurts like hell, but limbers me up. A little. My journey from the vehicle to the front door feels like I'm taking the first steps on a planet with twice the gravity, but I make it to the door. And from there, using every wall and surface for support, I make my way through the house to where I can hear Graham cursing under his breath.

When I enter the kitchen, he's seated at a kitchen table and tearing at a loaf of bread. He munches on it and points to a laundry basket sitting beside a closed door. "Might be something in there that fits you."

The clothes are a crumpled pile, like they were either headed for the washing machine, or fresh from the dryer. Either way, it would be nice to not have my bloodied ass in the wind. So I dig through clothes, and dirty or clean, I feel relieved when I find a pair of jeans. They're covered in old, dry paint—a working man's pants—and they're two sizes too big, but there's still a belt in the loops. Definitely dirty.

While I'm changing, Graham dials the phone. He then listens to the phone for a moment and hangs up. "Damnit."

"No power?" I ask, cinching the belt tight around my waist. The house has no power, but phone lines often have their own power source and continue working even during blackouts. I didn't see any above-ground phone lines, so they're underground and maybe still connected.

"I'm having trouble reaching anyone," he says. "We don't use phones on mission. And when I call anyone, it's from my cell phone."

I wrote an article about the phenomenon just a year ago. With the emergence of cell phones, people are no longer memorizing phone numbers. While most people could recall the numbers of childhood friends, girlfriends and pre-911 police stations, they couldn't recall the number for their present-day spouse, friends or workplaces. After writing the article, I made an effort to memorize a few important numbers—work, Mina, Bell—but since I never have to actually dial them, I'm not sure I'd remember them. "Have you tried the operator?"

He extends a finger. "One, we're in the Ukraine. I couldn't understand the operator, even if someone picked up." He extends a second finger. "Two, no one is picking up."

I sit down at the kitchen table and take the phone, as he slides it to me. It's an old, yellow, plastic phone with oversized buttons. At least it's not a rotary. I pick up the receiver and start dialing.

"You have to hit zero twice first," he says.

"Right," I say. "Ukraine." I punch zero twice, followed by a one and the area code. Then I freeze up.

"Who are you calling?" Graham asks.

"My wife."

"Which one?"

"I'm only married to one woman," I say, wracking my brain for the digits. "I remember the last four digits, but not the first three." I take a guess, punching in 923, followed by the rest of the number. I wait through a series of clicks and then hear an answering machine. Definitely not Mina. I hang up the phone. "Good news is the phone is working."

I pick up the phone again and dial, trying 932. I get an automated disconnected message. I hang up and start to dial again, but stop five digits in. I can suddenly see the notebook page that I wrote Mina's number on. I close my eyes, letting the memory sharpen. "Three, nine, two." I hang up and redial, using the new numbers.

It rings three times without a pick up. I start to feel discouraged, but then remember that I'm calling a cellphone. The first few rings are phantom rings, while the cell networks on the other side of the planet route the call. They're designed to make the caller think the connection went through immediately. There's a click and the ringing resumes, this time for real.

After the second legitimate ring, I hear Mina's voice, soft and a bit shaken, say, "H-hello?"

"Mina!" I shout.

"Abraham?" My name is followed by a deep breath and then, "You're alive?"

"You thought I was dead?" My chest constricts, as I picture my sons' reaction to the news.

"They *told* us you were."

I nearly explode. We'd been given up for dead and the news delivered to my family in the same time it took Graham and I to escape said death, find a phone and call in. "Mina, listen. You need to tell them. Tell them we're alive and on the ground in Ukraine..." I look at Graham, and he sees the question in my eyes.

"Fifteen miles south of the LZ."

"Fifteen miles south of the landing zone. We need an evac, now."

I hear a sniffle and know she's crying, something I've only seen a handful of times during our marriage. "I don't understand. You're still in the Ukraine? Still near...it?"

"We can see it from here."

"Oh, God," she says, going from sad to hysterical, which is truly unheard of for Mina. "You need to get out of there. Now."

"What?" I ask, but I figure she must be thinking of the nuclear reactors not far from here. "We're far enough from the reactor that we can—"

"It's not the reactor," she says. "Russia is attacking. They're inside Ukraine already. They want to kill it before it reaches Russia. Abe, they're going to throw everything they have at it. Everything."

While Russia's military might is significant, it still pales in comparison to the U.S. in all but one category, which certainly falls within the realm of 'everything'—nuclear warheads. The largest nuclear warhead, Tsar Bomba, or King Bomb, has a fifty megaton explosive yield, 1400 times greater than 'Little Boy,' the bomb dropped on Hiroshima during World War II. The minimum safe distance for King Bomb is twenty-eight miles. At that distance, we won't be vaporized or immediately exposed to lethal radiation, but when King Bomb was tested, the shockwave still leveled entire towns up to thirty-five miles away. We are well inside the effective kill zone for a weapon like that, and if conventional weapons don't slow the Machine down—and I don't think they will—I have no doubt Russia will escalate things faster than the Kardashian family's bank accounts. And that means a ride is not coming.

"Listen, Mina. Tell them we're alive. We're heading south. We'll try to reach one of the bases in Bulgaria. Tell them we have a sample." Graham gets up from his seat, taking the loaf of bread and a bowl of fruit with him. He heads for the door, understanding our situation without the need for an explanation. I haven't given him the details yet, but the expression on my face and the quiver in my voice says enough. He knows that help isn't coming and that our time is short.

"I love you," I tell Mina. "Tell Bell and the boys the same."

"I will. And I love you, too."

"I'm sorry I left," I say, and her silence breaks my heart.

"Just come back," she finally says.

"I'll find a way."

I don't mean it to sound dire, but it does, and it is. Getting home is not going to be easy. And who knows what state the world will be in when I do make it back. "Do you know how long we have? Before Russia—"

The roar of a jet answers for her. If it's a Russian fighter, moving faster than the speed of sound, that means it's already passed and is closing in on the target. It's not a bomber, but it won't be long before Russia figures out that missiles are useless. And if we hear a bomber, it will already be too late.

"Love you," I say again, and I wish I could somehow tack on a thousand more. "We're leaving now."

"Go, Abe," she says, knowing I'm having a hard time putting down the phone. "Go now."

"I—I—"

I'm about to say something else. I have so much to say. But then there is a click, followed by a dead line.

She hung up on me?

She *hung up on me!*

She's trying to save your life, idiot, I tell myself, and then I hobble for the door, following Graham's lead and grabbing a container of cashews and bag of chips. I'm sure there are more and healthier options in the kitchen, but it's going to take me long enough to reach the SUV. I hear the engine turn over and for a moment, I fear that Graham is leaving me.

Then he appears in the doorway. "We've got company."

"They're Russian," I say, knowing he wouldn't be able to see, let alone identify, the jets through the ash hovering above us.

"Shit," he says, clearly understanding that this is bad news for us. He gets up under my left arm and helps me to the SUV. The sound of more jets fills the air with a painful shrieking.

There's a flare of light above us, followed by a new kind of rushing howl. *They're launching missiles,* I think, and I watch two bright orbs slide through the ash cloud, closing in on the Machine, its body still tall over the horizon, rising up into the ash. A moment later, more missiles fire—more than I can count—all following the first pair. *How many jets are up there?* I wonder, but I don't bother considering the answer. I slam my door shut, buckle my seatbelt and then grip the door handle as Graham slams his foot on the gas, tearing from the driveway and into the long field lining the congested road.

We bounce across the field, moving fast enough to make the most seasoned soldier clench. When I relay the information gleaned from Mina, and mention the details of King Bomb to Graham—news to him—he drives even faster. A mile from the small house, we reach an intersection and come across a still smoldering accident involving dozens of cars. The road headed north, which we're driving alongside, is blocked, but the other directions are clear. The cars no doubt turned around and headed back the way they came, not that anyone would have had a reason to head north. The field ahead ends in a five foot incline that leads to the road. We hit it hard and fast, but at an angle that carries us up and onto the road. Tires shriek as we tear across the pavement and accelerate down the now empty road, heading south.

The sounds of explosions chase us, echoing across the landscape and thumping against the SUV, each shockwave giving us a little jolt and reminding us we're not yet far enough away. I watch the action in the rearview, hoping that each flash of light will be the last, that the Machine will keel over and die. But it never flinches, and its pace never wavers.

Miles later, we can still hear the battle, but the monster's silhouette has faded into the ash. I take some comfort from this until I look at the odometer that Graham tripped after I told him about King Bomb. Converting kilometers to miles and then tacking on the roughly fifteen mile distance we started out at, and tacking on another ten for the Machine's movement, we're close to thirty miles. Not quite enough to unclench yet.

I'm about to tell Graham this, when a sound unlike anything I've ever heard before rolls past us. It's like a symphony of instruments, amplified to ear-splitting volume and unleashed in a five second blast.

That's what it sounds like, I think, realizing that we've just heard the Machine's roar. We're thirty miles away and facing the opposite direction of its head—assuming it has one. We never saw it, if it does. Flashes of light burst in the sky, some close to where I think the monster is now, many further away, the light barely visible thanks to the ash.

Those are jets exploding, I think. The Machine has just defended itself, decimating warplanes and probably everything in front of it for miles, with soundwaves.

There's a tap on my shoulder, and I turn to Graham. He's shouting at me, but I can't hear him.

"What?" I shout back, but I can't hear myself, either. My ears ring with a droning high-pitched squeal.

He shouts again, and I try to read his lips, but I stop seeing his mouth when his face lights up as though the sun has suddenly burst through the ash. I start to look back, but Graham grasps my face, shoves it forward and then pushes my head down between my knees.

The nuclear shockwave strikes us a second later.

The SUV is lifted off the ground and tossed end-over-end. I feel the powerful force slam through my body, but I don't hear a thing. I see the ground below and the gray sky above several times. We land on the roof, which folds in and nearly strikes my head. The SUV spins several times, stopping so the front end faces north. It gives me a clear view of a mushroom cloud, rising forty miles into the atmosphere, from the back of the still standing Apocalypse Machine.

24

"Why are we landing?"

I look out the helicopter's side window. The land beneath us is dry and barren, dust billowing out around us. There are homes in the distance, and people standing outside them—the men wearing scarves, the women dressed in hijabs. They're watching us, but not moving.

"One doesn't simply fly into Israel," Graham says.

"Did you just web meme your reply?"

He smiles.

"You know that just about every character Sean Bean plays gets killed, right? And the character you just meme-quoted was turned into a pincushion."

His smile fades. "We made it this far."

He's right about that. Neither of us believed we'd make it out of the Ukraine alive. While I did suffer some mild radiation sickness, it faded faster than the lump on Graham's head. He'd been knocked unconscious when the SUV flipped. I dragged him out of the vehicle, and then for several miles on gelatinous legs, watching the mushroom cloud billow upwards and to the east, mingling with ash and the radioactive fallout plume rising from the nuclear power plant's remains. And within that death cloud, the undaunted Machine lumbered on its way, headed for Russia.

I can only guess where it is now. The few people we came across on our journey—most of whom didn't speak English—knew far less about the Machine than we did, but they revealed that entire populations, including border guards, were migrating south. Our drive to Bezmer Air Base in Bulgaria was mostly uneventful. Most towns were deserted. Those that weren't, were occupied by unsavory people who'd made themselves kings without subjects. A few tried to stop us, but not one of them was prepared to face down an Army Ranger.

The most poignant moment in our trip was our arrival at Bezmer. No guards at the gate. No planes in the hangers. No one home. The base had been evacuated. Everything capable of making the long flight home was gone. Despite the power being out, we tried to make landline and satellite phone calls, but couldn't get through. The short range radios in the vehicles picked up a lot of people talking, but no one was speaking English. Alone in the wrong part of the world, we absconded with a Bell UH-1Y Venom utility helicopter that had been left behind. We also took several containers of fuel, a dozen MREs (Meals Ready to Eat) and several gallons of water. We flew during the day, landing only to refuel or to eat and sleep. Sometimes we had to fly out of our way to find a safe place to land. Once we reached Turkey, the land below us was filled by an endless sea of refugees, all headed south.

We flew low to avoid radar detection, but that also meant I was able to look into the haunted eyes of millions of people who would never see their homes again, and were likely to perish on their journey into foreign, probably hostile lands. We saw evidence of battles and mass killings along the way, but if Turkey had tried to keep people out, they'd failed. The country had been overrun.

And after all of that, we arrived here. "Where are we?"

"Lebanon," he says, as the skids touch down on the hard earth. The already slowing rotor blades are casting dust into the air around us.

"Lebanon," I say. "Great. Nothing bad ever happens here."

"Much closer and Israel would shoot us down. Remember, the country we're trying to enter is the one nation in the world that excels at keeping people out. When all those refugees we flew past reach Israel, they're going to bounce off her border and go right around."

"And what makes you think we're going to have any more luck?"

"We have the golden ticket," he says.

"Your dry wit and charm?"

He looks at me, deadpan, so I know it's not a joke. "You. We have you."

With the chopper set on firm ground, Graham unbuckles and reaches into the back, recovering two backpacks that we filled at the air base. Next he recovers two M4 assault rifles and two M9 Berettas, also recovered from Bezmer. I'm about to comment that the weapons seem like too much for one man to carry when he hands one of the rifles to me.

"What's this for?" I ask.

"We're in Lebanon, remember?" He pushes his door open, letting in a blast of dry heat. "Even when the rest of the world is kicking up its feet, the Middle East is a volatile place."

"I've never shot a weapon like this."

He reaches over and yanks back the slide, chambering the first round. "Just point and shoot. If you don't intend on shooting, don't put your finger on the trigger. Now gear up. It's about four klicks to the border."

Klicks are 1000 meters. Four thousand meters works out to about two and a half miles. My legs still ache, but I should have no trouble covering the distance, and I guess that, with our gear, we'll reach the border in forty minutes.

I'm tossing my backpack around my shoulders when I see Graham go rigid on the far side of the chopper. He's like a dog who's suddenly caught a scent. "What is it?" I ask through the chopper's two open doors.

"Engines," he says without looking back.

I follow his gaze to the distant hillside, which is covered in several single-story, flat-roofed homes. The people who had been watching us are now gone. A dust cloud rises up on the side of the hill, moving down, the vehicle still unseen.

Graham slides the chopper's side door open the whole way, revealing our half-used supply of fuel. He unscrews a single container and tips it on its side. Pungent fuel glugs out, covering the floor and filling every crevice. Then he steps back, draws his M9 sidearm and fires a single round onto the fuel-soaked floor. The resulting spark ignites the fuel, the blaze melting through the remaining containers, which erupt with a *whump*. I step back from the inferno, and when Graham runs past me, I turn and follow him.

I'm about to complain about running when I hear the incoming engine revving louder. Graham leads us downhill and around a rise, turning toward the border and running only a few steps before shouting, "Lose the pack!" He sheds his backpack, which contains food, water and survival gear. I do the same, and I'm able to double my pace. This is a Hail Mary play. If we don't get past the border, we're going to be a couple of Americans, with guns, in the Middle East.

Despite this do-or-die tactic, I feel strangely calm. I've survived an erupting volcano, landed on the back of a living mountain, been pursued by oversized mites, been cooked by radiation and walked away from a nuclear detonation. A couple of guys in a truck seem almost boring.

But it's not a truck. It's three. And one of them is a 'technical,' meaning it has a very large machine gun mounted on the roof. The other two are pickup trucks, the backs holding six men each, all wielding AK-47s, the most common rifle in the world.

Graham ducks down behind a large rock and motions for me to do the same. I'm about to ask why we're stopping when he says, "They haven't seen us yet."

All three vehicles turn for the blazing chopper, engines roaring as they approach the scene. When they're no longer in view, Graham breaks from our hiding position like an Olympic sprinter. I do my best to match his pace, but he puts a little distance between us with each long stride.

After a few minutes, I start to gain on him again, but not because he's getting tired; he's stopping to look back. His brow doesn't furrow until his fourth stop, when I'm within twenty feet of him.

"Here they come," he says, and then he takes off again. "Just keep moving!"

When he leaves me in the dust, I realize he had actually been holding back.

The sound of engines grows loud behind me. They've definitely seen us, and they're probably a little upset about Graham torching the chopper, which had clear U.S. markings, including a flag.

I nearly dive to the ground when Graham spins around, drops to one knee and raises the M4. But he waves me on and then takes aim. I nearly fall when he squeezes off a three-round burst, and then again when I look back to see the lead pickup truck tilt to one side, its suddenly flat front wheel digging into the hard-packed dirt. The technical swerves around the disabled vehicle and barrels toward us. When the man behind the machine gun takes aim, I turn forward again and push myself faster. The loud clatter of machine gun fire tears through the air behind me. A line of pock marks explodes in the desert, ten feet to my right, tracing a line heading for Graham. But the Army Ranger doesn't flinch, not even when the line of rounds scores the earth beside him. He calmly adjusts his aim and fires again.

The machine gun falls silent.

Graham aims and fires one more time. An engine roars. I glance back to see the machine gunner slumped over. The windshield has three holes, the inside of the cabin splattered with blood, the driver nowhere to be seen. The way the vehicle swerves to the side and speeds away uncontrolled makes me think he's fallen over the steering wheel, the dead weight of his foot on the gas.

"Move it!" Graham shouts, waving me on before standing up and running to the top of a steep rise. Bullets tear through the air behind us, fired wildly by the men now standing in the truck bed. But Graham doesn't fire back. Instead he holds out his M4 and drops it. He draws the M9 next and drops it as well.

"Lose the weapons," he says as I draw near.

I shed the weapons, happy to have not fired them, and I join Graham at the top of the rise. I nearly charge down the other side, but he catches my shoulder, stopping me in place, ignoring the bullets buzzing past us. He raises his hands, and I do the same.

"Slowly," he says, and he approaches the thirty-foot-tall, concrete wall three hundred feet ahead.

"A little closer than four klicks," I say.

He nods, but says nothing, his eyes flicking back and forth, watching the men standing behind the wall, aiming an array of weapons straight at us.

The truck engine roars loudly behind us, close enough to run us over, but the sound is quickly replaced by the grinding of locked tires on the hard earth. Most of the Israeli soldiers guarding the wall adjust their aim at the vehicle. I don't turn to look, but I hear frantic Arabic shouting and hands slapping against the metal roof. The engine revs again, but this time fades. The relief I feel is soured when the men on the wall redirect their attention to us.

"Are those flamethrowers?" I ask, seeing several men with distinctive fuel tanks on their backs. They really are prepared to fend off hordes of refugees. Not even desperate people will allow themselves to be set ablaze. Given the surprised expressions on the faces of the men on the other side of the wall, we're the first ones to risk it.

When a stream of flame jets down ahead of us, setting a patch of brush on fire, Graham stops. "We're Americans," he shouts. "U.S. Army. We're seeking safe passage to—"

"No," one of the men shouts. "No passage. Border closed."

"We're allies," Graham says.

"Your military left you," the man says. "Left all of Israel. Returned home."

"Damnit," Graham whispers, glancing at me. "We bugged out. No wonder they're on edge. Apocalypse Machine or not, they're still surrounded by enemies." He looks back up at the soldier. "We'll be killed out here."

"You'll be killed if you come any closer."

"We have a sample," I shout, and Graham gives me the biggest 'what the fuck' face I've ever seen. Apparently, he wasn't ready to play that card yet.

The soldier looks confused for a moment, and then asks. "Sample of what?"

Graham's face is still warning me to stay quiet, but the Apocalypse Machine isn't a U.S. problem. It's a global problem. "Golden ticket," I say to Graham, and then turn to the soldier. "The creature. My name is Abraham Wright. I'm a scientist sent by President McKnight." I point my finger at Graham and myself, waggling it back and forth. "We're all that's left of—"

The soldier turns away, consorting with one of the other men. He picks up a radio and has a conversation we can't hear.

Graham tenses, which generally predates something horrible.

A moment later, a ladder is lifted up and slid down to the ground. No words are exchanged. They simply wait.

Despite my fear, I'm the first to move.

Grumbling a string of curses under his breath, Graham follows. At the top of the ladder, two soldiers help me over the wall and onto a metal catwalk on the far side. I thank each of them, thrilled to be alive and in friendly-ish territory.

Graham arrives a moment later, helped by two other soldiers. But he's not relieved. He's anxious. He looks me in the eyes and says, "Just so you know, this next part is going to suck."

Before I can reply, a black hood is thrown over my head, and I'm clubbed by something solid. Consciousness fades, as I fall. It's mercifully gone by the time I hit the hard metal catwalk.

25

In the hours following our abduction, I learn how to avoid being tortured: tell them everything.

Like Chunk in the clutches of the Fratellis, I hold nothing back. My past. My job. I direct them to websites where they can find articles written by me, and my bio. I tell them about Iceland. About my time at the White House. About our mission and every detail about what we found and how we ended up outside Israel's border. For the first few minutes, I'm pretty sure they are going to water board me anyway. They have the towel and bucket ready. The concrete room I'm kept in has a drain. Layers of brown stains cover the floor. The faint smell of past horrors lingers in the air.

I'm pretty sure my interrogator, who is wearing a black mask that reveals only his cold blue eyes, thinks my story is a smoke screen. I can't say I blame him. I find it hard to believe, as I retell it. But he lets me say my piece, listening to every word without comment, staring me down the whole time.

When I finish, his eyes narrow, but he still says nothing.

"Sir, I'm telling the truth. I have no reason to lie. The Machine—the monster—threatens the whole world."

"The threat of annihilation is nothing new to Israel," he says, breaking his long silence. "And we face it still, from your Machine, and from the enemies who surround us still. But now, our ally, *your* country, has abandoned us to our enemies."

While I doubt the decision to call back U.S. forces worldwide had everything to do with me, I *did* advise the President to take that kind of action, to prepare for a mass southern migration and a possible war with Central America. So it's hard to hide my blossoming guilt. And I'm pretty sure he can see it.

He leans forward, menace in his eyes. "You will tell me everything."

I'm about to insist that I have, aside from my advice to the President, when the metal door behind him opens.

The first sign that things are turning around for me is that the woman who enters isn't wearing a mask. The second sign is that she gives me a smile. It's the kind a receptionist at an emergency room might offer—welcome mixed with pity. Her large brown eyes look kind, her curly hair barely held back by an elastic band. She looks almost Muppet-like, compared to the black clad terror seated across from me.

She steps up next to my interrogator and hands him a tablet. He takes it without a word, looking at what's on the screen. He then swipes several times, his eyes scanning with military efficiency. Then he hands the device back and pulls off his mask, revealing a kind looking face that hasn't been shaved in a few days. And he's actually smiling. "Your identity checks out, Mr. Wright. We can't confirm the rest of your story, obviously, but your friend, who has remained undaunted by the threat of torture, is clearly U.S. Military."

"An Army Ranger," I offer.

The man grins. "You've said that, yes."

The woman walks around behind me and unlocks the handcuffs holding me to the metal chair, one-by-one. When I'm freed, I lean forward, stretching my spine. The chair's back is angled just over 90 degrees, making it incredibly uncomfortable, which I suspect is the point. I put a hand to the back of my head. There's a bandage where I was clubbed, but the swollen lump still makes me wince when my fingers graze it.

"Have you considered that he might not be pleased that you've spoken to us so candidly?" the woman asks, and then she drops three maroon pills into my hand. "For the pain."

I put all three in my mouth and swallow them dry, like a bona-fide action hero. "I'm only considering the fate of our world. I don't care about politics or rivalries or ancient squabbles. There isn't going to be a human race left, if we don't put all of that behind us."

The woman stops in front of me, still smiling. "I'm glad to hear you say that."

"You are?" I say.

"I agree with you."

"So I didn't just take cyanide pills," I say, mostly joking.

"Ibuprofen." She offers her hand, and I shake it. "I am Agent Aliza Mayer." She motions to the man sitting across from me. He doesn't offer his hand, but looks far less threatening than he did a few minutes ago. "This is Agent Yehoshua Zingel." She heads for the door, and Agent Zingel motions for me to follow her.

We leave the interrogation room and enter a stark white hallway that's just twenty feet long and has only two exits—one that opens to another featureless hallway, and a second at the far end, where a closed metal door awaits.

"Where are we?" I ask, and then I pose a follow-up question. "What agency do you work for?"

She pauses at the far end, hands on the door's push bar. She gives me a grin, shoves the door open and says, "Welcome to Mossad."

The vast room on the far side of the door, filled with large view-screens, an array of high tech computer consoles and a beehive of activity from people in lab coats, suits and combat armor, catches me off guard. The massive digital maps and countless video feeds displaying different parts of the world, from ground level, and from high above, put the White House's situation room to shame—as does the newness of this place. Everything is bright, shiny and new, like the bridge of some kind of starship. But the surprise I feel at the room's futuristic feel and activity level pale in comparison to the revelation that my host is Mossad.

The secretive intelligence agency is Israel's version of the CIA. They're well known for being the most ruthless, dangerous and efficient intelligence agency in the world, performing covert and counterterrorism operations in some of the most hostile locations on Earth. They're also one of the most high-tech agencies on the planet, employing a dedicated team of scientists covering just about every discipline imaginable, including creating future-tech combat and defense weaponry. They're not a broad military force, but for surgical strikes and covert operations, there is no one better. And I'm pretty sure that even Graham would agree. This also means that the interrogation room wasn't a prop meant to scare me, and those stains on the floor were very likely real.

Standing at the back of the room, just a few feet away, is Graham. Like me, the back of his head is bandaged, but as I walk to his side, I see his face took a beating as well. He sees me and offers a head nod.

"They work you over?" I ask, looking at his bruised face.

"Until they showed me a video of you spilling your guts," he says.

"Better figurative than literal, I always say. Well, I've never said it before, but I stand by it."

He grins, and then winces. "You'd make a horrible Ranger."

"That's why I'm a journalist. You don't seem that angry about me spilling my figurative guts."

"I was, at first." He shrugs. "Then I decided you were right. This is bigger than any one nation. The Machine doesn't recognize borders. We shouldn't either."

When Agent Mayer steps up beside me, eyes on the large, movie theater-sized screen at the center of the far wall, I ask, "Do you know where it is?"

She turns to me slowly, eyebrows furrowed. "How long have you been out of communication with your superiors?"

"Since we touched down," I say. "Almost two weeks."

"A lot has changed," she says. "The... you called it 'the Machine.' The Apocalypse Machine."

I nod.

"It out-paced the ash cloud after destroying Moscow and made its way across Siberia." Mayer pulls a small device from her suit-coat pocket, pointing it at the large screen currently covered in an array of frames, each displaying different information and images. A cursor slides across the screen, grabs one of the frames and drags it to the center, following the motion of the device in her hand. The frame expands, taking up a large portion of the vast screen. A video starts playing.

It's a security camera pointing down an empty street, lined by business buildings, their signs all in Russian. And in the distance...the Machine. Its legs are still below the horizon, concealed by buildings and terrain, but the top half of its immense body can be seen clearly stalking straight toward the camera, and the city in which it's mounted.

It's a horrifying view. Despite the image being black and white, it's still easy to see the luminosity seeping through the Machine's shell and glowing from the coils of giant tubes collected at its underside. There are also several long spines jutting out from the bottom of its...neck, for lack of a better word. The towering spines on its back, doubling its height, sway back and forth with each step. All of this is horrible, but nothing compared to seeing the Machine's head for the first time. It's really just an extension of its shelled body, but its large black eyes, framed by glowing light, reveal something far worse than the menace I expected to see: indifference. It's strolling across the countryside, decimating civilization, and it's not even noticing. Comparing the Machine to a human stepping on ants isn't even appropriate. We're even less significant to it than ants are to us. We're more like the tiniest of insects that people step on all the time without even noticing. A shiver quakes through my body.

"You okay?" Mayer asks.

"Hadn't seen it head-on yet," I say.

"It is...unnerving," she says, and then continues. "It didn't cause much direct damage in that part of the world, aside from the earthquakes generated by its passing, but the radioactive ash settling to the ground decimated the population that hadn't evacuated. In response to the crisis, the Russian military, in cooperation with the former southern Soviet states, pushed south into the Middle East, making way for millions of refugees. This is the primary reason Israel's enemies have yet to attack.

Russia had less luck moving into China, and the two countries are now effectively at war.

"The Machine then crossed the Pacific Ocean, creating a tsunami that decimated the western coast of Alaska, and nearly wiped Hawaii off the map. It moved across northern Canada, through mostly uninhabited lands, where the combined Canadian and U.S. militaries tried a brute force attack even more powerful than the Russian assault you witnessed. While the resulting loss of human life was minimal, the assault dumped more radiation into the northern hemisphere and proved equally ineffective."

Between the image of the approaching Machine being displayed, and Mayer's tale of woe, I'm beginning to feel sick. But there is a glimmer of hope. She hasn't said anything about the contiguous 48 U.S. states, which means my family might still be safe.

I'm about to ask about Washington, D.C. when the Apocalypse Machine's lumbering walk becomes a flurry of action. The large plates on its back quiver. "What's happening?"

Mayer turns her attention back to the video. "We're not sure."

Fluid leaks from several of the Machine's dangling tube-like appendages, spraying back and forth, as each step sends them swaying. They look like giant leaky hoses, the liquid occasionally bursting out from escaping air bubbles. Mounds of material slide away from the sides of the Machine's back, propelled by the vibrating plates.

"Oh, no," I say. "I know what it's doing."

Mayer looks at me, but doesn't say a word. She's waiting for me to continue, and she looks ready to beat the words out of me if I don't start talking.

"Have you gone through my pack?" I ask. "Did you find a sample container?"

"Holy shit," Graham whispers. He's just figured it out, too.

"We did. Both. The sample is in a biohazard containment unit. What is it?"

"I haven't confirmed this yet, and—"

Mayer grips my hand in hers, hitting a pressure point that numbs my arm from wrist to elbow. "*What* is it?"

"Eggs," I say. "It's shedding eggs like a fiddler crab."

She releases my hand. "It's *multiplying?*"

"Maybe," I say. "Though I doubt our planet could sustain more than a few of them."

"We haven't seen it eat yet," she points out. "We're not even sure it has a mouth."

"You have my sample. Run tests on it. Maybe we can destroy the eggs before they hatch?"

"Backtrack the Machine's movements," Graham chimes in. "Napalm the egg sites." He shakes his head. "Won't be possible under the ash."

My mind whirls with possibilities, conjuring worst-case scenarios involving the billions of eggs being scattered by the Machine. But despite all of this new information, my thoughts return to my family. "Where is the Machine now?"

"Greenland," Mayer says. "It's been there for a week."

"A week? What's it doing?"

Mayer points the remote at the large screen and drags a satellite feed to the center of the screen, expanding it. The view is high above Greenland, recognizable because of its distinctive shape and the massive ice sheet covering three quarters of the world's largest island.

The image zooms in on the southern portion of the island nation. The landscape looks ravaged.

"It's been crushing mountains," Mayer says. "One by one. It tramples them to dust and then moves on."

"Is there anything there?" I ask. "You know, things the public might not know about?"

Mayer raises an eyebrow at me. "You mean like secret nuclear launch sites?"

"Things like that, yeah."

"No."

"And it's just destroying mountains?"

"Flattening them, from the ice sheet to the coast."

My legs grow weak and wobbly even before the realization fully resolves in my mind. "I know what it's doing. It's going to kill them."

"Kill *who?*" Graham asks.

"My family."

"Your family?" Mayer scoffs. "Why would it—"

"My family...and every single person anywhere near the Atlantic ocean. They're all going to die."

"When?" Mayer asks. "How long do we have?"

I point at the satellite feed. "Is this real time?"

"Yes."

"Then now. It's happening now."

26

The room goes silent when everyone sees what's taking place on the big screen. All 1,062,544 square miles of Greenland's ice sheet, resting on a layer of liquid water, and held in place by a range of mountains. With most of those mountains now destroyed, the rest give way to the immense weight of all that ice, allowing it to slide away, toward the Atlantic Ocean. Because of our perspective, witnessing the event from far above, everything appears to be happening in slow motion, but the ice is covering a vast distance, in seconds, scouring all life from the coast and then plunging into the ocean, sliding into the depths and displacing a mind-numbing amount of water.

"Zoom out," I say, my voice cracking, as tears well.

Mayer's hand shakes as she raises the remote. Our view pulls back, revealing the northeast coastline of Canada and the U.S. on the left, and the already ravaged northwest coastline of Europe. Lit by the sun, and viewed from space, we can actually see the wave rise up and slide across the globe, spreading out in a ring of destruction that will wipe the landscape clean and sweep entire cities away. It will roll over the northern continents' coastlines, followed by South America, Africa, and then Antarctica. Anyone within hundreds of miles of the ocean will be killed. Island nations will cease to exist.

The volcanic eruption and nuclear fallout killed millions of people, and would have slowly killed millions more. The event we're now witnessing is going to kill billions.

Including us.

When that wall of water rushes over Spain and through the Strait of Gibraltar, tsunamis will race across the Mediterranean, decimating the refugee-laden southern coast of Europe, the northern coast of Africa and then the Middle East. While that wave will be less substantial, losing energy as it strikes Spain and Italy, Israel will take the hit head on.

I start to calculate how long it will take the wave to reach us, when I see the wall of sun-glittering blue sweep over Newfoundland and race south, toward the United States and my family.

Please don't let them be there. Please, God, let them be gone.

I feel a tap on my left hand. I look down. It's Graham, flicking my hand with his finger. He leans closer and whispers a barely audible, "How much time do we have?"

If he's figured it out, there must be other people in the room already thinking the same thing. It won't be long before even these hardened Mossad agents start to panic at the realization that they'll be dead in... I lean closer to Graham. "Depends on where we are."

"Mossad HQ is in Tel Aviv."

Tel Aviv... Geez. The city is positioned dead center, right on Israel's coast, about as far away as you can get from her enemies in every direction, without actually wading out into the Mediterranean.

I don't bother trying to figure out the math, and guess. "Ten minutes."

"Stay close to me," he says, and he takes a slow, subtle step back like he's got nowhere to go and isn't in a hurry.

I want to remind him that we are inside some kind of Mossad headquarters. And while there very well might be helicopters around that he can pilot, the odds of us absconding with one, while everyone outside this room is still oblivious to their impending demise, are slim. But I keep my mouth shut, because the odds of us dying inside this room, in ten minutes, are astronomical.

Mayer senses our departure, looking to where we had been standing and then back at us. Her hand goes for her weapon, but she doesn't draw it. Instead, she walks toward us, calm and collected. The hand over her weapon never wavers, as she stops in front of us and says, "Where are you going?"

I glance at Graham, and when he says nothing, I reply with my usual candor. "Up. Preferably very high."

"This building is ten stories tall," she says.

"This building isn't going to be here in nine minutes," I tell her.

Mayer's face pales. She hadn't figured it out yet. She turns back to the screen, watching the wave roll over the entire U.K., unhindered by its cliffy coast, or mountainous highlands. She takes a step back into the room, urgency in her step.

She's going to tell them. And when she does...

Graham grasps her shoulder. She spins around, drawing her weapon and leveling it at his face.

He doesn't even flinch. The two warriors glare at each other for a moment, and then Graham breaks the silence. "No borders, remember?"

"They'll all die," she says.

"They'll all die, either way."

She sneers, her finger wrapping around the weapon's trigger. "What makes your life more valuable than theirs?"

"Not my life," Graham says, and then he pokes my shoulder. "His."

Mayer's eyes snap to mine while the gun remains pointed at Graham's gut. Agent Zingel looks back at us, but doesn't move. I think he's in shock, but Mayer has also positioned herself so that no one else in the room can see the gun. Given the circumstances, anyone looking on would probably think she was grilling us about the wave, not debating whether or not to tell them it will soon be crashing through the building's walls.

"Since the very first moment that thing emerged from Iceland, he has been one step ahead of it. He's survived multiple encounters, while millions have died. He stood on its back and took a sample. He understands it, and the ramifications of its actions. He might not agree with me, but I'm certain that if anyone is going to figure out how to stop this thing, it's him."

He's right, I don't agree, but at the moment, I'm not going to argue, either. The only way I might ever see my family again—assuming they're able to escape Washington, D.C before it's decimated—is if we leave this place in the next few minutes.

She glances back at the room full of people, many of whom she likely knows, as colleagues, maybe even as friends—all of whom have families. Her body language shifts, becoming rigid. Stoic. She might care about a lot of these people, but she's also a Mossad agent, trained to make life-and-death choices without flinching. She looks back at the big screen. The U.K. is submerged. Water eats its way across Europe, sliding over Spain, toward the Mediterranean. In New England, the states of Maine, New Hampshire and Vermont have been consumed.

When she turns back to us, her face is transformed. The friendly woman who freed me from the interrogation room has been replaced by someone I have no doubt could get the most hardened enemy to talk. "Turn around. Second door on your right. I will be right behind you." Even her voice sounds different. Tight. Sharp. Lethal.

Graham nods and heads for the door, walking casually, like nothing important is happening. He stops by the door and waits for Mayer.

She presses her hand against a print reader mounted beside the door. A light shines green, and the lock snaps open. She pushes the door inward, motions to a flight of stairs and offers a smile that looks genuine. "Head on up." The killer is gone once more, but this time, I know it's an act.

Graham starts up the steps, his pace casual. I have a hard time not prodding him to move faster. My imagination is continuing the satellite feed in my head. The water will be nearing Gibraltar. It won't be long before everyone else in the control room knows they're doomed. And when that happens...

The door behind us closes. I look back expecting to see Mayer at the door, but she's already surged up the stairs, taking the steps two at a time. She passes me in seconds. When I follow her passage around me and turn forward, Graham is already gone, sprinting upwards a flight above me.

"Shit," I whisper, and I charge up the stairs, my legs once again reminding me that they have been severely abused. But I don't waver. Charging up ten flights of stairs isn't easy, but I've gone through and survived worse. My legs are stronger for it, but so is my will. By the seventh flight, I catch up with Mayer and pace her all the way to the top.

We exit onto the roof where there are two landing pads, both occupied by olive colored Black Hawk transport helicopters. Graham wrenches the door open and slides into the cockpit. Mayer walks to the far side of the chopper and does the same, leaving me to open the side hatch and climb in the back.

While the rotor starts to whine and spin, Mayer takes out her phone, taps the screen a few times and places it against her ear. After waiting for a moment, she says, "Get out of there," and hangs up. I'm about to ask her who she called, when the rotor chop grows too loud to be heard. I put on one of the headsets, sit back in the seat and buckle myself in. When a powerful wind slaps up against me, I realize I never closed the side door. The chopper can fly just fine with it open, so I stay in my seat, white knuckle-clutching the straps over my chest.

Then I look through the open door.

My mental calculations were off.

The wave is here. And it's bigger and faster than I thought.

"Lift off!" I scream.

There're a few seconds of raw terror-filled stagnation that seem to draw out in slow motion, the wall of water growing steadily closer, and higher. And then we're airborne, lifting up and away from the rooftop, ascending fast enough to crush me into my seat, while at the same time moving inland, away from the wave.

But not nearly fast enough to outrun it.

I watch the water's approach through the open side door. High above Tel Aviv, I see the water slide away from the coast, gather into the wave, arc up and then return with a vengeance, sliding not just through the city, but over it, rising higher as it climbs up onto dry land, and crests a thousand feet up.

The rotor whines.

The pressure on my body increases as my blood pressure spikes. I feel like a cooked sausage, ready to burst. I try to scream, but fail.

The water races at us, a wall of gray-blue.

We rise steadily higher as the Black Hawk tilts at a steeper angle, turning my view upward to the sky, and the frothing white crest of a nation-devouring wave.

The water arcs high, blots out the sun and then crashes downward, rushing toward the chopper, the open side door and my shrieking form. And in that moment of abject horror, of knowing that my life has come to an end, I find myself back in that foxhole mindset, begging an all-powerful being I don't believe in to spare my life. My silent plight rises up, no doubt mingling with a chorus of others around the world, all crying out to be heard, to be spared.

But there is no one listening.

The roar of water and screaming voices, the scent of salt rushing past on the tsunami-propelled wind, the sight of civilization's eradication; that is the only response forthcoming, and it's not God speaking.

It's the Apocalypse Machine.

Crashing water snuffs out my voice, and moments later, my soul.

FIFTEEN YEARS LATER

27

AYERS

The Great Inland Eyre Sea provided life, and took it away. That was the first lesson the children of Uluru were taught. Over the years, the lesson had been retaught, again and again, as each fishing venture returned either food or death. Often both. And while that was the framework that guided daily life, it was not the only instruction passed on by the elders, the last of whom had perished more than a year previously.

The eldest child of Uluru, Jon Ayers, was a descendent of the ancient, who had once renamed the island upon which they eked out a living. Like the elders before him, he remembered the calamity that had reshaped the world. Their land had been larger then. A continent. A country. Australia. A desert then, humanity settled along the coast, where most perished when the waves rolled in and the waters surged up. Entire cities, unimaginable to the children of Uluru, now resided under the vast ocean. Eighteen million people had drowned in those days. Five million more had starved in the deserts. And the last million had become food for the *Moyh-ma Lamang*, the wild animals who rose up in the Destroyer's wake. While the deadly energy that exploded out from the crushed nuclear power plants along the coast added to humanity's suffering, it had spurred the Moyh-ma's growth.

That was the theory passed on from one of Uluru's founding members. A scientist. In his time, Uluru had risen up from the barren earth, glowing red in the setting sun's light, a marvel to behold that attracted visitors from around the world. Now, it was an island, providing refuge to the last of Australia's human residents.

Ayers stood on the shore, dressed only in a pair of cargo shorts passed down from the elders who had come and gone. They were torn and frayed, but the pockets and belt loops still functioned well enough to hold some of the tools of his trade: pliers, two knives—one for defense, one for filleting—spare line, bandages, a magnifying glass and a pair of binoculars.

His dark skin warmed in the morning sun. It was, he thought, the only true pleasure left in the world, aside from his wife, Adina. At sixteen, she was young enough to have no memory of the world before. Uluru and the one hundred twenty-one people residing on the island, were all she had ever known of the world.

At twenty years old, Ayers remembered his parents, his house in Port Augusta, cartoons, fast food and the waters that rushed in to take it all away. His faint childhood memories served no purpose in the world remade, though. They brought him pain. Nothing more. So he squelched thoughts of the past and spoke of them only when Adina asked.

The water was calm, but looked a little higher than the previous day. Each year, the tides rose higher, climbing the steep island shoreline. Before dying in the jaws of a Moyh-ma shark, the thirty-two year old elder had calculated that if the waters continued to rise steadily—as the world's ice caps melted—Uluru would sink beneath the waves within fifty years. But he also said the waters would never reach that high. Uluru was safe. The rest of Australia...was not.

Ayers had set foot on the mainland only twice, the first on a quest to find supplies, including soil, and the second to gauge the possibility of establishing a beachhead from which the children of Uluru could colonize the mainland. Both ventures had resulted in several deaths at the hands of the Moyh-ma, some at sea, and many more on land.

The countryside had been overrun by new life, both animal and plant. While the former elders had recognized some of the creatures as 'mutations' of what had existed in the Old World, many of them were new, and hostile. While there was prey in abundance, feeding on new plant life, predators lurked in every shadow. Some of the Moyh-ma posed little threat, but the ones that did were larger than twenty men and had insatiable appetites.

If one of them managed to cross the open sea without becoming a meal in the process, Uluru would be lost. Ayers knew he would have to lead his people across the Eyre Sea and stake a claim on the mainland. The survival of humanity depended on it. But to do that, he needed strong warriors, and to build that strength he needed food. So for now, they remained fishermen.

"How are the winds today?" Adina asked.

"Gentle." Ayers slid his hand around her back and pulled her close. The canvas tunic she wore was rough against his arm, and it hid her body, but Adina's light skin burned on cloudless days. When the rains came, she would shed her clothing, like most of the darker-skinned residents of Uluru, who had once been known as Aborigines. Ayers knew even less about his ancient ancestors than he did of the world he'd been born into, but he understood that they had mastered the dangerous bushlands of Australia, and he hoped that he could lead people to do so again.

"I wasn't asking about you," she said, snuggling against his broad chest. Adina was a strong woman, a master fisher and a warrior, but she would not be joining today's hunt, because she was also with child. When her stomach swelled and a sickness had overcome her, Payu, who at nineteen was Uluru's eldest woman, had recognized the symptoms. She had helped with births before, but Adina's would be the first she oversaw.

Two years ago, during the Destroyer's last passing, detectable only as a repeating earthquake, the air had become hard to breathe. Those born long before the calamity had grown ill and perished. Twenty three elders in six months. Ayers was the oldest child of the Old World to survive. Those born after the calamity never fell ill, their bodies already acclimated to the New World's shifting atmosphere.

Ayers pointed at the placid water. "The sea is far more gentle than me. I will need the oar team for today's hunt." The children of Uluru had six seaworthy vessels, two of them pillaged from the Old World, and four built by Uluru's founders. The pillaged boats had towering sails and carried a large number of crew, or supplies. They were also safer, because of their size. They were crewed by two, five-man teams, who knew every knot and rigging, what the sound of a snapping sail indicated and how to predict the wind itself. The other four boats—long, slender craft—also required five-man teams. But those were comprised of four thickly muscled men to row and one woman, to hunt fish or defend against predators. With Adina pregnant, Ayers had taken her position as a hunter.

"You will be careful," Adina said.

"When am I not?"

She smiled up at him. "Every time your feet leave Uluru."

"I take risks," he said. "But I'm not reckless. I will live to see our child born, and the children of Uluru return to the mainland."

"Unless the Destroyer returns."

He looked down at Adina, whose gaze had fallen to the ground. "There is little left for it to destroy."

"There is you," she said. "The last change nearly killed you."

"My strength sustained me," he said, squeezing her tightly. "It will continue to do so. During the hunt. Against the Moyh-ma. And in the Destroyer's wake. Now..." He kissed her forehead and removed his arm from her canvas-wrapped waist. "Fetch the others. Two teams. The sun rises."

Alone once more, Ayers walked down the steep path that used to lead to the desert floor, but now stopped a hundred feet down, where they tied off the boats. He stopped at a tall shack that would eventually have to be moved higher up the path. He took eight oars and two long spears, each tipped with the sharpened bones of slain Moyh-ma. He then distributed the gear between two of the boats and stepped into the water. The scent of salt water had once invigorated people, connecting them to something primal. That was the way the elders had described it. But for Ayers, it reminded him that they lived on an island prison.

We will be free, he thought, looking to the northeast, where land could be found, beyond the horizon, now glowing orange in the morning's sun. *But first, we must eat.*

Eight groggy men and one woman walked down the winding path, their bare feet slapping against the warm stone. Each of them was a seasoned hunter, but would have been considered children in the Old World. Now they were Uluru's best hope of survival, of expansion and of freedom.

Without words shared, they took their position in two boats and shoved off, paddling into the deep, dark blue, where food and monsters lurked. Ayers stood at the front of his long vessel, spear in hand, but not yet at the ready. His counterpart, Yindi, whose dark skin and hair matched his, stood at her bow, eyeing him. "You do intend to catch a meal today, I hope."

The men rowing behind her chuckled. The two teams had developed a friendly rivalry since Ayers had taken over for Adina. She and Yindi were close friends, and neither believed Ayers could do the job. He had done well enough, but he never brought home quite as much food as Yindi. Luckily, the sea was bountiful. There was food to spare. But the sea was also dangerous.

"And live long enough to eat it." Ayers hefted his spear into position and raised his chin to the water ahead. "There."

Yindi looked forward and frowned.

A portion of ocean, eight feet across, was smoother than the rest. The 'footprint' could have been left by a whale, which would benefit them greatly, or it could have come from a Moyh-ma shark—a mutated shark still recognizable from the Old World—or from something worse. Ayers preferred hunting seals or large fish, as they were easier to haul back inside the boats, which left less blood in the water. Larger prey were considered worth the risk, but they usually had to fight for them, first against the prey animal, and then against creatures drawn by its blood.

"A second," Yindi said, pointing with her spear and shouting, "Yiyah!"

The men behind her dug their oars into the water, chasing a creature they had yet to identify.

Ayers felt unsure, but ordered his men to follow. The hunt was on, and it would require both ships to complete. His fears faded as the wind whipped through his long hair. He held his ten-foot-long spear in his left hand, and cupped the bottom of it with his right.

A turquoise glow slid past beneath the hull, white flesh reflecting the morning sun.

"Beneath us!" he shouted, turning to watch the massive form pass by, hoping to identify it. The creature's shape proved elusive, broken up by bands of darker color. All he knew was that he had never seen anything like it, and that was bad.

Very bad.

They had books on Uluru. Through study and experience, he could identify most creatures of the Old World, even those that had mutated. But something new...that meant they were dealing with a pure-blood Moyh-ma. The greatest danger from a new Moyh-ma was that no one knew how it would behave. Was it docile? Was it hunting them? Unpredictability made the Destroyer's spawn lethal, even when they weren't predatory.

As the boat turned to follow the creature, he saw its footprint swirl to the surface ahead of them. And then again to the side of Yindi's boat.

"It's circling!" he shouted, and they all knew what that meant. Prey moved in a straight line, away from them; predators circled. Luminous water surged up on the far side of Yindi's boat. The beast was charging. "Yindi! To your side!"

The four men holding oars did their jobs well, tipping away from the creature, plunging their bodies into the water, and flinging Yindi away. The reinforced hull would protect the oarsmen, but Yindi, the more valuable crew member, would need to be retrieved.

A set of jaws, lined with human-like teeth, emerged from the water, a thick purple lip peeling back. A loud crack filled the air, as the jaws clamped down on the hull and squeezed. Wood cracked and splintered, but held, protecting the men still inside. Yindi hit the water and started swimming toward Ayers's boat, which surged through the water, straight for the floundering craft.

Yindi saw them coming on fast and kicked out of the way. "What are you doing!"

The answer to her question became clear a moment later, as his boat's bow struck its counterpart. The impact jolted the vessel to a stop and shot Ayers forward. Spear cocked back, he looked down at the Moyh-ma. Its broad body warbled with color. It wasn't just striped light and dark. The color of its body shifted, pulsing with energy. Its six eyes, mounted atop flimsy looking, translucent skin sacks, gazed up at him. He saw fins in the ocean, at least eight of them, beating backward. The creature released the tipped boat and shifted back, away from Ayers.

Too late.

Using speed, gravity and weight, Ayers thrust the spear downward. It plunged into the Moyh-ma's head, slipping through flesh until it connected with something solid. Ayers clung to the spear, and when his body yanked to a stop, the pressure shoved the sharp blade through the creature's skull. By the time he hit the water, the Moyh-ma was dead.

Ayers stood atop the creature's slick back, holding his buried spear for balance. "Survivors?"

He watched the tipped boat right itself, the four oarsmen still inside. A moment later, Yindi hoisted herself back inside the long ship. She stood up, dripping wet, and shouted back. "Survivors, all!"

28

KABA

Invasions were nothing new for the Awáni people. Over the past few hundred years, their deep jungle territory had been visited by strange peoples with undecipherable languages and odd clothing, ill-suited for the jungle's moist air.

Kaba had heard the stories told by firelight, while the tribe dined on fish, turtle and mango, her favorite dishes. Invaders came, sometimes for slaves, sometimes for trees, sometimes for sport, but they always left, turned away by Awáni warriors, whose understanding of nature made all the difference. Before newcomers reached the Awáni territory, they first had to fend off the jungle's assaults. Biting insects, wild beasts, hungry fish and ceaseless moisture turned many invaders back before they even found the Awáni. Those who passed the jungle's trials were greeted with kindness, but few reciprocated, and those who became violent, met their end at the poisoned tip of a warrior's arrow.

Kaba, a woman of thirty and a mother of three, remembered the loggers, who had come to their jungle in search of trees, using iron monsters to cut down everything in their path. They destroyed the homes of Awáni and animal alike. They used loud weapons to repel warrior attacks. Kaba's father had been injured by one such weapon. It tore a hole in his arm, from a distance, without need of an arrow.

She had been fifteen when the loggers had come, beginning what the Awáni referred to as the Desperate Times. Warriors died. Lands were lost. Hunger was rampant, and they were forced to expand their territory, bringing them into conflict with neighboring tribes.

One day, the loggers got inside their mechanical transports and abandoned their iron monsters. They never returned. The jungle reclaimed the land, swallowing up all evidence that the men had ever come. Then the skies changed. The jungle smelled different, like fires without a source. The Awáni had no contact with the outside world, though they knew it existed. They understood that something drastic had changed in the world around them. They felt the earth shake several times. The river swelled, forcing them deeper into the forest, where tribes fought for new lands. And then, over the course of many years, outsiders invaded once more.

At first, they came in droves, crashing through the forest in pitiful waves, most of them perishing from exposure and starvation. The rest were hunted. For a time, the jungle and its creatures fed on humanity, growing strong from the endless source of blood and flesh. The Awáni considered helping, but there were too many. If the new invaders learned to find food, they would take it all. So the Awáni kept their distance, watching from the trees, until the invasion slowed to a trickle.

In the past few years, the historical roles of the region's sparse tribes and the invaders shifted positions. Neighboring tribes began taking survivors as slaves, bartering them, the way they might meat and fish. And the newcomers never complained. The tragedy that had befallen the world outside had broken their spirits, making them susceptible to influence, and the women submissive. As Kaba aged, she found that the men of her tribe preferred the more docile outsider woman, so she too was forced to marry outside the tribe. Her husband was kind, pale-skinned and weak. But his mind was sharp. He'd brought the river to the village, allowing them to grow crops and create a permanent settlement. The Awáni were no longer nomadic, and their strength and numbers had grown, while the surrounding tribes struggled to feed all of their new slaves.

As one of the original tribe, married to an outsider whose influence had improved their lives, Kaba was now regarded with high esteem. She regaled the tribe with stories of old, oversaw the fermenting of drinks and participated as an equal on hunts. But life had become busy, and she found herself pining for the nomadic days of her childhood. She sought refuge from her busy life, disappearing into the jungle for days, dependent on the trees for food and protection.

But there was one friend who never left her side. She had found Rapau when she was twenty-five, between her first two babies. His mother had likely been slain by outsiders. So she took him in and let him suckle alongside her middle son. And now, he was her constant companion, protector and guide. No matter how well she knew the jungle and how adept she was at moving through it, the howler monkey would always be better.

When she settled down for a rest, she knew the monkey would keep watch, and if danger arose, she would be warned well in advance. She placed her long bow and arrows down against the tall, winding root of a two-hundred-foot-tall Kapok tree. The coils of roots provided homes for frogs, birds, bromeliads and countless insects. But she wasn't interested in the tree's living bounty, she wanted its bark. Using a machete taken from a dead outsider, she dug a tall rectangle into the tree's paper-like bark. The woody sheet peeled cleanly away. She cut off a small section and sat against a curving root that hugged her body and scratched the insect bites on her back. The sharp blade swept over the sheet of bark, peeling away thin layers of fiber with each pass, leaving behind a thin, flexible sheet.

Kaba dug her fingers into a small tobacco pouch that hung from the belt around her waist. It was the only article of clothing she wore, or owned, holding machete, arrows and tobacco. Everything else she needed was provided by the jungle. Fragrant tobacco crumbled out from between her twisting fingertips, lining the inside of the paper. She then rolled the paper between her palms, coiling it tightly. She licked the loose opening, careful not to cut her tongue, and then she gave it a squeeze. Traditionally, she would have had to make a fire using Achiote wood and a stick rolled between her hands, but that was no longer necessary. One of the many treasures left behind by the droves of dead outsiders was what her husband called a 'lighter.' She pulled the bright red device from her tobacco pouch, gave it a flick and lit the end of her smoke. She pulled in two deep breaths, flaring the tip to a bright orange, and then she leaned back.

The tobacco, mixed with a few other dried plants, relaxed her mind and body. This was what she needed. Life in the tribe was hectic, but out here, alone in the jungle, she remembered who she was. Who the Awáni were.

Rapau chortled in the tree high above her. His booming voice echoed through the jungle. Distant monkeys cried out in reply. She glanced up at Rapau's black form. He danced among the branches, shaking leaves free.

Is he alarmed, or having fun?

Rapau's play often became overzealous, especially when he met other monkeys, so it was sometimes hard to tell. She would normally act on his cries, either way, but the smoke's effect was strong, and she had just sat down. She held her machete in one hand, and puffed on her smoke with the other.

Ten minutes later, despite Rapau's continued warnings, Kaba drifted into sleep, a trail of white smoke snaking into the trees above.

It wasn't Rapau that woke her, or the stub burning her fingers, but the sound of voices, close and speaking a foreign tongue.

Eyes closed, she listened.

Two men. The baritone suggested outsiders, not tribal men. Her mind painted pictures of them: hairy, tall, bearded and overdressed. Were they newcomers or did they belong to one of the other tribes? She didn't recognize their language, so she assumed they were new, which meant they didn't know the rules of the jungle.

Clutching her machete, ready to swing, she cracked her eyes and found that she was only partially right. The men were tall, bearded and fair-skinned, but aside from the heavy packs hanging from their backs, they were naked. These two had apparently eked out a living in the jungle for some time. They looked comfortable in the wet heat, and carried spears and blades, weapons that would serve them well. They clearly had been influenced by neighboring tribes. But while they had adapted to life in the jungle, they had not truly become part of it. The packs they wore, while dulled with grime, were still bright red and blue. And their senses had yet to be honed.

They stood ten feet away, their backs to her, eyes turned up at the branches, where Rapau thrashed and howled.

Kaba's tan skin helped her blend in with the surrounding terrain, but her weapons and lit smoke should have drawn them right to her. She let the stub fall from between her fingers, bounce off her flat stomach and fall in the mud beside her hip. She pressed it into the earth, leaned forward and stood without making a sound. She could leave without the chance of conflict, or perhaps invite them to join the Awáni. They appeared capable enough, and she had considered taking a second husband or two.

As she considered her options, the pitch of Rapau's warning changed.

She tensed. The monkey had several different warning cries. One for friends. One for strangers. One for rivals. And one for predators. But the deep hoot tearing from his curled lips was unlike anything she'd heard before. The monkey wasn't just calling out a warning, he was terrified. And then, he did the unthinkable. Rapau fled, sweeping through the canopy faster than she could move on land.

Feeling merciful toward the men, she snapped her fingers. When they spun around in fright, stepping away from her, she knew she had nothing to fear. Even if they worked up the courage to attack her, everything about the way they moved said that they weren't killers. When the two men had settled down, she placed an index finger to her lips. She'd learned the sign for 'quiet,' a universal gesture all outsiders understood, from her husband. The men parted as she approached them, sniffing the air. The newcomers were rancid with sweat and their own waste. The scent of her smoke lingered. But there was something else. Something raw, and new.

She pointed at each of the men, then at herself and then to the jungle behind her in the direction Rapau had fled. They nodded vigorously, docile like most outsiders lost in the jungle, and they started in the direction she had pointed.

The repetitive thud of heavy footfalls stopped them.

When the two men started whispering between themselves, she placed her finger to her lips once more, but was ignored.

Fools, she thought, and she planned to abandon them at once. But before she could leave, the footfalls doubled in pace. A guttural rumble rolled through the air, like a crocodile's warning. The creature was attacking.

While Kaba dove behind a sheet of tall kapok root, the two men shouted in surprise, and then terror.

She looked over the root in time to see the creature attack. It had a body like a bird, but its featherless skin resembled a crocodile's, as did its long, slender, sharp tooth-filled snout. The eyes, however, bobbled atop puffy sacks of flesh, as did several other organs, like transparent teats, hanging from its underside. The creature stood on two legs, a long sweeping tail providing balance. Before the men could react, the beast snapped down on one of their arms. As the man pulled away, the sharp, slender teeth slid through meat and bone, severing the limb.

The wounded man screamed.

His partner fled. And as he ran, two more of the creatures sprang from the shadows. They leapt onto his back together, crashing to the ground and silencing the man's screams with a loud crack. A merciful death compared to his friend. Another two creatures arrived a moment later, the first biting the wounded man's face, the second sniffing the air for a moment, and then turning toward Kaba. Unlike the two men, these creatures were perfectly adapted to living and hunting in the jungle.

She stood and raised her machete, slapping the flat blade against the tall, hollow root. She struck the root four more times, the rhythm practiced, the sound echoing through the jungle for miles.

And then, she ran.

And the monsters followed, leaving their two dead prey behind to chase down a third.

She fired her arrows while on the run, striking the neck of the creature closest to her. Each arrow stumbled a predator, but didn't stop it. She sent her fifth and final arrow soaring at a creature's bulbous eye, piercing the flesh with a wet pop that sprayed clear fluid. The predator moaned, staggered to a stop, and then began scratching at its head with one of its three-toed feet, tearing away the injured flesh.

Although it was slowed, it was quickly replaced by the remaining four pack members.

Kaba wound her way through the jungle, following paths that only she could see, and following turns only she knew were coming. Though the creatures snapping at her heels were larger and faster, her knowledge of the jungle kept her one step ahead of them. But after five minutes of running, it became clear that one step ahead was still several steps short of safety. The creatures split up so that the next sharp turn she made would still lead her directly into the jaws of a waiting monster. She leapt between two trees, forcing the closest predator to sweep around them, but it was right behind her, and gaining.

She could feel its vibrating chortle, rumbling through her chest.

The creature's hot, wet breath burned the back of her neck and carried the scent of human blood into her nose with each inhalation.

She swatted the flat of her blade against several Kapok tree roots as she ran past. The creatures didn't flinch at the resounding booms, but they weren't intended to.

When she heard a pattern beat out in reply, she wondered how the others had reached her so quickly. Then she saw Rapau in the trees above, running toward her, leading the charge.

"There are four," she cried out. "One on my left. One at my back. Two at my right."

"We are near!" came the reply. It was Pacon, the lead hunter. And the 'we' he spoke of would be the rest of the hunters. All thirty-seven of them. She grinned, and when Pacon shouted, "Down!" she obeyed.

Kaba launched herself onto the leaf-littered jungle floor, just as thirty hunters sprang from the jungle ahead of her, launching arrows, spears and darts. The creatures, suddenly impaled and outnumbered, slid to a halt, barking and snapping their jaws. When the largest of them took an iron-bladed spear tip to the throat and toppled over, the others turned tail and fled back into the jungle.

Pacon offered Kaba his hand, pulling her back to her feet. They stared down at the creature together.

"What is it?" Pacon asked.

Kaba wasn't sure. Her husband had mentioned the great monster destroying the outside world, but he had never mentioned anything like this. No matter what it was, Kaba knew better than to turn down the jungle's offering. She grinned at Pacon and said, "Lunch."

29

LOPEZ

There is nowhere more remote on planet Earth than the middle of the Pacific Ocean. So when the end of all things reared its ugly head, Captain Aurelio Lopez left San Diego behind and headed out to sea, planning to live off the ocean's bounty and ride out the world's end—including the massive waves rolling across the oceans. He stocked the hold with supplies, and with no loved ones to bid farewell, and no crew he trusted well enough to bring along, he struck out alone, early one morning.

While the world fell apart, he sailed northwest into the open ocean, stopping once the North American western coast, the Alaskan southern coast and Hawaiian northern coast were all equal distances away. His only company were the whales, sharks and fish that seemed drawn to the hundred-foot-long maroon hull of his fishing vessel, the *Red Sky*. It was as if they knew life on Earth was dying on a vast scale, and they were banding together, drawing comfort from each other, and from his ship, all the while eating one another.

Over a period of weeks, Lopez collected large patches of floating debris—parts of the Great Pacific Garbage Patch. The floating mounds of trash, bound together by fishing nets and coils of rope and seaweed, expanded the shadow cast by the Red Sky, which in turn increased the amount of sea life taking refuge beneath it. He was securing his future by turning his ship into a floating island, all the while keeping the stern clear so he could move and steer, should the need arise.

When the first of many waves arrived, he knew he had made the right choice. It rose beneath the Red Sky, lifting the vessel and his island high into the sky. It slid over the broad, arching top of the wave and back into calmer waters. It had been like surfing over a mountain that stretched from one horizon to the other. Even from the top, several hundred feet in the air, he could see no end. The wave left as quickly as it had arrived, racing east for California. It didn't take much imagination to know what kind of destruction the wave would unleash on the densely populated coast. The wave's cause wasn't a mystery, either. The monster that had risen from Iceland and stormed across Europe, had reached the Pacific, and it was headed for North America.

In the months that followed, Lopez expanded the island, binding the garbage so tight that he could walk across it. He left holes in the surface through which he could fish. He ate, and he grew his kingdom. He survived. But he had also made a tragic mistake. Every day that passed, alone under the blazing sky and star-filled nights, he grew more and more lonely.

So when the first ship—a yacht—arrived, its seven Japanese occupants nearly out of food, he welcomed them with a bright smile, feeding them and providing water from the small pond he'd built in the trash island. The sailboat was tied into the floating mass, and once again, the island grew. Since the Japanese couldn't speak Spanish and knew only limited English, communication was reduced to hand gestures while they learned each other's languages. The first word Lopez taught them was 'Captain,' and that he was it.

As more months passed, more stragglers arrived, one ship, boat and yacht at a time, each one becoming a new way station on an interconnected mass of trash and ships that could rise and fall with the waves, no matter how vast. They picked up vessels and crew from New Zealand, China, Russia, Fiji, Hawaii, and the mainland United States—all people who thought to flee to the open ocean before the waves came. Within two years, their community had grown to a hundred.

They collected rain water, and syphoned it from the humid air itself. Fish were abundant. Colonies of edible seaweed grew from the fringe of the expanding six-acre garbage and boat patch, which Lopez had deemed the Red Sky Flotilla.

It seemed they would not just weather the end of the world, but they would flourish through it.

Until it found them.

The wave came first, more powerful than any they had experienced before. They lost two ships recently connected to the flotilla, but no people. Lopez realized too late the wave's power came from the fact that the monster was headed straight for them. It arrived early the next morning, its spines cutting through the ocean like mile-high dorsal fins. And they sliced the flotilla in half, destroying ships and years of work.

Thirty-seven people were lost, some killed by the creature's passing, some lost at sea and drowned and others consumed by the sharks that had made their home beneath the floating island.

But Lopez rallied his people. Using small boats, they brought the severed halves of the island together, closing a miles-wide gap that had formed. They fought for their homes, against the monster and the elements, and eventually, they won. Lopez was revered by the people. He married a Russian woman. He had a son.

And then, the world changed again.

Floating organic debris left in the creature's wake clung to the flotilla's edges, growing spindly white tendrils. They attempted to tear it away, but it spread too fast, moving beneath the water, filling in the cracks. After a year of this strange growth, the flotilla was stronger than ever, bound by living roots. New life grew up from the trash, lush, green and soft underfoot. He could almost feel it pumping out fresh oxygen. Soon, Red Sky was growing on its own, expanding miles, bulging with terrain, all of it rising and falling with the waves, and all of it kept at the Pacific's core by the same cyclical currents that helped form the original garbage patch.

That was the beginning of a new prosperous life, and in the many years since, Red Sky had grown into a small town of three hundred forty-seven souls. They lived like a commune, with each person doing their share of the work and reaping their share of the reward. No one went hungry or starved. Crops, *actual crops*, grew on the spongy terrain, which was moist with fresh water. The white roots dangling hundreds of feet down sucked up the water and filtered out the salt, forming a small lake at the island's core, partially submerging the original Red Sky vessel.

There had been threats to their colony in the past, rising from the ocean. Strange beasts with bulging eyes. But the sea life around them, who now called the island home, reacted to the new creatures' arrival with territorial aggressiveness. And those too large to be chased away were trapped by the island's roots. At first, Lopez thought the creatures, some fifty feet long, were getting trapped in the twisting system of roots the way dolphins used to find themselves coiled in his fishing nets. But then he saw it for himself, watching through a fishing hole one day. While all of the fish and sharks, and other new species of smaller ocean dwellers, swam in and around the roots, they never came into contact with them. When the larger creatures tried to swim beneath the island, the roots reacted to their touch, wrapping around the large bodies and paralyzing them, and then slowly consuming them.

The island wasn't just growing, it was *alive*.

A new symbiotic world.

So when Lopez woke to the jarring sound of a fog horn, it took him a few confused moments to remember what the sound indicated.

It was a warning.

They were under attack.

He stumbled from his cabin below-deck on a yacht they had collected five years previous, its occupants long dead. The boat was now fully enveloped by the island, a half mile from the coast. "Stay inside," he said to his wife and five year old son. "Don't come out until I get you."

The early morning sun was just over the eastern horizon, casting the sky in a violet hue. Lopez looked to the coast beyond his home. There were a dozen more vessels between them and the shore, but they were close enough that something large could pose a threat. He saw nothing there. Aside from other members of the Red Sky clan emerging from their homes, armed for a fight, he saw nothing. No threat.

If someone sounded a false alarm...

He heard shouting in the distance and headed for it. The voices came from the far side of a cargo ship. It was small by cargo ship standards, but the largest vessel on the island, and it had brought them many amenities and supplies, not to mention several tons of plastic and rubber goods that had been adapted for life at sea. Ping pong balls became fishing bobbers. Toys became bait. And tire tubes became floatation devices and buoys.

The raised voices echoed off of the metal hull, urgent and afraid.

Lopez rounded the bow, spear in hand, with a dozen men now behind him.

"Captain," Pietro, the Russian who was on watch, shouted. "They took Harry."

Lopez noted the crazed, fearful look in Pietro's eyes. He had been with Lopez for eight years, and he had seen and survived some horrible things. But the man was terrified. And Harry, a large Hawaiian man, could not have been carried off by anything small. Lopez searched the land around them, looking for something still dragging the man back to the sea, but he saw nothing. He looked to the nearby fishing holes, but the water was calm.

"Where did they go?" Lopez asked.

"Go?" Pietro asked, sounding bewildered. "They have yet to leave."

That was when Lopez noticed the pale Russian was looking *up.*

At the sky.

Lopez craned his head up and saw them right away. They looked like manta rays, with broad, undulating, fleshy wings, and sacks of flesh on their backs propelled them like breathing jets, sucking in air and then squeezing it out. There were six of the creatures, circling like vultures. And one of them held a man in its jaws, revealing the truth behind Pietro's story and the creatures' size—at least fifteen feet long, with a thirty foot wing span. Lopez didn't see any limbs on the creatures, but he soon understood why. When the flying ray carrying Harry passed the shoreline, it dove down and plunged into the ocean.

"Get everyone inside!" Lopez shouted to Pietro. The Russian wasted no time climbing back into the cargo ship. He'd be safe behind its metal walls. And with its fog horn, he could signal the entire colony to stay indoors.

"The rest of you, come with me!" Spear in hand, Lopez ran out into the open.

A handful of the men followed him, less sure, but loyal. The rest remained hidden in the cargo ship's shadow.

"Captain," Jones said, "we can't possibly hope to fight creatures that big." Jones was a skinny man. A hell of a fisherman and cook, but not a fighter.

He was also right.

"I don't intend to fight them," Lopez said, watching the skies, waiting for the creatures to notice them. "Not all of them." He held his spear at the ready. The five-foot metal rod, tipped with a razor sharp harpoon, could slay a whale if thrown with enough force. It would work on the flying monsters, too, if he could hit one. "Aim for the first of them that comes. Wait for my signal. Then throw."

"To what purpose?" Kai asked. He was a Korean man and one of their most skilled hunters, taking down mammalian sea creatures when the colony felt the need for red meat.

The fog horn let out three quick blasts, warning everyone to stay inside, and giving Lopez time to consider his answer.

He had a secret. He'd kept it from everyone. Mostly because he didn't want his wife to worry, but also because he wasn't entirely sure how the others would react. Fear of the island on which they lived helped keep everyone in order. He'd been fishing, alone, when something large and deep caught him sleeping and pulled him into the fishing hole. He had plunged thirty feet down before he'd fully understood what had been happening and let go of the rod. That was also the moment he'd become tangled in the long white tendrils dangling beneath the island. He had seen them before, from a distance when diving off a boat, but he had never been so close, and he had certainly never touched them.

The roots meant certain death.

Only, they didn't.

Not only did the coiling tendrils not kill and consume him, they had held him in place for a moment, twisting around his body, gently, almost like a caress. The moment was almost intimate, and he'd returned the roots' affection, rubbing his hand over the undulating vines. They then had lifted him back to the surface, sinking down again only after he was safe, back on shore.

He wasn't certain what the colony offered the living roots—nutrients from their waste, a habitat to cling to, company—but they weren't just carnivorous plants. They were intelligent. They were protectors. And he needed their help now.

One of the flying creatures dove at the group of men before Lopez could explain the plan. They might not have believed him anyway. The ray swooped low, and cruised over the landscape, jaws open to reveal broad, flat teeth meant for crushing and chewing. *Poor Harry*, Lopez thought, and then he opened his mouth to shout the command to attack.

But he never got the chance.

He was interrupted when one of the ray's undulating wings slapped against the green, spongy island surface. The reaction was immediate and violent. White spears punched up through the ground and then through the creature's body. The ray's momentum turned into a downward arc, smashing its face into the ground, where more white tendrils snapped up, enveloping the creature, pulling it down.

"You *knew* this would happen?" Kai asked, eyes wide.

"I hoped," Lopez replied. "Red Sky is alive. And friendly."

The group of men looked down at the squishy ground beneath them, aware for the first time that the pile of trash and boats had become much more than their home. It could, at any time, slay them all, but instead, it protected them, and provided for them. The colossal monster had destroyed continental humanity, but at the same time, it had provided a protector.

Far in the distance, Lopez saw the land rising up.

The fog horn blasted again, warning of an incoming tsunami, which they had no trouble riding out now.

He and the men ran back to the cargo vessel, climbing inside the cabin and holding on, while the big wave rolled beneath the island and moved on its way. Given the wave's direction, he guessed the monster was headed back toward the West Coast. If there was anyone still alive on the mainland, he wished them luck, but what they really needed was to adapt, and to make a new life for themselves, like the people of Red Sky had done, and would continue to do.

30

ABRAHAM

Hope, like what little remains of humanity, has become nomadic. Elusive. Always on the move. Never where you left it, or where you think it will be. And on occasion, it surprises you. Like the Nepalese mountain people living in caves. The Iranian desert dwellers, their tents never in the same place. The Egyptian raft villages outside the ruins of the now coastal Cairo, subsiding on the sea, ready to float away. And then, at the base of the Loma Mountains in what once was Sierra Leone but is now part of the Atlantic, we found a seaworthy vessel, cast aside by one of many civilization-crushing waves. The sailboat had the name *Daisy*, but I rubbed it away and duct taped a new name to its aft: *Hope*, the nomadic ship with three passengers.

"Abraham." Graham sounds tired, and he should. For weeks, he has piloted us through a storm-ravaged sea and over a rolling tsunami that carried us miles backward before setting us back down into the ocean. Waves like those sweep across the oceans every time the Apocalypse Machine enters and exits one, reminding us of its presence. We've only seen it once since Ukraine, watching it from a mountaintop in Nepal, with the mountain men who took us in. It lumbered over the horizon, its miles-tall spines visible for a full day.

For years we dodged its path and the natural disasters created by its passing, pushing us further east, and then south, and then north again. Our lives became nomadic. The longest we stayed in one place was for a year, recovering after nearly starving to death. I'm not even sure where in the world that was—somewhere in southern Asia—but the tropical jungle provided enough food for the three of us. Until it dried up. All of it. Starvation nearly claimed us again as we headed back west for the first time, stopping our travels long enough to recover from them.

Sometimes we found ourselves uprooted by the Machine's chaotic influence on the world, sometimes by lingering humanity, many of whom didn't want to share their now precious resources. But we three, bolstered by each other, never descended into the animal-like life we saw in others. I came close, the first time I killed a man. It nearly broke me, but I did it to save Mayer's life. And it wasn't the last time. The world had turned violent, and the three of us, lacking a tribe, were always in danger.

It was many years before we got the chance to head west again, and our journey to the coast was two steps forward, one step back. Sometimes ten steps back. But we pressed on, mainly for me. My family has never been far from my mind, and every step in the wrong direction felt like torture. But traveling isn't what it used to be. You can't just pick a direction and strike out. For a time, we thought heading east to the northern Pacific was the answer. We could have crossed to Alaska in summer and worked our way southeast toward home. But a drought forced us west again, to Africa.

"Abraham," Graham says again. "Do you see that?"

He's sitting behind the wheel of the outdoor helm station. He doesn't sound concerned, but it takes a lot to ruffle his feathers these days. Mine, too.

I'm seated below in the cockpit, which sounds official, but it's really a nice back deck with a dining table and navy blue-cushioned lounge benches. Over the past fifteen years, we have struggled to survive, pushing through the Machine's—and humanity's—worst offerings. We are perpetual refugees, without homes, countries or families, in search of a way back to the United States, more curious about its fate than hopeful about what we'll find.

After cutting across northern Africa, which is still primarily barren desert, the Leopard 48 dual-hull catamaran is a luxurious change of living situations. It took months to prepare for our cross Atlantic journey, but we have managed to enjoy the trip—when not fighting for our lives. The galley, stocked with fruit, game and fish, has a working propane stove for cooking. There are multiple quarters with actual beds, and soft blankets. The polished white interior and stylish accents are almost futuristic, making it easy to pretend that the rest of the world hasn't reverted back to a primitive, pre-civilized state. And when the winds die down, or there's a tsunami to overcome, the propane powered engines provide all the kick we need to continue forward.

It's what we do now. We push onward, no matter what lies ahead.

We live.

We explore.

And occasionally, we hope.

I climb up into the small helm station, standing beside Graham, who has one hand still on the wooden wheel. His long dreadlocks that I have deemed his 'Marley do' wiggle in the wind, but they're too heavy to really blow. My salt-and-pepper hair is still cut, but sloppy, with a knife. Completing my bedraggled look is a bushy beard that matches my hair, and a pair of sunglasses straight out of the 1980s, with neon green temples.

He points again, and I see it right away. There's a distortion in the ocean ahead, almost invisible, but imperfect enough to see. We've come across more than our fair share of deep sea trouble, including large and hungry Machine spawn that have no fear of mankind. I called them Scion, short for *Scion Divergentibus*, the quasi-Latin name I created for their phylum, which basically means 'Divergent Descendants.' On the surface, they're completely different from the animals that populated the Earth before the Sixth Great Mass Extinction was kicked into overdrive and the world was reset. But I've come to believe they're not completely different from us, primarily in that we can trace our origins back to the same source: the Apocalypse Machine.

There is one thing every single mass extinction has in common— nature out of balance. Starting with the first mass extinction, triggered by a worldwide bloom of photosynthetic, oxygen-pumping micro-plants. This time it was humanity who had kicked things off. I don't think it was our pollution, global warming or the rape of the natural world that triggered the Machine's rise. It certainly wasn't Kiljan's toe. I think it was the combination of humanity's effect on the planet. We reached a tipping point. Scorch the Earth and start anew, or let the world die. Those were the options we created. Had we known about the Machine's existence, I'd like to think humanity would have made different choices. But I'm not sure it would have mattered. We saw the writing on the wall. We knew where our destructive lifestyle was leading the planet. But we continued forward, comfortable with our blinders on—until they were torn away and most everyone died.

As with all mass extinctions, not every living creature on Earth was killed. The heartiest living things, like sharks, thrive through the ages, weathering mass extinctions the way New Englanders used to do harsh winters. Others adapt and evolve. And still others rose from the seeds strewn by the Machine itself. Once upon a time, humanity was the result of such a mass seeding—Scion themselves, who evolved over the ages into human beings. But like so many species in Earth's past, we triggered our own demise at the hands of the Machine.

I wish I could say that I came up with all of this on my own, but I've been plagued by dreams inspired by my two fifteen year old visions. As things have played out, I've become even more convinced that physical contact with the Machine generated some kind of communication, or transfer of knowledge. But I'm also convinced that they were both flukes. There was no real wisdom imparted to me for the benefit of mankind—now on the brink of extinction—or for my own. The Machine has nearly killed me on multiple occasions.

Nearly, my subconscious says, and I squelch the thought. Death looms. In the air, on land and at sea. If the Machine doesn't crush me underfoot, or drown me in a wave, the Scion will eventually consume me. Part of me misses the good ol' days, when it was just the Machine and people trying to kill us. The rise of Scionic life forced us to re-learn how to survive. We had to evolve from nomads to predators on the prowl, always ready to fight, always ready to eat when something was killed, because no one knew when the next meal might try to eat us.

And they would have already if not for Graham, whose job when we first met all those years ago, was to protect me. Funny how so much has changed, except for his job description, which is no longer carried out because of a sense of duty, but because of friendship. We're no longer Science Guy and Supernatural, though we continue to fill those roles, and I think it's part of why we're still alive. Without Graham, I would have died a thousand times over. He has saved me from floods, starvation, poisoned air, human marauders and the Machine's spawn. But I've also saved him, finding shelter, water, food and other resources in places he would never think to look.

I raise a pair of binoculars to my eyes, scanning back and forth until I see the strange shape in the water ahead. I flinch back, surprised. "It's a boat!"

"Describe it," Graham says, still sounding calm.

Recovering from my initial shock, I place the binoculars to my eyes again. "I see two sails. White. Two hulls, like *Hope*. And...there! A man. He's looking at us." I raise my hand to wave at exactly the same time as the man in the approaching vessel does. My hand stops mid-wave. My counterpart stops as well.

A reflection.

Feeling foolish, I lower my hand and search the area. Several large rectangles reflect the ocean ahead of us. I turn my view higher and stop when I recognize the shape above the reflective rectangles, which I now know are windows. The tower at its top has fallen over, but there is still enough of its unique shape for me to identify it.

"It's a building," I say. "One World Trade Center."

Graham smiles, but it feels off. Not only are we seeing what remains of one of the world's greatest cities, we're looking at a symbol of perseverance in the face of vast loss, now sunken beneath the waves. And the city really must have sunk. The sea levels have risen a lot, but One World Trade Center stood 1792 feet tall. For us to be seeing just the top, the island had to sink. It's not surprising, really. Just another terraforming project for the Machine. And while the events of 9-11 seem small in the face of the apocalypse, the symbolism strikes home.

"Abandon all hope," I say. "Ye who enter here."

Graham chuckles at me and shakes his head. We've had a long time to come to grips with the world's end. He's moved on. Accepted his role in the New World. I still need closure...which is part of the reason we're here.

"We're bringing hope to America," he says, patting the steering wheel. "Remember?"

He's quoting my own words back to me, when I sold him on the idea of sailing across the Atlantic to South America and following the remade coastline north. It didn't work out quite that way. We ended up heading northwest across the ocean, taking the longest, most dangerous possible route across the open sea, traveling from what little remains of Sierra Leone to the submerged New York City.

He slaps his hand on the galley roof. "Liz! Get up here!"

The sliding door below us, which leads to the galley, lounge and below deck cabins, swishes open. Aliza Mayer, dressed in cargo shorts and a black bikini top, steps onto the back deck. She looks the part of vacationing Yacht owner, but is actually the most deadly person I've ever met. As many times as Graham has saved me from certain doom, she has saved us both. She's been with us since we narrowly escaped the tsunami that swallowed Israel. After some time in Nepal, fleeing the drought, we returned to Israel, finding no human life, and the Mediterranean expanded into the Sea of Galilee. There was nothing left for her there, and the Scion who inhabited that part of the world were very large and very dangerous. Their size and energy was supported by an excess of oxygen in the atmosphere, which was a nice change after the season of poisonous air. We first survived that by wearing gas masks, and then by living deep underground, where the air was still clean. That was before we entered Africa, which required using a much smaller boat to cross the two mile stretch of water now bridging the Mediterranean and Red Sea.

"Coming up," Mayer says, stepping up into the cramped helm station. She takes the binoculars from my hand without asking, her explosive hair tickling my face, getting in my eyes and mouth. I press her hair down, and make spitting noises. We're comfortable with each other. We've survived by not worrying about personal space. So she doesn't comment or care when I pull her hair back and tie it off. She just looks through the binoculars for a moment before lowering them. "We made it?"

"Welcome to New York City." I sweep my hand out to the distant sunken skyscraper. "Home of absolutely nothing."

"Not exactly," Graham says.

We both turn toward him, waiting for an explanation, but already suspecting. Graham has a habit of delivering bad news with unnatural calm.

"I saw water spouts," he says. "Beyond the building. They're what made me notice it in the first place."

"Whales?" I ask. As far as we know, the ocean's largest living residents—ever—still live. We haven't seen any during our voyage, but whales tend to stay near coastlines, where deep water wells up to the surface, bringing nutrients and plankton into warmer waters.

"No idea," Graham confesses. "And no desire to find out."

"Agreed," Mayer says. "Something that large..."

She doesn't need to finish. We've faced a handful of Scion, ranging in size from ten to twenty feet. There was also a school of mutated hammerhead sharks. Hundreds of them, but with two hammer-shaped protuberances, and four eyes. While the sharks paid us no attention, the more aggressive Scion had to be fought off.

Whale-sized Scion...that is a horrible thought.

"Just get us to shore," I say. "Then I'll lead the way." Assuming the landscape is at all familiar.

My stomach twists with thoughts of home. By car, it would be an hour drive from the city. On foot, it will take a few days, give or take, depending on what life on shore is like. I'm terrified by what I'll find. I don't know if my family had returned home by the time Greenland's ice sheet slid into the ocean. I don't know if they survived the resulting wave, the rise in sea level from a surprising rise in global temperature, the poisoned air or the Scion repopulating the planet. I have no knowledge about this part of the world. All I really know is that everywhere we go, we find death. And if that's what's waiting for me at home, if there is a home to find, then at least I will be able to find some kind of closure.

That's not going to happen, I think, as though determining it will make it real. "Grains of sand," I whisper.

"What was that?" Mayer asks. Her hand is interlocked with Graham's. While there are no religions or governments to confirm their union, the pair married five years ago. We held the ceremony in a tent, using rings scavenged from the dead. When I brought up the lack of paperwork, Mayer rolled her eyes and said their union was real in the eyes of God, and that was all that mattered, to which I rolled my eyes.

I don't speak of, or to, God. I haven't since the very Holy Land that He had promised to Mayer's ancestors was washed away.

"Remembering a lie someone told me once." Before she can ask me to elaborate, an explosive spray of water and air bursts from the back of a large creature, curving up through the water's surface, headed straight for us. Something the size of a whale poses a serious threat, but if our ancestors found ways to slay creatures that big, so can we. When two more humps join the first, I realize the name of our catamaran is the punchline to a joke. In a world like this, hope will get you killed just as quickly as facing down a pod of sea monsters.

31

I'm the last to reach the bow. No matter how strong I become, Graham and Mayer remain a few steps ahead of me. They had a head start, from their various military trainings, but also from the genetics passed down by their parents. Keen eyesight, fast-twitch muscles for strength and speed and teeth that can saw through rope and never need care. They've had to pull three of my teeth. While I might be the last to arrive, at least now I can keep up.

I catch the long speargun Graham tosses me, and then I step to the rail. We tie lines to the spears when using them to fish, but not this time. The three brown humps rolling through the water maintain their collision course. I can't really make out any details, but they're large...large enough that the spears will be little more than a deterrent. Even the largest predators will flee if they've been injured. No meal is worth dying for. Of course, those were the rules in the Old World. We've encountered Scion in the past that haven't quite mastered that survival rule. And with creatures as large as these, it might never become a rule.

"I'll take the left," Mayer says, loading her spear and stretching the black rubber bands down into place, using all six to ensure maximum power. It would also create one hell of a kickback. The weapons are designed to be used underwater, where the fluid around the speargun absorbs much of the reverse force generated by all those rubber bands snapping free. But with practice, and a high tolerance for pain, they can be used effectively from the boat deck. And they're far more effective than conventional firearms, since bullets tend to fracture upon striking the water, and they lose their deadly energy just a few feet deep. Even at point blank range, the spears are going to penetrate deeper, and thanks to the sharp barbs at the tips, they'll do more damage.

"I'll get the right." I pluck a spear from the open case on the lounge bench and load it into the gun. Propping the gun handle on the bench, I use both hands to pull down the six black rubber bands, one-by-one, until they're all locked in place, their deadly force held back by a small trigger. I lift the long weapon and lower the end of it toward the creature on the right.

Graham takes aim beside me, and we wait. Without having to discuss the plan, I know it. We'll fire as one, and if we're lucky, the three injured animals will panic in unison and flee without confrontation. That's the best case scenario. And if it doesn't work, Graham will handle strategy, Mayer will lead the assault and I'll use my noggin to find a weakness. We know our roles, and we don't question or doubt them. It's how we survive.

"On the next rise," Graham says, his voice a whisper.

The three creatures slide beneath the waves, leaving footprints behind them. Tracing the footprints back through the water, I can see that they're rising and falling every fifty feet. The next rise will bring them within sixty feet of *Hope*. It's a long shot, but allowing them to dive once more would allow them to come up right beneath us.

I adjust my aim to where I think my target will rise. My index finger slides over the trigger.

The ocean swells.

The creatures break the surface.

Sunlight gleams off of gray-blue skin.

The long bodies bend, arching back into the water.

My finger tightens on the trigger. But doesn't pull. Why can't I fire?

"Stop," I whisper.

Graham and Mayer obey without question. They don't ask for an explanation, either, but I owe them one. "They're not Scion."

"What are they?" Mayer asks, her eyes still on the water, muscles tight and ready.

The distinctive dorsal fin, seen for just a moment, brought back nearly forgotten memories of a family trip. "American Princess."

Graham's focus wavers as he glances in my direction. "Excuse me?"

"The name of the ship." I raise my speargun, keeping the tip pointed up and away from us. "We went as a family. The five of us. The boys were both five." I horde the details, precious gems, just for me.

"Abe." Graham's serious tone pulls me out of the painful memory. "What are they?"

The ocean beneath us glows as sunlight reflects off of white skin, the underbelly of a creature whose twenty-foot long, rough-edged flippers appear angelic. "Humpback whales. They eat plankton. Not people. Or boats."

The fifty-foot-long whales perform an underwater ballet, swimming around the catamaran, rising and falling, offering up their light-reflecting undersides like submissive dogs, an Old World greeting that says 'we mean you no harm.' And I believe them. After a few minutes, even Graham and Mayer have abandoned their weapons. We watch the display in silence. Mayer sheds the first tear. I'm not far behind her.

When the dance slows and the whales rise to the surface, their big black eyes just staring back at us, I move to the stern dive deck. One of the whales meets me there, raising its barnacle encrusted head. I see my reflection in its eye and reach out my hand. The boat bobs on a wave, and when it settles again, my hand comes in contact with the cool, solid skin of one of the world's most majestic creatures. "You're still alive."

The whale lets out a resounding call, the sound audible above water and reverberating for hundreds of miles underwater. Then it sinks away, leaving me to fall back against the hull, choked up.

"I think they were happy to see us," Graham says, his smiling face above me, looking out at the sea with a newfound wonder.

"The world is as different and frightening for them as it is for us," I say. We might have hunted them near to extinction once, but with the arrival of the Scion, we're almost kin now. Our encounter might be as meaningful to them as it is to us.

I shout a "whoohoo!" as one of the humpbacks rises up next to the ship, breaching forty feet of its massive body out of the water, before toppling down again. Water explodes away from its girth, leaving me laughing and spitting salt from my mouth. I'm drenched in salt water, which will dry crusty and itchy, but this is the best day of my life in fifteen years. Graham and Mayer stand above me, soaked and smiling. Graham has his arm around her.

This...this right here, is why we're alive.

I'm not talking about the three of us as survivors, I'm talking about humanity as a species. Only we have the kind of minds capable of fully appreciating a moment like this. There's no evolutionary benefit to regarding beauty, in art, music or nature. It's just part of what makes us unique. Of all the Machine's creations, we had to have been its finest. Until we nearly destroyed it all.

Another whale call freshens my smile. But there was something different about it. The tone. It wasn't the long droning call of a satisfied humpback. It was sharp, and short.

Worried.

Afraid.

I stand to my feet and turn to warn the others, but they've already separated. Graham scans the ocean, binoculars to his eyes. Mayer runs for the forward deck where we left the spear guns.

A swirl of light blue pulls my attention back to the water. The whales are there for just a moment, their flukes pounding hard. Soon, all I can see are their bright white flippers, sliding away into the abyss, where they can stay for fifteen minutes before needing to surface for another breath. Our friends have fled.

But from what?

I climb back onto the deck beside Graham. "See anything?"

He scans from left to right, looking out at the Atlantic, then snaps to a stop. He focuses the lenses and then very calmly says, "Secure the sails."

The Leopard 48 has two large sails. In strong winds, we've hit 15 knots. On a day like today, we're cruising at a comfortable 8 knots, which is basically nine miles per hour, or about my average jogging speed. That Graham wants to lower the sails means he's about to start the engine and hit our 'under power' top speed of 20 knots. The motor hanging off the back of the boat isn't the original. We pilfered it from a speed boat. Using Graham's mechanical know-how and my scientific—what Mayer calls 'crackpot'—ideas, we blew up one motor and converted the second into a propane-powered work horse. I draw down the sails, pulling them in tight so they can't create drag.

The motor roars to life, filling the silent ocean with the long forgotten sound of human technology.

Mayer returns to the back, wielding two loaded spearguns. She puts both down on the padded lounge bench and ducks back into the galley, headed for the forward deck.

"Keep an eye," Graham hands the binoculars down from the helm station.

I move to the back deck, gripping the chrome crossbeam above my head, and I place the lens to my eyes. "What am I looking for?"

"Not sure," he says. "But it's the only thing out there. And it's big."

The motor growls. The blades spin and bite into the ocean. Graham shoves the throttle forward and stands, as the dual hulls tilt upward.

I cling to the bar as my body leans out over the churning water. My view is shaky, swaying back and forth. I steady myself from the bouncing as we cut through waves. Even with all of that, I see it.

At first, it's a swell in the ocean, water sliding over something large. But then several long spines, like exaggerated dorsal fins, cut through the surface, each one ten feet tall.

Are they killer whales? I wonder, trying to keep the binoculars steady. Orcas do prey on larger whales, attacking as a pack, especially if there are calves present. That would explain the humpbacks' hasty retreat. But the long black dorsal fins approaching us from behind are nearly twice the size of the largest killer whales. And they're moving in perfect symmetry, undulating up and down in two single file lines. It's a single, very *not-whale* creature. A Scion. Enemy of human and humpback alike.

I nearly fall over backward when the thing lunges out of the water, turning its massive head and bulbous eye toward us, sneaking a peek.

As it splashes back down into the ocean, I stagger back to the lounge bench to grab a speargun.

Mayer returns at the same moment carrying the third speargun and extra spears. She nearly drops them when she sees the Scion plunging back into the sea. "Holy shit."

"Graham," I say, trying to mimic the calm he's perfected over the years. "Any chance you can go any faster?"

"We're pegged," he shouts over the wind blowing through his dreadlocks. "But I see the shore on the horizon. You're going to have to hold it off."

A quick calculation using our rough speed and the approximate four miles to the horizon from Graham's elevation gives us about 10 minutes to fight and survive, or die trying. It's the best we can do, and it's gotten us this far, but I'll be damned before I die now, with home and its potential horrors, so close. Speargun in hand, I walk to the back rail, and like Jonah or Ahab, I wait for my sea monster to arrive.

32

EDWARDS

The world had gone to shit, but the five men stationed at Outpost Hood had it made. The once frigid summit of Mount Hood, covered in snow year round, now rarely dipped below fifty degrees. At lower elevations, including the Timberline Lodge, where the five men bunked, the average temperature hovered around eighty. The lodge had been a hotel and ski resort before the aberration leveled the planet, and while there were no chefs, maids or hosts to attend them, they still had access to the many beds, kitchen, fireplaces, pool tables and a wine cellar. The brass knew about the cushy accommodations. They didn't know about the wine.

Despite having access to alcohol, and a lot of it, the men understood the importance of their mission, and they never drank within five hours of their shift. While four men recuperated in the Timberline, the fifth manned the lookout tower constructed atop Mount Hood's peak. The hundred-foot-tall tower, topped with a solar powered communications array, combined with the mountain's 11,249 feet, allowed the lookouts to see 130 miles in all directions. On a clear day, they could see the Pacific Ocean as a streak of blue outlining the horizon.

And since their target was taller than the mountain upon which they eked out a living, Corporal Bryan Edwards estimated that its spines had risen into view when it was still 250 miles away. If it was in a hurry, it could close that distance in less than an hour, but it hadn't been seen moving anywhere fast in the last ten years.

They'd been watching the aberration's meandering approach for two days. The beast seemed content to languish in the water. But Outpost Hood's five-man team remained on high alert, camping out at the tower's base, observing every movement and reporting every detail back to Command, which was currently located in the Raven Rock Mountain Complex—a nuclear bunker buried beneath Blue Ridge Summit in Pennsylvania. Before the aberration's rise, it was often referred to as an 'underground Pentagon.' Now it was the last vestige of the United States government and military command, perhaps the very last organized resistance to the creature left on the planet.

From what Edwards understood, humanity, including most of the U.S. population, had been reduced to tribal living. People had to compete with 'Fuck-Jobs'—*Fobs* for short—Outpost Hood's name for the smaller, funky looking monsters that had sprung to life in the wake of the giant's passing, and had since inhabited every corner of the Earth.

After the days of mass destruction, when the aberration followed a path of devastation, setting off every natural disaster already poised to happen and leveling every single nuclear reactor—not to mention the large number of nuclear warheads that had been launched at it— survivors primarily had to fear the Fobs. While there were docile species, roaming in great packs, migrating across the terrain like they weren't planetary squatters, the predatory Fobs were savage things. Large, hungry, savage and unpredictable.

Outpost Hood routinely fought off individual hunters roaming the mountains for food. Solo predators weren't the biggest threat. It was the pack hunters that really concerned them, moving in numbers ranging from fifteen to fifty.

Fob packs were responsible for wiping out many of the larger North American tribes that had refused government support, which included soldiers and weaponry. The only real defenses against predatory Fob packs were training and a lot of bullets—two things the men of Outpost Hood had in excess.

The oldest of them, a Master Sergeant, was just twenty-three. He was about ten years too young for the rank in the Old World, but with few men to choose from, the smartest and most capable of them rose through the ranks quickly. The Master Sergeant could fight, like a soldier, or like an animal if need be. They'd faced three assaults by Fob packs, losing only one man in the past five years. But this was the first time they'd spotted the aberration in all that time.

There were outposts scattered around North and Central America, reporting on Fob movements and populations, but their main task was creating a network of warning stations. Communication with advanced satellites had been lost a long time ago, and most information was now shared via radio, or in person. The most important outposts at key locations, were manned by military trained teams. Some were operated by cooperative tribes. But the vast majority of them were under the oversight of solo operators, most of whom were civilians who had 'gone native.' The men used to joke about people like that—Fob-Crazies—until they learned the Master Sergeant's step-mother was one of them.

Edwards yawned. He would have never guessed that watching a planet-conquering monster would be boring, but the thing hadn't even made landfall yet. He peered through the telescope aimed out the long window, one of four that provided a 360 degree view. He could see the creature's face. Its armored, black carapace burned hot from the inside out. Long tubes dangled and twisted, luminous with energy or bioluminescence. After fifteen years, no one knew for certain. Fluid drained from the tubes, sometimes spraying, sometimes oozing.

"C'mon, you big bitch," Edwards grumbled. "Do something."

And then it did.

Edwards gasped and stood from his chair, but he kept his eye glued to the eyepiece.

"Uh..." He knew he should call the others, that they would need to report this, but astonishment stole the words from his mind. He'd heard about this, but had never seen it. Few people living ever had. Most people who got close to the aberration died. He'd only heard of one man ever touching it, but he was pretty sure that guy was 1) dead, and 2) a legend.

The big plates lining the aberration's back lifted up, giving it the look of something about to spread its wings and fly off. But when the city-sized shell panels dropped back down, a lake's worth of chunky mush squeezed out and fell to the ocean. From this distance, and because of the creature's great size, everything looked to be happening in slow motion, but the globs of mush—eggs if the stories were to be believed—had miles to fall before reaching the water. The plates pulsed up and down, shedding more material in the Pacific. In a few years, all that stuff would grow and evolve, becoming new lifeforms. *New Fobs for us to kill*, Edwards thought, and then he remembered his job.

"It's shedding!" he shouted, and then he banged on the tower's solid metal floor with the aluminum baseball bat they kept at the tower for hitting rocks, not for self-defense. "Get up here!"

Edwards knew he was forgetting all kinds of protocols, and how things like this were supposed to be communicated, but he was just twenty. No one—at least no one in Outpost Hood—would blame him for acting his age, and he could feel the others scaling the ladder beneath him. The message had been received.

The hatch behind him squeaked open. He glanced back as Wittman climbed into the tower first. He looked more excited than afraid. At just sixteen years old, he was the youngest of them. Wittman hadn't been with them during the last Fob assault, and he had no memories of the world before all this. Edwards didn't remember much, but there were flashes of things he loved, including his parents, his dog and SpongeBob SquarePants. "Let me see!"

Edwards stepped aside, letting the lanky kid bend over the telescope for a look. Despite being the youngest, he was also the tallest of them, and the most childlike, sporting a mop of blond hair and vibrant blue eyes. The kid didn't mind the end of the world, because he didn't know anything else. He was...content.

"Ho-lee-shit." He was more than content. "Badass."

"Hardly." The Master Sergeant's silent approach and sudden arrival made both men leap. Edwards had heard the man referred to as 'Sergeant

Ninja' before. At first, Edwards had assumed it was a quasi-racist term stemming from the Sergeant's Asian heritage, but the man was half-Korean, not Japanese, and Edwards had learned over time that the nickname had been earned. The Sergeant was a stealthy man. Light on his feet. And though he was an inch shorter than Wittman, he was built like an athlete, or rather, like what he was—an Army Ranger. One of the few left. All of the most important outposts were led by Rangers.

The two young soldiers stepped aside for their slightly older, but far more authoritative comrade, letting him look through the telescope. The Sergeant looked up from the lens a moment later and turned to Edwards. "You're on watch. Call it in."

Edwards nodded and moved to the radio station on the far side of the lookout tower. He sat down at the desk and powered up the radio.

Behind him, Felder and Gutshall ascended through the hatch, looking bleary-eyed. Despite it being three in the afternoon, the two men had been sleeping in preparation for their night shift. Without talking, they each took a peek through the telescope, shaking their heads and muttering curses.

"Can I go back to sleep?" Felder muttered, rubbing his fingers through his greasy black hair.

"Can you take a shower?" Gutshall replied, though he wasn't much cleaner.

The pair chuckled. Two weeks of night shift could leave you with a looser sense of humor.

"Uhh," Wittman said. "I don't think you're going to get to do either."

Before he could explain why, the Master Sergeant nudged him out of the way and looked through the lens again. He spoke without taking his eye away from the telescope. "Edwards."

Edwards sat up straight. The Sergeant's tone had shifted toward ominous. "Sir."

"Inform command that the aberration has shed into the Pacific Ocean off the Oregon coast, and it is now moving inland."

"Yes, sir. How...how fast is it moving?"

The silence that followed the question filled Edwards with a new kind of nervous. It felt like his organs were moving around, like some invisible specter had reached inside his guts and shifted them about.

"ETA, thirty minutes."

"Thirty minutes?" Felder said, nearly shouting. "Is it coming for Hood?"

Part of what made Mount Hood such a strategic location for an Outpost was that it provided staggering views in all directions. But as one of the region's still active volcanoes, it was also a potential target. And yet, there were bigger targets in the geographic neighborhood. Just under six hundred miles away to the east was Yellowstone National Park, one of the world's largest natural disasters waiting to happen, still untouched. The park sat atop a super volcano capable of expelling 240 cubic miles of magma. Its ash cloud would consume the northern hemisphere, and whether or not the warmer Earth would freeze without sunlight, most life of the non-Fob variety would perish.

The codename for the potential disaster was GONE—Game Over Now, Earthlings—coined by a post-apocalyptic science-fiction author turned science advisor. They all knew the term. They'd heard about it growing up. And as members of Outpost Hood, it was their job to report the possibility of such an event, should the aberration appear in this part of the world.

After a few more minutes, the Sergeant—a God-fearing man—let out an uncharacteristic curse, "Shit." He stood and looked ready to punch something, clenching his fists. The men near him stepped back.

Edwards sat still, finger hovering over the transmit button. Things had been changing so fast, he had yet to send a single message. "Sir? What message should I send?"

"I'll do it," the Sergeant said, taking the mic from Edwards's hand. The relieved Corporal retreated from the chair and moved to the telescope that the others had abandoned. He looked through the lens and flinched when he saw the aberration moving. It had reached the shore and struck out across Oregon. Its eight massive legs carried it miles with each step. The towering spikes on its back, rising at an angle, cut through the air, slicing through clouds. Its long tail swept back and forth, countering each step and maintaining perfect balance. He watched its broad feet strike the Earth, spreading wide, dispersing weight and reducing the impact it had on the land. The creature weighed untold tons, but with two pairs of legs always in contact with the ground, its girth never pushed down on a single location—unless it intended to. The thing had flattened mountains by stomping on them. The black armor, glowing red-orange from the inside, gave it the look of a mountain-sized demon.

There are monsters like this in the Bible, Edwards thought, and then he made a mental note to ask the Sergeant. He'd know.

There was a part of him that felt relieved the aberration wasn't heading for Mount Hood. He liked it here. And it was possible that the ash cloud rising from Yellowstone might never reach them. Despite being just six hundred miles away, the ash would be carried east, and then around the globe. If they were lucky, and the Pacific wind currents pulled the ash south, this part of the world might remain an oasis. But that wouldn't help their friends on the East Coast, nor would it help humanity's struggle against extinction.

He moved the telescope down, following the creature's limbs to the ground, overshooting the feet and peering into some distant, but much closer, forest. He saw motion. "The hell?"

Edwards focused the lens.

The motion was still hard to see. At first it looked like a flood, like the land itself was moving through the trees. But then he understood what he was seeing: Fobs.

And not just a pack of them.

A herd.

An *army.*

He couldn't tell if they were leading the aberration's charge, or just trying to steer clear of its path, but what he could determine with ease, was where they were headed. He stood up straight and turned to address the Sergeant, who had just started speaking.

"This is Master Sergeant Ike Wright, at Outpost Hood, calling Raven Rock. Do you read, over?"

"Sir," Edwards said, the word a hissed whisper.

Ike held up an index finger.

"This is Raven Rock. Good to hear you, Ike."

Ike flinched, and grinned. "Katelin?"

Edwards had never seen the Master Sergeant disarmed, but the feminine voice on the other end managed it in just a few words. She must have meant something to him.

"They put me on the radio a week ago. Can you believe it? Hey, is this a private call?"

Ike straightened up and glanced at the men. "We're on the *radio*, Katelin. And all communications are recorded...Kate. And I'm afraid this isn't a routine check in, so let's catch up later. Over."

"Understood," Katelin said. "Your report, sir? Over."

"At approximately 1500 hours, the aberration arrived at the Oregon coast. It was observed shedding and has now made landfall. It is currently headed east toward Yellowstone National Park. We are looking at a potential GONE situation. I repeat, GONE may be imminent. ETA at current speed, under four hours. Over."

"Holy shit," Katelin said. "Um, copy. I have protocols to follow now. Maintain position until someone contacts you. Over. Again."

"I know what to do, Kate. Take it easy. Just relay the information. Okay? Over."

"I'm on it. And Ike, love you. Be careful. Over."

Sergeant Major Ike Wright glanced at his men, his eyes conveying a threat should this moment ever be repeated. Then he toggled the mic, and said, "I will. Love you, too. Over and out."

Edwards raised his hand, an instinct instilled during years of subterranean schooling at Raven Rock. "Uh, sir. We might not be able to wait very long."

Ike squinted at him, waiting for the reason.

Edwards hitched his thumb behind him, toward the endless swath of forest between them and the still-mobile aberration, its footsteps now reverberating through the mountain. "We have incoming."

33

ABRAHAM

How can something like this exist? I wonder, watching the Scion sea monster slowly gain on us.

But I know how.

Or at least, I think I do.

At first, I thought that the Machine's destruction of nuclear power plants was a well thought-out plan revealing the monster's ruthless intelligence. Covering the world with ash, ocean water and radiation was a good way to wipe out every living thing. But that's not exactly what happened. Mankind, and much of the animal kingdom we had been slowly pushing toward extinction, were killed, but not by radiation. Not in the long term, anyway. Those in the direct path of radioactive clouds died horribly, but those of us who avoided lethal exposure were spared the longer, slower death of a poisoned environment. Something had *absorbed* the radiation, cleaning the air, land and water.

That left two possibilities: the Apocalypse Machine or the Scion. I suspect it's both, the former using all that energy as fuel, the latter using it to kick start mutations and rapid evolution. Previous mass extinctions might have taken thousands of years to complete, wiping out one ecosystem and seeding the next. Thanks to the nuclear age, we super-charged the process, expediting our own demise and fertilizing our replacements' growth.

That's the theory anyway. None of my mental projections have come to fruition. Not only is the world not radioactive, it's also not in the grips of a renewed ice age. New York is the farthest north I've been in fifteen years, and the weather is tropical. While I'm sure the Arctic Circle is still choked by atmospheric ash, sea levels suggest that both ice caps have melted. That means that the North Pole is not frozen. In fact, it's probably warm. New ocean and wind currents circulating warmth from the southern hemisphere could make that happen, a result of higher concentrations of greenhouse gases. From volcanoes. From new life. From the destruction of mankind. The planet has become a veritable greenhouse, with more oxygen in the atmosphere than at any time in human history—but not high enough to be toxic.

And all of that, the oxygen, the radioactivity, the warmer and wetter climates, has given rise to Scion, like the one behind us.

Its two lines of eight dorsal fins are the most normal thing about it. Two bulbous eyes are mounted atop its broad, flat, head. While its skin is dark, like an Orca's, the eyes look more like two translucent peeled oranges, crisscrossed with white veins and filled with liquid. The strange sacks seem to be a feature that unite most of the Scion, though it's entirely possible that some have evolved without them. The twin orbs bobble about with each vertical thrust of the creature's wide, shelled tail. Although parts of it are whale-like, some features smack of shellfish—lobster or shrimp. But it's the jaws at the front of the long, undulating sea worm-like body that hold my attention. With each surge through the water, twin pairs of mandibles spring open to reveal what looks like a wide, smiling mouth—full of teeth that look human. Bobbit worm on the outside, Cheshire Cat on the inside. Topped with those large, bobbing eyes, the thing looks maniacal. At the very least, the way it's pursuing us, lunging up and down like sea serpents are supposed to, suggests that its ravenous.

"Halfway there," Graham calls down to us.

Judging by the rate the Scion is closing in, it's going to reach us a good minute before we plow into the shoreline.

"We're going to need the go-packs on the forward deck," Graham says. His view from the helm is higher than the ceiling above Mayer and me. That means he has a clear view of the monster. And that he's the least protected of us. Leaving the aft deck will give him one less protector, but without the go-packs, we might not last long on land.

If we make it that far.

"I'm on it," I say, wedging my speargun down between the back rail and a support beam. If Mayer needs to take two quick shots, she can use my weapon. She's a better shot than me anyway, but reloading will take her a long time without my help.

I nearly crash through the sliding door leading to the galley, but manage to recover and shove the door open. I descend the staircase into the port hull, turning into the aft cabin, which has been converted into a storage area. I sleep in the forward port cabin, while Graham and Mayer have the starboard side to themselves. Technically, the boat is always 'a-rockin,' but I don't need to know why. Being alone for fifteen years has been hard enough. I don't need to know when they're enjoying the pleasures of marriage.

The three go-packs are at the foot of the unused bed. Each one contains food, clothing, survival gear and ammunition. Attached to the outside of each pack are sound-suppressed firearms—noise attracts hungry attention—and blades. Each pack weighs in at eighty pounds, with half the weight being dedicated to weaponry.

I pick up one of the packs and nearly topple over backward when the ship surges over a wave and crashes back down. I'd hoped to do this in two trips, but it's better to do three and not break a leg in the process. Taking one pack at a time, I bounce my way up to the forward deck and back down, three times, making each trip in about forty seconds.

The third pack lands with a thud at my feet. My muscles burn for just a moment, but quickly recover. I'm not the out-of-shape science-nerd I used to be. I'm not even breathing hard, but that has more to do with the higher concentrations of oxygen in the atmosphere.

I look up from the go-pack and flinch at what lies ahead.

It's the coast, but it doesn't look like the northeast American coastline I remember. Granted, the entire coast has been redefined by a massive

rise in sea level caused by melting ice and the rise of Antarctica, once
freed from said ice—another pet theory, but the swath of green earth,
polka-dotted with splotches of red is not something I could have predicted, or even imagined.

What the hell is that?

The strange terrain stretches along the coast for as far as I can see
in either direction, rising up out of the ocean and coating the land for a
few hundred yards inland, where a mix of old ruined homes and new
tree growth form a border. Despite the strangeness of the land, it's the
ruined homes that surprise me most. While New York City's skyscrapers
were designed to withstand a beating, especially One World Trade
Center, I didn't expect to see homes here. My last view of the wave,
propelled by Greenland's freed ice and cascading over continents,
showed it moving steadily south.

It must have lost its destructive energy moving over all that land, I think.
Or maybe the flow was diverted by New Hampshire's White Mountain
range. I'm sure some of that water reached the area, scouring it clean of life,
but maybe some remnant of civilization remains intact here.

Maybe my home?

"Abraham!" Graham shouts. "We have incoming!"

Funny, how after all these years, Graham's language is still so very
military. Then again, there's never really been a time it didn't feel
appropriate. We've been at war for a long time now.

I arrive on the aft deck in time to watch the sea Scion rise up out
of the water behind us. While its spreading mandibles are blocked by
the ceiling, I get a clear view of its underside. Most sea creatures on
Earth have sleek bodies designed for sliding through the water with as
little resistance as possible, but this thing has several bulging sacks
lining the bottom of its body. They're similar to the eyes atop its head,
but I can't guess at what they're for.

Then it shows me.

The two lines of liquid-filled sacks compress. Jets of water shoot
out, spraying down into the water, propelling the creature higher and
faster. It's combining the pulsing tail motion used by whales with the
jet propulsion utilized by squid. This thing is clearly a Scion, but its

various parts reflect adaptations to sea life acquired by many different species that took millions of years to evolve.

It's borrowing, I think, *acquiring genes from its meals—squid, shrimp, lobster, whales. Is that how they're adapting so quickly? Is that why life on Earth, throughout history, has common links despite extinction events, and without many obvious transitional species in the fossil record?*

I pick up my speargun and raise it to fire, but never get the chance.

Mayer tackles me to the floor. "Down!"

On my back, I see four mandibles snap closed on the ceiling above us. The thick white plastic sheet doesn't stand a chance against the massive jaws, which must be packing an unimaginable amount of pressure. The ceiling is crushed and then yanked away, leaving us with a clear view of the blue sky overhead. As we pull away, the creature gives the plastic panel a shake and then discards it. With a spray of water from its ventral jets, the Scion continues the chase.

"Sixty seconds," Graham shouts.

Aiming at the Scion is a lot easier now that the roof is gone, so that's good, but the monster is a flurry of movement, rising and falling as it charges through the water. Hitting it at all is going to be a challenge. Hitting something it cares about is going to be impossible...unless we wait until it's nearly on top of us.

As though to prove me wrong, Mayer leans forward, braces herself and fires a spear. She's nearly flung off her feet by the force of it, but takes the impact without complaint. The spear is nearly invisible as it launches out over the water, slipping past the opening mandibles and shattering one of the Cheshire teeth.

The monster doesn't falter.

Mayer sets about loading a second spear, while I take aim and wait.

The tip of my speargun rises and falls with the Scion's motion, my gaze locked on the bulging right eye. One of the easiest ways to deter a Scion is to pop one of its eyes. It doesn't kill the creature, or even blind it— the eyes heal and inflate anew—but the pain, or sudden disorientation from the limp orb, stops most Scions in their tracks. The questions are, will my slender spear be enough, and can I hit the creature before it crashes down on top of us.

The monster disappears beneath the wave for a moment. *Going deep for a jump*, I think, and then I watch as the creature explodes out of the water right behind us, jets of water streaming from its underside, filling the air with a fishy stench. It arcs high above us, mandibles split wider than the catamaran, poised to grasp and puncture our hull.

We're out of time.

I pull the speargun's trigger with no time to brace myself against the high angle. The spear soars upward, while I'm slammed down onto the deck, the air shoved from my lungs. Coughing, I watch the spear punch into the flat space between the creature's eyes. The spear went deep, but it's either not deep enough, or too fine a wound to garner any real reaction.

The Scion descends.

The Cheshire smile parts, revealing a second and then a third, each one opening in sequence, powerful enough to reduce human and boat alike into a fine pulp.

Mayer lifts her reloaded speargun and fires, off balance. The force spins her around and casts her sprawling onto the deck's tabletop, but the spear, aimed and fired by an expert warrior, finds its target.

The eye seems to fold in on itself for a moment. Then liquid sprays from the two small holes made by the spear as it punched in one side and out the other. The small holes give way to pressure from within, tearing and letting loose a deluge of clear and red gore. The Scion coils its body as the once balloon-like eye falls limp and flat against its head.

As the creature crashes back to the sea, one of its retracting mandibles catches the starboard hull, punching through wood and fiberglass. The boat pulls away, listing slightly, but not enough to stop us. As long as we keep moving forward, physics will keep us from sinking.

Graham leaps down from the helm station. "Let's go!" I look up at the steering wheel, now held in place with a belt, the throttle still pegged all the way forward. Mayer peels herself from the table top and chases after Graham, moving to the forward deck. By the time I catch up, they've both got their go-packs on and are standing at the bow. I sling my heavy pack over one shoulder and then slide in the other, buckling it tight around my waist and chest. Feeling like I've just stepped onto the surface of a planet twice the size of Earth, its increased gravity tugging me toward the ground, I head for the bow in time to see the green shore with red polka dots rushing at us. The incline looks smooth. We might just slip up onto the smooth surface and glide to a stop.

But nothing is that easy. Not anymore.

Twenty feet from the shore, the now very angry Scion strikes again. None of us see it coming, and as the boat twists counterclockwise beneath us, I stumble backward and slam into the starboard rail. Then, pulled by the weight of my go-pack, I tumble over the side just as the ship collides with the shore. As I fall, I see Mayer and Graham leap away, landing in waist deep water. Then I plunge into the frigid ocean, and sink.

I hit the bottom on my hands and knees. There's a moment of indecision about whether or not to open my eyes. There's no way to know which direction I'm facing, so I have no choice. Salt water burns my eyes when I open them, and my view is hazy, but I can see the surface eight feet above me. The sloping shore is ahead, which is sandy until the water is shallow. I try to swim, but my pack pushes me down into the sand, sending crabs scurrying away. Then I crawl on my hands and knees. I move in slow motion, the drag from the pack slowing me down. I think about shedding it, knowing this is how a large number of soldiers perished while storming the beaches of Normandy during World War II, but I don't give up yet. We'll need the gear to survive on land. Survive now to survive later.

I'm pushed back down by a sudden blast of water. I twist around and see the warbling underside of the sea-Scion. Water jets from its underside, pushing me away. Its head slams down into the water, thrashing back and forth. I slide across the ocean floor on my stomach, lungs burning as my muscles eat up the oxygen in my veins. A scream carries away the air in my lungs, but I hardly notice as the Scion curls over my body and surges back into the deep, dragging *Hope* along with it.

Light from above draws my attention back to the surface. So close. I plant my feet in the sand, tilt my body forward and shove, one step after another. Half of my effort goes to pushing small mounds into the loose sand, but I move forward.

My body aches.

I trudge on.

Then I feel myself about to inhale.

The top of my head clears the surface, but I'm still unable to breathe. I can't even jump up for a quick breath. My hands fumble with the pack. I need to set it free.

Need to breathe!

My mouth opens.

Water rushes in, sucked down into my lungs, flooding my oxygen-deprived body with salt.

34

IKE

Master Sergeant Ike Wright watched the approaching wave of Fobs through the lens of the high powered telescope, but he knew it wouldn't be necessary soon. He didn't think the creatures knew about the five men keeping a vigil from the top of Mount Hood, but they were certainly going to pass by close enough to pick up the scent. If the Fobs had been of the more docile variety found on the plains, competing with bison that had made a comeback, he wouldn't be worried. But the creatures, racing through the forest thirty miles out, had the look of predators.

He'd never seen this sub-species of Fob before, but that wasn't unusual either. The creatures were ever evolving and migrating, searching out a niche to call home. The bulky four-limbed creatures, with their squat heads, long tusks and bulging eyes, could have come north from Central America, or south out of Canada. Hell, they could have come out of the ocean, for all he knew. It didn't really matter where they came from.

His job, right now, was to keep his men alive. And that meant making a choice. Dig in and fight, or abandon the outpost. Loyalty to his men and a dedication to the job were at odds for the first time in his military career.

We've already served our purpose, he thought. *There's nothing more we can do.*

His military training countered. *I swore to defend this outpost with my life. I knew I'd probably die here. So did my men.*

Call it in. Report the situation. Let someone else make the call.

But give the men a fighting chance.

"Edwards," Ike said. "You're on point. Back to the Lodge, double time. Prep for a fight."

The young man's voice quivered as he said, "Yes, sir."

"Felder." The four men stopped by the hatch, eyes expectant and nervous. They had seen action before. They'd fought and killed Fob packs. But not this many. No one had faced this many and survived. "Prep the chopper for evac. I want both options ready to go when I get there."

Hope sprang into the faces of all four men, and Ike prayed it was justified. He was putting their lives, all of their lives, in the hands of someone more than two thousand miles away.

He waited for all four men to start down the ladder before closing the hatch and sitting down at the radio. He raised the mic to his mouth, pausing for a moment. Katelin was on the other end. Hearing her voice after nearly a year away from Raven Rock was hard enough, but knowing she still loved him after all that time made it painful, too. Clouded his judgement.

He wondered if his thoughts of retreat stemmed from speaking to her. He couldn't discount the possibility. But he also didn't want to sacrifice the lives of his men if they'd already fulfilled their duty to the fullest. If the aberration really was headed for Yellowstone, there really wasn't a good reason to stick around.

He pushed the call button. "Raven Rock, this is Sergeant Major Ike Wright. Do you copy? Over."

"I'm here, Ike," Katelin replied. "Over."

Ike shook his head and smiled. She wasn't very good at her job, but he was glad to hear her again. "Katelin, I need you to listen, and I need you to act on your training. Forget about us. Forget about how you might feel. There are protocols to follow for a reason. Okay? Can you do that? Over."

"Y-yeah, Ike. I've been doing this for a while. But it's you, so you know, I figured I could be myself." She sounded annoyed, but that wouldn't last long. "Over."

"I need to speak to General Lorenti. ASAP. Over."

"I need a sitrep. Over. Has the aberration's trajectory or speed changed?" She was trying to sound detached and professional, but he could still hear the worry in her voice, masked slightly by annoyance. "Over."

"Please, just put him on the line. Over."

"Protocols. Over."

Ike didn't curse often, reserving what his stepmother had once called 'harsh language' for special occasions. He had never once sworn at Katelin, but he came close now. With no time to waste, he followed his own advice and obeyed the protocols, which said that any request for communication with the higher ups—who were undeniably busy trying to organize the salvation of the human race—be made along with a situation report. "Outpost Hood is in imminent danger of being overrun. We have incoming Fobs. A new species. Too many to count. ETA..." He closed his eyes, running the calculations he should have before making the call. "One hour."

It was a guess really. He didn't know exactly how far away the Fobs were, and he didn't know how fast they were moving, but they looked too close, and too fast. An hour was about how long it would take him to climb down the six thousand feet of steep trails to the Lodge, so he hoped they had at least that long.

"I need to know if we should attempt to repel the Fobs, or if we should evacuate. Timing is essential, Kate. Please pass this on, now. Over."

He took his finger off the call button, waiting for confirmation. The radio remained silent. Was she already passing the information along? Was she panicking? Had the message even gotten through? Radio wasn't always reliable.

He pushed the call button. "Kate, do you copy? Over."

He waited again. Each second of silence felt like another nail in his coffin.

"Kate!" he shouted into the mic. "Do you copy? Over."

Her reply came fast and firm. "I copy, Ike. But I'm not passing the sitrep on."

He wanted to respond. Wanted to shout at her. To beg her why. But until she let go of her transmit button, she wouldn't hear a word he said. Radios were great for communicating in a world on the brink. Not so great for lover's spats.

"You're going to listen to me, Ike. And you're going to do what I tell you, not some general who sees you as an expendable asset, and not your mother, who is even more detached from her humanity than ever."

Ike shouted and punched the radio table.

She's going to get me killed. Going to get my men killed!

"So calm the fuck down, Ike, and listen." Her language caught him off guard. Like him, she rarely used harsh language, and apparently she could also read his mind from across the country.

He sat still in the metal chair, gripping the sides, trying not to explode.

When she spoke again, her voice had changed. She sounded softer. Sad. "Ike...they wouldn't let me tell you. Your mother wouldn't let me tell you. She said you wouldn't finish the tour, if you knew. I told her that was a good reason to tell you, but like I said, she's detached. I'm not sure she sees you any differently than all the other soldiers she's sent..." She sighed, long and hard. "Look, why I'm not passing this up the chain, and why you're going to evac, now, without arguing..."

Ike's fingers had gone flaccid. His whole body felt weak. He knew what she was going to say, and his thoughts were already turning toward abandoning the outpost—screw the consequences—but he needed to hear her say it. He needed to know for sure.

"You're a father." A pause, and then. "Over."

Ike's shaking hand clutched the mic. "A name? Over."

"Edom," she said.

Edom. One of the names they had talked about when fantasizing about the future. He had a son!

He lifted the mic to speak, but realized she still hadn't disconnected yet. "And Akiva."

Akiva? Was that Edom's middle name? It was another of the more unique names on their list, but—

"Twins," she said. "Over."

Ike was stunned. His body shook from nerves and adrenaline. When he didn't respond right away, Kate's voice returned. "Ishah and Layla have been helping. They already have a brood. Five kids. Can you imagine? Ike, please tell me you're coming home. Over."

Ike crushed the call button down and said, "I love you. I'm on my way. Over and out."

He heard her reply as he retrieved his gear and weapon, and flung himself toward the hatch. "Love you, too. Be careful."

He didn't bother closing the hatch behind him. He simply grasped the ladder's metal sides with his fingerless gloves, placed his boots outside the rails and slid one hundred feet to the bare stone surface of Mount Hood's summit. He ran for the trail, leaping stones and sliding over steep slopes. Before the outpost had been set up, Mount Hood was a technical climb. There were crevasses, rockslide threats and quickly changing, often freezing weather. But now, the southside path to the lodge was hewn into the stone face, the crevices were bridged, and the loose rocks had been removed. He knew the path well, but had never descended it so quickly. It was dangerous, but not nearly as much as having to fight off a horde of oversized Fobs.

He reached the lodge forty minutes later, out of breath, legs burning, but more determined than ever. He slowed to a fast walk as he approached the broad concrete staircase leading to the hotel's massive stone façade, which was topped with an American flag. Shooting from the sand bag-walled doorway, which could be sealed if necessary, and the two octagonal windows on either side, they could repel an assault on the hotel's front. But the building had weak spots, and it would take just one smart Fob to exploit those weaknesses. Not that they were sticking around.

Ike unclipped the handheld radio from his belt and raised it to his mouth. Before he could speak, the coughing of sound-suppressed gunfire filled the air. A moment later, it was followed by screaming.

35

ABRAHAM

Pain spikes from my head on down, and as I drown, I think, *that's weird.* I then begin to evaluate this odd line of thought; *why am I not freaking out? Am I not afraid of death? Am I grateful for it? Do I* want *to die?* That doesn't sound like me, or at least the person I want to believe I am. But maybe after all this time fighting for my life, I really just don't care anymore. Or maybe I haven't at all, since I lost my family. What's the point? *Burying them,* I conclude. *Closure.* Then *I can die.*

A moment after the revelation comes, I feel air on my face. My vision clears, and I see Graham standing beside me, one hand on my arm, the other gripping a handful of my bushy graying hair. Then I heave, coughing ocean water all over him, and gasping in one ragged breath after the next, as he carries my wet weight and both of our go-packs onto the squishy shore.

Panting follows gagging, and after a few minutes I'm breathing normally and wincing at the overwhelming flavor of salt in my mouth. Burning my throat. Coating my lungs. My stomach convulses, and I vomit onto the spongy, green shoreline.

"You okay?" Mayer is seated behind me. Her hand is on my arm.

"At least...I can't...taste the salt now," I manage to say before puking again.

Mayer pats my arm. "It will pass in a minute."

As I lie there, staring down the emerald shoreline, waiting for my body to equalize, I start making observations. The beach, or what used to be a beach, is coated by a thick green fungus. I rub my fingers against the surface. It feels like a mushroom, but it's far less fragile, having no trouble supporting our weight. I push on it with my fingers, expecting to punch through the surface, but it just bends and springs back, like a memory foam mattress. Smells like a vegetable smoothie, though, and I swear I can feel the oxygen pumping out of it. My attention turns to the red spots. They start a few feet up from the current waterline, probably just outside the high tide waterline. Each ruby spot ranges from baseball to basketball in size, spaced out every five feet or so. The larger spots have far fewer neighbors.

I ponder the spots, while my insides twist and coil. My veins feel like they're pumping cement that's hardening and expanding. Who knew surviving drowning could hurt so much? At least I didn't need CPR. Then I'd have broken ribs to boot.

Graham is on his feet, searching the area, slowly working his way toward the high tide waterline. I blink my eyes, focusing on the red spots. There's more there than just spots. Debris, washed up by the ocean. Sticks. Old world trash still floating about. Dead animals.

Too many dead animals.

Mostly crabs and sea birds, but I can see the carcasses of larger creatures further down the beach, all of them congregated around one of the spots.

"Stop!" My voice is ragged and stings from bile and salt, but the message is loud and clear.

Graham freezes in place, one foot still in the air. He backtracks a step and turns to face me, eyebrows raised, waiting for an explanation. He's not impatient or annoyed. He trusts my warnings, but he's not a fan of being startled. We're also supposed to use 'inside voices' when we're on land. Loud noises tend to attract unwanted attention, and my shout broke that rule and then some.

Mayer stands and offers me her hand, yanking me to my feet. After making sure I've got my land legs back and am not about to puke again, I walk to Graham's side and look down at the softball-sized red spot he was about to walk over. I let out a chuckle.

"What's funny?" Graham asks.

I shake my head. "My inner monologue. I'm still comparing things to Old World objects." I point down at the spot. "Softball." I point to a smaller one. "Baseball."

He points to a much larger spot, closer to the forest's edge. "Faule Mette."

Mayer snickers. "Really?"

He shrugs. "Old habits." He looks at me. "Right?"

"What's a Faule Mette?" I ask.

"Cannon," Graham says. "Fired 735mm rounds. About three times the size of a basketball. So, you're not the only one. Now, what has you spooked?"

I locate a long dead branch, smoothed by life at sea before being deposited on the shore. It's about the size of my arm, and should do the trick. I move the branch toward the spot, planning to poke it and see what happens. But the moment the branch hovers over the red blotch, it's yanked from my grasp. I shout and stumble back. The branch has been run through by what looks like a spear-tipped tubeworm. The top splits and opens, unleashing a writhing mass of white tendrils that wrap around the wood, caressing its contours. Then the tendrils snap back inside, the sharp tip closes and the four-foot-tall creature retracts back into the red spot, freeing itself from the stick, which rolls away, stopping at Graham's booted foot.

"Okay," Graham says. "That wouldn't have felt—" He cocks his head slightly in a way that is his equivalent of shouting, "Oh shit!" It means we're about to be in big trouble. And then I hear it, too.

Water. Spraying. Rushing toward us.

I turn back to the ocean.

The sea-Scion hasn't given up. It's rushing the shore, one eye deflated, the other trained on us, not *Hope*.

As one, we turn and run. In situations like this, we react as a unit now. No one needs to shout 'run' or remind the other to not step on or over the red spots. We just act, charging up the spongy shoreline, evading living spears and following the leader to safety. Or death.

I glance back again when the fungal beach quivers beneath my feet. The massive Scion has reached the shore, but can it pursue us? It is, without a doubt, a creature of the sea. It won't be able to chase us over land.

And then it proves me wrong.

Jets of water shoot from the liquid filled sacks covering its abdomen, launching the creature forward. It glides up the shoreline like a hover-craft, moving on a liquid carpet ride, closing the distance between us, as we try to not be impaled by the land itself.

But the Scion takes no such precautions.

The beast quivers. Its massive mandibles snap open wide. Its three Cheshire mouths gape in a silent scream. Forward momentum snaps to a stop, and then with a deep welling shriek, the creature rears up, arching back. A dozen living spears are torn from the beach, their bodies ranging in size from five to fifteen feet. Long white roots wriggle at the end of each stalk, each one tipped with a red sack similar to the Scion's eye, and marking the strange subterranean worms as Scion themselves.

As water gushes from the punctured fleshy balloons, we continue up the beachhead, each step slower than the previous, as the density of red spots increases. At the border of the forest, the spots are in tight proximity to each other. Without debating, Graham launches himself at the spots and dives over. Spears jut upward like a trap worthy of Indiana Jones, but Graham is already gone by the time they're fully extended.

Mayer and I pause, waiting for the spears to retract. Once they're underground, Mayer makes the leap and is nearly struck in the leg, but she slides into the dark forest and rolls to her feet. They make it look easy. They always do. I'm far more capable than I once was, but I still lack their natural grace.

The enraged sea-Scion lets loose a gurgling roar and lunges up the beach. It's impaled once more, but seems oblivious to the pain this time, perhaps because the ruptured sacks have already been drained. Or it sees us as the source of its pain and is out for vengeance.

I take two steps closer to the forest, getting ready to leap. The heavy pack over my shoulders pulls me forward, threatening to topple me over the mass of red spots. Using the momentum of my fall, I shove off and leap into the air. The backpack's weight pulls my back forward and my head down. Instincts draw my hands out toward the ground. Something strikes my legs, and then I'm beyond it. My legs flip over my head, continuing their arc with enough energy to propel me back to my feet. When I rise back up on the far side, cloaked in the shade of an unfamiliar forest, I look into the shocked faces of Graham and Mayer.

"Did I just flip?"

"Something like that," Graham says. "You're getting better at this."

"It's been fifteen years."

He grins. "You're a slow learner."

The solid earth beneath us quakes. The Scion is halfway up the shore, and writhing closer. A veritable beard of Scion-tubes hang beneath its jaws, surrounded by limp sheets of popped orange flesh.

"Let's go," Graham says, backing away into the forest, his M4 assault rifle now pressed against his shoulder.

Mayer unclips her sound-suppressed TAR-21 assault rifle, chambers a round and follows after him. The weapons, now wet with salt water, will probably still function, but we're going to have to take them apart and clean them soon. Even when the water dries, it's going to leave a sticky salty residue that can keep a gun from firing, or worse, cause a backfire.

Exhausted from my near drowning, I opt for my handgun, a sound-suppressed Sig Sauer P229. It's easy to use, and reliable, just like my assault rifle, a sound-suppressed AK-47. We picked it up in what once was Iran. According to Graham, its simple design, lack of dainty parts and environmental protection make it the perfect weapon for someone who doesn't know much about weapons, which also accounted for its popularity world-wide...before the world ended.

The forest is a mix of old and new. I see maples, elms, pines and oaks, all mixed in with mossy heaps of green that remind me of the shoreline, but lack the red spots. Still, we do our best to avoid any foliage that can't be identified. When we reach a patch of what looks like fifty-foot-tall, fuzzy green Muppet legs, we have to risk it. We need to move inland, not just to distance ourselves from the sea-Scion, but to reach our goal.

Downsville, New York.

Home.

The tall trees, many of which grow up through the remains of decrepit Old-World homes, smell sweet, and they're topped with plumes of bright flowers. Buzzing clouds of what Graham thinks are bees attend the open petals, but when one of the small creatures zips past, we realize that they're hummingbirds, adapting to the new environment by forming new symbiotic relationships with Scionic life.

On the far side of the Muppet forest, Graham stops. At first, I think he's taking a break, but when I catch up and see the large white sign, tilted at an angle and half absorbed by a Scion-tree, I understand. I read the sign aloud, "Welcome to Harriman," and then adlib the rest, "Population, zilch."

"Zilch?" Mayer asks.

"Means, zero."

"Huh." She settles down, slips out of her backpack and starts disassembling her TAR-21.

"How far to Downsville?" Graham asks. He's never been there, but we've talked about our pasts in depth. With no TV and few books remaining, when we're not fighting for survival, we're talking. Mayer resisted joining us the first two years, evading familiarity to stay sharp, but when it became clear we were something like the Three Muske-teers—Graham's comparison; mine was the Three Amigos—she started getting to know us, which led to her romance with Graham. They really are kindred spirits, which is great for them, but sometimes hard on me. All those years I spent running away from my family... I try not to dwell on it. I'll see them again soon. Or what's left of them...if they ever made it back home at all.

Fighting a sudden wash of melancholy, I reply. "Seventy miles. As the crow flies." I point up at a Scionic bird, flying past high overhead. The red sacks on the bottom of its body fill with air during each downbeat of its wings, then fart it out as the wings rise again, keeping the creature's flight path smooth. "Or whatever that is."

"The great red-titted queef," Mayer says, revealing nothing more than a smirk, while Graham and I try to silence uproarious laughter. Of the three of us, Mayer has the most sinister and filthy sense of humor. It lifts the spirit, but sometimes makes stealth a challenge.

I wipe tears out of my eyes, while Graham sheds his pack and erases the humor from his face like a pro. "I'm going to scout the area. If we get a good night's sleep and rise with the sun, we'll cover the seventy miles in two days."

He leaves without another word, leaving my insides to cramp, while I think, *two days...two days...oh God...*

"You going to puke again?" Mayer asks, that trace of a smile still present. "You look a little—"

"Terrified. Horrified. Squirrelly. Take your pick."

"We've survived worse." She waves her hand in the air like she's brushing away a fly.

"I wasn't talking about the Scion."

She removes the magazine and ejects the single round already in the chamber, catching it and popping it back in the magazine. Then she lays her weapon on a white rag, disassembling its various pieces and laying them out. She picks them up, one by one, wiping, brushing and oiling with the attentive care of a new mother. It's a full five minutes before she speaks again.

"I felt like you on our return trip to Israel. Questions about what I would find plagued me. Friends. Family. Rotting corpses. Destroyed memories. I pictured horrors piled atop horrors. Do you remember what we found?"

"Nothing," I say. The land had been scoured clean. The only living things in that part of the world were Scions, plant and animal alike. A new world, promised to no one.

"Nothing."

"You have a point?"

"The Old World is dead, Abraham. All that remains of humanity is scattered across the globe, pockets of survivors like us. Fighters. Most people...most normal people...perished in the waves and in the mad years that followed. Your wife, and your lover—"

"Mina and Bell," I correct.

"They were strong?"

"Strong-willed."

"We both know that is not enough, just as we know that you would not have survived this long without us."

"Thanks."

"Your boys," she says, and I don't have the heart to say their names. "They were young. Too young."

I start taking apart my AK-47, handling the parts a little more roughly than I should. "Again. Are you trying to make a point?"

She stops cleaning her weapon and looks me in the eyes. "They have been gone for a long time. You were a husband and a father for far less time than you have been a survivor and a warrior." She places her palm down on the disassembled rifle. "This is who you are now. But you still need us to survive. You won't become the man you need to be until you let them go. I hope visiting your home provides that for you, but I also hope you find nothing there. Graham is the strongest of us, but he needs us both. Heart and brains. We need you, okay. That's what I'm trying to say."

She throws herself back into her work, avoiding my eyes.

Her words sting, but she's also right.

No matter what I find at the house, I need to stay strong. For Graham, and for Mayer, and for all of humanity. We *are* humanity now. And when we're done here, we'll find a tribe of our own, push back the Machine's spawn, and begin to reclaim the planet. It might be a losing fight. Some evolved Scions, millions of years from now, might dig up our fossils and theorize about how our primitive species lived before going extinct. But we'll at least *try* to survive.

It's all we have left.

36

IKE

Ike raced east, toward the sound of suppressed automatic gunfire, flinching when the noise of a flashbang grenade boomed. Most Fobs had acute senses, and flashbangs worked better on them than they did on people. But the thunderous boom was akin to ringing a dinner bell.

The lodge was a long building that looked one-part ski resort, one-part castle. The entire first floor was stone, built to resist the mountainous cold, heavy snowfalls and occasional avalanches. Despite being at an elevation of 6000 feet, it still appeared to be at the foot of Mount Hood, surrounded by open space, thinning grass and short pine trees that disappeared from the mountainside a few hundred feet higher.

Rounding the corner, the lodge's vast, open parking lot—now serving as a supply drop-zone and helicopter pad—came into view.

As did the monsters invading it.

Like most living things in the Old and New World, the Fobs had followed the path of least resistance when scaling the mountainside. In this case, it was the old, winding road that led directly to the lodge.

There were three of them.

They stood twice the size of men and four times the girth. They exuded power, like gorillas, but they were hairless, their bodies covered in striking patterns of green and brown. It was natural camouflage, perfect for the forest. He suspected that these creatures had been living in Washington's lush forests all along, but had been flushed out by the aberration's arrival. Separated from the giant at birth, now evolved into their own species. Perhaps the behemoth had no more allegiance to the Fobs than it did to humanity? That was how they beat him here. These Fobs weren't part of the larger incoming army, they were already nearby, living below the timberline.

But now they were here.

And that made them the enemy.

Ike lifted his SOPMOD M4 assault rifle, but held his fire. Felder and Gutshall, aiming over a sandbag wall facing the lot's entryway, were between him and the Fobs, two of which were still charging. The third had been shot by a large number of rounds. Blood oozed from the wounds. It was staggering, but was that because of a mortal wound, or the flashbang?

Ike dropped to one knee between the two men and raised his weapon over the wall. His instinct was to pull the trigger and hold it down. But winning wars wasn't about unleashing some ancient berserker rage of uncontrolled violence. He squeezed off a three-round burst. Two of the three bullets struck the nearest creature's left kneecap. It let out a deep whooping sound and nearly collapsed, but rather than fall, it continued running on three limbs, falling behind the new pack leader.

The Fobs had broad heads and long, tusk-like incisors, as if an ape had mated with a sabretooth cat—and a jelly fish. The forelimbs, coiled with twitching muscles, ended in what looked like three-fingered hands and no thumbs.

Ike adjusted his aim a little higher and pulled the trigger again, this time striking the creature's bulging eye, splattering its face with gore. The Fob coughed out a bark, but didn't slow. Ike pulled the trigger three more times, putting nine rounds into the creature's face. Its charge slowed and then stopped. The Fob sat and pawed at its face, suddenly looking pitiful. The bullets had apparently punctured skin, but not skull. Not deep enough to hit its brain...if its brain was in its head at all.

The three-legged Fob was still incoming, but moving slow and still a hundred feet off.

"Where's Wittman and Edwards?" Ike asked.

"Edwards is in the lodge," Felder said. "Wittman..." He nodded his head at the chopper, a long range Black Hawk armed with a machine gun and packing enough fuel to get them home. It was their lifeline, and the only means for Ike to ever see his sons.

Sons...

Between their position and the chopper was a fourth Fob, its face and a portion of its upper body missing. *What the hell did that?* Ike wondered, and then he saw a mash of red gore, identifiable as human because of the coiled entrails and the legs attached to them. *Wittman.* It hadn't been a flashbang grenade that he'd heard, but a frag grenade, the sound of it muffled by the two bodies it tore through.

"It was headed for the helo," Gutshall said. "Kid saved us."

Not yet, Ike thought, and then he drained the rest of his magazine into the third Fob, center mass.

One of the rounds must have hit something vital, because the monster twitched and fell to the side, its legs pawing at the air and then going still. Its body seemed to deflate a bit, and then fluids leaked from its backside and four nostrils.

"Felder, fire up the Black Hawk. I want us in the air in three minutes."

Felder's eyes went wide. "We're bugging out?"

"That's the plan."

Relief oozed off the two men, but it was short lived. Deep, resounding calls began echoing through the forest. The crack of branches snapping filled the air with a crackle that sounded like a gun battle.

"Go!" Ike shouted, and the younger man sprinted for the chopper. He swapped out his magazine for a fresh one and then toggled his radio. "Edwards, we are leaving in three mikes. Drop what you are doing and get out here. Over."

"Copy that," Edwards's crackling reply came. He sounded out of breath, probably already on his way. "En route to you now."

"Should we take them out?" Gutshell asked, motioning to the two still-living Fobs.

Ike wanted to kill them. He might have been a religious goody two-shoes, but he wasn't above putting down a pair of Fobs. Still, he shook his head and said, "Save your ammo."

The helicopter engine coughed and then started whining as the rotors spun up. It would take a few minutes for the whipping blades to reach lift-off speed. Felder climbed out of the cockpit, something he would never do under normal circumstances, and opened the sliding side door. He climbed inside and slid the mounted M-240H machine gun into position. The weapon could fire a large number of heavy hitting 7.62×51mm NATO rounds, with a one mile effective range. While the M4's smaller caliber bullets struggled to penetrate the big Fobs' hides, the machine gun would punch dime-sized holes in one side and Frisbee-sized holes in the other. Felder chambered a round, gave a thumbs up and then climbed back into the cockpit. The big weapon would help, but it was currently facing the wrong direction.

Ike resisted the urge to make for the chopper yet. He wouldn't move until Edwards was with him, or there was no other option. So he stayed in position, behind the wall, eyes south on the entry road and the forest surrounding it. When the first Fob broke from the trees, beating a large branch into the ground, Ike opened fire.

"Go down," he mumbled to himself, as the creature took round after round. It flinched and thrashed, but it didn't fall. Instead, it got angry, beating the ten-foot-long branch into the ground until it shattered into splinters. It raised its head and let out a bass-thumping chortle. A cacophony of voices replied to the call, rolling up the mountainside like the cries of lost souls, wounded and angry.

Ike let out his breath, aimed at the target that had just been revealed, and fired a single round. The Fob's thick throat, bubbling like a frog's, burst. The monster tried to cry out, but the air flowed through its ruined throat without making a sound. And then, finally, the beast fell.

But it was replaced by another.

And another.

The big Fob was dead, or dying, but too late. Its battle cry had gone out, and was already being answered.

Trees shook. Some toppled over. The sheer mass of the approaching Fob horde was more than the five—now four—men could ever hope to repel, even from within the castle-like lodge walls. They didn't have enough ammunition. One by one, the army of new lifeforms rolled out of the forest. Some looked at the Fob at the edge of the parking lot, its ruined throat quivering with each labored breath. Some looked at the two injured Fobs in the parking lot. But they all reacted the same way.

With rage.

Many of the beasts stood on their hind legs, like bears or apes, letting out uproarious hoots from the air-filled sacks beneath their chins.

The rest...charged.

Ike put the radio to his mouth and shouted over the now chopping rotor blades and the even louder Fob calls. "Edwards, we are leaving! Now!" He grabbed Gutshall's arm, yanked him up and shoved him toward the Black Hawk. "Get on the 240!"

Gutshell ran for the chopper, while Ike shouted into the radio once more. "Edwards!"

"Right behind you!" The reply didn't come from the radio. Ike spun around to find Edwards, carrying two heavy packs and an M3 Carl Gustav recoilless rifle—what Ike had called a bazooka when he was a child. The 84 mm anti-tank weapon packed the kind of punch they needed, but they'd only get one shot.

And it was his to take. Not because he had a macho need to fire the big gun, but because he'd be damned before leaving a man behind. He'd be the last one in the chopper, sons or not. He took the weapon from Edwards, and pointed him to the helicopter. "Go, go, go!"

The man obeyed, and Ike spun around to face the oncoming wall of Fob death. "Fucking fuck-jobs," he grumbled, letting the words fuel his last stand. Then he raised the weapon atop his shoulder and looked through the sights, targeting the lead creature.

He pulled the trigger.

He barely felt the recoil, but he heard it. The boom beside his head was followed by an even louder one two hundred feet away. The lead Fob disappeared in a ball of flame. The resulting shockwave sent five of the nearest creatures sprawling away. The sound set off several more, shrieking and thrashing their hands against their heads. Blood and gore from the disintegrated target sprayed over a large area, coating the bodies and faces of a dozen more Fobs, throwing them into further chaos. But still they came. Hundreds of them rushed from the forest, drawn by the sounds of battle and the pained cries of the injured.

Ike dropped the big gun and sprinted for the Black Hawk.

He could feel the paved lot shaking beneath him.

The chopper rotated toward him. At first he thought the others were giving him an easy entrance into the vehicle, but then he saw Edwards behind the machine gun and read his lips. "Get down!"

Ike dove to the ground.

The machine gun roared.

Bullets zipped past overhead.

Ike rolled onto his back in time to see a large Fob, just twenty feet away, bucking and thrashing as high caliber rounds chewed through its body.

When the gunfire came to a stop, Ike launched to his feet and threw himself into the chopper beside Edwards, just as the machine gun roared again. Three Fobs took the rounds head on, flinching back as their bodies were shredded, but still moving.

Still reaching.

Then the chopper canted to the side and peeled away, lifting out of reach and swinging east.

Ike's momentary relief was short lived. They had survived the Fob assault, but the view from the still climbing chopper robbed him of any sense of victory. The aberration moved at the horizon, plowing across the landscape, heading steadily east, toward Yellowstone, and the super volcano that could end modern man's last hope of survival.

37

ABRAHAM

"Does any of this look familiar?" Graham stops in the center of what used to be a paved street. It's still mostly clear, but foliage, both Old World and New World, rises through the cracks. Broken down homes still line both sides of the road, slanted, crumbling and rotting. Some have trees growing from their roofs. Some appear to have been hollowed out and turned into nests for creatures that are either gone, hiding or hunting us. I'm impressed that the buildings are still here at all, but they won't be much longer.

Scionic life has what's left of human civilization in a sleeper hold and is tightening its grip.

"Some," I admit. "We're just a few blocks away now."

The neighborhood is nearly unrecognizable, but some distinct features remain. The hot pink mailbox. The arching tunnel formed by old oak trees growing on both sides of the road, untrimmed for fifteen years. The blue mailbox the boys dumped their sodas in.

"You're on point," Graham says. "Lead the way."

I head down the street, maintaining the even pace that got us here in two days. Once upon a time, I would have had nothing but complaints after walking back-to-back marathons, but now it's just another day. We've gone further, and faster, in the past. And nothing has tried to eat us in 48 hours, which is always a bonus.

I keep my now clean AK-47 in my hand, the barrel pointed at the ground to my left, safe, but ready to snap up and fire, the way Graham taught me. Despite my even pace, I find myself breathing faster, each inhalation bringing back familiar smells. Igniting memories. There is new growth all around, but so much smells the same. *Lilacs*, I think, and then I spot the purple flower. Their distinct, flowery scent used to fill the neighborhood. I listen for the sounds of children, but I hear only the forest and its denizens. Bird calls. Chattering squirrels. And things I can't identify.

I stop at an intersection, looking at the canted-over, vine-covered, green sign reading 'Desert Spring St.'

"This is it."

My voice cracks around the lump in my throat, and I flinch when Graham pats my shoulder.

"We're doing this togeth—"

I glance at Graham and see concern in his eyes, as he looks down my street, something I have yet to do.

I raise my eyes and take a step back, lifting the AK-47 a bit.

"I'm assuming it didn't always look like this?" Mayer asks.

The street is littered with flowing tan sheets that ruffle in the breeze, like living things. Some are tangled in the trees, dangling cut ropes. Others are wrapped around the remains of crates, strewn about the street.

"What are they?"

"Supply drops," Graham says. "Military."

I point into what once was a neighbor's yard, but is now a forest of sapling oaks and faster growing Scionic trees. Resting atop a few crushed limbs is a supply crate, still in one piece. Smaller boxes are spilled out around it. The parachute was stuck in the trees above, ropes cut. Someone went to a lot of trouble to free the crate, but they haven't taken the supplies.

A growl turns Graham and me around to Mayer. "Stomach," she says. "I'm thinking about MREs."

MREs were the U.S. military's prepackaged food for soldiers in the field. They contain everything needed for a hot meal, reminiscent of what we once enjoyed. Main courses, side dishes, desserts. My favorite part is the moist towelette. The lemon scent—like the Pledge furniture polish my mother used to use—brings back memories, and I enjoy how clean my hands feel after rubbing the gunk off. It has been years since we found an MRE, and that one had spoiled.

"I'll check it out," Graham says. Hunting for food is how we survive, but all of us would much rather scavenge it. And the promise of Old World food, real food with all its glorious spices and preservatives, would be a welcome change, perhaps even a feast to say goodbye, once and for all, to my past.

Mayer and I take up positions, weapons shouldered, ready to fire, our backs to Graham. We call this the 'triangular watch,' providing a broad defense for the person whose back is turned and whose guard is down. We use it while hunting, scavenging and sometimes while going to the bathroom in a particularly unfriendly environment.

I scan back and forth, looking over the barrel of my weapon, searching for movement and listening for aberrant sounds. Behind me, Graham pushes through the flexible, young trees. He grunts and shoves, slipping further into the new forest. Then I hear him cutting through plastic, shifting things about.

"What is it?" Mayer asks. "What did you find?"

I grin. She really is hoping for an MRE.

"Mother-lode," Graham says. "Food, water, survival gear. There's no ammunition, but...arrows."

"What?" Mayer asks.

"There are arrows. Metal ones. The kind hunters use."

"Is there a bow?" Mayer asks.

"No, but—ach!"

Mayer and I turn back toward Graham, raising our defenses.

He sounded like he was stung by a bee, but I've seen him stung before. He doesn't even flinch. He moves through the woods with a swiftness I recognize, the kind that means trouble is behind him, but I'm still caught off guard when he emerges from the woods with an arrow sticking out of his triceps, in one side and out the other.

Did he stab himself with an arrow? Did he trip and fall on it?

I quickly dispel these ideas. He would never do either. And that means he was shot.

Whoever this drop was meant for is still here.

And then, the person who shot Graham, is among us.

A black blur springs from the forest behind Graham, slamming into his back and sending him sprawling into Mayer. The pair fall to the ground, Mayer unleashing a string of curses in her native tongue.

I raise my AK-47, finger already on the trigger, already squeezing. But the attacker is too fast. A whirling, spinning kick strikes my rifle, twisting the barrel away from my target, sending four rounds shooting into the sky. I reach for my P229, while thinking I should have gone for my knife instead—Graham always said a knife beat a gun in close quarters—but neither choice would have helped. The stranger is too fast, moving with a kind of primal elegance, fueled by rage. The best word to describe the attack is 'wild,' but also coordinated and practiced.

"Wait," I say, before two feet slam into my chest, knocking me flat on my back and driving the air from my lungs.

Gasping for air, I get my first good look at the attacker, whose shape reveals we're dealing with a woman. She's covered in mud and plants, perfectly camouflaged. Had we not stopped to pilfer her supplies, we might have continued on past without ever knowing she was here. Her hair is coiled into muddy, inch-thick strands embedded with leaves, which make the tendrils look more like tree branches or some kind of new Scionic life. For a moment, I wonder if that's what she is, but her distinctly human shape, lack of bulging sacks and the fact that she is wearing clothing, albeit dirty rags, mark her as a fellow human.

Someone who can be reasoned with, if I can catch my breath and find my voice.

Mayer frees herself from Graham's sprawled form and raises her assault rifle too late. The woman leaps to the side, landing on her hands like an animal, and then she springs further around Graham, using his body to shield herself. Then she hurls a stone. I don't know if she picked it up while leaping around, or if she had it in one of the many pouches hanging from her waist, but she whips the stone like an expert, striking

Mayer's head. She follows that up by leaping on Graham's back like an ape, gripping the arrow in his arm and tearing it free. Then she punches him in the back of the head, sending him into a near unconscious state that matches Mayer's.

She's not trying to kill us, I think. But she's definitely delivering a message. This is her territory. And we are not welcome.

"We'll leave," I say, between gasps.

Her face snaps toward me. Covered in dry mud and leaves, she looks inhuman.

But her eyes, dark brown and wide, they're...

She leaps at me using Graham's back as a springboard.

I lift my hands, disarmed. "Wait. *Wait.*"

She draws a knife from behind her back, closing in on me. Her eyes lock on mine. I see anger and ferocity, desperation and loneliness.

And then confusion.

She sees what I'm seeing. Familiarity. Some sense of something nearly forgotten.

It can't be...

It's not.

I'm seeing what I want to see, because of where we are, conjuring the distant past, jogged by fresh memories.

And she proves it by pouncing, knife gripped to strike.

Catch her striking arm, I think. *Twist it. Free the knife. Punch her in the side of the head. End this before she ends you.*

I have killed before, animal, Scion and even human. I loathe the latter of the three. It makes me sick. But sometimes, people remove the choice, and you do what you have to. Survival depends on it. And not just mine. As much as I need Graham and Mayer, they need me. Without me, they'd be pincushions back on the polka-dotted shoreline, not to mention a hundred other deaths avoided, thanks to not brawn, but brain.

But this time, those big black eyes disarm me.

The woman, built like one of Edgar Rice Burroughs's jungle Queens, wielding a blade and dressed like a cave woman, has a kind of power over me.

I can't kill her.

I can't even fight her.

On the off chance that there is something to those eyes, I manage to shout just two words before she lands on me.

"It's me!"

Then her thighs are wrapped around my chest, pinning my arms to my sides.

I could lift my legs up, wrap them around her head and pull her off. I've practiced the move with Graham. But I don't. Instead, I watch as she takes a fistful of my thick beard, lifts my chin and swipes down with the knife. I feel a tug and a sting, and I hear the knife cut.

Is that it?

Am I dying?

I wait for the pain. For the warmth of blood oozing from my neck. But I feel nothing until she grabs another handful of hair and cuts it away.

"No," she says, her voice deep and gravelly—practiced—but not her own.

She cuts and grabs, cuts and grabs.

"No!" Her voice is full of anguish now.

The sneer revealing bright white teeth loses its power, her lower lip quivering.

"No! No!" She takes a handful of shaggy hair on my head, cutting it away with a swipe of the blade, repeating the process around my head, weeping now, the warm tears weakening the mud on her face, chipping it away as new expressions break through.

Pain.

Disbelief.

And then joy.

She's trembling all over as she makes the final cut, revealing a face that I haven't seen in over a decade. The mask of dirt covering her face crumbles away, falling on my chest. I see her for the first time in fifteen years, older, a little wrinkled, gray creeping into her brown hair. But her eyes. Her lips. Her cheeks.

"Are you real?" I ask.

She responds by leaning down and placing her lips against mine. Dirt becomes mud as our mouths join, slowly and gently at first, but then with a passion that can only come from love lost and regained.

When we finally separate, I rub her cheeks with my thumbs and say a name that has only brought me pain for fifteen years.

"Bell."

38

The past rears up like a tidal wave, overwhelming with sights, sounds and smells I thought would never be part of the world again. I'm sitting in my house. *My* house. In the kitchen, listening to the tea kettle whistle, smelling hot food and hearing the sound of Bell's soothing voice as she apologizes to Graham and Mayer, tending to their wounds.

Wounds *she* inflicted.

While much of the old duplex is still as I remember it—the furniture, the fixtures, framed paintings, family photos and lines on the hallway wall charting the boys' growth—much of it has changed. The windows have been barred. Some boarded up. The doors are metal and have reinforced locks. Weapons are everywhere. Most of them blades or bow and arrows. But there are a few firearms and buckets of ammunition laid out beside windows and doors.

But the biggest change is Bell. The woman before me now...She's no longer the Christ-like pacifist who would turn the other cheek even at the risk of life. She's a hunter. Maybe a killer. The way she fights, savage and primal, says a lot about who she has become. I don't hold it against her. Just the opposite. I adore her for it. I had called her strong-willed, but she's shown herself to be so much more. At the same time, there is something missing.

She's no longer at peace. She used to face down life's challenges with a smile on her face. The kids. Work. Bills. Nothing seemed to faze her. What was it she said? Tomorrow will take care of itself. Each day has enough trouble of its own. That and something about birds and bees being taken care of, and how much more important people were to God.

But now, with the human race on the brink, that belief must have been shaken.

Not shaken, I think. *Lost. That's what's different. She's lost her faith.*

Bell has washed away the mud and living camouflage, and replaced rags with an old pair of shorts and a t-shirt, both of which are too large for her. But she still carries herself like someone used to roughing it, squatting instead of bending, tearing with teeth instead of cutting. Gone are the smooth movements that accentuated her curves. Gone too, are most of the curves. She's slender and wiry from living in a hostile world. *No wonder she was willing to fight for those supplies.*

She stands up from bandaging Mayer's head. Back in the days of hospitals, Mayer might have gotten stitches for the wound opened up by the flung rock, but these days, duct tape did the trick. The hole through Graham's arm took more work, but Bell sealed it closed with superglue before wrapping it in a copious amount of gauze. "Sorry again," Bell says, closing up her first aid kit and carrying it back into the bathroom.

Mayer and Graham give me concerned glances. They're no doubt wondering if this is the Bell I remember, or if she's off her rocker. Mayer calls it 'going native.' Some people we've come across have devolved into a kind of tribal living, not just in how they interact with their land, but with how they treat outsiders. Like rival chimpanzee troupes, some tribes just start wailing and attacking, chasing the outsiders until they're either dead or far outside their territory. There are more civilized tribes, particularly in former third world countries already accustomed to living off the land, but they're harder to find. Solitary survivors, ones with little or no human contact...they're traditionally the most dangerous.

I raise my palms to them and mouth the words, 'She's okay.'

Bell reenters the kitchen before I can hide my hand gesture. She stops, eyes me for a moment, and then the others. "You're wondering if I'm nuts, right?"

"You have that air about you," Mayer says with her normal direct approach.

Bell grins, either finding humor in Mayer's comment, or she's proud of it. "How did you three survive?"

"Us?" I say. "He's an Army Ranger. She's *Mossad*."

"And you used to be a nerd." Bell bends down and kisses my forehead, which has been wiped clean with a facecloth and bowl of warm, now dirty water resting on the kitchen table beside me.

"Thanks for the past tense," I say.

She grins. "Still kind of a nerd."

Bell pours four cups of hot water without asking anyone if they're interested in a drink. It pretty much goes without saying. Then she drops a tea bag in each and sits down beside me. Her hand slides up my leg. Her fingers find mine and weave their way into my grasp. The skin-on-skin contact sets my heart racing and wakes up long dormant parts of my psyche. I squeeze her hand, wanting the moment to linger.

And then I ruin it by asking, not just *a* question, but *the* question. "Where are the others?"

Her hand pulls away. She stands up and fiddles with the tea bags.

"If it's too painful," I say, "we can—"

"Painful," she says, "but not in the way you're imagining. They're alive."

I nearly fall from my chair.

Even Mayer gasps.

"Mina. Ike. Ishah. All of them."

I'm on my feet, desperate to move, to run to them. "Where are they?"

"Not here," she says, deflating my urgency, but not my desperate need for knowledge. "I haven't seen them..." Her hands are shaking. I reach out and take her hands, guiding her back into the seat.

"I'll take care of the tea," Mayer says, helping herself to the silverware and pretending to fuss over the steaming cups. But I can tell she was really just listening. While Mayer and Graham had never met my family, they'd heard enough about them, and my feelings for them, to be fully invested in this moment. I have been hunting and hoping for answers about them for all this time, and now that I have them, the news is impossible to comprehend.

Alive. All of them. But Bell is here. Alone.

Something went wrong.

"Take your time," I tell her, but I can see she's already called up a reserve of strength.

"I haven't seen them in fourteen years."

The news sucks the air from my lungs. It's been longer than that for me, but I've had Graham and Mayer by my side.

"You've been *alone* all that time?" The question comes from Graham, who is now leaning forward, elbows on knees, his full attention on Bell.

"Visitors come and go," she says. "Most of them never come back. Some of them are chased away. But yeah, alone."

"Why?" I ask.

"The First Lady...what was her name?"

"Susan," I say. "McKnight."

"Right. She kept their promise. Our family stayed with the government's core for that whole first year after you left... After you went missing."

"I'm sorry," I say, but she continues without acknowledging the apology.

"Then we ended up in Raven Rock."

"What's that?" I ask.

"Underground bunker in Pennsylvania," Graham says. "One of the few places on Earth designed to wait out an apocalypse."

"Six months later, there was a military coup. People who were considered useful, and their families, were allowed to stay. Mina is an engineer. The boys share her last name. And I was just a Bible-thumping, homeschooling mother. But they didn't just kick us to the curb. They set us up around the country, let us choose where we wanted to live." She motions to the house around us. "I chose home. They dropped supplies four times a year at first, but that increased to eight when internal strife settled down and the thousand VIPs living there voted for a new President.

"I could have gone back then. She invited me. But I stayed here in case..." she rubs her temples, hands shaking again. "In case this... In case you came back."

"You've been waiting here for me?"

"Told Him I would believe, until you returned."

"Told who?" Mayer asks.

I point to the ceiling and say, "Him. *Him* Him."

"Ahh," she says, scooping sugar into the tea, and licking it off her fingertip with a slightly orgasmic look on her face.

"And now?" I ask.

"We'll talk," Bell says. "Him and me."

I smile. "I'm glad to hear that."

She squints at me. "You are?"

"I've had a few words with Him over the years. Most of them angry." I shrug. "The whole world is a foxhole now."

Bell laughs, and the sound of it nearly breaks my heart.

"If you don't mind me asking," Graham says. "Who is the president now?"

That there is still a President of the United States means that Graham still has a boss. I don't think Mayer will see it that way, but once a Ranger, always a Ranger. Or something like that.

"It's Mina."

I flinch back like I've been slapped. "What?"

"Apparently her engineering skills kept everyone alive on two occasions. She's organized. Direct. You know how she is. She's the opposite of me, which means she could run a country better than I could a household."

I'm more aghast than surprised. "And she *left* you out here?"

"I chose to stay," Bell says. "She tried to get me back. Sent choppers to pick me up a few times. Even sent the boys after me. Don't blame her."

It's a lot to absorb. Too much to absorb. So I move on. "The boys. They're okay?"

"Ishah." She says her son's name with a bright smile. "He's got a wife and five kids. Three boys, two girls. He's a nerd, like his Dad. And like his Dad, he's trying to find a way to kill it."

"Kill what?" I ask.

"*It.*"

"The Machine."

"They still call it 'the aberration.'"

"*It* calls it the Machine."

Her brows furrow. "I'm not following you, Abe."

"Every time he touches it, he sees things," Mayer says. "Visions. He talks to it. It tells him things. Old news and probably delusions brought on by fear."

"You've *touched* it?"

"Twice," I say. "And I *wasn't* delusional."

Mayer hands the tea cups out, one by one, while we observe this solemn moment in silence. Graham takes a sip, closes his eyes and says, "Black tea?"

"Mmhmm." Bell takes a sip. "Whoo. Lot of sugar there, Aliza."

Graham tilts his head back and chugs the tea until it's gone. "Oh, God that is good."

"Been a while since you had tea?" Bell asks, smiling.

"Caffeine," Graham admits. "Rangers take caffeine pills to stay awake on long missions. We end up addicted to the stuff. It's been too long."

"Well, I'll have to ask Ike about that. See if they still use the pills." She gives Graham a wink. "Maybe he can sneak you some."

"Wait," I say, putting together the pieces, albeit very slowly. "Is Ike in the military?"

She nods. "Ranger, same as him. Deployed at an Outpost like me."

"Mina deployed Ike to an outpost, too?" My fatherly ire is up. It was bad enough that Mina didn't send a whole Special Forces platoon after Bell, but to let her own son...their son...fend for himself in the wild instead of the safety of a mountain base...

"Mount Hood, on the West Coast," Bell says. "Keeping watch for the...Machine. He volunteered. And he's good at his job. One of the best, I'm told. Mina's quite proud of him. And she's a good grandmother to Ishah's kids."

Frustration rears up, catching me off guard. I'm beyond thrilled that they're alive, but I can't say I'm happy about some of the decisions they've made. My family is alive, but scattered and still very much in harm's way. "I should never have left."

"That's true," Bell says, inflicting a deep emotional wound. "But we share the blame. I could have stopped you. Mina could have stopped you. And if we're honest about it, if you had stayed, we wouldn't have been taken in by the First Lady. We'd all be dead. But we're not." She shakes her head with a grin that reveals some of the old Bell that I've been missing is still there, just beneath the surface. "Mysterious ways..." She looks me in the eyes. "It's been a long time, but we're alive, and we'll be together again."

"How?" I ask.

"Finish your tea," she says.

I follow Graham's lead and swig the tea down. "How?"

She stands and heads for the stairs. "Follow me."

She leads us up the staircase to the second floor, where Ishah's room was. I resist the urge to open the door and look in. If it's still decorated like it was fifteen years ago, I'm not sure I'll be able to take it. He's alive, and I might well see him again, but he won't be the little boy I remembered. He'll be a man... My thoughts flash back to the vision, of Ike and Ishah, fully grown.

Did it know? Did it allow me to live?

"In here," Bell says, leading us to the master bedroom, where a different set of memories reside. But when I step inside, nothing is how I remember it. The bed is gone, replaced by stacks of supplies and a table, upon which is a radio. "The antenna's in the back yard, strung up over the trees."

She sits down at the radio, turns it on and keys the mic. "Raven Rock, this is Black Widow." She lifts her finger from the call button. "I chose my handle. Always liked those movies, and..." She points at herself, moving her finger up and down, indicating her body. "I like to think I've got Johansson's figure. Used to anyway. Not as curvy as I used to be, but there hasn't been anyone around to disagree."

She pushes the button again. "Raven Rock, do you copy? Over?"

"Reading you loud and clear," a man replies. "Just in time. President Wright was just about to contact you."

There's a crackle of static, during which Bell looks up at me, worried.

Mina's voice fills the room, threatening to pull fresh tears from my eyes. I thought fifteen years of struggle had hardened me, but all those walls are crumbling. "Bell. It's Ike. I need you." After a moment she adds, "Over."

"Is he okay?" Bell asks. "Over."

"I don't know. The outpost was lost. We don't know if he made it out. I—I don't think I can do this without you. Please. Over."

"Of course," Bell says. "But there's something you need to know. Over."

"Yes," Mina says, sounding more like her put-together self. Just knowing Bell was going to join her helped her calm down. They might not have seen each other in fourteen years, but they were still family, and that, for me, was worth the years of hardship traveling around the world. "You called for me. Over."

"Actually," I say. "*I* called for you. Over."

Silence for a full ten seconds.

"Abraham?"

"I'm here. I'm alive." As I say the words, my eyes roam around the room, looking at the piles of supplies. They stop at a vaguely familiar backpack. I take my finger off the call button and point at the pack. "Is that..."

"Yours," Bell says. "I found it inside the front door when I came back. The airline delivered it. I haven't opened it."

I kiss her hard on the lips and then speak into the mic again. "Baby, listen, I have something for you. Tell Ishah I'll need his help. We're not beaten yet. Over."

"Choppers are already on the way," she says, her voice hiccupping in a way that tells me she's crying. That's when I notice that I am, too. So much for macho, post-apocalyptic Abraham. "I have to go, but I'll see you soon. Over."

"Love you," I say.

"You too," comes the soft reply.

"Over and out."

"What is it?" Mayer asks. "What do you have?"

I head for the backpack and unzip the top. Inside is a heap of clothing and equipment, but stuffed down the side is a folded up tool. I remove it carefully, unfolding the ice ax's blade without snapping it into position. I lean close and look at the streak of red on its surface. "A sample."

39

Our ride arrives ridiculously fast, in just over twenty minutes. A roaring Black Hawk helicopter dangling a rope ladder to the empty supply crate-littered street. One by one, we climb out of the savage New World and into the modern old. The transition would have been jarring a few months ago, after fending in the wilderness for so many years, but our journey across the ocean on *Hope*, and our time in my old house, has acclimated us to the idea that the world as we knew it still exists.

The chop of the rotors is probably attracting the kind of attention that would get us killed, but there are two Apache attack helicopters circling the area, looking for trouble. When they first appeared overhead, roaring past and sweeping out and around the neighborhood, Graham and Mayer were all smiles. While the world I left behind was full of loved ones, the pair of soldiers saw the weapons of war as old friends. They might not run up and hug a chopper, but they looked noticeably more relaxed and confident when the world's most dangerous attack helicopter—then and now—showed up for escort duty.

Ascending the rope ladder is far easier than I expected. In the past, while on location for various stories, I struggled up similar ladders as they bent and twisted around. But now, I could ascend the rungs with just my arms if I needed to. Even Graham, with a fresh wound in his triceps, makes short work of the ladder. Once we're all inside, the cargo door is slid shut and we're offered headsets. There aren't any mics, but they dull the thunderous roar of the chopper blades. Tired and unable to talk, we settle in for the ride.

Graham and Mayer sit across from Bell and me, fingers interlocked, heads leaning against each other, sound asleep. While the pair operate under a 'sleep when you can' philosophy, I think the helicopter's vibrations and monotonous rotor chop is comforting to them.

I sit with an arm around Bell, my hand rubbing her side, each stroke convincing me that this isn't a dream. Her left leg dangles over my right, our bodies intertwined as much as they can be while sitting in the back of a helicopter. But the intimacy our closeness promises makes my heart beat a little faster. I've been alone for a very long time.

For the first twenty minutes, my mind wanders, wondering about Mina, Ike and Ishah. Will my reunion with Mina go smoothly? Or has she changed so much I won't recognize her? I still have a hard time accepting that Bell has been out here by herself all this time. And Ishah. He became a father while he was still a teenager and has five children now, none of whom Bell has met. That she stayed away all that time on the hope that I would return... It breaks my heart. But I'm also grateful she made the sacrifice. Without it, our family wouldn't be coming back together.

Thinking of myself as a grandfather feels strange. I don't feel old. But I've got gray hair, both of my sons are grown, and with Ike's two sons—twins—I'm the patriarch of a growing family, perhaps one of the largest still living on the planet, about to be reunited.

While trying to picture my grandchildren's faces, I fall asleep.

I dream of monsters. Of running. Of death.

The normal stuff.

But when I wake again, hours later, all of that is a distant memory.

A hand grips my shoulder.

I knock it away with my left hand, and reach down for the knife on my hip with my right. It's all reflex. Muscle memory. My brain is still catching up as my knife hand comes up, finding my attacker's chin, and

I shove. Then I'm gripped from behind and yanked back. I start to struggle, but full awareness returns just a moment before I slam my elbow into the side of Bell's head.

I raise my hands, looking up at the stunned soldier who is fumbling for his sidearm. Had I not shed my weapons upon entering the chopper, he'd have a five-inch blade stuck up into his head.

"Sorry," I say, to Bell, not the soldier. I'm gripped by shame at revealing my savage side to her. Graham, Mayer and I always woke each other from a safe distance, with bird calls or tossed pebbles. We've become dangerous people, ready to kill or be killed, even in sleep.

But my shame is short-lived.

"That was slick," Bell said, squeezing my shoulders, her smiling face beside mine. "Those reflexes kept you alive. Kept both of us alive."

"Yeah," I say as Graham and Mayer stretch, both smiling, both enjoying the show.

"At ease, soldier," Graham says to the man still fighting to draw his weapon in the helicopter's tight confines.

The man hears the familiar words and stops. He eyes each of us with the wild look of someone who realizes they've just stepped into a swamp full of gators. We're wild animals. We could bite. We could kill. He's only just now realized this.

Graham leans closer to the soldier, offering friendly advice with a smile. "You should know better than to shake a warrior when he's sleeping."

"Yes, sir."

"Sorry," I say again, this time to the soldier. "We've been out there a long time."

And that's when I realize I can hear what I'm saying. The rotors have stopped spinning. We're on the ground. That's why he was waking us up.

Through the side window I see forest, but there's a razor wire-topped chain-link fence holding it back, a hundred yards off. The two Apaches have landed beside us, their crews still inside, waiting.

For what? I wonder, and then I see the first helicopter start to sink. Then the next.

What the...

I flinch as the Black Hawk jolts and is swallowed up by the ground. I tilt my head upwards, watching the light of day shrink to a square above us. A hatch slides shut, plunging the chopper into momentary darkness. But then we emerge from the vertical tunnel, lowering down into a vast subterranean hangar. There are many more helicopters lining the vast space, along with Humvees, armored personnel carriers, a half dozen M1 Abrams tanks and assorted other military vehicles I can't identify. No jets. If the U.S. military still has planes, they're not here.

There's a loud clunk as our descent stops. The soldier slides open the door and hops out, still looking rattled. He looks about to say something, maybe some kind of official welcome to Raven Rock. But then Bell grips my arm and sucks in a quick breath. She points beyond the soldier, who now looks bewildered in addition to nervous.

It's Mina.

She's walking toward us, flanked by well-dressed and well-fed people. Some wear business suits. Some wear military uniforms. And a handful of them wear black suits, making them easy to identify as Secret Service. While I knew Mina was alive, and the new President of the United States of Apocalyptic America, I didn't expect so little to have changed. I half expect a marching band to emerge, playing Hail to the Chief.

But I lose focus on all that when I make eye contact with Mina. Her facial expressions are subtle. They always have been. But I can read them. While her gait and poise remain unchanged, I see the desperate longing hidden from the others. It pulls me from the chopper and past the soldier. He says something to me, and repeats it a moment later more sternly, but I don't hear it.

Mina looks almost like she hasn't aged. There might be a few stress lines in her forehead, but she still looks sharp and beautiful, her angular face smooth, her long black hair tied back in an impeccable bun. As always, she is a complete contrast to Bell, who's become wild, like me.

Two of the Secret Service men converge on me. I ignore them until one of them blocks my path, placing his hand on my shoulder.

Three quick strikes later, both agents are on their knees, gasping for air. They might have been well trained, but they've been living a protected life. I might not be a soldier. Never will be. But I'm hard now.

Mina is startled by the sudden violence, but as weapons are drawn and men start shouting, she holds out her palms and says, "Stand down. All of you. Now."

And they listen.

She stops a foot short of me.

Have I made her afraid of me? Did I misread her longing of me?

I glance down at her left hand, and she must see me, because she lifts her fingers, revealing the wedding band and engagement ring given to me by her mother. Still there. Still married. I get the message, but not the distance. This feels cold, even for the more reserved Mina.

"I'm the President now. There are expectations." As far as explanations go, it's horrible. "I need to appear...in control."

I can see that she's struggling. She might not show her emotions the way Bell does, but she's not a robot. What has she endured here all these years to make her think these people would expect a reunion with her husband to be an emotionless affair? *The coup*, I think. Raven Rock might have survived the end of the world, but at what cost? How much blood was shed? How much violence did these people see? How many of their own people did they murder for peace? I look around at the rigid faces watching us. In many ways they're less human than those of us who have been living like our primeval ancestors. Control is everything here.

But control is an illusion.

In the world of the Apocalypse Machine, there is no such thing.

So I step forward, closing the distance between me and my wife. We're standing nose to nose. Out of the corner of my eyes I see guns rising back up.

"You wouldn't shoot the First Lady, guys, would you?"

A hint of a smile slips onto Mina's face. "First Gentleman."

"Same thing," I say, speaking softly, so only she can hear me. "Anyone whose opinion of you changes because you express affection can deal with me."

She glances at me. Then at the two agents behind me, still picking themselves off the ground.

"I can see that."

"I'm going to kiss you now."

A tear rolls down her cheek. She gives a curt nod.

I lean in and press my lips against hers. It's soft at first, but slowly becomes an urgent pressure. Her fingers find mine, intermingling and then pulling. Her lithe body presses up against mine. My arms enfold her. And all at once, years of self-control are undone.

A sob slips from Mina's lips and undoes us both.

We fall to our knees, weeping and hugging, saying everything that needs to be said without uttering a word.

When Bell arrives, dropping to her knees beside us, wrapping her strong arms around our backs, I feel something break within me. A wall. Erected to protect myself from the pain of love lost. It's destroyed, and all that trapped pain slides from my body with heaving sobs.

And just when I think it's going to subside, when I think we might regain some composure, I hear a single word that opens the floodgates anew.

"Dad?"

I look up into the blue eyes of Ishah, my son.

"Dad!"

He runs across the hanger, a grown man with the desperate cracking voice of the eight year old who lost his father a lifetime ago. His six-foot-tall form falls into my arms, two grown men sobbing.

I grasp the sides of his face, pulling him back so I can see him. He looks like the same kid I remember, but his features are distorted. Elongated. But I've seen this face before, too. Fifteen years ago.

The sound of little feet rushes over me.

I resist the instinct to defend myself. And when the first small face appears, innocent and smiling, I don't have a single instinct guiding me.

It's a child.

A girl.

And though I know I've never met her, I feel like I know her. And the way she's looking at me, she knows me, too.

"Are you grandpa?" she asks.

"I think I am," I say, and I'm dive tackled. I fall back, remembering vaguely what it was like to be a father of young children. And then more faces appear, smiling and laughing, trusting me outright. The ages range from maybe seven to two. I'm overwhelmed by joy and look up to see Bell in the clutches of more children, these even younger. They're an interesting mix of nationalities. Black, white, Asian and hints of other things. I look up at the throng of military personnel and government advisors. To my relief, I see tears in most of their eyes. Control or not, they know what they're seeing: the future. And maybe for the first time in a long time, it looks good.

Two smiling young women I don't know stand behind the kids, watching the unfolding scene with teary eyes and wide smiles. One looks Arabian. The other is white. Neither of them are dressed for work. *The mothers,* I guess, and offer them my best smile. I mouth the words, 'Thank you,' and get nods in return.

I look back at the kids, now wrestling and tickling and kissing and laughing. Though I've never met any of them before, I recognize pieces of me in each of them. In their hair. Their eyes. Their bone structure. Each one of them carries a piece of me.

I've seen this before.

Grains of sand.

On a beach.

In a vision.

40

"While I'm enjoying family fun time, there might be other things even more pressing."

All eyes turn to Mayer. She's her usual direct self, but I don't miss the glisten in her eyes. She's not a sap. Never was. But she knows what this moment means for me. She might not love me the way she does Graham, but she does love me. We're family. And the people swarming around me are now her family as well. There will come a time when this gaggle of children call her auntie.

But that time might never come if we don't do something about it. If we don't stop the Machine.

And for the first time, we have a way to learn something about it.

Graham clears his throat and lifts the backpack holding the now plastic-bagged ice ax, still smeared with red from the very tip of the Machine's still ice-locked spine.

The kids dance around for a few moments more, slowing to a stop as they sense the shift in tone.

"What is it?" Mina asks.

I grip Ishah's sleeve, fighting against the urge to hug him again and again. "You're a scientist now?"

He shrugs. "I know a lot about a lot."

A laugh leaps from my throat. His twist on my constant claim to know a little about a lot makes me happy, mostly because it means he remembers me. Really remembers me.

Despite my frequent absences.

"And *he's* not joking," Mina adds. "He's our lead scientist now, and that has nothing to do with me."

Swelling with pride, I reach out to Graham, who hands me the backpack. I put it on the floor between Ishah and me. The kids swarm around for a closer look, like I'm opening a gift on Christmas morning. Do people still celebrate Christmas? I haven't in fifteen years. Not Christmas. Not the Fourth of July. Not a single birthday.

To my surprise, the mob of advisors, military personnel and Secret Service crowd around, too. This moment might carry the historical impact on par with the nativity scene that Bell put up every year, and they recreate the feel of it by encircling us, eyes on the backpack baby Jesus. I unzip the pack, reach inside and pull out the sealed plastic bag. There's an audible sigh of disappointment as the group sees the ice ax. But not Ishah. I was an absentee father much of the time, and though I did not share Bell's beliefs surrounding the holiday, I always gave the best Christmas gifts.

"What is it?" the oldest of the children asks.

I carefully turn the ice ax around, so Ishah can see the smear of red. "When we first encountered the Machine—"

"The Machine?" Ishah asks.

"The monster," I say, and then I search my memory for the term used by the White House and the military fifteen years ago. "The aberration."

His eyes widen with recognition. They're still using that initial non-descript name, which also tells me they know nothing more about it than they did all those years ago. "You call it 'the Machine?'"

"*It* calls it the Machine. Also 'the Ancient,' but 'Machine' struck me as more authentic, given its lack of emotion and relentless progress." I wave my hand, shooing the subject away. "All that can wait." I pat the ice ax and continue, "When the Machine was still encased in ice, when—"

"A man from your party, Kiljan, stepped on it." Ishah grins. "I've read the report. More than once."

I nod, wondering if he was trying to glean information about the Machine or his father. "I struck the exposed spine with this ax. And I scratched it."

Grumbles erupt all around us. They don't believe it. One of the men in a military uniform says, "It seems to enjoy nuclear warheads, and you expect us to believe you scratched it with an ice pick?"

"I don't care what you believe at all," I tell the man, and I turn back to Ishah. "I think it was still waking up. Or it could have been a dead outer layer, like skin. The scratch healed in seconds. It doesn't matter how it happened, only that it did, because scratches are formed when material is removed."

I turn the blade around and lift it close to his eyes.

Ishah takes the bagged ice ax from me, holding it with religious reverence. "Is that?"

"A sample," I say. "From the Machine. It's been at the house all this time. I didn't remember it until after our second encounter with the Machine."

"When you died," Ishah says. "We all believed it." He glances at his mother. "Most of us." He frowns. "I'm sorry."

"I should have never gone."

The frown transforms into a smile. "What matters is that you're back, and you've brought another gift from your travels. Let's just agree that your life leading up to your death was all preparation for this moment."

"That sounds good, hon," Bell says, leaning her head on my shoulder.

Ishah stands, sample in hand, and looks down at me with a grin. "Would you like to see the lab?"

It takes us an hour to actually reach the lab. Mina has returned to her duties. Graham and Mayer are being officially debriefed by a collection of generals who Graham would have outranked by now. The kids and their mothers, who I'm looking forward to spending time with, have returned to their quarters, where homeschooling is the norm. There are a few other families in Raven Rock, but not many. With space at a premium, procreation isn't exactly encouraged.

That hasn't slowed down Ishah and his wife, though. From his perspective, our chance to successfully repopulate the planet began when the Machine started killing people. He's been hard at work since he was sixteen, filling his every waking hour with two things: family and science. In many ways, he's a lot like me, but smarter and a better father. He's the man I should have been, and I don't think I could have asked for anything more in a son.

On our way to the lab, with just myself and Bell clinging to his arms, he told us a bit about Ike. He hasn't seen his brother in more than a year, but they remained close. Ike, in Ishah's eyes, is something like an action hero. Strong, brave, noble and deadly. His description sounds a lot like how I would describe Graham, so I was surprised when Ishah said, "He's a lot like you."

Our arrival at the lab ended the conversation and sent me into full on nerdgasm. They have everything, absolutely everything, a scientist— of any field—could need. From gene splicers to supercomputers. There's even an observatory atop the mountain above us, projecting the images it pulls to a screen in the lab. The large warehouse-sized space is partitioned into sections by clear glass walls, etched with the name of the field and a list of the equipment found therein. Within each partition are rows of long worktables, peppered with equipment. Between each work station are low shelves holding an array of equipment, some of which I don't even recognize. I could play in here for years and never get bored.

The immaculate space is also very empty. Through the rows of glass partitions, I see just a few lit work lamps and even fewer people. "A little understaffed?"

"More than a little," Ishah says. "Most of us don't specialize, either. There are a few experts left over from the Old World, but most of us are young, and focused on ways to undo the damage done to the Earth."

As Ishah leads Bell and me down an aisle, I say. "Maybe you're looking at it the wrong way."

"How do you mean?"

"You can't undo what's been done." I say it as a fact, not a theory. "We need to adapt. To evolve. Not resist. All of this happened because we bent the natural world. We warped it. The Machine is setting the world back in order."

This stops both Ishah and Bell in their tracks.

"By destroying it?" Ishah asks.

"Not all of it."

Ishah looks disappointed in me for the first time since our reunification. I don't think it will be the last. "The human race is almost extinct."

"Almost. But not quite. Look at it from the Machine's perspective. We don't know what it is or where it came from, but we do know why it's here."

"We do?" Bell asks.

"To something as ancient and vast as the Machine, humanity is insignificant, no more or less important than all the other species living on Earth. And yet, we were pushing all species toward extinction as fast as any mass extinction in the 3.5 billion years that life has existed on this planet. And we were doing it in a way that prevented new life from evolving. We weren't just wiping out species, we were killing the Earth. All of it. The only way to prevent that from happening was to usurp the mass extinction started by the human race, and finish it the way it has before."

"You're saying the Machine is responsible for the previous mass extinctions on Earth?"

"Maybe not all of them, but I'm guessing the hole left by the Machine's emergence in Iceland is going to look a lot like an asteroid impact in a few hundred years." I put my hand on Ishah's shoulder. "I'm not saying I like what it's done, or that I'll be opposed to destroying it if we find a way. But I understand its rationale, even if I don't appreciate its methods."

"It's a forest fire," Ishah says.

I snap my fingers and point at him. It's the same example I used when explaining this to Graham. "Yes!"

The fire burning in his eyes shrinks down to a flicker.

"That's why it's changing the world," Bell says, "not just destroying it."

"It's reseeding," I say, "using radiation to accelerate adaptations and mutations. It's treating our impact on the planet with the same aggressive tactics we use on cancer."

After a moment, he nods. "I get it." He strikes out once more, moving deeper into the lab. "C'mon."

We turn into an aisle labeled Microbiology. I'm about to question the choice when I see his destination. A microscope. He's starting simple, getting a closer look before we try to break the sample down and figure out exactly what it's made from.

He sits down at the work station, dons a pair of binocular loupe magnifier spectacles that look like sports glasses with two high power-ed lenses mounted on the front. They're similar to the kind worn by surgeons and dentists. He carefully removes the ice ax from the bag, laying it down on the counter. After preparing a glass slide with a small water drop, he leans in close and uses a scalpel to scrape the tiniest fleck of red away from the ax and into the drop. He seals the miniscule sample with a clear cover slip, flattening the water drop and finishing his preparation.

I let out the breath I was holding and step a little closer. He moves the slide into position beneath the microscope lens. Then he looks through the eyepiece, adjusts the focus and leans back.

"What is it?" I ask. "What did you see?"

He smiles at me. "I was just making sure it was centered. I haven't turned it on yet." He flicks a switch and the microscope lights up, illuminating the sample. He then turns on a flat-screen monitor beside the scope. The image on the screen is out of focus, but soon resolves into an angular red shape, like a fractured scale.

"It's still out of focus," Bell observes.

Ishah sighs, making minute adjustments that only make it worse. He stops after a few tries, confounded by his inability to clean up the edges.

"It's not out of focus," I say as the epiphany slams into my mind. "It's moving."

41

Raven Rock isn't just a subterranean backup Pentagon, it's also a vast military complex and backup White House, complete with its own Situation Room. At any other time in the history of the Situation Room's existence, fifteen years would have brought a lot of changes. From landlines to cellphones and then smartphones. From notepads to PDAs and then tablets. From paper maps to interactive touch-screen displays with satellite imagery. But now, despite the passage of fifteen years, this duplicate Situation Room looks identical to the one I remember. The long desk. The office chairs. The wall-mounted flat screens, most of which are turned off, having no outside feeds to display. The furniture looks worn from use, no longer able to be replaced with each new presidency.

I sit beside my wife, the President, who is seated at the head of the table. Her fingers are tented in front of her weary face. She glances around the room, making eye contact with several of the people seated with us, no doubt trying to gauge their reactions to the information bomb dropped by Ishah. He's not the most senior scientist in Raven Rock, but they seem to trust him, especially Mina, though she has questions.

"What do you mean, it's not alive?" she asks.

Ishah's first declaration silenced the room, but it achieved its purpose. He has their attention, not necessarily because of the information that he's given them, but that he's given them something for the first time since the last Situation Room meeting I attended. I look around at the faces watching him, searching for someone I recognize. The science advisor, or generals, all of whose names I have forgotten. But I see no one familiar, and most of them are younger than me. *How many of the old guard were lost in the coup,* I wonder, and then I turn my thoughts back to Ishah's answer.

"In many ways, it resembles life. It takes in energy, we think, from radiation, from the sun and from biological matter, most likely from the oceans, which it then excretes, or sheds, as new biological matter. My father calls it Scionic life, divergent from all previous life on Earth, but still related."

"Related?" someone asks. "To us? How?"

The question is off topic, but I tackle it head on with the hopes of getting back on track. "The human race and most of the plants and animals we shared the planet with evolved in the wake of the Ordovician–Silurian extinction event."

"You're saying that the human race..."

"Evolved from the Machine, yes. We were shed into being, created from the elements of this Earth and allowed to be fruitful and multiply, until we nearly destroyed the garden we were given to tend."

"You're suggesting that the Machine is...God?" The question comes from Bell this time.

I shake my head. "It's a tool, created by and left here by a higher power. Whether you believe that's God or aliens or beings from another dimension, is up to you."

At the back of the room, the door opens and a man steps inside. I only see his head, but the tight shave tells me it's another military man. I wait for him to push through and take a seat, but he seems content to linger behind the circle of aides and advisors, ready to spring into action.

"You keep calling it 'the Machine'," one of the generals points out. He wasn't around for my earlier explanation of the name, and Ishah wisely leaves that story out, focusing on the newfound scientific facts.

"That's because it *is* a machine," Ishah says. "The sample provided by my father contained thousands of microscopic nanobots." He points a remote at the large screen mounted at the back of the room. It shows a video captured by the microscope. At first glance, it looks like a close up view of tiny biological creatures flitting about. "Each one of the individual units you see is smaller than a speck of dust. Yet, they are machines, containing no biological elements. Separately, they are even more primitive than a virus. Their primary function is to seek out other nanobots and form more complex matrices, which we were able to modify with various electrical charges. Each one acts as a stem cell, able to become part of whatever is needed, whether that is part of a self-healing exoskeleton, or a more complex machine capable of genetically engineering new life.

"We believe that the Machine is composed of more nanobots than we could ever count. Basically, a googol. And combined in that number, the Machine would be sentient, far more intelligent than any of us, and very capable of managing life on Earth, from the planet's conception to its eventual demise at the hands of the sun."

It's Mina who hears the silver lining in all that. "How were you able to modify it?"

"Certain charges triggered changes in the nano behavior," Ishah says. "We were able to instigate a merging, or tightening, in which the nanos coalesced into a dense ball. And we were able to separate them again, putting them in a kind of temporary dormant state."

"Could you do this to the Machine?"

"Theoretically," Ishah says. "But the effect would be momentary and would likely wear off before the effect even reached the far side. It would be like a ripple of dormant activity, moving at the speed of light. The best it would do is make it stutter, for just a moment."

"Can the nanos be destroyed when they're dormant?" Mina asks.

"Individually, they are quite fragile. I would guess that the nuclear blasts used against the Machine in the early days destroyed layers of them as well, but when pulling from a resource numbering googol, it's virtually impossible to run out of replacement parts, especially when new parts can be constructed from the very Earth itself. And it's conceivable that the nanos could form a structure sturdy enough to not sustain any damage."

The look in Mina's eyes is one I haven't seen before. She's always been intelligent and logical, but now I see cunning. "And if a nuclear blast were to follow in the wake of a dormancy ripple?"

Ishah looks as stunned as I feel. Did Mina just unravel a way to not only defeat, but destroy the Machine?

"Uh," Ishah says.

"In theory," Mina says.

"In theory." Ishah gives a nod. "Yes, but—"

"How fast can we—"

"I think we need to take a moment and consider not just whether or not we can, but whether or not we should."

Mina has always hated being interrupted, especially by me, because I know better than anyone how much it annoys her. But the shock in her eyes is more than simple annoyance. And it's not just her. Aside from Ishah, most of the people filling the situation room now stare at me like I've got bulbous peeled orange eyes.

Like I'm a traitor.

"It's here for a reason," I say. "And that was *our* fault. *Humanity's* fault. We inherited the Earth and set about annihilating it and each other. If we destroy the Machine, there will be nothing to stop us from killing the planet in the future."

"That could be millions of years in the future," Mina says, her voice strident, but not quite angry. This isn't a personal argument between husband and wife. I'm talking to the President, who can do whatever she pleases, whether or not I agree. "I have to believe we are capable of learning from this. We can harness the power of nature without destroying it. We can expand into the stars. We can even learn to live with the...Scionic life. We can be responsible stewards. There's a lot we can accomplish if we are focused on the task and present to get it done."

I don't miss the slight dig at the end, and I nearly congratulate her on speaking like a polished politician. But those petty quibbles can't compete with the affection I feel for my wife. And, I admit, her words are inspirational. I don't believe our responsible stewardship of the planet is probable, but maybe it is possible, given the right start. Maybe that's the real solution. Maybe the Machine is simply waiting for one of its evolved spawn to take responsibility? To grow up. That might be the furthest thing from the truth, but I'm not going to stand on the sidelines and let this happen without me.

"Well then, I suppose the next obvious question is, do you have any nukes left?"

Mina smiles. "We're still the United States."

That's a big, fat 'yes.' The only country with more nuclear warheads than the United States was Russia, and the last I knew, we had roughly 7,100 —enough to destroy the world more efficiently than the Apocalypse Machine, several times over. With that number in mind, I still think it's entirely possible that the Machine has saved us from extinction, rather than caused it.

"We have twelve." The man who entered late steps through the crowd and presses his fists against the tabletop. He's dressed in military fatigues and wears a dirty olive-drab shirt stained with blood over his large, powerful body. His cheek has a fresh cut, sewn up by someone lacking a surgeon's steady hand. There isn't any military situation in which his current state would be found acceptable, especially in the Situation Room, in the presence of the President. He's young, but carries himself with the air of a seasoned warrior, like Graham and Mayer, confident and in control, totally oblivious to the rules of diplomacy.

Normally, the man's appearance and insertion into the conversation would have earned him a strong rebuke, if not worse, but no one says a word. This isn't just some random soldier, it's the President's son.

My son.

Ike.

"The aberration stopped thirty miles outside Yellowstone, and since we haven't heard the eruption yet—and we will, when it happens—we can assume it's remained stationary. This might be our last chance to do something, anything to stop it." Ike turns to Ishah, his eyes glancing past my face, not seeing my teary-eyed fascination, as my son-turned-powerful-man volunteers to save the world. "If you can give me something to create that electrical charge—" he turns to Mina, "—and if you can give me a nuke, my men and I will get the job done."

"Sir," someone says, "you just got back."

"There is no one better trained or with more experience than—"

"That's not exactly true," I say.

Ike appears to enjoy being interrupted as little as his mother does. He reels around on me. "I don't know who you are, or what...you..." My heart breaks in time with his hard shell. He goes from anger to confusion and visible denial in seconds.

"It's him," Ishah says, smiling wide.

"It's me," I say, and I stand to my feet. For a moment, I think Ike is going to close back down, that after all this time he holds nothing but contempt for me, but then he leaps across the table with all the grace and speed of a soldier in action. "Dad!" His big arms enfold me, lifting me up. I'm dropped back down onto my feet and then pulled close again. We stand there, two men hugging in silence, the room watching us, not interrupting, understanding the significance, or perhaps simply not wanting to mess with Ike.

There's a moment where I wonder why he's not saying anything, but when I feel his big, muscular form shaking up and down, I realize this hardened soldier is crying. There's nothing else that needs to be said. He's still my son. I'm still his father.

I look down at Mina, who's holding back her own tears. "I'll do it. Don't let him go."

Ike pulls back. "I'm going. My men are ready."

I motion to Mayer and Graham standing across the room, dressed in military garb and looking rock solid. "So are mine. And you have kids now. You need to meet them. You need to be with them."

Ike wipes both of his eyes. "So did you."

"I shouldn't have gone."

"I've always been proud of you for it."

His words stun me. Proud of me? For abandoning them? For running away again and again?

"'Sometimes the best thing you can do with your life, is risk it for others.' Those were your words. The night you left. When you thought I was sleeping. They're why I am who I am today. Why I'm a Ranger. You inspired me then. And here you are, alive? After fifteen years, out there? You inspire me still."

We stand there, eye-to-eye for a moment. Then I turn to Mina and say, "We'll both go."

42

Things get done fast at Raven Rock, mostly because they've spent the last fifteen years dreaming up ways to attack the Machine, but never implementing them. They've literally been waiting for this moment for much of their lives. Like that Phil Collins song about a lover longing for vengeance. They have new weapons systems, a variety of nuclear payloads and delivery systems, body armor designed to protect soldiers from sudden environmental changes. But they've never field tested any of it, and they've avoided all direct contact with the Machine since the failed assault in Canada, all those years ago.

The best way to survive the apocalypse, they thought, was to hide from it.

But not now.

With a plan in place, the entire base rallies to make it happen, and fast.

We're all aware of the ticking clock. Every slammed door makes people jump, wondering if Yellowstone has finally erupted. When it does, the sound will reach the East Coast, but beneath the mountain, it might just be detectable as a quivering rumble. Still, we will know. The many outposts scattered around North America will all hear humanity's final death knell, loud and clear.

But until that moment, when we know all hope is lost, the residents of Raven Rock move with a purpose.

I shouldn't be surprised when I find myself dressed for battle, standing outside the door of an Osprey. The vehicle is one part helicopter, one part airplane. Its tiltrotor design makes it capable of vertical takeoff and landing, as well as a 310 mph top speed, which means we will reach Yellowstone in roughly six and a half hours. It's the fastest anyone has traveled anywhere in a very long time, but with the Machine poised just outside the super-volcanic National Park, it doesn't feel quite fast enough.

Despite that painful urgency, leaving...actually leaving—again—is the hardest thing I've ever done.

We could live here. Survive. Under the mountain. The world above us might wither and die, but I could live to be an old man with Mina and Bell and my sons. But what about their children? What about all those faces I saw in the vision, for generations to come? They won't exist. The human race will be extinct. Every time I feel doubt and my own selfish desires creep back in, I look at the faces of my grandchildren. I know that if we don't do this, if we don't succeed, then they will die here. Miserable, likely watching their own children, my great grandchildren, die as well.

So I have to go, no matter how painful.

And Ike feels the same. He's met his twin sons. He's wept over them. And loved them. And he's proposed to their mother—a promise to return. But he is still going, because it's the most loving thing he can do for them.

I don't know if he'll make it back.

I don't know if any of us will.

But even if they grow up without a father, they will learn about his sacrifice, and be better for it. Just like my sons. Despite my absence early in their lives, traveling for one story or another, hiding from the awkward situation that was my love life, all my sons really remembered is that their father went off to face a monster with the power to destroy planets. It helped define them as men. As fathers. Ike and Ishah became very different men, but each of them is a reflection of me—the man I was, and the man I became.

Saying goodbye to Ishah is hard. He volunteered to come, but his request was denied, quite strongly, by Ike. The two had a hushed but heated argument, at the end of which, Ishah agreed to remain behind. And now, as I hug my son goodbye, I get a sense that he doesn't expect to see me again. There is a finality to his goodbye.

"You did the right thing," he says into my ear. "You're doing it again. Thank you." He pulls back and glances at his wife and five children. They're standing with Ike's fiancée and two sons. "My family thanks you."

His family.

"Time for you to go," says a warm, loving voice. I'm freed from Ishah's embrace and wrapped in Bell's arms. Her hug is firm and powerful, and part of me thinks she should be coming. But she's needed here, for Mina. The women balance each other. Always have. And the pressure crushing Mina's spirit needs the kind of support only Bell can provide.

"In a hurry to get rid of me?" I joke, my eyes moving from her smiling face to her hair, which has been shaved short, like mine.

She slaps my body-armored chest. I barely feel it. "In a hurry to get you back. The sooner you leave, the sooner all this will be over."

I appreciate her confidence, whether it's genuine or not.

She kisses me, gently this time. Then she pulls back and gives me a playful slap on the cheek. "Take care of Ike."

I nod and turn to Mina, who's approaching. She looks serious. Presidential. "Abraham. I wanted to—"

"You know, I can't say I've ever fantasized about being with a President before, but you've changed that." I pull her close, holding her until she remembers she's more than just a president, and she relaxes into my arms. "Seriously, it's like a sexy librarian thing, but forbidden."

"We're married," she says.

"Even better." I lean down and kiss her. She starts to unravel, all her pent up emotions threatening to spill out in front of everyone, again. I understand why the illusion of control is important, so I separate from her and say, "Are you going to slap me, too?"

She smiles. "If it takes you fifteen years to come back, yes."

The Osprey rotors start to whine, spinning slowly. We're still underground, so it's not about to lift off, but it's our signal to wrap it up. Graham and Mayer are already inside, getting to know Ike's crew: Edwards, Felder and Gutshall. They're all very young, but willing and able. They're still more civilized than Graham, Mayer and me, but they've seen action. They've faced their fair share of Scions and come away alive. They might not have found their inner savage side yet, but they're not going to flinch in the face of mortal danger.

Mina surprises me with a hard kiss. "Love you," she says, and then she steps back.

"Love you," I say, stepping back toward the Osprey's open rear hatch. I turn to Bell. "Both of you."

Bell wraps an arm around Mina, who leans her head on the other woman's toned shoulder. I give Ishah a wave, and all his children return it, smiling brightly, unaware that they might never again see the grandfather they've just met.

I walk up the ramp backward, each step feeling like a knife in my heart. The hatch rises, sealing shut with a *thunk* that hides my family from view.

When I turn around, I'm greeted by the soldier named Edwards. He extends his hand. "It's an honor to be serving by your side, sir."

I shake his hand. "I'm not doing anything more than you."

"No offense, sir, but you are." Edwards motions to the rest of our crew. "We've all been trained for this. It's our job. The Sergeant Major told us about you. About how you faced the aberration. You were a civilian. A *writer*. But you answered the call when your country needed you. You risked your life. And you fought, for all those years to get back to your family, to get back to us, to bring us this gift." He motions to the nuclear device attached to an armored ATV with oversized wheels, all of which is strapped to the Osprey's floor. "And now, after finding your family, you're answering the call again, this time for the world."

"You trying to talk me out of going?" I joke, feeling a real tug toward the hatch. I could still leave. I could let them do this without me. But Edwards's next words root me in place.

"I don't think we could do it without you. Without your strength. And courage. And leadership."

"Leadership?" I ask.

"You're the boss," Graham says.

I look around Edwards and see the others seated on the benches lining both sides of the gray, utilitarian Osprey. All eyes are on me. Graham is the ranking officer on this mission, recently promoted to General, his knowledge of combat and the world outside Raven Rock dwarfing his counterparts. Technically, he shouldn't even be here. He's still got a hole in his arm, now patched up right, and Generals don't go on missions. But being a General, no one could really stop him, either. "We need brains and brawn this time around. You're making the calls."

I'm dumbfounded.

And intimidated.

But then I look at Ike and see the confidence in his eyes, and the assurance he feels that his father is larger than life, fully capable of tackling any problem. And like the good father I should have been, I do my job, and fake it. "Well then, what are we waiting for?"

Graham gives me a knowing grin and a nod, seeing through the charade, but approving. Then he thumps his fist against the cockpit door and shouts. "Take us up!"

Edwards and I take our seats and strap in, as the Osprey shakes and then heads for the surface, lifted by powerful hydraulics. Light streams through the windows as the hatch above us opens and we ascend into the noon-day sun. The rotors spin faster, reaching a relaxing hum, and then lift us off the ground. We rise a few hundred feet in the air, and my stomach churns as our upward motion shifts forward. I watch the wings rotating, transforming the dual prop helicopter into a fixed-wing aircraft. Then we're hurtling through the sky, accelerating to full speed and cruising west, chasing the sun and our fates.

Six hours later, I'm woken from a sound, dreamless sleep. As my eyes blink and my mind sharpens, I try to recall the words that roused me, but fail. I know it was one of our two pilots, speaking over the intercom, but I'm not sure what he said. I rub my eyes and turn to see Edwards looking out the window. He notes my attention and says, "Sure is an ugly sonuvabitch."

His words are punctuated by a clap of thunder that shudders through the aircraft.

I shift around in my seat and look out the window.

My guts seize.

I'm gripped by an old fear.

Anxiety blooms like a long forgotten flower, surprising in its sudden and vibrant potency.

I half expect the Machine to turn in our direction and face me down. But it doesn't. It remains motionless, standing still amidst Wyoming's natural splendor, now mixed with a variety of Scionic life, both animal and plant. Despite many of the trees below us standing a hundred feet tall, the forest looks like a close-cut lawn around the eight massive legs. A miles-wide path of destruction leads west. It stretches all the way to the coast and ends at this point, just outside Yellowstone, where the Machine's incalculable mass will punch through the landscape and set off the largest eruption Earth has seen, since the last time this super volcano erupted.

Which begs the question, why hasn't the Apocalypse Machine set it off yet? Its efficient remaking of the world has been performed without pause or hesitation for a decade and a half.

Why has it stopped now?

Lightning arcs through the roiling, dark gray sky, illuminating the scene as a torrent of rain lashes the Osprey. Rivulets of water run across the windows, beading and sliding away. A second lighting strike makes contact with one of the tall spines reaching up into the sky, spearing the clouds. Light crackles over the black surface, and then dissipates. For a moment, I doubt our plan. The Machine is unaffected by lightning strikes. But then I remind myself that the electrical charge we'll be hitting it with is a very specific frequency, far less powerful than lightning, and we've seen it work in the lab...under controlled conditions.

Stop worrying, I tell myself. *This is happening.*

I scan the creature's body, searching for clues as to why it stopped, but it's like looking at Manhattan from a distance and trying to figure out what its population is thinking. The Machine's black, translucent shell, burns with orange-red energy from within, the nanobots that comprise the body still hard at work, generating energy, maintaining the most powerful form to ever walk the Earth. The coils of tubes outside its body glow brightly, but they aren't quite how I remember them. The color is constant. Steady. They were swaying before, slowly undulating. But is that because it was moving? I've never seen it standing still before. Long tubes and spikes dangle from its body. Limp.

And dry.

That's the difference.

The few times I have seen the Machine, in person or in video, it had been expelling material. Sometimes leaking, sometimes spewing, it seemed to be in a constant state of matter regurgitation. Or shedding.

My eyes move down the miles-high spines, now still, like great towers, to the vast plates lining its back. I look at the seams and find them smooth. There is no mash of goo and eggs between the plates. The Machine is no longer shedding new life.

"It's done," I whisper.

"Done what?" Mayer asks, standing behind me, looking out the window.

"Done shedding."

"Then what's it doing?" Graham asks, looking out the window with Edwards.

I shrug. "Evaluating its work? Making sure it set things right? Maybe it's looking for us. Seeing if we're still around."

"Here we are," Ike says, looking out the window, defiance in his eyes.

"But I think there's no doubt about what it's here to do. It might be done reseeding the planet, but I don't think it's—"

All six soldiers in the plane, and myself, see the Machine's big black eye shift in our direction. We step back as one, gripped by primal fear. We've been spotted. Fight or flight instincts kick in.

Was it waiting to see if we'd show up? Should we have stayed hiding in Raven Rock? Maybe it would have avoided Yellowstone, if it thought us contained. But here we are, flying through the air, toting a nuclear payload that it probably can detect. Maybe this is what it wanted? A boost of radiation to kick off another round of accelerated shedding and rebirth?

Calm down, I tell myself. *Evaluate the situation. Find a solution.*

I step forward and return the Machine's stare. It might see me, but I see it, too. We're not defenseless anymore. And whether or not this thing had a hand in making the human race, it's our planet, too. My children's planet. My children's children's and generations to come.

As though sensing my brazen contempt, the massive eye shifts forward, and the Machine takes a step, toward the park.

Toward humanity's undoing.

I turn to the cockpit and shout, "Get us down there! Now!"

43

My stomach lurches when the Osprey shifts back to vertical flight. The change in momentum feels like a fast-moving elevator that travels front to back and side to side, in addition to up and down. But it's not just the movement making me uncomfortable, it's the knowledge that I'm about to return to a living landscape that I had hoped to never see again, let alone set foot on.

But the visit will be short this time. The plan is simple, the way good plans are.

Get the bomb into position.

Lock it down.

Run away.

Then we will set off the bomb from a safe distance. The explosion will take place in two stages: a very specific and not even very powerful electrical charge, triggering the nanobots' dormant state, and then a nuclear blast to eradicate them and keep the robotic cells from reforming the Machine. It's a theoretical and completely untested weapon. It could have no more effect than all the other nuclear warheads thrown at the monster since it emerged from the volcanic depths of Iceland.

But we have to try.

Graham steps away from the cockpit, relaying a message from the pilots. His voice comes in clear through the comms built into the tactical helmets we're all wearing. The visors can provide night vision if needed, and display tags for every member of the team. Even in complete darkness, we wouldn't lose each other. The rest of our gear is a mix of radiation blocking armor, weapons and survival gear, should one of us be separated and be forced to abandon ship using the parachutes built into the armor's back. We also have facemasks and an hour-long air supply, though we should only be out there for a few minutes tops. "Touch down in sixty seconds. We will have thirty to unload. They'll pick us up when we call it in."

"All right," Ike says, his voice somehow more masculine and commanding than I've yet heard. But I've never seen him in action. In his element. "Circle up!"

Edwards, Felder and Gutshall are on their feet, unsteady as the Osprey descends, but showing no fear. They link arms around shoulders, waiting for the rest of us. Graham is the next to join the incomplete circle, perhaps recognizing what I'm guessing is some kind of pre-mission ritual. Mayer follows his lead, and I'm the last to join. I've never played sports. Never taken part in a huddle, or even stood on a football field. So this feels foreign. It's somehow intimate and powerful at the same time. And then it's something else entirely.

"Our Father who art in heaven, hallowed be thy name." Ike's words catch me off guard. I'd always assumed he would take after his mother and me, but as the words slip from his mouth with the earnestness of a true believer, I see that I was wrong.

Edwards, Felder and Gutshall join him at, "Thy kingdom come," and then Graham chimes in with, "Thy will be done, on Earth as it is in Heaven." Mayer remains silent, but her eyes are closed. She might not know the words, but she understands the meaning of this moment, and the bond being forged between soldiers and with, perhaps, God.

Memories of dinners past, seated around the kitchen table with Mina, Ishah and Ike, listening to the musical cadence of Bell's voice reciting the prayer, return. I smile and join in, finding comfort in the words. "Give us this day our daily bread, and forgive us our trespasses, as we forgive those who trespass against us, and lead us not into temptation, but deliver us from evil. For thine is the kingdom, and the power, and the glory, for ever and ever. Amen."

The group separates, and Gutshall shouts out, "Yea, though I walk through the valley of the shadow of death, I will kick evil straight in the fuckin' nuts!"

"Hooah," Edwards and Felder shout in response.

Graham once explained the various military shouts to me. While they all mean basically the same thing—heard, understood, and acknowledged—'Hoorah' was used by the Air Force, 'Oorah' belonged to the Marines, 'Hooyah' was preferred by the Navy and 'Hooah,' as we've just heard, was used by the Army, to whom the Rangers belonged. That said, the Rangers generally avoided using the term, in part because it revealed their higher standards of conduct and skills, including with language, but also because the movie *Black Hawk Down* so overused the term that every Ranger who saw the film stopped using it out of embarrassment. So I'm a little surprised when Graham offers a hearty, "Hooah!" as well, before pushing the button for the rear hatch. "Visors down, masks on!"

I pull my visor down, activating the display. I see small sword icons appear over the others' helmets, each followed by a callsign. Ike's is 'Ehud,' whatever that means. Graham's says 'Supernatural.' Mayer's reads 'Mossad.' I tap Felder's arm, whose name is displayed as 'Night Terror,' and I point to my helmet. "What's this say?"

He chuckles. "'Science Guy.' Not very intimidating."

I catch Graham smiling before he puts his facemask on, and I have to do the same. *Bastid.*

The Osprey's rear door lowers to reveal a chaotic, hellish world. The rough terrain of the Machine's back is nearly how I remember it, but it's now covered in large lumps, like growths or tumors the size of mini-cars. Rain whips across the surface, propelled by swirling winds. Vast networks of puddles reflect the turbulent sky and the lighting streaking across it.

For a brief moment, the team looks out at this otherworldly landscape, frozen by its strange violence. In the next moment, it's falling away below us. The illusion is that we've just ascended several hundred feet, but we haven't moved; the Machine has. With each step, the Machine's body shifts from side to side and up and down. I remember the roller coaster-like feel from Graham's and my previous visit. And I prepped the team for this possibility.

"Get ready!" I shout, bracing myself at the end of the ramp. I cling to a rung in the ceiling as wind and rain slap against me, trying to peel me away.

The terrain rises up below us.

When it's ten feet away and slowing, I shout, "Go, go, go!" Then, I leap from the ramp. By the time my feet touch down, the vast back has nearly stopped rising. The impact is still enough to buckle my knees. But I now know how to take a hit. I roll back to my feet, vaulting away to make space for the others. They each run to the side, allowing Edwards to drive the ATV onto the Machine, just as the ramp comes in contact with the surface. While the vehicle could have managed the jump, jarring a nuclear bomb isn't a great idea. There's no risk of it accidentally detonating, but damaging it could certainly prevent it from functioning.

We regroup and start moving, as the Osprey lifts away from the shifting landscape.

"Where to?" Edwards asks.

I search the area, looking for a break in the plates. Ishah and I determined they would be the best place to secure the bomb, and a logical weak spot, making the device more effective. I spot the rise a few hundred yards away and strike out for it. "This way!" I want to run and get this over quick, but I'm still adjusting to the moving terrain.

How fast is it walking? I wonder.

It won't be long before it reaches the Yellowstone caldera, and all that pressure... The explosive force released might not affect the Machine, but the sound alone will be loud enough to liquefy our brains and end our lives, long before we realize it's happening.

I motion to Edwards and wave him on. "We'll be right behind you." The ATV has no trouble handling the rising and falling landscape, and Edwards heads for the fault line ahead of us.

"What the hell?" Felder says. I glance back and find him following us, but walking backward. He's got his XM25 assault rifle, equipped with explosive rounds, aimed back at something.

"What is it?" I ask.

"Thought I saw something moving," he says.

Darkness is settling over the landscape as the now setting sun is all but blocked by the thick clouds. Lightning carves across the sky, lighting the Machine's back for miles around. At first I don't see it, but then I catch a glimmer of movement.

It's the lumps.

"Abraham," Graham says, his voice a chilling warning. "It's the Crawlers. They've grown up."

Flickering light blooms beneath several of the creatures, illuminating the ground around them in hues of orange and red. One by one, more of the creatures stir and blink on. Legs slide out from the rough, rounded shells, scratching across the Machine's surface, as though irritated. They flex and stretch, popping the shells into separate plates, elongating their rounded bodies into something shaped more like a merger between a lion and a scorpion. The nearest Crawler snaps open its six-pronged mandibles at us and lets out a squeal.

All across the landscape, behind and ahead of us, lights blink on.

"We'll cover you," Graham says. "Get the bomb into position!"

"Ike," I say. "With me!"

I can tell he wants to stay and fight, but activating the weapon is his job. Once the bomb is locked down, he needs to turn it on.

I turn for Edwards, still a hundred yards ahead of us, when the Machine reaches the bottom of its stride and starts rising back up. The added pressure beneath my twisting boot makes it catch. I stumble back, fall and catch myself. The initial fall probably looked clumsy, but my recovery was graceful.

"You okay?" I hear Ike ask, but I don't reply.

My fingers feel cold.

Not just cold, *wet.*

I look at the digits, the white tips exposed at the ends of my fingerless black gloves. My hands are submerged in a puddle, making direct contact with the Machine's shell.

"Aww, shit," I say, before losing consciousness.

44

Barren brown stone stretches out around me. It looks like Arches National Park, sans the arches. There's no life here. I can feel it. I can taste it. This is how I've pictured Mars, devoid of even a hint of life. On Earth, organic material litters everything, adding flavor, even in the remotest locations, whether still living or long decayed.

My mind has been kidnapped once again, thrust into a vision. Communion with the Devil himself. I should feel afraid, but I feel nothing, as empty as the landscape.

"Your future denied."

I spin around toward the deep voice and find more rocky terrain.

My future? I wonder, looking at the emptiness. But that doesn't feel right. It's not talking about me. This is Earth's future.

Or was.

"This is what you were preventing? This is why you had to wipe out the human race?" I turn in circles, addressing the emptiness.

When I receive no reply, I try to control the vision, to reform it. But this is still not a lucid dream. I'm not in control here.

"You are not in control, anywhere."

The voice is right behind me. I turn with a gasp.

Nothing.

A light twinkles in the distance, flickering in the light of a sun that does not exist here. And yet there is daylight. And blue sky.

Because this isn't real, I think, eyes still on the blinking light, beckoning me forward.

I'm halfway there when I realize I'm walking. *When did I start walking?* I don't remember deciding to start.

Control, I think. *I'm not in control. I'm just along for the ride.*

"Your will is free," the voice says, and this time I don't bother looking for its source. "There are choices to make."

"What do you want?"

"To walk with you."

"I don't see you." I look back and forth, wondering if the black figure from my previous visions is going to make an appearance. "You're not here."

"I am."

"Then show yourself, Machine," I shout. "Speak to me plainly. Tell me what you need. Tell me how to save my people. My family."

I scuffle to a stop, somehow crossing the great distance to the flickering light in just a few steps. A lump of stone juts from the ground. Beneath its shadow is a cave entrance, blocked by a door. A key, looped around a twine cord, dangles from the knob, glinting light with no source. It's shiny, gold and new. Completely out of place in this primal, lifeless place.

"Life is not yours to give or take," the voice says.

This statement riles something inside me. I scoff and say, "And it's *yours?*"

"YES." The reply booms across the land, shaking the solid stone beneath my feet.

I wait for more, but an all-consuming silence follows. Minutes pass, and my impatience grows. The key taunts me.

"Fine," I grumble, taking the key and unlocking the door, making a show of my reluctance. "Let's walk."

The door opens to reveal a long, dimly lit tunnel carved into the stone. A smooth, stone staircase leads down. I look for the light source, but see none. It's like looking at a movie. The scene is lit, but you can't see the source.

It's not real, I remind myself, and I start down the stairs. "You usually don't make me do this much work when we talk." The echo of my voice is the only reply.

The staircase appears to stretch on forever, but I find myself at the bottom three steps later. The cave opens up into a tall cavern. The walls look like vertical waves frozen in time, like a photograph of a curvaceous woman dancing, intercut by horizontal lines of strata. Beams of light stab down through holes in the ceiling, illuminating airborne dust and a single figure seated at the center of the cave.

The hooded man's back is to me, all features hidden by a black cloak.

"Here you are," I say, and I realize my mistake without being told. The black figure from my previous visions was impossible to look at directly. And its body seemed almost immaterial. Flowing. Like smoke. This person looks very solid and present. I rephrase the sentence. "Who are you?"

"The first born." It's the formless voice still speaking to me, not the figure.

"What are you?" I ask.

"An offering."

I point at the cloaked figure. "I wasn't speaking to him."

"Expiation."

The word throws me for a moment. It was uncommon in the world before, and one I've certainly not heard in the past fifteen years. It takes me a moment to delve into my former life as a writer and recall the word's meaning. "Atonement. For what?"

But there is no answer. None is needed. I get it. "Because this is what we would have made of the world. Lifeless nothing."

"And yet you still expect to inherit it. To claim it. To take it."

Oh, shit, I think. It knows why we're here. Why I've returned. Of course it does. It can probably see all my thoughts. What we're doing. What the plan is. Is it offering expiation because it fears the plan will work? Or is it genuinely giving us—giving *me*—a chance to show we've changed our destructive ways? Could triggering the bomb doom us, or set us free? Is my response, here and now, the litmus test for the human race?

"Make your choice," the voice says.

I consider the options, weighing the odds of our mission's success against the odds that its offer is an honest one. Would a creature as ancient and powerful as this resort to lying or trickery? And what about our previous encounters? It showed me a future with my family, and I have seen the first generation of them with my own eyes. But how did it know I would survive? That *they* would survive? Coincidence or grand scheme? Why bother communicating at all? If its purpose truly is the complete eradication of mankind, the only reason to speak to me would be if it derived some kind of sadistic pleasure from my confusion. But again, that doesn't make sense.

"I'll do it," I say, choosing what I think is the right path. Deep down, beyond my concerns for the people I adore, there is a scientist who knows that the world was dying, that humanity was responsible for the sixth great extinction, and who understands how the Machine's actions have already spared the planet from the fate I've been shown.

"I'll do it," I say again. "Sacrifice."

"Look upon the offering."

I step around the seated figure, giving it a wide berth, not fully trusting the Machine, despite it providing a chance for redemption. Could it really be that benevolent? After destroying nearly all of humanity and replacing us with new life, could the Machine be willing to give us another shot, based on my actions? Granted, I'm pretty sure I'm the only human being it's come into direct contact with on multiple occasions. I suppose I shouldn't be surprised it's deemed me the sole representative of homo sapiens. What other choices does it have?

Standing in front of the hooded figure, I still can't see his face.

"If you're screwing with me..." I don't complete the threat. It's hollow, and the Machine surely knows that, even more than I do.

I reach out, pinching the loose hood between my index finger and thumb. The fabric is rough, and cold. With a flick of my wrist, I flip the hood up and over the shaved head.

"No," I say, stumbling back and falling onto my ass. "No, God damnit."

The man staring back to me, with striking Asian features and dark brown eyes, is my son, Ike. The wound on his cheek is a scar, like it was in the first vision, matching the wound now on his cheek.

How did it know?

"How did you know!"

Darkness flows down from the ceiling, flowing behind Ike. I divert my eyes as though staring into the sun itself, watching the flowing darkness spread out behind my son, dark tendrils wrapping around him, claiming him.

"Expiation," the Machine's spirit says. "Make your choice."

The darkness surges at me. A black hand wraps around my face, shoving me down onto my back. It shouts again, in time with impact. "Eligo!"

I jolt upright and am accosted by peals of thunder, stinging rain, the pounding of firing weapons and screaming voices. In the distance, I see Ike, hunched over the bomb, setting it to explode. Edwards is already running back toward me, and the others are now fully engaged with grown-up Crawlers.

Eligo. I don't need someone to translate the word for me this time. I understand it easy enough. *Choose.*

"Ike," I say, knowing he can hear me over the comms.

"Dad!" He glances back at me. "Are you okay?"

"Fine."

"You were speaking," he says. "Latin, I think."

"It happens," Graham says, sounding calm despite the near constant din of gunfire. "What did it show you this time?"

"It?" Edwards asks. He's nearly reached me and looks confused.

"The Machine speaks to him," Mayer explains. "When he touches it. Did you touch it?"

I look down at my hands, still submerged, still in contact. "I still am." Lightning cuts through the sky, reflecting in the water beneath me, forcing my eyes shut for a moment.

"What did it say?" Ike asks.

"That I need to make a choice."

"What choice?"

"Whether or not to let you stay."

The conversation falls silent. So do the guns. Even the storm seems to be contemplating my words.

Then it all starts back up again, like a bomb, like *the* bomb.

"What's he talking about, Sergeant Major?" Gutshall asks.

"The bomb," I say. "We can't trigger it remotely, can we?"

"No," Ike confirms.

Edwards arrives and offers me his hand. He pulls me up and then rushes to join the others, who have formed a defensive line, tracer rounds streaking across the glistening landscape.

I look back at Ike, hunched down beside the bomb, waiting to do his duty. Waiting to kill the Machine, and for it to allow him to do so. That's the sacrifice. That's the change in heart it's looking for. The future it promises can only come if I sacrifice my son.

Plagued by doubt, I make my choice. "Cauldron, this is Science Guy. Do you copy?"

"This is Cauldron," the Osprey pilot replies. "We have eyes on you."

I search the chaotic sky and see the plane cutting a wide circle around our position.

I look at Ike again. He's far away and hard to see through all the rain, but I see his nod. "You better be telling the truth," I say to the miles-wide armored plate beneath my feet. I follow them by the hardest words I've ever had to say. "Cauldron... We are ready for Evac. Come and get us."

45

"Negative, Science Guy. LZ is crawling." The plane cruises past overhead, tilted to the side, so the pilot can look down at us. Lightning streaks above it, turning it into a silhouette. "Clear the area."

I don't like it, but he's right. The Machine is moving forward, and hundreds of feet up and down with each step. Not crashing into the massive plates, while avoiding the towering spines sweeping back and forth, viewing the world through a rain spattered windshield and being blinded by near constant lightning, is already going to be a challenge. If the Osprey is attacked, we're not leaving.

And part of me is content with that. I don't want to leave Ike.

But he's making this sacrifice for our family, and I should honor that by returning to them, and making sure that vision comes to fruition. He has two sons. His family will grow. And I'll be there to protect them.

I free the XM25 assault rifle from around my back, chamber the first explosive round and shout, "All right, you heard the man. Let's clear some room!"

I falter for just a moment, when I look up at the scene before me. Lightning flickers, giving us a strobe-light view of the incoming creatures, still visible in the moments of darkness because of their luminous undersides. White-hot tracer rounds zip away from Graham, Mayer, Gutshall and Felder, who have formed a defensive line fifty feet away. Most of the rounds deflect away from the bulletproof shells, but the rest of the explosive rounds perform as advertised, bursting on contact, or at a predetermined range. But they're not even slowing the large creatures still barreling toward us, aiming beyond us, at Ike.

I glance back at my son, still working on the bomb, securing it in place and entering the passcode that will allow him to arm it. "Ike, if they get past us..."

"I'll take care of it," he says. "I just need another minute."

I catch up to Edwards, who's running to join the others at the defensive line. He looks afraid. Maybe because we're in the worst possible situation imaginable, but I think it has more to do with leaving his team's leader behind. Ike's confidence fueled these men and kept them alive behind enemy lines for years. So I try to be that for them now. "Graham. Shock and awe!"

I see him reach to his chest and pluck away two small devices. "Flashbangs out!"

He tosses the two grenades at the oncoming wave. The closest of the Crawlers is just fifty feet away. It will arrive in seconds. I raise an arm over my visor to block the light, trusting distance and the helmet's audio filter to protect my ears. I see the flash around my arm, and I hear the boom as a loud pop.

When I look up, nothing has changed.

"They're not Scionic," I shout. The strategies we've developed over the years for dealing with the new life forms evolving on Earth might not be effective against these creatures, which have evolved over billions of years, hatching and growing for generations with each rise of the Machine.

What can we do?

How do we fight them?

"You son-of-a-bitch!" I shout at the Machine. "I made my choice! Call them off!"

I take aim at the nearest Crawler, unleashing six rounds. I feel the heat and shockwave of each explosive round bursting against its shell, having no effect. I turn down in defeat, and that's when I see the solution reflected in a puddle beneath the Crawler's glowing underside. The orange light's source is a twisting coil of loose flesh, reminiscent of the Machine's belly.

I pull the trigger, firing from the hip, the recoil nearly yanking the weapon from my hands. Three rounds zip toward the creature, the first two exploding against the front of its carapace, the third sliding beneath the body, striking the Machine's hard shell, and exploding.

The explosion tears into the creature's softer underside just as the Machine begins a downward step. The combination of the explosion's upward force and the ground dropping away propels the creature over our heads, trailing a luminous arc of gore.

"Aim beneath them!" I shout.

As one, the six of us redirect our explosive rounds to the gap between the Crawlers and the terrain beneath them. The battle shifts in an instant, as the creatures are sent spinning through the air, their insides hollowed out. But for each Crawler that falls, several more take its place. And our ammunition supply is limited.

Lightning strikes the Machine's back just to our left. I turn away from the earsplitting crack and the blinding light to see that we're being flanked. Five Crawlers are nearly upon us. I open fire, launching two of the creatures into the air, their guts spiraling away, and slapping against Felder's visor, blinding him.

He stands and lowers his weapon, confused by the sudden blindness caused by the viscous, glowing gore blocking his view. "What the hell?"

I kill one more of the creatures and mortally wound another, now twitching and writhing in circles. But the fifth reaches Felder before I can shoot it. "Look out!" I scream.

Gutshall hears the warning and turns to fire at the creature, but his weapon just clicks when he pulls the trigger. He's out of ammo.

The Crawler skewers Felder's chest, the powerful limbs punching through his armor with ease.

With the dead man stuck on its limbs, the Crawler rears up, twitching its leg, trying to shake Felder's body free.

"Felder!" Gutshall shouts, launching himself at the creature's underside. He draws a knife from his waist and plunges it into the thing's gut, swiping the sharp blade upward. A wave of innards spills out over his body, but he keeps cutting and pushing. The Crawler's limbs jut out straight, gripped by pain and then death. With a final shout, Gutshall pushes the dead Crawler onto its back.

Covered in gore, he slumps down beside Felder, trying to pull him free, totally unaware that another Crawler has reared up behind him.

I take aim for the creature's underside, but to hit it, I would have to put a bullet through Gutshall's chest. I don't even have time to shout a warning.

The Crawler's mandibles close over Gutshall's head, and with a quick bite, severs it from his body. I nearly vomit into my facemask as Gutshall's callsign: Dim Reaper, shown in my visor's heads-up display, slides into the monster's gullet, following the helmet's signal. But my horror turns to fear when I raise my weapon to fire and it's knocked from my hands by one of the Crawler's flailing limbs. It lunges over the bodies of Gutshall, Felder and its fallen comrade, two limbs raised, ready to plunge into my chest.

I stumble and trip, falling hard on my back, defenseless. I fumble for the knife on my side, but fail to pull it free, and even if I did, I don't have the reach or speed to fend off the monster.

But someone does.

Three rounds punch into the Crawler's exposed underside, exploding inside the creature. A wave of guts and shattered limbs fall atop me while the shell is launched back, slamming into the next Crawler intent on killing me.

I scramble back to my feet, wiping at my visor, letting the torrential rain help clean me off.

"You alright?" Ike asks, his voice clear in my comm despite the distance between us, the storm's roar and the cacophony of gunfire.

I turn and see him facing me, XM25 raised to his shoulder.

"Thanks," I say. "Felder and Gutshall—"

"Did their duty," Ike says. "And I'm ready to do mine. You need to bug out. Now. Cauldron, what's your status?"

"We can attempt a mobile pickup," the Osprey pilot listening in says. "That's the best we can do, and we'll only get one pass. Incoming in one mike, half a klick east from your position."

I look to the sky and see the Osprey banking toward us, the dual-prop rotors in their upward position, allowing the vehicle to fly like a helicopter.

"Frags out!" Graham shouts, as he and Mayer roll a half dozen fragmentation grenades at the oncoming Crawlers, now climbing over the bodies of their dead to reach us.

I turn and run with Graham, Mayer and Edwards, only to be slapped down by the concussive force of all those grenades. I'm yanked back to my feet a moment later and shoved from behind by Mayer. "Move it, old man!"

Did she not even fall? And here I thought I'd been toughened up.

While the three soldiers take turns running, reloading and firing, I sprint ahead, weaponless.

A quick look back reveals the Osprey swooping down, a hundred feet above the action. Landing would be impossible. The Crawlers would set upon the plane before it could lift off again. Beneath it, the monsters continue their pursuit, slowed by the explosive gunfire peppering the frontline, but not stopped. A flash of lightning reveals a moving torrent of the creatures, stretching as far as I can see. The Crawlers haven't just been growing, they've been multiplying.

Gunfire draws my eyes back to Ike. He's far to the right, hunched by the ledge where one plate overlaps another, firing up into the gut of a Crawler that approached from the east. A fresh cascade of lightning, streaking through the clouds above, reveals what lies ahead. Crawlers. Hundreds more, rushing to meet the wave pursuing us like the two walls of Red Sea water that crushed the Egyptian army in Cecil B. DeMille's *The Ten Commandments*.

But we have something Ramses didn't have.

"Here comes the ladder," Cauldron's pilot says.

I look up and back to see a rope ladder unfurl from the Osprey's side door. It drops down, twenty feet above the horde. Several of the creatures leap for it, but they fall short, either not strong enough to make the jump, or beat down by the twin rotors' wash.

The Osprey roars past me, still descending as the Machine reaches the apex of its step.

"Go, go, go!" the pilot shouts.

The first rung of the ladder descends right beside me, and it's about to pass me. I reach out, hooking my fingers around the bottom rung, and then suddenly I find it yanked tight in my hand.

My feet leave the ground.

They're pulling up?

"What are you doing?" I shout.

"It's not us," the pilot replies.

It's the Machine, dropping down as it takes another step, moving ever closer to the Yellowstone caldera. *How far away are we? How long has it been?* Time feels surreal and slow, but we must be nearly past the point of no return. I look down and forget all my questions. I'm hanging from a ladder now a hundred feet above the surface, and growing. The illusion is that we're ascending, but the tug on my arms remains steady, and I'm able to pull myself up.

The gun battle shrinks away beneath us, but keeps moving.

"Maintaining speed and course," the pilot says. "We'll be here when you come back up. But that's your last chance."

I'm about to argue, when I get a good look at the scene from above. There are Crawlers incoming from all directions. The mass approaching from ahead will reach the others around the same time the now-ascending landscape reaches us. If the others don't get on the ladder then, they never will.

The battle rushes back up, and my mind says that we're going to crash, but the massive body slows at the top of its step, giving Graham and Mayer precious seconds to leap onto the ladder.

Graham and Mayer, but not Edwards.

I look for Edwards, expecting to find a torn-apart body, but instead I find him sprinting toward Ike and the bomb. "Edwards, what are you doing?"

"You need time to reach the minimum safe distance, sir," Edwards says.

"He's right," Graham says. "Cauldron, you are good to go!"

I grip the rope ladder as the Osprey ascends and peels away. After looping my arms around a rung and linking my hands, I look down expecting to see Graham and Mayer clinging to the ladder below me.

But I'm alone.

My only friends and company for the past fifteen years are with Edwards, running back to Ike, buying time so that I might live.

"No!" I shout, and I nearly let go. But we're several hundred feet in the air now. I couldn't join them if I wanted to.

"The world needs you more than it does us grunts," Graham says. "Take care of yourself."

Lightning streaks past the Osprey, drawing my eyes up to see if the plane's been struck. But we're still moving, pulling away from the Machine. That's when I notice I'm only twenty feet from the hatch now. The ladder is being winched back inside.

"Graham..." I find myself at a loss for words. He and Mayer are as much my family as anyone.

"Suck it up, buttercup," Mayer says. "A soldier couldn't ask for a better death than this."

"Minimum safe distance in two mikes," the pilot says.

The response to this statement is garbled by the sound of gunfire and shouting.

The last words I hear, are my son's. "Beside you! Three o'clock! Get down!"

46

IKE

Master Sergeant Ike Wright had seen combat before, but nothing like this. They weren't fighting back a wave of Fobs from the familiar setting of the Mount Hood Lodge, the forest or even on the bare mountain peak that vaguely resembled the current battlefield; they were fighting strange new monsters atop the miles wide and long back of the creature that had nearly destroyed the human race. It wasn't just a living land-scape, it was mobile. The wind shifted as the massive body lumbered forward, sliding side to side and up and down. Ike's stomach churned with each new descent and rise. He had never been on a roller coaster, but he imagined they felt something like this, only without the man-eating beasts, lightning and pelting rain.

Ike had never believed in the fire-and-brimstone version of hell popularized by the Middle Ages, carried to American shores by the Puritans and adopted by modern conservatives—before most of them were killed—but it no longer seemed that scary. At least fire would be warm. As the nearly absent sun fell below the living horizon, and the rain continued to saturate his body, a chill ran through him.

His hands shook as he worked the bomb's control panel, thankful that his brother had thought to make the whole system waterproof. Ishah had always been the smarter of the two, more like Mina, while Ike took after Sabella, the religious, passionate mother turned warrior. It was funny how that worked out, but he and Ishah identified both women as their shared mothers, with love shared equally among them, bonded by a common element—Abraham.

Ike had dreamed up scenarios where his father returned to them, but in them he was always kept at a distance. Ike loved his father and remembered him fondly as the brave man who set out to save the world. But as he and Ishah grew up, he knew his brother had more in common with their science-minded father.

But now, after living in the wilds for fifteen years under the tutelage of a fellow Ranger and a Mossad Agent, his father was one of the finest warriors he'd ever seen. But his mind hadn't lost its edge, either. They had a chance to win after all this time, because of him. His father was the kind of man the world needed. The kind of man who could bring humanity out of the darkness once more.

Ike would happily die for him, and knew he would have to before he'd stepped on the Osprey. Ishah had told him how the bomb worked, that there hadn't been time to create a remote trigger, and even if they had, it might not be reliable. Looking at the storm overhead, there was no doubt about that now. Leaving his sons before getting to know them broke Ike's heart, but he understood the sacrifice. He'd never once felt angry at Abraham for leaving all those years ago. He respected the man for it. Let the sacrifice guide his life. And now it was *his* turn. What Ike couldn't have predicted was that so many others would be willing to die for his father, too.

Ike finished setting the bomb. All he needed to do now was push a button. And then he, Edwards, Mayer and Graham would be vapor-ized, hopefully along with the Machine. He could push the button now, and end it, but he was determined to hold out as long as possible. It wasn't just the world that needed his father, but his family as well. Mina, Sabella, Ishah, Layla, Katelin and all the kids, for generations to come.

"Suck it up, buttercup," Mayer, the Mossad agent, said to Abraham over comms, as she ran toward Ike. "A soldier couldn't ask for a better death than this."

She was right about that. As far as deaths went, this was by far the most epic. If they were successful, their story would be told for generations, to his sons and hopefully by his sons to *their* children. He was about to add to her words, to let his father know that he didn't fear death, that he'd made peace with it a long time ago, but a crack of lightning arced down and hit the aberration's back, just a hundred feet behind Mayer. The boom and bright light forced Ike's eyes closed, but in the afterimage projected on his eyelids, he saw one of the creatures, which his father had dubbed 'Crawlers,' surging at Mayer from the side, unseen.

He swiveled his weapon in her direction, eyes still closed, and shouted, "Beside you! Three o'clock! Get down!"

Ike lifted his XM25, opened his eyes, seeing the chaotic world through streaks of green afterimage, and pulled the trigger. Three rounds launched from his rifle. The second was a yellow-hot tracer round, revealing the two explosive bullets' course. Mayer's head twisted as she dove for the rough terrain, tucking into a roll. Her quick reflexes and trust in Ike saved her life twice, first when the rounds passed within inches of her face and second, when they struck the underside of the airborne Crawler descending toward her back.

The Crawler's forward momentum came to an abrupt end as the two explosive rounds burst beneath it, shattering its underside and spinning it away. But the explosions, just a few feet behind Mayer, struck her as well. Her dive and roll turned into an ugly sprawl as metal fragments struck and flung her forward.

"Liz!" Graham shouted, reaching down for her with his left hand, while firing with his right. That he was able to maintain control of the weapon, which had a considerable kick, while lifting Mayer off the ground, was a testament to his strength. He was the consummate Ranger, and he had won Ike's immediate respect.

"I'm okay," Mayer grumbled, though she didn't sound okay. "The armor stopped most of it."

Most.

Not all.

But there wasn't time to argue or even worry. They were set upon by the enemy.

With Edwards by his side, just like old times, Ike picked his targets one-by-one, firing over and around Graham, covering the pair of warriors until they reached the bomb. Mayer was in obvious pain when they arrived, but Graham didn't place her gently on the ground and fawn over her. He lifted her up, depositing her on her feet and returning her weapon to her hands, bringing her back to the fight.

They were all going to die here. Wounds weren't going to be healed. Their lives couldn't be saved. They were simply buying time.

With their lives.

The four soldiers fired at the encroaching horde. The dead Crawlers created an obstacle course of carnage for the living. Their bodies needed to be climbed over or around, and their guts, mingling with the rain water flowing over the Machine's back, made the landscape slick. Their efforts slowed the assault, but couldn't stop it.

"How much time?" Graham asked, while changing out his magazine.

Ike looked for the Osprey, but couldn't see it in the sky. Lightning crisscrossed above them, lighting up two of the massive spines rising up into the clouds, cutting through them like a witch's spoon through a steaming brew. "Cauldron, ETA to safe zone?"

No response.

Ike fired the six remaining rounds in his XM25, killing two more Crawlers and then dropped the weapon, drawing his sidearm and his twelve inch knife. The next Crawler he faced would be up close and personal. But Graham pushed him back and stood in front of him.

"Don't even think about it, kid," Graham said. "Your job is to push that button. If we go down, don't wait. Your father has survived worse."

Ike smiled at Graham's confidence in his father. He'd only heard a handful of stories about their time in the wild, about what they saw and how they survived their first encounter with the Machine, but those were enough for him to share Graham's confidence. Still, as strong as his father was, he wasn't indestructible. If he didn't reach the minimum safe distance before the bomb went off, he would die with the rest of them.

Ike crouched down beside the bomb, finger hovering near the button that would detonate the electric charge and the nuclear warhead.

It would be a violent, but painless death. "Cauldron. Do you copy? ETA to safe zone?"

Silence.

"Cauldron, answer me, God damnit!"

"Down!" Edwards shouted.

Graham, Mayer and Ike ducked. Looking down into a puddle, Ike saw a Crawler launch over the ridge behind which they'd planted the bomb. As it soared above them, reaching down with its talons, Edwards fired up into it. The explosions tore into the creature's underside and Edward's helmet with equal force, tearing both apart.

It took all of Ike's focus to not scream out and dive to his friend's aid. He'd already lost Felder and Gutshall, but Edwards had been his closest friend over the past few years. *Honor him by completing the mission,* Ike told himself. *He came here to die. Like the rest of us.*

"Master Sergeant," Graham said, his voice a warning. They were about to run out of time. To punctuate the fact, Graham dropped his now empty assault rifle and drew a long blade. Mayer did likewise, opting for the .50 caliber hand gun strapped to her waist.

"Cauldron," Ike shouted. "Do you read? ETA to safe—"

"Ike?" It was his father. He sounded desperate and afraid, but not for his own life.

"Dad," Ike said. "Are you clear?"

"Clear," came the response. "Ike, I'm sorry."

"Nothing to be sorry for, Dad. Your actions taught me how to live in this world, and how to die in it. Love you, Dad."

"Ike!" Graham shouted. "Do it!'

Ike didn't hear his father's reply as his thumb shoved the detonation button down.

Bright white light flashed.

A thunderous boom tore through the air.

Heat coursed through his body, tingling every cell.

But there was no bliss to follow.

No choir of angels.

No white tunnel.

Just more of the same. Rain. Darkness. Lightning...

It was a lightning strike, slamming into the Machine's back nearby. He looked up and saw several Crawlers, unmoving and steaming, cooked by the electricity.

"Do it, Ike!" Graham shouted.

"Push the button," Mayer screamed at him, reaching for it herself.

Ike pushed the red button one more time.

Nothing happened.

"It's not working!" Ike said.

Graham reached down and pushed the button several times, but the bomb didn't explode.

They'd failed.

"Ike?" His father's voice. "What's happening?"

"The bomb failed," Ike said. "Dad, we failed."

The pause before his father spoke again was filled by the booming of Mayer's handgun. The powerful rounds punched into a nearby Crawler's eyes, making it rear back in pain.

"I don't think so," Abraham said.

Ike stood, armed with his handgun and knife, ready to go out fighting. "Dad, the—"

"Son," Abraham said. "Ike. Look up."

As Ike turned his eyes up to the turbulent sky, the gunfire around him fell silent. Were they out of ammo? Or were they seeing what he was seeing and stunned into inaction? He didn't bother checking. It didn't matter now. Their mission was a success.

The massive towers that had been rising up into the clouds just moments before, fell inward, toward the Machine's back. But they weren't like falling trees. They were turning to dust. Caught by the wind, the disintegrating particles swirled and coiled away, churning downward.

"It's coming apart," Abraham said. "The spikes. The tail. All of it."

"But..." Mayer sounded stunned. "How? The bomb failed."

"The electric charge," Abraham said. "It must have been enough."

Ike looked back at the device, still armed, still ready to fire, but not functional. The nuclear device hadn't fired, but neither had the electrical charge. Whatever was happening, it wasn't them.

"Get out of there," Abraham said. "Go! While you still can!"

The possibility of survival sharpened Ike's senses.

They were still surrounded, but the Crawlers seemed confused. They staggered about, twitching, black eyes tilted up at the disintegrating body they called home. Ike turned north. The Crawlers had closed in from every other direction, but the path north, along the plate's seam was clear to the horizon.

He turned to Graham. "Take her. I'll cover you."

Mayer opened her mouth to protest, but found herself flung over Graham's shoulder before she could say anything. She reluctantly handed Ike her weapon. He nodded in thanks and said, "Go!"

Thirty seconds into their retreat, Ike thought they would escape unnoticed, but then whatever state of confusion that had transfixed the Crawlers, faded away. The creatures attacked the bomb first, assaulting it with savage efficiency, tearing it apart and ensuring that it could never be repaired or used. Then, they turned toward the fleeing soldiers and charged.

"Here they come!" Ike said, but he held his fire. The handgun only held eight rounds. If he was lucky, he might be able to stop or slow down four of the creatures, but he didn't trust his aim with a handgun while running. And he wasn't about to stop.

Being Rangers, and survivors in the wild, Ike and Graham could run long distances while carrying heavy weights. It was a necessary survival skill. Sprinting wasn't as easy. Sprinting for a mile pushed them to their limits. But stopping, or even slowing, meant a certain and gruesome death.

Ike fired two rounds, the second of them striking the nearest Crawler's eye. It stumbled for a moment, and would have kept charging, if the creatures behind it hadn't plowed into its backside. All three Crawlers thrashed and kicked, until they were free of each other. The rest of the horde widened out around them, looking like a football defensive line from the seventh circle of Dante's hell. The line steadily closed the gap, their hard limbs clacking against the Machine's shell.

Taking the two shots slowed Ike's speed, and he found himself lagging twenty feet back. He poured on the steam, willing his legs faster. He looked down at his feet like he did when he was a kid, imagining himself as the Flash, watching his boots blur as he ran. *Faster*, he thought. *Faster!*

Ike blinked when he saw what looked like smoke billowing out from his feet. For a moment, it looked as though he was running fast enough to set his boots on fire, but then he noticed the entire landscape was smoldering.

Not burning, he thought, *coming apart.*

The nano-particles were separating, top to bottom. If they didn't reach the edge soon, they'd be falling through the creature's insides. *If we make it that far*, he thought, and he glanced back. With a shout of surprise, he aimed the high caliber weapon back with one hand and pulled the trigger. The bullet punched through the leaping Crawler's underside. It didn't have the explosive force of the XM25's ammunition, but a fifty caliber round mushrooms and breaks apart on impact. The hole in the creature's underbelly was neat, but the damage on the inside was enough to topple the creature when it landed, right behind him.

The bullet had saved his life, but firing the weapon one handed had pulled the gun from his hand and broken his wrist. Defenseless, Ike turned to run, but he was hammered in the back. He sprawled to the ground, now covered in a foot-deep layer of loose nano-particles. If not for the mask over his mouth and nose, he'd be breathing them in. When the attack didn't continue, he pushed himself up, using his good hand. He looked back. The dying Crawler had managed one last attack, but it was now curling up on itself.

When another Crawler leapt onto the back of the fallen creature and let out a shriek, Ike focused all his energy on running. Within seconds, he was catching up to Graham and Mayer at the same rate the horde was gaining on him.

"Nearly there!" Graham shouted.

Ike looked past them and saw the terrain drop away.

Graham leapt over the edge feet first, but he didn't let go of Mayer.

Ike followed them over the side, diving forward, expecting to see a drop off to the ground. Instead he found himself falling down to a steep incline, which Graham was now sliding on. Ike fell past his fellow Ranger and struck the incline moving fast. His armor absorbed some of the blow, but instead of sliding down the side, he toppled, completely out of control.

As he spun, he saw flashes of lightning above. Black mist whipped away by the wind, and a horde of Crawlers plummeted toward them. The creatures had followed them over the edge, just as they had the first time Graham and Abraham had fled the Machine's back. When Ike first heard the story from Graham, he thought it had been embellished, like the myths of old. But now he was living it, following in his father's footsteps, down the side of a planet-destroying monster. Each impact brought jarring pain, but less than expected. The aberration's side was coming apart as well, providing a cushion of loose nanobots.

Slowed by his tumble, Graham and Mayer slid past him. As they did, Graham shouted, "Here we go!"

Ike spun through the air, waiting for the next impact, but it never came. Instead, he fell through open air, his body no longer tumbling, but facing up, toward the raging sky, where Crawlers spilled out, surging for him. The nearest reached for him, its sharp-tipped limbs just inches away.

With a snap of fabric, Graham's parachute deployed. Still clutching Mayer in his arms and legs, he glided away from the descending chaos.

Ike let out a roar and swiped at the creature with his knife.

The blade passed through it, as though he was cutting through air. And then, as one, the horde burst into dust and was carried away.

Ike dropped his knife, reached up to his chest and pulled the ripcord for the parachute built into his armor. The chute deployed a moment later, but he didn't feel the sudden slowing that comes from an open parachute. He looked up and found the open chute whipping through the wind, limp and useless, shredded, by the Crawlers' final attack.

He soared past Graham, who had Mayer clinging to him like a baby monkey. Her parachute would be shredded as well, something Graham had no doubt realized before committing to the jump.

"Ike!" Graham shouted, his voice clear in the comm. But there was nothing else the man could say. They were miles in the air, but there was no way to stop his fall.

Ike saw the Osprey fly overhead and bank away.

His eyes moved to the Machine, its body coming apart, its glowing insides flickering and going dark.

"I see him," came the voice of his father. "Twelve o'clock, Ike."

Ike's eyes widened as he saw a human missile cut through a cloud of nano-dust and plummet toward him, arms outstretched.

"Lose the chute, Ike," Abraham shouted.

Ike slapped the button on his chest, freeing the useless parachute. It billowed in the air above him while he fell even faster. But as the ground rushed up below him, his father, a man turned legend, rocketed down above him, no trace of fear in his eyes, hands outstretched.

"I've got you, son."

47

ABRAHAM

I'm terrified.

I thought I had lost my son, leaving him as some kind of sacrifice to the Machine. But the bomb failed. Now, despite that failure, the ancient world-destroyer is coming apart. The moment I saw it, I understood what was happening, and ordered the Osprey to turn back.

But now we've arrived too late to pick up the surviving members of my team. From high above, I watch them tumble down the Machine's side, sliding through clouds of nanobots the consistency of dry flour, despite the rain. The Crawlers chase them down the side, as mindless in their pursuit of prey as ever.

Go, I think, willing them to fall faster. *Go!*

Graham and Mayer reach the edge and fall into open space. I hold my breath. When Graham's parachute opens and slows his and Mayer's fall, I breathe a sigh of relief. *They're going to make it.*

Then Ike spills over the edge, a Crawler reaching for him, inches away.

If he pulls his chute now, he'll—

The Crawler bursts into black dust.

The horde follows its lead, like miniature Machines, disassembling into their nano-components. *They were part of the whole,* I realize, like some kind of external, defensive pruning system, or perhaps just the caretakers for all those shed eggs.

Nanobots swirl into the air, and for a moment, I assume it's the wind. They twist and curl, sliding into the air and merging with larger clouds, all of it moving forward, and then down to the ground. The Machine's head is nearly gone. Its underside flickers, the brilliant light fading as it comes apart. But it's not the wind carrying the dust away. The rain, and the wind carrying it, is blowing in the opposite direction. The nanos are still in control, still operating under some ancient function. *But to what purpose now?* Is it attacking in some new way, or abiding by its promise? Ike lives, but not because either of us was unwilling to make the sacrifice.

The moment Ike's chute deploys, I know he's in trouble. It doesn't billow out. It just flutters, limp and useless, torn apart. Before I've fully registered my actions, I've leaped from the back of the Osprey as it flies over the scene.

Graham's voice booms loud in my ear as my son falls past him. "Ike!"

"I see him," I say, leaning forward into the fall, gaining speed. It's been a long time since I did this, but I'm far more calm than all of my previous sky dives, and I have no trouble angling myself toward my son. As I come in from above his head, I say, "Twelve o'clock, Ike."

When our eyes meet, I actually smile. Miles in the air, rushing toward my plummeting son, while a city-sized monster disintegrates behind me, and I'm smiling.

Because he's been spared.

And I know that I can save him. I might have been the king of nerds once upon a time, but now, *this* is who I am.

"Lose the chute, Ike" I say. The tangle of flaccid canvas and twisting ropes could keep my parachute from functioning right, and then I'll just be a very confident stain on the ground. When the parachute flutters away, yanked in the opposite direction of the nano-clouds, I reach my hands out.

"I've got you, son."

I flare my arms and legs wide, increasing the drag on my body, trying to match Ike's speed. We fall together, nearly within reach of each other, trying to get closer without colliding too hard. Our fingers touch, but a gust of wind separates us, pulling us apart.

"Dad," Ike says. His voice carries a tone of finality. And it's not hard to know why. We have just seconds until impact.

"I'm not letting you go," I tell him. "We both live, or we both die. Now get your ass over here!"

We both lean in, diving toward each other. Before we collide, I open my arms and bring my legs down. Ike slams into me with enough force to break a few of my ribs, but I barely notice them when I feel his arms wrap around me, linking behind my back. Then his legs wrap around me, link and squeeze.

"Hold on!" I shout, and when the grip around my body is so tight that I can't draw a breath, I pull my parachute's ripcord. The chute rips out and deploys, filling with air and slowing our descent. Ike slips a little, but he holds on.

At the mercy of the whipping winds, we're tossed from side to side, and then slapped against the Earth three times, before coming to a stop.

On the ground, at the center of a wide open field.

Alive.

On my back, wracked by pain, I reach up and yank my helmet and facemask away. Water pelts my face, disguising my tears. Ike doesn't move when I take off his helmet and facemask. "Ike," I say, fearful that he didn't survive the impact. "Ike!"

He smiles. "Remember when we used to wrestle like this? How much Mom hated it?"

"That's because we knocked the perfectly folded laundry on the floor." I grunt. "You were a lot smaller then."

"Sorry," he says, and he starts to move away.

I hold him tight, not wanting to let him go.

He rests his forehead on my chest. "Thanks for saving me."

"I don't think it was me."

I know he's referring to the parachute maneuver, but he should have died a few minutes before that, too. Did the Machine honor his sacrifice, by sparing his life? Did that seemingly insignificant act of expiation apply to the rest of humanity?

"Heads up," Graham says, his voice coming through the comm still in my ear. I look beyond Ike and see Graham and Mayer descending toward us.

Ike and I roll apart in separate directions, giving Graham room to land, which he does, while holding Mayer, without falling over.

I'm about to call him a show off, when I notice the epic display taking place in the sky above us. I climb to my feet and watch in silence as the others join me.

The Apocalypse Machine is almost wraithlike now. Its massive form is still present, but sifting apart in great churning clouds of black, stretching down to the ground, into Yellowstone. The now-dark form is backlit by near constant streaks of lightning, as though the entire natural world is aware of the Machine's passing and has come to bid it farewell. Or perhaps mourning its savior's passing. Without the Machine, the world would have become a wasteland, and now the whole world will flourish. And mankind...we've been given a second chance.

"You all want to get out of the rain?" the Osprey pilot asks.

I turn my eyes upward into the now lashing rain propelled by the Osprey's rotors, as it descends to the field.

Graham removes his helmet and lets it fall into the grass. "In a minute." He helps Mayer remove her helmet, too. She's injured, but not mortally. Ike and I join them, watching the Machine peel itself apart, sliding down into the ground itself.

"How is this possible?" Graham asks.

"I wasn't sure fifteen years ago," I tell him. "And I'm still not."

"But you spoke to it." Mayer asks. "Another vision?"

I nod. "The deal was simple, my son for the world. I thought he had to detonate the bomb.

"I tried," Ike says.

"And it seems our willingness to do so was enough." I smile at the dark cloud that only slightly resembles the Machine's massive form.

"Then it's over?" Ike says. "We beat it?"

"Over? I think so." I pat my son's shoulder. "But beat it? No. Not a chance."

"Then what's it doing?" Mayer asks.

"Returning to the volcanic hell from whence it came," I say. "Where it will watch, and wait, and the next time we, or our ancestors a thousand generations from now, threaten life on Earth again, it will return."

I turn toward the Osprey and see the pilot watching us. I wave him down and squint my eyes against the water as the big aircraft descends, rotating so its opening rear hatch is facing us.

Ike steps forward, raising his hand in a salute. "For Edwards, Felder, Gutshall and Wittman."

Graham joins him, offering a salute as well, and naming the members of his squad who died on our first mission, ending with, "Baker, Tremblay and Somers."

"And Zingel," Mayer adds, naming the Mossad agent we left behind on the day we escaped Israel.

"For Holly," I say, surprised when I start to choke up. "Philip, Diego and Kiljan."

We finish the salute to our fallen comrades and then enter the Osprey in silence. As we lift off and start east, knowing we'll have to land within a hundred miles to refuel, I watch the last of the nano-cloud slip into the Earth and disappear.

The world was evaluated and found wanting. But it seems we've also been forgiven. If not forgiven, at least given a second chance.

If we can survive the trials ahead.

Our world is now full of Scion, hungry and happy to claim the planet as their own.

I don't know if the human race will survive.

But I know we're going to try, and if the Machine is true to its word, my family will one day be like grains of sand on a beach.

How did it know? I wonder. *How could it know? That I would survive? That I would be here, at the end of its time on Earth, able to offer my son as a sacrifice?*

Long before I come up with an answer that makes sense, my thoughts drift to my family. To Mina and Bell. To Ishah and my grandchildren. We'll be home before morning, and then for the first time in fifteen years, Hope will be more than just the name of my boat.

ONE YEAR LATER

EPILOGUE

"Did you ever think this would be possible?" Mina asks.

She's standing beside me atop Raven Rock Mountain, overlooking New Washington. It's not much as far as cities go, resembling a medieval fortress more than a modern city. But its tall stone walls protect a modern-enough neighborhood, with streets, running water and electricity, supplied by Raven Rock. Our territory stretches for miles, and the Scionic predators in the area have already learned to avoid humanity. There are still roving packs to worry about, but we have safe houses scattered throughout the mountainous region, not to mention modern weapons. Fuel and ammunition is limited, and will one day run out. We're using what we have to give civilization a kick start, but we're under no illusion that we'll be able to live at a twentieth century comfort level forever. But we'll use it while we have it, and not just to grow our small city, but to reach out to others around the world.

Let them know the Machine is defeated.

That humanity carries on.

That they are not alone.

"I never really thought this far ahead," I reply, smiling down at my wife, dressed in a black military uniform, long straight hair tied back—her preferred hunting garb. Since freeing the world from the Machine, Mina has been working hard at adapting to the New World. No longer hiding beneath a mountain means learning how to defend yourself, how to fight and kill. She's efficient at all three, from a distance, preferring the bow and arrow to close up combat. And with a compound bow, there isn't much game that can escape her. She's become one of our best hunters. And she's no longer President.

That title has fallen to me.

There was no election. No coup. Everyone, including Mina, agreed to put me in charge. I didn't ask for it. But I didn't fight it either. I get it. I know a lot about a lot—Old World and New—and with so much at stake, there's no room for misguided leadership. So I took the job, and the first thing I did was retask the Secret Service. New Washington needs more protection than I do. And I've got three deadly shadows nearby at all times. I told Graham, Mayer and Ike that I didn't need protecting, but Graham and Mayer pointed out all the times they'd saved my life over the years. I have yet to need rescuing, but I do feel safer knowing they're lurking nearby, keeping watch.

I smell Bell's arrival before hearing or seeing her. She's fragrant. Earthy. From working the farms, where we now grow crops and raise livestock, which requires the most guarding. We're domesticating wild pigs and turkeys that managed to survive and later thrive. We've also got a few different Scionic animals, which show promise of domestication and are somewhat tasty. Bell is in charge of it all, working the land and finding the peace of her old self again.

"Thought I'd find you two up here," Bell says, as she steps from the woods and onto the ledge overlooking the town. She steps to my right and takes my hand in hers. I look down at her fingers. At the ring. Funny thing about being a leader in a new world without formal laws, bureaucracy or squabbling councils? You can pretty much do whatever you want, within reason. So I married Bell, no wonky religion required. And I'm not alone. The end of the world has left humanity with a two to one ratio of women to men. And since repopulation is one of our goals, men—especially the younger generations—are making like it's 1700 B.C. and marrying multiple women.

Not Graham or my sons, though. Of course, Ishah and his wife, with their sixth on the way, could probably repopulate the planet on their own. While I'm technically in charge, my focus is mainly on growth, infrastructure and defense. Ishah has become a man of the people, using his mind to better people's lives, and keep them healthy. Especially the children, of which there are now fifty-three, more than half of which are under a year old. He's also in charge of our outreach program.

It sounds corny, like something an Old World church might have done, but it now involves trying to contact other pockets of humanity around the world. Most communication is via radio, but since Graham and Ike led a team to Cheyenne Mountain, home of the North American Aerospace Defense Command (NORAD), we've been able to reconnect with several satellites. And we use them to find people by looking for the one thing humanity always seems to generate: heat. Fires mostly, burning at night.

We now know there is a tribe of people living in Australia. They survived the end on Uluru, that massive red rock rising out of the desert. It's an island now, but they recently managed to create an outpost on the coast. Like us, they're using Old World skills and knowledge to push Scionic life back, while at the same time, preparing to join the New World, not as conquerors, but as part of the new order.

The Amazon is home to one of humanity's largest outposts. First World people fled to the rainforest when civilization fell apart. Many of them died, but those who didn't were adopted by tribes. Some were enslaved, or at least indentured, but from what I understand, as Scionic life encroached on their land, the tribal peoples were eager to learn about modern technologies that would help them fend off the savage new threats. Nothing unites people like monsters.

Perhaps the strangest of all New World civilizations is a place called Red Sky Flotilla. It's a floating island in the middle of the Pacific Ocean, formed by what was once the Great Garbage Patch, which I wrote about eighteen years ago. They're a collection of ships and their crews, who survived the end of the world by fleeing to the sea, along with a Scionic lifeform living symbiotically with people. I suspect it's something like the

Redwood Forest. On the surface, we see separate trees, but beneath the ground, their massive roots are connected to form a single, massive organism. And with the disappearance of the Machine, Red Sky is now the largest living creature on Earth.

We have returned to Yellowstone just once. Volcanic activity is at an all-time low. Even old Faithful lacks the pressure to erupt. The heat, it would seem, is being absorbed by something...something large, beneath the surface. But perhaps the most poignant reminder of what the world faces should it be thrown out of whack again, are the six, twenty-foot obelisks rising from the ground. They look like structures erected by some ancient civilization, but we know better. The Machine is watching. Testing the air. Listening to our broadcasts. Maybe even sensing our thoughts. We know very little about the creature, including where it came from, but we do know why it's here. We're going to make damn well sure future generations understand that there are rules governing the planet, and a Machine—a literal machine—that is judge, jury and executioner when the world is at risk.

The sounds of people at work, building and growing, echo through the valley below. I smile and close my eyes, my face warmed by the sun. The scents of pine and flowering Scionic trees fill my nose with the odors of a world remade. My hands are held by the two women I love, the mothers of my sons. There has never been a time in the Old World or New, where I was more content. That urge to run and hide from my life is gone. I'm fully immersed in it, reveling in it, and thankful for it.

Something crashes through the brush behind us.

Mina spins, nocking an arrow.

Bell holds her spear at the ready.

I raise my sound-suppressed AK-47 to my shoulder, taking aim at the sound. At my son.

Weapons lower as Ishah emerges from the forest, looking winded. He's run the whole way here.

"Why didn't...you bring...your radio?"

Three figures slide out of the trees behind him. Their approach was completely undetected. Even now, as Ike, Graham and Mayer step into the light of day, Ishah hasn't heard them behind him.

"You're too loud," Ike says, surprising his brother. "You might as well run through the forest ringing a dinner bell."

I agree with Ike's assessment, but I also know Ishah wouldn't have run all the way here without a good reason.

"What is it?" I ask, leaning down to look at Ishah's face. His hands are planted on his knees as he catches his breath. "Is something wrong?"

He shakes his head, showing a slight smile.

It's good news.

"We made contact," he says. "With a new colony. Their leader said he's been expecting to hear from you."

"They know about New Washington?" I ask, wondering if word is spreading on its own.

Ishah shakes his head. "About you."

"Where is this colony?" Graham asks.

"Iceland."

"Iceland?" I reel back from the word like it's some kind of reanimated voodoo corpse. Iceland was ground zero for the Machine's rise. Between the volcanoes, flooding and remote locations, not to mention a small population, I would have never thought to even look there. I work through the problem. The volcanic ash was blown away from the more densely populated western coast. The flooding could have flowed out to sea, following natural gorges and rivers carved by ancient glaciers. There were no nuclear weapons or power stations on the island nation. And it's located north of where Greenland's ice sheet plowed into the Atlantic. The wave that scoured countless other nations would have missed Iceland entirely. And the island's height above sea level means it would be mostly unaffected by the rising oceans. "I suppose it makes a strange kind of sense. What was the man's name?"

Ishah's smile widens. He knows the name. Knows it means something to me. I'm about to shout at him to spit it out when he says, "Árnason. Kiljan Árnason."

I break into a run, heading for the nearest Raven Rock entrance. The others follow close behind. Only Ishah has trouble keeping up, but he manages, and we reach the entrance as a group. I move through the complex with some urgency, arriving at the communications room with enough speed to panic the people manning the radios. I raise my hands to put them at ease. "Are you still in touch with Iceland?"

One of the men vacates his chair. "He's waiting for you."

I fall into the chair, snatch up the microphone and push the call button. "Kiljan, you son of a bitch! You're alive! Over."

"You are son of bitch," Kiljan's deep voice replies. "I have been waiting many years to hear from you. But you keep me waiting." He lets out a hearty laugh. "I should not have doubted. Over."

"Your family," I say, remembering Kiljan's desperate quest to save them. "Did they make it? Over."

"All of them," he says. "But I knew they would. Over."

"How? The last time I saw you... The water...the earthquakes." I pause for a moment, reliving the last time I saw him. All this time, I believed he'd died shortly after we flew away. "Over."

"I was shown how," he says. "Like you. Was difficult. But I am Icelander. Naturally resilient. Not as hard for me as for you." He gets in a good chuckle, and it brings a smile to my face. It's been a long time since I got a ribbing like this, and I suspect it's because the man Kiljan is picturing is skinny, out of shape and a bit nerdy. He probably wouldn't even recognize the man I've become. "Over."

"What do you mean, you were 'shown?'" I ask. "Over."

"The vision," he says. "When you touched it. Over."

I nearly fall out of the chair. "But you... You said you didn't see anything. Over."

"Didn't want you to think I was crazy. *You* looked pretty crazy. I didn't really understand it was real, until I found my family where he said I would. Over."

"He?" I ask. "You mean the Machine? The monster? It told you where to find your family? Over."

"The Machine? Is that who you think you were speaking to?" he asks. "It wasn't the Machine. It was never the Machine."

ACKNOWLEDGMENTS

Apocalypse Machine has been a long time coming. The epic storyline has been percolating for years, but the number of people involved in bringing this monstrous title to life has been relatively small.

First is my trusted editor, Kane Gilmour, who years ago opened my eyes to the idea of writing original Kaiju novels. Next is Matt Frank, the amazing talent behind Nemesis's design, who lent his Kaiju illustration skills to the cover, bringing the Machine to life. Roger Brodeur once again helmed the effort to seek out and destroy typos, and he was joined by amazing advance proofreaders, Jeff Sexton, Dustin Dreyling, Lyn Askew, Kelly Allenby, Becki Tapia Laurent, Jamey Lynn Goodyear, Julie Cummings Carter, Dee Haddrill, Jennifer Antle, and Elizabeth Cooper.

Special thanks, as always, to my amazing wife, Hilaree, for supporting my whacky career choices and my children, Aquila, Solomon, and Norah, for sharing my excitement over stories and art featuring monsters. Love you guys!

ABOUT THE AUTHOR

Jeremy Robinson is the international bestselling author of over fifty novels and novellas, including *MirrorWorld, XOM-B, Island 731,* and *SecondWorld,* as well as the Jack Sigler thriller series and *Project Nemesis,* the highest selling, original (non-licensed) kaiju novel of all time. He's known for mixing elements of science, history and mythology, which has earned him the #1 spot in Science Fiction and Action-Adventure, and secured him as the top creature feature author.

Robinson is also known as the bestselling horror writer, Jeremy Bishop, author of *The Sentinel* and the controversial novel, *Torment.* In 2015, he launched yet another pseudonym, Jeremiah Knight, for a bestselling post-apocalyptic Science Fiction series of novels. Robinson's works have been translated into thirteen languages.

His series of Jack Sigler / Chess Team thrillers, starting with *Pulse,* is in development as a film series, helmed by Jabbar Raisani, who earned an Emmy Award for his design work on HBO's *Game of Thrones.* Robinson's original kaiju character, Nemesis, is also being adapted into a comic book through publisher American Gothic Press in association with *Famous Monsters of Filmland,* with artwork and covers by renowned Godzilla artists Matt Frank and Bob Eggleton.

Born in Beverly, MA, Robinson now lives in New Hampshire with his wife and three children.

Visit Jeremy Robinson online at www.bewareofmonsters.com.

WHEN THE DAIKAIJU ARRIVE
THERE IS ONLY ONE WAY TO FIGHT:

SUPPORT   POINT   BASE

TOGETHER

UNITY

A KAIJU THRILLER BY JEREMY ROBINSON